John Burdett is a former lawyer who worked in Hong Kong until he found his true vocation as a writer. An Englishman by birth, he has lived in France and Spain, and is now back in the Far East.

He is the author of A *Personal History of Thirst* and *The Last Six Million Seconds*, as well as his previous novels featuring Sonchai Jitpleecheep, *Bangkok Eight*, *Bangkok Tattoo* and *Bangkok Haunts*.

For more information on John Burdett and his books, please visit his website: www.john-burdett.com

'Like no other novel that's come my way lately.
Ironic, sexy and trailing an odour that reminds
me of a Bangkok street after hours . . .
Expect to be enlightened!'
Literary Review

'Open *Bangkok Tattoo* and you will read on and on,
with wide-eyed fascination, some horror or disgust,
and considerable delight'
Washington Post

Also by John Burdett

BANGKOK EIGHT
BANGKOK TATTOO
BANGKOK HAUNTS

and published by Corgi Books

THE GODFATHER
OF KATHMANDU

JOHN BURDETT

CORGI BOOKS

TRANSWORLD PUBLISHERS
61–63 Uxbridge Road, London W5 5SA
A Random House Group Company
www.rbooks.co.uk

THE GODFATHER OF KATHMANDU
A CORGI BOOK: 9780552153607

First published in the United States in 2010 by Alfred A. Knopf,
a division of Random House, Inc., New York
and in Canada by Random House of Canada Limited, Toronto.
First published in Great Britain in 2010 by Bantam Press
an imprint of Transworld Publishers
Corgi edition published 2010

Addresses for Random House Group Ltd companies outside the UK
can be found at: www.randomhouse.co.uk
The Random House Group Ltd Reg. No. 954009

The Random House Group Limited supports The Forest
Stewardship Council (FSC), the leading international forest
certification organisation. All our titles that are printed on
Greenpeace approved FSC certified paper carry the FSC logo.
Our paper procurement policy can be found at
www.rbooks.co.uk/environment

Typeset in 10.5/13.25pt Electra by Falcon Oast Graphic Art Ltd.
Printed in the UK by CPI Cox & Wyman, Reading, RG1 8EX.

2 4 6 8 10 9 7 5 3 1

For Nit

Acknowledgments

I thank David Giler for his usual invaluable comments, and Douglas Mays, who taught me all I am ever likely to know about padparadschas.

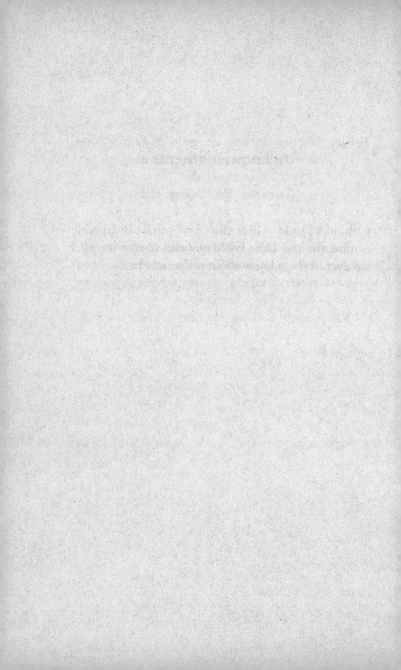

Few are there amongst men who go to the Farther Shore;
the rest of this mankind only run about
on the bank.
– Gautama, *The Dhammapada*

The third kind of suffering and pain that the soul
endures in this state results from the fact that two other
extremes meet here in one, namely, the Divine and the
human.
– San Juan de la Cruz, *The Dark Night of the Soul*

THE GODFATHER OF KATHMANDU

1

Ours is an age of enforced psychosis. I'll forgive yours, *farang*, if you'll forgive mine—but let's talk about it later. Right now I'm on the back of a motorbike taxi hurtling toward a to-die-for little murder off Soi 4/4, Sukhumvit. My boss, Colonel Vikorn, called me at home with the good news that he wants me on the case because the victim is said to be some hyper-rich, hyper-famous Hollywood *farang* and he doesn't need poor Detective Sukum screwing up with the media. We'll get to Detective Sukum; for the moment picture me, if you will, with a Force 8 tropical wind in my face causing eyes to tear and ears to itch, on my way to one of our most popular red-light districts where there awaits a larger-than-life dead Westerner.

I'm nearly there. With a little urging my motorbike jockey drives up onto the sidewalk to avoid the massive traffic jam at the Soi 4 junction with Sukhumvit, weaves in between a long line of cooked-food vendors busy feeding the whores from Nana Plaza who have just gotten up (it's about eleven in the morning), slaloms between a mango seller and a lamppost, returns to the tarmac with the usual jolt to the lower spine, and now we're slowing to swerve into Subsoi 4. (Should one add the two fours to make the lucky number eight, or should one accept the stark warning: two fours mean death twice within the Cantonese luck system, which has taken over the world as a vital component of globalization?) Finally, here we are with a couple of squad cars and a forensic van in the parking area of the flophouse to welcome yours truly on this fair morning.

Also waiting for me is my long-haired assistant, Lek, a *katoey*—transsexual—who has not yet scraped together the courage or the funds for the final op. He avoids the supernatural brightness in my eyes (I've been meditating all night) to inform me, sotto voce, that Detective Sukum is here before me and has already developed possessive feelings toward the cadaver. The good Sukum is half a grade above me, and we are rivals for promotion. Like any jungle carnivore, Sukum is hunched over the kill as if it were all his own work—and who can blame him? Necrophilia is a professional hazard on any murder squad, and I have no doubt my rival is slobbering over his magnificent prize, just as if he had come across the Koh-i-noor diamond in a sewer. Within the value system into which we were all inducted at cadet school, this murder is everyone's definition of *ruang yai*: a big one. It will be interesting to see how Sukum handles my inconvenient arrival. I think I might be able to surprise him.

Lek leads me past the guards' hut into the parking deck which is also the entrance area for a ten-story apartment building that was erected in a hurry fifteen years ago in order to profit on a no-frills basis from the sexual frustration of Western men over the age of forty: a fail-proof business decision, the owners got their money back in the first three years and it's been honey all the way ever since. Paint is chipped and flaking from the walls, revealing white plaster with occasional graffiti (*Fuck you, farang,* in Thai; *Sarlee, you were so good last night,* in English); the lift is tiny—even the slim Lek and I find ourselves embarrassingly close for a moment. (Our clash of colognes reveals our sexual orientations. He will use nothing less than Chanel No. 5, which he begs from my mother, Nong; mine is a rugged, take-no-prisoners little number from Armani.)

"This could be one for the FBI," I say in the elevator.

"She's stuck in Virginia," Lek says. "Poor little thing broke her arm during combat training. She was fighting two instructors at the same time, and of course they both came off worse, but she still can't really call herself one of the boys because she's in love with *me*. Don't tell her I said that."

"Kimberley? Really?"

"She sent me an e-mail yesterday."

Kimberley Jones, an FBI agent, is a friend of mine and Lek's. Especially Lek's. It's a long story. She worked with me on a few cases of an international nature and fell in love with Lek, which awkward fact has confused the hell out of her. Does her lust for a transsexual make her a dyke or not? I fear there is little in your culture, *farang*, to provide guidance on this conundrum—so she calls me all the time.

The corridor on the fourth floor leads to room 422, where two uniformed cops are stationed.

They part to let us into the apartment, where a massive American at least six feet long waits propped up in semi-sitting position on a bed wearing only a gigantic pair of shorts, over the top of which a great wormy mass of intestines has flopped like tripe in a butcher's shop. (His bed is so narrow that parts of his flesh sag over each side, and one has to wonder how he coped when engaged in sexual congress.) The drama of this center-screen image at first makes the various slim Thai cops and forensic technicians seem like a chorus to a Greek tragedy. Then Sukum steps forward.

Detective Sukum Montri is a good-looking Thai cop in his early thirties, very upright and proper when not consumed by fear, aggression, and lust—like the rest of us; but right now I discern in his eyes the fire of one who has decided that this is the moment when the fig leaf of comradeship must be dropped by both protagonists to reveal the competing stiffness of their virile members. Well, I have good news for him: today, thanks to the way my psychosis is hanging, I'm all *metas*—Sanskrit for "loving-kindness." However, it is important not to spoil people. I shall break the good news that I don't give a damn about promotion today—or for the rest of my life—later. For the moment, let us enjoy Sukum.

He wears a black jacket, black pants, white shirt, thin pink nylon tie (pink because it's Tuesday—our days of the week are color coded), all items generic, i.e., not good enough to qualify as fakes. The jacket is particularly narrow at the shoulders, pinching under the arms and badly crumpled, even though I'm sure it was freshly pressed yesterday. (Our gifted imitators of French and Italian haute couture would never be so crass; Sukum's tailor, if he has one, must be Thai Chinese of the old cloth-saving school.)

"Good morning, Detective." I take careful note of the position of his hands as he *wais* me (palms pressed together and raised to mouth level, with precisely the right mindful pause), before I *wai* him back in exactly the same way. Sukum coughs. "It's very kind of you to rush over to help me out," he says. I grunt non-committally, causing a brief grin to cross Lek's face.

"Of course your special input will be most welcome." Sukum is talking about my perfect English, which I learned from my mother's customers, and my half-*farang* blood, which gives me a unique insight into the mysterious Western mind.

"Yes?"

"Oh, yes. But let's not get carried away."

"Oh, absolutely."

Here Sukum drops his tone almost to a whisper. "Let me be frank: the unwritten rule that you get

19

farang murders only applies when the *murderer* is also *farang*. It doesn't apply when a Thai whore snuffs a *farang*."

I insert the pinkie of my left hand into my left ear, which is still itching from the motorbike ride, and work the wax around a bit. "Really? Forgive me, Khun Sukum, but is there not a failure of logic in what you have just said? How would one know until the end of the case if the perp were Thai or *farang*?"

"I knew you were going to say that," he snaps. "Look, this is obviously a Thai hit." I ostentatiously move my eyes up and down the gash from the victim's solar plexus almost to the pubic area; the corpse is so massive it is hard to imagine a little Thai girl standing on tippy-toe so she can get a good angle with the boning knife. I allow Sukum a skeptical stare. "Okay, it's a bit ambitious for a girl, but you know how they go when they get angry. Maybe he insisted on bugger-ing her and she got mad—our girls can be picky these days."

"But didn't I hear someone say that he's famous?"

"You mean it's a paid hit? Maybe, but if it's a hit, it's bound to be by a Thai. In Thailand ninety-nine point nine per cent of professional hits are by Thais," he says patriotically.

"Is that an official statistic? Perhaps you are right, Khun Sukum. Mind if I look around?"

Mostly I'm staring at the dead American. His hair is long and gray and swept back in a ponytail; a gray beard expands an already gigantic face. His mouth is half open, and a little blood is trickling from one corner. When I shift my glance to the rest of the apartment, I immediately become mesmerized by the books. It occurs to me that Sukum has no English.

I take a couple of surreptitious steps in the direction of the bookshelves, which are thinly populated with a set of novels and screenplays. My eyes fixate insanely when I come to a collection of short stories by Edgar Allan Poe. I turn my back so Sukum cannot see the intensely puzzled frown on my face, which only increases when I check the other titles. I finally manage to tear my eyes away, and pace the room for a moment. I am careful not to take any more notice of the bookshelves. For a moment my eyes rest on the cheap cathode-ray TV on a stand with a DVD player hooked up to it on a lower shelf.

"Khun Sukum," I say, my hands clasped gently behind my back as I pace, "would you do me the honor of indulging a whim of mine? Would you open the victim's mouth and tell me if you see there either a small pebble or an imago, or possibly both?"

Suspicious, Sukum opens the giant's mouth and slips in his fingers, then pulls out a large black imago and a pebble. He is staring at me with fear, loathing, and envy-driven hatred. "How in Buddha's name did you—"

"And I think, Khun Sukum, you had better examine the top of the victim's skull, in the area of the fontanel; you might want to pull at the hair in that area, give it a good tug, that's right."

As he does so, a large circular section of the skull, which amounts to the whole of the top of the head, comes away with the hair. Now we have a clear view of the victim's brain, still bright red under the protective membrane, but with a few folds missing from the left lobe.

When Sukum stares wildly at me, I allow my eyes to divert to a small and squalid coffee table on which a paper plate and a plastic spoon have been left. Now Sukum is shuddering involuntarily, Lek is astounded at my brilliance, and everyone is staring at me. I shrug. Sukum shakily replaces the victim's scalp, carefully trying to fit it into place like a piece of a jigsaw puzzle that might get damaged if he forces it, then looks up at me. "I don't know how you did that; it must be your *farang* blood." I feel bad for him as I watch his ambition sag, his identity crumple. Finally, with weary detachment after a heroic inner struggle: "Okay, it's your case, obviously the assassin was a *farang*, we don't have any Thai murderers that crazy."

I shake my head and tut. "No, no, my dear Khun Sukum, I would not dream of standing between you and your life's ambition of becoming a detective sergeant. Wouldn't dream of it, my dear chap. Look, why don't you simply use me as a resource—here's my private cell phone number, call me whenever you get stuck, hey?"

Lek is pulling at my sleeve; he has something private and confidential to communicate. "Look, I've got to go now, let's meet for a brainstorming session sometime soon. It's okay, your name will be on the file, I don't want any credit, just the honor of helping out in a spectacular case." I smile as Lek pulls me out of the room. At the door I add, "I know you've thought of it already, Detective Sukum, but just in case it has inexplicably escaped your notice, the victim was not staying here. No clothes or other signs of habitation, you see, only a few books. I would check with all the five-star hotels hereabout, if I were you." Sukum knows so little about *farang*, he still doesn't get it. "He was probably hiring the room for sex, while living in some five-star suite at the Dusit Thani or something." Sukum nods, trying to get his head around the idea that someone might rent two hotel rooms at the same time, just to be discreet. Now that really does say *ruey ruey* in Thai: fabulously rich.

In the lift on the way back to the ground floor, a silent trickle of tears flows down Lek's cheeks.

2

Lek has me trapped at a cooked-food stall on the sidewalk off Soi 11. It's lunchtime by now, and all the tables are full. There is a traffic jam to my left and iron railings to my right. Lek sits opposite, staring resentfully. "I can't believe what you just did," he says. We have ordered and the food has arrived—*tom yam gung* for Lek, green sweet rabbit curry for me; neither of us can eat.

"I told you, I've found the path, you should be pleased."

"For five years you've been the guy who has to get promoted next. It's outrageous that the committee hasn't promoted you yet. If it was up to Colonel Vikorn, you would have been promoted years ago. Even your enemies think you should get promoted. Sukum's okay, but he's not inspired. You're a genius."

"They'll never promote me. You know that. People put up with me as a lowly detective. If I rise any higher, people will start talking about my *farang* blood. You know how Thais are. Totally fair-minded Buddhists, until their personal income is threatened.

Anyway, I told you, I'm almost there, Lek. A few more sessions with Tietsin and I'll be an awakened being."

"That charlatan. I hate him."

"You've never met him."

"I hate him for what he's doing to you in your time of grief." Lek covers his face, lest I see my suffering there. He has become like the picture of Dorian Gray: I see in him the reality I dare not see in myself. I turn away.

"I'm not really a genius. It's just that my English sometimes gives me an advantage. D'you know how I guessed about the pebble and the imago and the trepanning? It's all in the titles of the books and screenplays—"

Lek wipes his face and tuts. "I don't give a shit how you did it, I only care about you, and that Tibetan witch is destroying you." He stares at me with simple country love, then calls for a can of beer. When the Singha arrives he says, "Drink it."

"I can't, Lek," I say, shuddering slightly at the can and its implications.

"If you love me, if you have any regard left for me, drink it."

"Lek—"

"You're scared, aren't you? That's an artificial high you're on, I think you were smoking dope last night while you were reading witchcraft—"

"It's not witchcraft, it's Tibetan Buddhism—"

"So, if it's not witchcraft, drink a can of beer. Just one. I've seen you sink ten in a row. But you're terrified of the comedown, aren't you? Just one little can of beer bursts your balloon—that's why he's a charlatan, that Tibetan witch."

Wearily, because I love him, I guess—he might be the only one left—I drink the beer. He's right, the very modest intake of alcohol bursts the bubble. I feel the onset of paranoia. Lek pays for the food and takes my hand, leads me to the nearest cab. It doesn't matter that we're going to sit in a traffic jam, it's the relative privacy of the backseat Lek is looking for. When I close my eyes I see what is always there, like a video playing on the back of my forehead: a car—it was a silver Toyota Echo—taking the turn into the *soi*, hitting my six-year-old son, Pichai, where he was standing in the street after getting out of a taxi. Chanya only slightly injured in her left foot, refusing help, taking Pichai to the hospital, calling me on my cell phone. I arrived at the operating theater just in time for his death.

Chanya couldn't handle it any better than I could. She became a novice nun at a radical forest convent out in Mukdahan, on the border with Laos. They still meditate over pictures of dead bodies there. She turned into a fanatic, observing and merging with every stage of human decomposition. For my part, I found Doctor Norbu Tietsin, the mad Tibetan mind master. Let's say he showed me how to orbit the earth, as an alternative to living on it. The technique doesn't go with alcohol, though. Even a small amount is inimical to spiritual evolution; alcohol is a death drug, a devil brew from the lands of the setting sun. It drags the spirit back into the body: more torture.

"I'm going to have to roll a joint, Lek," I say, suddenly feverish.

"Not in the taxi, for Buddha's sake." He stays my hand, which is reaching for the small bag of pot I'm never without these days. "Master, face it, you're bipolar. Your tragedy has done this to you. With help you can get over it. Real help, hospital help. *Farang* help."

"Sorry, Lek," I say, and pull the handle to open the door and get out of the cab. "It's an emergency."

It's been no more than an hour, but I've forgotten all about the gigantic dead American and the theatrical circumstances of his murder. I'm concerned with how to survive the next five minutes. It happens that the cab has stopped in the jam outside the Rose Garden on Soi 7, where I'm quite well known. I dash through the bar to the toilets, where I find a booth and roll a joint, but I can't stand the claustrophobia, so I leave the booth as soon as the joint is rolled. While I'm feverishly smoking, I check out some of the signs on the wall above the pissoirs, which warn that the establishment is not responsible for the behavior of the women who use the bar to solicit customers, and advises patrons to take note of a girl's identity card before taking her back to a hotel. There's a female worker in the process of cleaning the toilets, but she doesn't seem to notice the acrid stench of my joint. I retreat to a cubicle to sit on the throne and soak myself in a damn good cry.

3

We were going to talk about *psychosis, farang*. The word, I believe, means perforation of the psyche: we must imagine a delicate net of filaments, like the old-fashioned mantles of gas lamps, which, due to ill-treatment by life, people, and gods, suffer irreversible damage, leaving cancerous black holes where the clear light of unimpeded consciousness once radiated. Actually, it is a mystery which cannot be penetrated without resort to myth, metaphor, and magic, but we'll keep it simple for now. Nor can it be understood without reference to the law of karma: cause and effect. I kick you, you kick me back. Confession: I provoked the world and the world turned on me. The private history of my fragmentation is as follows.

I have only myself to blame. For years my boss, mentor, and surrogate father Police Colonel Vikorn nagged me to get him a set of DVDs of the *Godfather* series, with Marlon Brando and Al Pacino. The problem all along was that I only could find editions with Thai subtitles, and Vikorn is too lazy to read and watch the action at the same time. Finally, Lek found an illegally dubbed set of a reasonable standard and I gave them to Vikorn on his last birthday. According to his Wife Four, who was down from his mansion in Chiang Mai to do her tour of duty at his house in Bangkok (he likes to operate a roster, which the wives appreciate since it enables them to know when they are free for full-time shopping and when they are required to perform marital chores), he devoured all the DVDs in one long, whisky-enhanced sitting.

His verdict, the next day, was carefully balanced. I have indelibly burned into my memory cells the image of him sitting behind his vast, empty desk, with the DVD set dumped in his out-box, like a solved case. His posture was both regal and forensic, although he brushed his hand over his short gray hair and stood up when he got bored with sitting down. He is of average height, muscular, given to wearing the homely brown fatigues of a police colonel the way Napoléon wore his old uniform to reassure the troops (Vikorn is a multimillionaire; some even use the B word to describe his wealth); but for a man in his mid-sixties he moves with an unusual suppleness; only gangsters are so feline at his age. In his considered opinion old Corleone was a total sissy for refusing to trade in smack, and Sollozzo was well within his rights to try to have him bumped off. My Colonel even honored me with one of his famous analects:

"What's wrong with trafficking in heroin? The smack goes to Europe or America. Some self-obsessed narcissist who otherwise would be causing untold pollution driving to and from work every day, probably in a car without passengers, only to go burning electricity in an overheated office somewhere—thanks to us he stays home in a stupor and gets the sack. His work gets outsourced to Bangladesh, where someone does the same job better for a fifth of the pay, which he uses to feed a family of seven, and to top it all he commutes to work on a bicycle—the whole earth benefits."

On the other hand, he liked the ruthless way young Michael Corleone cleared out the opposition after the Don had been shot, but doubted it was really necessary to flee New York and start over in Las Vegas. With better planning and more efficient use of funds, contacts, and leverage, the Corleones could have bridged the country like a colossus with a foot on both coasts. He loved the way they severed the head of the racehorse to intimidate Jack Woltz, but despised them for failing properly to capitalize on the wheeze: "They could have had the whole film industry wrapped up after that. This is the problem with *farang jao paw*: they're shortsighted, triumphalistic, and they don't have Buddhist restraint or humility—that's why I hate dealing with them."

But there was one feature of the Don's setup that intrigued Vikorn and brought that gleam into his eyes which invariably spells danger for someone, usually me. "That light-skinned *farang* who's not as hairy as the others—what's his name?"

"Hagen. He's light-skinned because he's Irish-born. Vito Corleone adopted him after Sonny Corleone dragged him in off the street one day. The Don sent him to law school."

"Yeah, that one. What do they call him, his job title?"

"Consigliere."

"Right," he said, looking directly into my eyes.

As usual, he had taken me by surprise. I had thought we were discussing an old movie nobody talks about anymore. I had not detected any signals that we were discussing the rest of my life.

"No," I said. "Don't even think about it. You know me, I'm the biggest wimp on the force, I only survive through your patronage, in ten years of active service I've never killed anyone, not even by accident—isn't that despicable? All the real men on the force think I might be a secret *katoey*, a ladyboy like Lek—" I was stuttering a little at this point, for while I was speaking my subconscious was delivering pictures of me full of holes bent over a car hood somewhere in Klong Toey, near the river. Or maybe in the river itself.

"I, I, I have this Bu-, Bu-, Bu-, Buddhist conscience, I really do try to follow the Eightfold Path, I mean I take it seriously, I don't juh-, juh-, just go to temple, I study Buddhism, I probably know more about Buddhism than the average monk, you said it yourself, I'm a monk manqué—no." I said it again, more to convince myself than him, "No. No, no, no way I could be anybody's consigliere."

He was gazing at me more with amusement than irritation. "Have you discussed it with your mother?"

Aghast: "My mother? Of course not, you've only just mentioned it."

31

He let me have one of his tiger smiles. "Don't get so excited, that's always been your weakness, your nerves are way too close to the surface. That's because your rising sign is a Wood Rabbit."

"I know, I know, and you're a Metal Dragon."

"Exactly. And you work for me." He raised a hand at my sudden anger. "It's okay, I'm not ordering you to do anything except think about it—and discuss it with your womenfolk. If you don't want to talk about it with your mother, at least discuss it with Chanya."

"My wife?" I was about to protest that no way would my devout Buddhist partner (we've started using that word over here, where—as we shall see—the definition of wife is somewhat loose) encourage me to play consigliere to a *jao paw*, a godfather; then I realized he must already have done some lobbying or he would never have mentioned my mother or Chanya.

"Okay," I said, because it was the only way to close the interview, "I'll talk about it with Nong and Chanya."

I was pretty sure he'd somehow gotten my mother, Nong, on his side, probably using the weight of his money—he owns a majority of shares in her go-go bar on Soi Cowboy, the Old Man's Club—but I was confident of my darling Chanya, a female *arhat*, or Buddhist saint, far more advanced than myself, an attainment all the more remarkable in that she spent years on the Game herself. No, Chanya was *my* conscience, not his. Furthermore, she had grown increasingly respectable in her attitudes since giving birth to Pichai, our now six-year-old son, to the extent that she had even started hinting at a legal marriage. So far, we had remained content with a Buddhist ceremony in her home village. I paid her mother fourteen thousand dollars in the form of a dowry, even though she was technically damaged goods within the village price structure: her mum knew I was a junior shareholder in my mother's business and shrewdly concluded I was worth a lot more than my cop's salary. (Chanya, by the way, had to wash my feet as part of the ceremony, a benchmark event which we reminded each other of from time to time — it's a two-edged sword in any argument.)

More terrified than depressed by Vikorn's offer of promotion in his import-export franchise, I rushed home that day. Chanya was playing with Pichai in the yard of our little house — Pichai was the reincarnation of my former police partner and soul brother, whose name was also Pichai, who died in the cobra case years ago — and I had to carry on the conversation while Pichai crawled all over me and tried to pull my gun out from where I had shoved it under my belt in the small of my back.

"D'you know what Vikorn is trying to get me to do?"

The innocence of her expression was compromised by the time she took to assemble it. "No, what, *tilak*?" *Tilak* means "darling" (literally: "the one who is loved"). She was particularly skilled in its usage for strategic and tactical purposes.

"He wants me to be his consigliere."

"His *what*?"

"It's like chief negotiator to a *jao paw*—it's a Sicilian invention. You saw *The Godfather*, with Marlon Brando and Al Pacino?"

"No. Who are they?"

"Actors. That's what's so ridiculous. We're in the field of fiction here."

Chanya gave one of her beautiful smiles. "Oh, well, if it's only fiction, why not indulge him?"

I stared at her for a long moment. "He's got at you, hasn't he?"

"*Tilak*, don't get paranoid. I haven't spoken to Colonel Vikorn for over a year, not since that—ah— Songkran party." Songkran is the old Thai New Year; everyone gets drunk. This one was about par for the course: three near rapes, nine traffic accidents, a couple of serious beatings—I'm talking here about cops and staff at the police station. Chanya loved it.

"Through my mother—Nong spoke to you, didn't she?"

Chanya puckered her lips a tad. "*Tilak*, when you spoke to Colonel Vikorn about this, when he offered you this new position, did it even occur to you to ask about salary?"

Aghast for the second time that day: "Of course not. I was thinking of my skin, not my bank account. And my—" Suddenly I felt silly saying it, so I let her say it for me.

"Your karma?" She came to sit on the bench next to

the outdoor shower, causing Pichai to change sides immediately and nestle up to her bosom, of which he was, in my humble opinion, inordinately fond. Only seven years ago he was a celibate twenty-nine-year-old Buddhist about to enter a monastery: there is no constant in life but change. "*Tilak*, I love you so much, and I love you most for your conscience. You're the most genuinely devout Buddhist I know. Everyone else just follows the rules. You really think about karma and reincarnation. It's very admirable."

"Well, if it's so admirable, why are you trying to corrupt me?"

I felt a friendly female hand run up and down my back a couple of times, followed by a caress of my thighs and a subtle little tug at my cock—there are many techniques she learned on the Game which have proven useful in married life. "You are a saint, but you mustn't make the mistake of being a cloister saint."

"That's what Nong calls me sometimes."

"*Tilak*, just think of all the good you've done by restraining Vikorn over the years. Only last month you got tipsy right here in the yard and boasted about— no, I mean, reluctantly let slip—all the lives you've saved merely by whispering words of restraint and compassion into his ear."

"I always have to make it look like good strategy. I play Condoleezza Rice while Sergeant Ruamsantiah plays Cheney."

"Exactly, *tilak*, that's exactly what I'm getting at.

What your mother pointed out as well. You're so smart the way you handle him—the whole citizenry of District Eight has reason to be grateful to you." Chanya started to use terms like "citizenry," and "reluctantly let slip" after she enrolled in a distance-learning course in sociology at one of our online universities.

"But don't you see, it only works because it's informal. If I become his consigliere, I'm on the payroll, I can't threaten to resign every five minutes the way I do now. He'll have me under his thumb totally." At this point I used Pleading Eyes, normally a fail-safe tactic. This time, though, she remained unmoved.

"Sweetheart, you're going to be thirty-seven this year. You're not the boy genius anymore. You need to consolidate. I think you'll do marvelously as his—whatsit. You'll save twice as many lives as you do now. He'll listen to you more carefully, he'll have to, how else will he justify . . ." Her voice faded strategically.

Feeling deflated, my eyes rested on Pichai for a moment, then I caressed his head. I gave a huge sigh. "So, how much did Nong tell you Vikorn told her he would pay me?"

"Actually, your mother negotiated a bit on your behalf. He started at a hundred thousand, but your mum is such a genius negotiator—she used all the arguments you just used, but much more effectively, and she really went on about the extra threat to Pichai and me, what a strain it was going to be on your whole family, the risks to your life. She referred to

Pichai—I mean in his last incarnation—a lot, how he got shot in the line of duty and he wasn't even bent." She paused here, smiled at the water tank, then slowly turned the beam on me. "She got him up to two and a half."

"Two hundred and fifty thousand baht a month?" I had to give credit where it was due; nobody has ever gotten that kind of money out of Vikorn.

"Your mother is brilliant, and she did it all for us. Just think, we can send Pichai to an international school, he'll speak English without an accent, he'll be a famous surgeon just like he wanted to be last time but couldn't because his family was too poor. And if I have another baby we'll be able to use international-quality hospitals, not that stupid pediatrician who couldn't get the milk right so we had to put up with Pichai screaming with colic every night. And we'll be able to buy a house in a gated community, no more worries about security."

"You and Nong have already accepted on my behalf, haven't you?"

She beamed and made eyes. I looked pointedly at Pichai.

"It's okay, my sister is coming back from the country this afternoon. She's promised to take care of Pichai for a couple of days. We'll have the night to ourselves."

It was sexual coercion of the most despicable kind, of course. Chanya thought so too and was proud of it. After I came for the third time (actually, I didn't really

37

want to come three times, but she was on one of those missions to prove she was as good as she used to be; I was quite sore afterward, but I didn't say anything), she said with undisguised triumph, "Was that a yes?"

"Honey, I don't mind risking my life—"

She put a hand over my mouth. "I know you'd die a thousand times and commit a thousand crimes for us, but that's not what we want of you, Sonchai. Being a consig-ee thing will be safer and better paid. Everyone thinks you're his consig-ee thing anyway." An utterly frank look: "Sonchai, since we've had Pichai I've grown up. In the country there are a thousand ways to be happy, but in the city only one: money. I can't bear the thought of Pichai turning into some dope dealer, running all over town doing *yaa baa*—like you did with him in his last life. It's very sick, but for his generation of boys it's going to be education or drug running. Just as for girls it's education or prostitution. Globalism and capitalist democracy aren't going to allow anything in between. What are you doing?"

I was waving my right hand while pinching my thumb and forefinger together. "Waving an invisible white flag."

As I recall, at this point we all sat back and waited to see how my Colonel would use me in my new capacity: what deeds of derring-do could possibly justify a quarter-million baht a month? It seems that Vikorn had it all worked out.

4

Or had he? I've witnessed so many brilliant strategies of Vikorn's over the years that I've come to understand something of the nature of his genius: improvisation. His plans tend to be pretty general ideas designed to best his archenemy, General Zinna of the Royal Thai Army, which can be adapted to whatever circumstances occur on the ground. I don't think even Vikorn ever contemplated anything as bizarre as a Tibetan named Tietsin.

It was at least a month since my appointment as consigliere to our cop godfather, and I'd even drawn my first paycheck, which amounted to the equivalent of thirty times what I was earning doing much the same sort of job without the title, when Vikorn's black-hearted secretary, Police Lieutenant Manny, called me. I was sitting at my desk feeling guilty that I was so much richer, all of a sudden, than all the other straight cops; except there weren't so many of them, so there was no real justification for the guilt, and I was simultaneously wondering if I'd inherited the *farang* disease of self-recrimination from my long-lost GI dad. But I realized I had to do something to earn my dough, even if it was illegal and bad and likely to land me in the drug traffickers' hell for a couple hundred years. (A Sisyphic adaptation: you are forever pushing your rock up a hill toward the gigantic syringe at the top; just as you're about to grab the smack, your strength gives out and you and the rock are at the bottom of the hill again; and that's only for small-time dealers—I didn't dare think what happened to heavy traffickers.)

"Get up here, the boss wants you," Manny said.

I knocked somewhat peremptorily at Vikorn's door, waited for his "Yeah," entered, and found him standing at his window with an expression on his face I'd never seen before. *Quizzical* doesn't quite describe it; he seemed to be suffering from the exquisite dilemma of deciding whether or not to believe in his undeserved good luck. He turned, stared at me, shook his head, and went to his desk without a word. I shrugged and sat opposite him without asking permission. For a long minute I was staring at the picture of His Majesty our beloved King that hung above a poster all about the evils of police corruption (which Vikorn was inexplicably fond of, perhaps because it showcased the source of his wealth and was therefore a comfort in times of stress).

"I've just had a call," he finally said.

"Yes."

"It's the weirdest thing I ever heard of. Really the weirdest." He seemed unable to develop the conversation further for a moment, the weirdness was too overwhelming. Finally he said, "The phone call was from Kathmandu, in Nepal."

Now I was starting to get a sense of what he meant. No one would dream of calling Vikorn on a matter of law enforcement, so who the hell from Kathmandu would want to talk to him? "The caller, was it a Thai or a Nepali or a *farang*, a he or a she?"

"None of the above." He grinned. "It was a Tibetan who claimed to be a kind of lama. You know about this stuff, that's pretty high up, isn't it?"

"Spiritually at the top. The Dalai Lama himself often says he can't match his lamas for technical accomplishment—you know, like living on a tea-spoon of rice in a freezing cave for fourteen years while meditating naked in the lotus position and making purple rain. Lamas are those kind of guys."

"But he could speak some Thai. Not well, in fact pretty badly, but somehow educated. Like he'd learned it all from tapes or something."

A Tibetan lama who speaks Thai? That still wasn't half as weird as a Tibetan lama who would want to speak to Vikorn. "What did he say?"

A frown passed over my master's face, and he shook his head. "He said a lot." He stared at me. "He knows all about us. He knows what we do. And he knows about the problem I have with General Zinna— our permanent feud. And he made an offer." He looked up at me. "An offer which, if it's real, we can't refuse."

"What sort of offer?"

41

"An offer to put Zinna out of business and allow me to clean up not only on the retail side, which we have pretty much under control, but on the supply side too." Here came the crunch, and he took the moment to check my face. "He offered to solve all of our supply-side problems—all of them, transportation from Afghanistan and Pakistan to Bangkok."

I shook my head. "So, it's just someone trying to get a piece of the action while dealing in fantasy. You haven't been able to solve your supply-side problems for thirty years. How could some religious fanatic in the Himalayas help?"

"I know, I know. So did he. That's why he's offering us first choice after demonstrating his credentials and effectiveness. If we say no, he'll sell his services to Zinna."

"This doesn't sound like a spiritual personality."

"If he was genuinely spiritual, he wouldn't be of any use to us, would he?" Vikorn scratched the stubble under his chin. "But when I say he knows all about us, I mean it. He knows about you. He mentioned you. He wants you on the team. You are the only reason he is favoring us above Zinna. Buddha knows how he got his information. Anyway, he's shrewd enough to point out that if we force him to go to Zinna, Zinna will get so rich he'll be able to wipe us out in five years."

"How do we know this isn't some hoax, maybe by the anticorruption squad?"

"By following his instructions, which aren't too difficult."

I jerked my chin. "What instructions?"

"You go to the Immigration desks at Suvarnabhum Airport tomorrow at about ten-thirty in the evening. Make yourself known to the officer in charge. Someone will try to pass through Immigration to take a KLM flight to Amsterdam. According to the Tibetan they will be detained. You are to watch and be there, that's all." I wait for the revelation. After a minute he reaches into his desk drawer and takes out a piece of paper with a photo on it. "He asked for my private Internet address and sent this."

Vikorn passed over the paper. On one side was a color photograph of an exceptionally attractive young blond woman in her mid- to late twenties. "He says her name is Rosie McCoy. She's Australian. A mule who works for Zinna."

"I don't understand. What does this prove, even if it's true?"

"It proves he's got the guts and the know-how to hurt Zinna—as long as we accept his offer." Vikorn stared at me until I lowered my eyes. He had success-fully transferred the full emotional force of the words *hurt Zinna*; could there be a better justification?

I took the paper and started to leave. When I reached the door, Vikorn said, "If this is the real deal, we'll need you to take a trip to Kathmandu."

5

We are a hub. Flights to Los Angeles and other American destinations leave early in the morning, flights to Laos, Cambodia, Vietnam, China, and all points north and south leave every few minutes during the day, and flights to Europe mostly happen late in the evening. So why are there so few toilets in our brand-new airport? The *farang* design team and the Thai approval committee obviously didn't feel comfortable with too many comfort rooms. I had three iced lemon teas on my way and now I needed to take a leak pretty bad. (Iced lemon tea: full of sugar and polluted ice; in this heat it's like heroin. Don't try it, so you'll never know how good it is.) I took my place in line.

One thing I had to admit, the designers were democratic in their incompetence: there were plenty of first-class-looking types with perfectly coordinated monogrammed luggage sets waiting, all of them doing the *mustafapee* dance according to their programming, along with grassroots types like me, everyone of us under the sway of the equality Buddha. We all watched with unnerving intensity while one guy shook hard and looked like he was about to zip up and let someone else at the relief trough—then an agonizing change of mind as he found more water to drain. Another shake, so vigorous I feared the thing might fly off—surely he was feeling the collective psychic pressure behind him?—then finally we moved forward by one man. By the time I got to the Immigration Police offices it was nearly ten-thirty, which was the moment when passengers for Europe hit passport control.

The police colonel in charge of Immigration was not as unhappy to see me as I expected. A woman and a devout Buddhist, she took the view that all help in stemming the evil tide of drug trafficking was welcome, and anyway her officers were pretty busy and could do with some backup. She hinted that she didn't really understand this particular tip-off, which seemed to originate somewhere in the Himalayas, so maybe I could be of some real help. In addition to being devout, conscientious, and good-looking, she was also single and about my age. I'm not bragging here, but she really did look as if she could eat me, before directing me to an obscure corner of the airport with a good view of passport control, where a couple of her "girls," in smart white shirts with epaulettes, navy skirts, and fierce mugs, were standing. They didn't mind my company, but wondered aloud how a man could help with this particular case. I said I was just there to observe, because Colonel Vikorn had gotten the same tip-off.

Basically, there wasn't anything much to do but

flirt. I loyally told them how happily married I was, with a son I was totally crazy about, and they told me about their families, which left the way clear for plenty of hints, nudges, and winks before the perp arrived. Suddenly we were all in combat-ready professional mode.

I took out the picture, just to make sure, but there was really no doubt about it: the girl who had just taken up her place in one of the lines for foreign passports was the girl in the photo from the Himalayas. If anything, she was even more stunning in the flesh: blond hair which was almost white—the kind Asian men would kill for—and one of those bodies which have been sculpted from the inside out by an abundance of female hormones, producing a bosom you couldn't buy in Hollywood, a centerfold shape, and a nonchalance that came from the certainty that she could get away with almost anything. I didn't think there was any conscious arrogance in that careless walk as she dragged her Samsonite carry-on across the floor, nor in the way she made her buttocks swing. It was genuine animal narcissism. Her true arrogance lay in the smack she had hidden somewhere about her person, if the tip-off was for real.

We all waited for her to reach the booth, because we had to be sure her passport corresponded with the information.

As the line moved up and she approached the Immigration officer sitting at the booth behind the isometric digital camera, I could almost hear her words of reassurance to herself (I worked the airport myself a long time ago): *It's okay, you're with the professionals, the people who run Thailand, no way are you going to get caught. How could you? Someone would have had to snitch, and you've joined the non-snitchers, right? You belong to the ones the snitchers snitch to, how can you lose?*

Now she took out an iPod and a set of white earphones and played some music. I wondered if it was Buddha Bar. By the time she reached the booth she had so successfully controlled her mind that she was able to smile at the Thai man in the white shirt with blue epaulettes without a shadow of guile. As he took in her face and upper body he gave a brief flick of a smile in return before plugging her passport details into his computer. Reassured by his smile and the magic her breasts were working in his imagination—she had taken care to show such cleavage as could reasonably be attributed to the heat in the under-cooled airport—she took the liberty of leaning on the front of the booth with one elbow in a slightly provocative manner. Even when he picked up the telephone at his elbow, she did not exhibit the slightest degree of panic. He was probably arranging a tea break, right? So when the three female Immigration officers and I arrived from nowhere, and the officer who had been the most exuberant flirt ten minutes before put a hand on her shoulder, and the rest of us stood close around in case she tried to run, she looked like her insides were turning over in one prolonged churning, sickening, soul-destroying motion, which caused her to stagger.

"Please, come with us," the officer said. Her hand had slipped from on the woman's shoulder to under it. Her English was very good, albeit with an unmistakable Thai accent. All of a sudden Ms. Rosie McCoy could not speak. She nodded helplessly, like a terrified child. We took her to a long room divided into two. At the near end were a few plastic seats; at the other a radiographer in a white jacket worked with some Immigration officers. There were four travelers in front of Rosie, all men in line for the X-ray machine.

The radiographer worked very fast: it seemed there was no need for the suspects to undress. Now they stood Rosie upright against the plate and stepped back. There was a click, and then it was all over.

Suddenly an outbreak of excited jabbering in Thai. The English-speaking officer was bringing the X-ray plate to show her, and the rest of us followed in a group infected with schadenfreude. There it was: a condom nestling inside her vagina exactly like an erect but sluggish penis, clearly packed with white powder, which seemed to shine with horrific brilliance in contrast to the gray contours of her bones and flesh. The contraband in her lower intestine was less brilliant, but quite obvious to an experienced eye: five cosh-shaped objects. According to our source, it was all 100 per cent pure heroin. In Amsterdam or

Maastricht she would have cut it to five times its present volume and sold it for sixty dollars a gram.

She freaked. Her life about to come to an abrupt end at age twenty-seven, a scream started from the bottom of her lungs and emerged from her mouth without any act of will on her part. The Immigration officer slapped her face very hard, which put a stop to the scream. Now she started feeling in her pockets for her cell phone and fished it out with shaking hands.

"No," the officer said, and grabbed it.

"Oh please, oh please, look, this is all the money I have, I'll give it to you if you let me make just one call. Please? I'm begging you."

The officer stared at her for a moment, then at the open money belt, then at the other officers. "Put your money away. I don't care if you make one call, but don't try to delete anything. If you do, you'll regret it, big time."

Rosie made the call. Apparently for weapons she had nothing but an extensive stock of Australian expletives.

"You slime bucket, you dag, you fuckwit, you fucked-up piece of dog shit, you motherfucker, d'you know what I'm going to do to you? I'm going to dob you in it so fucking deep you'll swing for this, you ass-hole, I'm not going down alone, you lump of green vomit, you string of colon plaque, I'm taking you with me, you said this was safe, this was the A-stream, no one working this one ever got caught in the last twenty years, they had customs under control, you stupid, fucked-up, lying asshole. YOU'RE GOING DOWN, YOU'RE GETTING THE INJECTION, NUMB NUTS."

Exhausted, she closed the phone and burst into tears. Calming her down the best they could, the officers led her to a female toilet, where she was given the choice of extracting the condom in her vagina herself or leaving the job to one of the officers.

They told me afterward that Rosie claimed she could manage it, but terror and despair had caused her vulva to shrivel like a walnut and her hands to shake violently. When they sat her on a chair with a rubber sheet, she urinated involuntarily. In the end one of the officers donned a pair of plastic gloves and, using K-Y Jelly to ensure the condom didn't break and spill its contents into her body, pulled it out with the gentleness, kindness, and compassion a Buddhist woman ought to show a fellow female. After that it was simply a matter of accompanying Rosie to a nearby hospital, where nurses experienced in these things would administer a laxative: with that much poison in her gut the officers were not taking any chances. In the meantime, I checked Rosie's cell phone in order to find the last number she dialed.

Which turned out to be the cell phone number of one Mark Whiteman, an Englishman who I happened to know was a minor player in a large and successful trafficking ring run by none other than General Zinna of the Royal Thai Army. I had the information I had come for. I fished out my own mobile to call Vikorn.

"The source is straight," I said. "His information is good. Zinna is hurt."

"Get a ticket to Kathmandu while you're there."

"I'm traveling first-class. I'm consigliere."

"Go business. First-class attracts attention."

"I'll get the first flight tomorrow, there aren't any tonight."

When I closed the phone I strolled over to one of the airport bookshops to buy a guidebook to Nepal.

Did I forget to mention that when I was finally given a glance at Rosie McCoy's passport I discovered a full-page visa for the Kingdom of Nepal, together with entry and exit stamps? She had flown to Thailand after three months in that Himalayan country. What a coincidence.

6

I am still in the men's room at the Rose Garden, but
I've finished the joint and stopped sniveling. *No one in
my state of mind should fool with this stuff,* I explain to
myself as I roll another joint. The thing is, you get
addicted to the emotional roller coaster. It becomes a
fascination to see how the great Ferris wheel of Self
gets stuck with you strapped into the top seat with
your legs dangling over the void.

How different would life have been if I had not
flown to Nepal that morning? *Totally, totally different,*
I mutter as I take a toke. *Would you do it any differently
today?* I ask the haggard face in the mirror with the
funnel-shaped joint hanging from its lips. *No,* I tell
the poor distraught fellow staring back at me, *for then
I would never have met Tietsin.* With the detachment of
the truly psychotic I start to cackle, then double over,
whether in genuine hilarity or some caricature thereof
is hard to say: *I wouldn't have missed him for the world,*
I say, cackling and shaking my head, *not for the
world, damn him.* And all of a sudden he is there, large
as life, in the men's room with me, in his old parka

jacket unzipped at the front, his long gray hair in a ponytail, his straggly beard somehow comic, his eyes rolled back, revealing only the whites. "Your problem is you're not remembering in enough detail," he explains. "Your Western blood makes you superficial — go deeper in. What have you got to lose?"

"Oh, nothing," I say with theatrical emphasis. "Only my mind, and there's not much left of that, is there?" But of course he was a hallucination and has disappeared like mist.

In Nepal we don't fly through clouds, because the clouds have rocks in them.

The guidebook used this quote from a Royal Nepal Airlines pilot to open the section on Nepalese geography. The poorest country on earth is also the most vertical. Anyway, why would you worry about national resources when you have Everest? Overachievers from developed countries pay tens of thousands of dollars to get frostbite, lose limbs, and die at twenty-nine thousand feet, so they can call themselves *summiteers*. I also learned, for the first time, that Mr. Everest was a humble surveyor of the British Empire who really did not want the biggest rock on earth named after him, and neither did anyone else within a radius of ten thousand miles, since they had had their own names for the mountain for a good five thousand years before the ever-ready Everest turned up with his theodolite: Chomolungma

(Mother of the Universe) in Tibetan; Sagarmartha (Goddess of the Sky) in Nepali.

Take a tip from me: if you're approaching Nepal from East Asia, try to get a window seat on the right. I'd never seen the Himalayas before, and they come up on you disguised as clouds, delicate white wispy things at first, you think, until it dawns on you: it's not a cloud, it's not a mountain, it's fifteen hundred miles of wall many miles high built by gods as a six-star dwelling place (there is no other rational explanation). As we landed I felt Vikorn's genius and influence evaporate after holding my spirit prisoner for more than a decade. He was vicariously out of his depth too.

But as a cop, I could not help falling in love with the airport. It's the only one I've found that insists on throwing your luggage through a security machine *after* landing; but the good news is the machine doesn't work, probably never has, and anyway the guy with the knitted topi on his head sitting behind it chatting to a friend probably wouldn't know what to do with a sizzling little electronic device if he found one. Outside, there was the usual collection of hustlers, hotel runners, half-legal taxis, and ragged people who like to watch planes land and take off. On a whim I grabbed a taxi hustler with a rag tied around his head and such an array of astrological charms and charts all over the windows and roof of his cab he put your average Bangkok cabbie to shame. His eyes were black oil wells with insane flecks of red. His name was Shiva, of course.

Shiva wanted to know where I was staying. After studying the guidebook I narrowed the short list down to two: the five-star Yak & Yeti (I was most tempted by the name), which used to be someone's palace, or the downmarket but internationally loved Kathmandu Guest House. To make a decision I really needed to think about the psychology of my business partners. I mean, in your line of work, *farang*, everything depends on projecting the right image, correct? Which was exactly my dilemma. On one hand, I was here to arrange a high-value supply-side contract, which would normally mandate the Yak & Yeti as the only joint in the whole Himalayas qualified to provide the appropriate ambience; on the other hand, it was not exactly my style and I was dealing, if my information was correct, with a mind master of considerable skill and insight—didn't he just destroy the life of Rosie McCoy and put one huge crimp in General Zinna's operation, without, apparently, leaving his cave? No, I didn't think the Yak & Yeti was a smart decision; with guys like Tietsin, you better go naked or not at all.

"Kathmandu Guest House," I told Shiva.

"Forget it, it's full, anyway very overpriced. How about the Himalayan Guest House?"

"How much commission does the Himalayan Guest House give you, per customer?"

"Five per cent."

"Okay, I'll give you five per cent if you get me a suite at the Kathmandu Guest House."

Shiva stopped the taxi for a moment so he could *wai* a Hindu shrine (much gaudier than the Buddhist equivalent, and with more flowers, not all of them boring white lotus, either—I do love marigolds), before saying okay. It turned out the Kathmandu Guest House was only at 50 per cent occupancy, so I got my suite and Shiva got his commission, and I found I liked his wacky taxi and dirty head cloth so much I hired him for the rest of the day for the knockdown price of five dollars. "Swayambunath," I told him, as soon as I'd checked in.

Some smart-ass Tibetan Buddhist prophesied about a thousand years ago that when iron horses ran around Kathmandu on wheels, that would signal the end of Buddhism. Well, it did. About the same time as the iron horses started to appear in this town, the barbarian Chinese invaded Tibet and the D.L. had to flee. The problem I had with the iron horses at that moment was more prosaic: the pollution was (believe it or not, *farang*) even worse than Bangkok's, and Shiva's rear nearside window didn't close. (He'd taken the lever out of the door; of course, these windows had never seen electricity; the car was an old Indian Ambassador.) The silver lining here, though, was that the open window enabled a welcoming committee of very skinny cows to come and pay their respects. One shoved her massive head into the back of the cab during a traffic jam, enabling me to fondle her shaggy, black-velvet jowl and wish her good luck in her next incarnation, which, after such patience, was likely to be celestial.

Swayambunath is generally known as the Monkey Temple, for the simian thugs who seem to run the place. They're everywhere, and they keep their beady eyes on you while you're climbing the million and one steps, sniggering at your feeble strength, openly deriding you for forsaking the rain-forest paradise and your hairy superbody for this pathetically inferior bare-skin version, which had me gasping for breath halfway up. It didn't help that Shiva, who decided to make merit by accompanying me, and who was an authentic third-world chain-smoker of a cigarette so foul they made our humble L&Ms smell like havanas, effortlessly took the stone stairway two steps at a time and patiently waited for me while I leaned on the iron rail that divided the steps, coughing my heart out.

Farang, I am ashamed to admit (but I know you'll understand) that my first thought on finally reaching the temple on the high summit was that my cell phone would surely work from there—it had been acting up since I arrived, and I hadn't been able to make contact with Tietsin. Well, it did work, and I told someone on the other end who promised to tell Tietsin that I was staying at the Kathmandu Guest House. That chore over with, I was ready for Shiva, Vishnu, and Buddha, for they all had holiday homes right here.

Forgive me if I'm teaching my grandmother to suck

eggs, *farang*, but when you do your tour of a stupa or chedi, please do so in a clockwise direction. I don't want to be responsible for the bad luck you'll accrue by going the other way—I know how perverse you can be. And remember to spin all the prayer wheels; it's your tendency to leave out the middle bit that got you stuck with a human body in the first place. At the top of Swayambunath this simple formula will introduce you to all the Hindu gods; then lead you inexorably to the Buddhist enclave, where, as like as not, you will find the Tibetans in their plum robes chanting their hearts out, when not engaged in territorial disputes with the Hindus; then—hold your breath—the nirvanic moment when the heavens open and you find yourself staring across the Kathmandu Valley at the greatest geological show on earth: *the mountains, the mountains.* With them as stark white backdrop, there is not a lot else to talk about. We are a miniature chorus in a theater built by the gods. And all the time I was thinking, *Tietsin, Tietsin.*

When I'd done my three and a half turns, I asked Shiva if he wanted to eat, but he shook his ragged head; perhaps he found my company impure, or perhaps he didn't like the way I spun the ancient brass prayer wheels. (Hindus are easily offended, but at least they don't decapitate you like Muslims, or ruthlessly exploit your natural resources for three hundred years like Christians.) I said, "Pashupatinath."

It's on the Baghmati River and is said to be the second most sacred Hindu site on earth, after Benares.

Suddenly eager to show his country in its best light, Shiva took me to an elevated platform where a yogin lifted a five-pound rock with his penis. (I don't want to sound deflating here, but he didn't do it by means of an erection—now wouldn't that have been divine?— but rather prosaically tied a string from rock to flaccid cock while squatting, thereby inexorably raising the phallic burden when he stood up.) The yogins here, by the way, really look the part: magnificent heads of uncut hair tied up in chignons liberally anointed with russet dye, a whacking great third eye called a *tikka* outlined on the forehead in a bright crimson stripe between two white ones, tridents and alms bowls, the whole shebang. They even have their own bijou hermit stations made of stone, with full views of the bodies burning on the ghats down below. Shiva and I watched the brawny fire tenders with their ten-foot bamboo poles prodding the flames while the white-shrouded corpses burned, surrounded by close relatives. When someone's brains exploded with an almighty bang, widow and children jumped back a yard or two, then laughed gaily.

I looked at Shiva and said, "Bodnath," in an inno-cent tone which did not betray my stage fright, for I had no doubt at all that Tietsin was there and would know I had visited, even though our first meeting was scheduled for the next day. Shiva surprised me by saying it was within walking distance.

Stupas may be Buddhist in this epoch, but their origin predates Gautama by many thousands of years.

Probably the Aryan invaders brought them ten millennia ago, along with their Vedic mysteries: those were the days, when *farang* knew more about magic than Asians. The stupa at Bodnath is a gigantic pure white breast about forty-five yards high and a hundred in diameter, surmounted by a pointed nipple and an all-seeing pair of eyes each about a yard wide; but what hits you the most are the prayer flags strung on great long cables that form a parabola from the earth to the top of the stupa. Blue for sky, white for air, red for fire, green for water, yellow for earth, generally in that order.

The flags, which carry the texts of a thousand prayers stitched into the cloth, are intrinsic to Tibetan Buddhism, and you find them all over the Himalayas. The wind takes the healing meditations of the holy monks and carries them all over our tortured world; to use the wind and earth as a kind of machine to broadcast the way of transcendence is to me one of those sublime cultural achievements: would you forgive me for suggesting it beats landing on the moon? I found the eyes particularly hard to look at. Sure, anyone can simply glance at something like that without suffering psychic overload, but try absorbing its significance on a deeper level—okay, okay, *farang*, you don't want to know about that, you want to know about sex, drugs, and murder, I understand. Anyway, I did my three and a half turns without neglecting a single prayer wheel, all the time surrounded by Tibetans, most of them monks and nuns—professionals, in other words—who talked on cell phones, chanted and gossiped and spun the wheels and laughed and ate (they seemed to be compulsive snackers, like Thais) their way around the fantastically oversized stupa like Canterbury pilgrims. I was at first offended by an elderly nun who begged me for a few coins. This was strictly un-Buddhist and for a moment very disappointing: the true meaning of alms is not to keep the monk or nun from hunger, but to provide an opportunity of grace for the lay donor. She should not have asked; she should have simply stood there to let me make merit. She was pretty decrepit, though, and perhaps not all that smart, so, feeling like a sucker, I dipped into my pocket to give her a bunch of coins and notes. Actually, I did my usual trick of not looking at what I was bringing out of my pocket. When I calculated how much I had given her it amounted to more than five dollars, a fortune for her. She took the money indifferently, as if it was no more than her due, then gave me a look which, in my mildly disorientated and slightly paranoid state, seemed to say, *What kind of international drug trafficker are you?*

Then that name flicked across the screen behind the forehead which some call the third eye: *Tietsin*, it said, in bright flashing neon. *Tietsin*.

On an impulse I went to find Shiva Taxi. The whole stupa was surrounded by teahouses, thanka shops, souvenir collections, and a thousand places where you can get your digital pix loaded onto a CD or access the Internet. It took me thirty minutes of running around the gigantic compound before I found him and told him it was time to go. He stared at me, wondering why I was suddenly exhibiting signs of stress.

When I got back to the hotel I found a message waiting. Tietsin's people would come for me about ten o'clock the next morning. Feeling restless, I left the hotel to walk on Thamel.

Which has a way of exploding in your face. Less than twelve inches from the perimeter of the guest-house, a couple of trishaw drivers pulled up and almost trapped me against a wall; a woman who might have been Tibetan held a dead baby in her arms while she thrust out a hand and sobbed; taxies honked as they tried to get past the trishaws; runners from some of the other guesthouses tried to persuade me to relocate; a young man almost in rags whispered that he had hashish as a couple of men in black leatherette jackets drove up on a mid-range Honda motorbike and offered the same thing at the same price, though with infinitely more gravitas. Someone—a man whose face I never saw—asked if I wanted a girl or two tonight. When I squeezed past the trishaws and crossed the street, I was accosted by chillum and pipe salesmen; craftsmen who had spent the day carving chess sets wanted to sell me their masterpieces; and it all happened against a specifically Hindu soundtrack of honks and yells and men making their habitual ablutions, which included some elaborate hoiking, right there on the street—but you can't really blame them, for the dust gets everywhere. Then there were the *farang* backpackers who moved heavily with their towering burdens which must have contained clothing for six months and medical accessories for a year. Some had aluminum tent poles sticking out. Quite a lot of them were single women or women traveling in pairs, both young and middle aged; Nepal was supposed to be safe, all the guidebooks agreed. I saw clones of Rosie McCoy. At the same time Nepali women in traditional dress (mostly saris, although a lot wore tapered pants under a long upper garment) were rushing in and out of shops and carrying groceries wrapped in gray paper, or cooking over gas burners in the open doorways of their medieval homes, taking care not to jostle the bony cows who also emerged to enjoy the evening. Then there was the music. *Om mani padme hum* boomed out from CD stores along with Robbie Williams and Ravi Shankar, and one corner shop never stopped with the deep-throat, low-note Tibetan chants which formed a kind of long-wave whale chorus to the whole zoological moment. Of course I was thinking, *Tietsin*.

I woke just after dawn, took a stroll around town, refused marijuana five times—only because I was meeting Tietsin—and gave some money to the woman still holding the dead baby; so maybe the baby wasn't really dead. When they came for me, the elderly nun from Bodnath to whom I had given money and whom I had thought decrepit was in the back of the minivan. She smiled warmly and mischievously. The driver seemed to be Nepali and didn't speak. "We're going to a lecture on Tibetan history," she explained with a smile in perfect English.

7

I had been shown into some kind of forum which had already started; indeed, it seemed on the point of finishing. The top floor of the teahouse had been converted into a meeting room with maybe a dozen chairs, eight of which were occupied by youngish *farang* who looked like backpackers. I had no choice but to sit at the back and listen.

Doctor Norbu Tietsin had a trick of throwing back his head and rolling his eyes all the way into the sockets, which might have seemed comic in a lesser figure, but with him seemed slightly sinister, like watching someone enter another dimension—or go into a trance.

He was more than six feet tall, in his sixties, very robust and muscular, and wore a battered parka-style coat, unzipped. He spoke English perfectly in what he himself later would describe as a UN accent, i.e., it contained hints of Oxford, estuary London, New York, and Sydney, with more than a little Scandinavian precision in the vowels—but had a tendency to morph into Brooklyn at odd moments.

He possessed a wispy, untrimmed gray beard that billowed under his nose and gray hair drawn back in a ponytail. Like a seasoned professor, he needed no notes and, when he was not looking out the window, limped up and down in front of the audience with his hands in his pockets. I was inclined to attribute his handicap to frostbite, though in another country one might have assumed gout.

"Captain Younghusband was the first white man to invade Tibet," Tietsin was saying. "Lord Curzon encouraged him and gave him the money, which, like most of the income of the British Indian Empire at that time, derived from the sale of opium. He slaughtered thousands of monks with his killing machines in the charming Anglo-Saxon way."

The crippled giant paused for a moment and coughed. "But we didn't mind the ambitious captain too much. We were already used to the cruelty of the Chinese, and as someone said, *When you know the scorpion you don't worry about the toad*. He did invade us, however, and the karmic price had to be paid." Tietsin took his right hand out of his pocket and raised it. The hand was no more than a stump, frostbite having eaten away at all the digits except thumb and forefinger. He brushed his brow with it, sighed, spared me a glance as he swept the audience, then said, "So we in turn had to invade him."

He stopped in mid-flight with his stump still raised and stared at us one by one for a full minute.

"It was touch and go," he continued, still apparently

talking about Younghusband. "You've no idea what a chore it is to develop a fetal psyche to the point where it can leave the womb of its culture of origin and begin to adapt to reality in one lifetime. Normally, with someone of that profile, you'd want a couple hundred years to be on the safe side—suicide is always the great risk. We did it, though. The good captain became an embarrassingly ardent convert to our spiritual path, without understanding very much about it, unfortunately, or necessarily realizing it was Buddhism that was rebuilding his character from the inside out." He shrugged. "Still, I guess as a way of introducing ourselves to the West you could say our strategy worked. It was Younghusband, really, who inspired the irrational distortion of our religion by people like the neurotic Madame Blavatsky, and the curious case of Dr. Rudolf Steiner, who somehow grafted gnostic Christianity onto it and called it Spiritual Science, for Buddha's sake."

I would grow used to his tendency to talk about events of more than a hundred years ago as if they happened yesterday. And they say we Thais have no sense of time. But I wasn't prepared for his erudition. I had vaguely come across Madam Blavatsky and Rudolf Steiner while surfing the Net: two early Western prophets of Oriental wisdom whose work was largely lost in that cosmic catastrophe called the Twentieth Century. I was out of my depth and knew it. I found myself wondering how *my* fetal psyche was going to adapt to this new reality.

Now Tietsin turned away from the window again and suddenly stared at me with the full force of his developed mind. "Then in '59, after the Chinese invasion, His Holiness went into exile and brought our spiritual science, if you want to call it that, to a world which had been at least partially prepared."

He paused again and frowned. "We've invaded the world. But we've lost Tibet."

There could be no doubt that this last phrase was meant for me. Suddenly it seemed everyone was following his eyes and staring at me. I nodded in full agreement with whatever the underlying meaning might have been, at the same time wondering what it all had to do with the price of smack. But you couldn't help but be riveted by the man himself. I was assuming he'd crossed the fifteen-thousand-foot pass on foot from Tibet to Dharamsala at some stage in his life. With the courage of a giant he managed to use his disabilities to project a spirit freer than an Olympic gymnast's. But it was his eyes: the speed of their movement together with the sharpness of focus indicated decades of meditation which cannot be faked.

There was nothing to do but listen while he expounded on the Chinese invasion: its barbaric cruelty, Tibetans reduced to slavery, forced to participate in the rape and pillage of their country, all in the name of glorious Socialism; young women forced into prostitution in Lhasa for the entertainment of Chinese soldiers—rough and brutalized peasant lads for the most part, children and grandchildren of Mao

Tse-tung's holocaust, called the Cultural Revolution.

It was pretty somber stuff and not the sort of thing your average Western backpacker comes to the Himalayas to hear about. But they seemed to be all attention, gripped by this maimed hero. For my part I think I would have been fascinated if he'd been giving a lecture on reinforced concrete; it was all about the man, and the man knew it.

Exactly as I was thinking this thought, Tietsin focused on me with such intensity I experienced it as a passing headache. I looked up in astonishment at that rugged face, which betrayed no loving-kindness. Indeed, for that moment it did not seem human at all; perhaps it wasn't. Then he looked away again.

After his unusual account of Tibetan history, Tietsin's summary of the principles of Buddhism was surprisingly standard. He took us through explications of the Buddha, the dharma, and the sangha in the usual order, simplifying for the *farang* audience. When he'd finished, everyone clapped politely and started to leave. I watched them, five white women and three white men, all of them under thirty. I could not tell if they were European, American, or Australian; they all looked innocent enough: travelers without commitment. Maybe Tietsin was aiming his discourse at the people they would be a couple of lifetimes hence. None of them looked like they were going to rush to ordain as monks and nuns. All of a sudden I was alone with the Doctor himself, who was staring out the window at the two great eyes on the stupa and ignoring me. I coughed.

He turned with a grin, came over, and twisted a chair around so he could sit and stare into my eyes. Finally he held out his right hand, the one with the missing fingers, and clasped my own between the two remaining digits. He held on until I had to tug to get my hand back. Those remaining fingers were extra strong. Now he jerked a chin at me, daring me to speak.

"Did you lose your fingers when you crossed the mountains to Dharamsala?"

"No. I lost them in Chamdo."

"I have no idea where that is."

"Extreme east of Tibet. Where the Chinese started the invasion."

I found myself nodding slowly while information I had absorbed in a vague way years ago began to filter through the memory cells. Somewhere the bio-computer was going through its elaborate calculations, which ended with a brief flash of inspiration on my part. "You were in the resistance?"

He inhaled deeply, then exhaled. "Thousands of us voluntarily disrobed so we could fight for our country. It didn't seem such a stupid thing to do; after all, we had America on our side, in the form of the CIA."

"Yes," I said. "I read about it somewhere. You were betrayed."

He shrugged. "You could put it like that. Or you could simply call it a flaw in democracy. America voted for Nixon."

I remembered now. The president with the meat-loaf mind saw China as a useful counterbalance to the Soviet Union—and to hell with human rights, which, as a part-time burglar himself, he'd never had any time for anyway. As soon as he got into power he ordered the CIA to hold back on support for the Tibetan resistance.

"But you must have been very young," I said.

"Fifteen. I'd already been in the robes for seven years. When I heard that my father and all the men in my home village had gone to fight, I joined the other monks who disrobed at that time. Of course, the Chinese slaughtered us. But that wasn't the point. Was it?" He stopped, waited for my question.

"You escaped to Dharamsala?"

He puckered his lips. "Maybe it's better you don't know what I did next." Another pause. "Sure, in the end I got to Dharamsala, paid my respects to His Holiness, accepted his gracious offer to find me a place in a monastery there so I could continue my religious studies."

Again a pause, as if he were calculating exactly how much information to let out. "But when the time came to take my vows again, I couldn't do it. In my soul the Chinese had replaced the Buddha with hatred. Things that happen when you're still young are hard to overcome." He sighed. "So I found a girl." He smiled. "Or, I should say, a girl found me. A Westerner, of course. A natural born do-gooder, which is the same as saying someone blind to their

71

own badness. It was her notion that love and marriage would heal me. I believed her. I was so new to the West, so disillusioned with everything else, I assumed she had the right answer. That's how naïve I was."

He looked at me with a comic expression. "I had a well-trained mind from my monastic studies, so I went through the usual third-world thing of collecting qualifications. I ended up with a doctorate in Tibetan history—really useful for joining corporate America, right? Naturally, love and marriage failed in the end, as they always must. The wife who would have died for me on day one was starting to think about having me bumped off by day one thousand. I had been brought up to take vows seriously, so there was no way I was ever going to leave her." Here he let a few beats pass while he contemplated me. "But when the self-righteous, hypochondriacal, self-pitying, life-fearing, man-resenting, competitive, criminal-minded, infantile bitch dumped me I wept with relief. Thank Buddha there were no children." He held up both hands, one deformed, the other whole. "*Me voilà.*" He cocked an eyebrow.

"You are a misogynist?"

"Nope. It can happen to anyone. Let's say the aspect she offered of her multifaceted humanity was pretty unvarying toward the end."

I stopped short. "The whole of humanity is that bad?"

"Actually, I was going easy on her. And the rest of us. I left out 'homicidal.' "

It would be a characteristic of his conversation that I seemed frequently to find myself at the receiving end of some kind of spiritual revelation when I thought we were having a normal chat. He leaned closer to me to whisper, "Do you really think that in the future it will be nations alone fighting for scarce resources? Don't be so naïve, we'll be fighting each other, all against all, down to the last square inch of commercially viable dust. Actually, that is what we're doing already. Without spiritual aspiration we revert, do you see? Not merely to the monkey state, that wouldn't be so bad. No, all the way back down the evolutionary spiral. Those are the stakes. How would you like to be worker number ten million and twelve in a termite nest?"

Something about Tietsin made you feel he wasn't just shooting his mouth off; it was as if he were read-ing from a text in the sky. I badly wanted to change the subject.

"You speak French?"

"French, English, Tibetan, Hindi, some Thai." He paused. "And Chinese. When your karma is that of the Homeless One, you'd better learn to be a linguist."

I remembered that "Homeless One" was a technical expression for a Buddhist monk.

It was at that moment I experienced for the first time a sensation which was to repeat itself a number of times in my association with him. It was a curious feeling that I was about to faint, then just at the moment of loss of consciousness a wave of energy flooded my mind and I recovered in what can only be described as a higher form of consciousness. I knew two things: that this was something Tietsin was doing to me deliberately, and that the exercise of such powers was strictly forbidden to genuine Buddhists.

All this time he had been watching me curiously, while the assemblage point of my mind hovered somewhere above the top of my head and sensory import became pleasantly blurred, as if the five senses didn't matter anymore.

Now he stood up and gave a great big benevolent smile which effortlessly wiped away the heaviness of the previous moment. "Let's get out of here," he said, and, limping, led the way down the stairs. I had to follow slowly, so as not to lose my balance, but the sensation was at all times seductively pleasant.

"We watched you yesterday, when you came with that Hindu with the rag around his head. We were very impressed. Without seeming to think about it, you started at the most easterly point of the stupa, walked around it exactly three and a half times, carefully turning every prayer wheel, which brought you up at exactly opposite the point where you started: west. When that old lady approached you for money, you didn't stick to the letter of the law but showed compassion over and above strict dharma and gave her rather a lot of dough. You are a terrible romantic, therefore: you broke the law for love. That makes you a high security risk on the one hand—and a dreadful sucker—but a sympathetic fellow traveler on the other. Let's say you already passed our interview yesterday, there's nothing more about you we need to know. So this day is your opportunity to interview me. Fire away."

I tried to say, *Interview you?*, but the words would not come out. We had reached the bottom of the stairs and turned right toward the great stupa, but all the people were gone. I gasped.

8

There is nothing magical about telepathy; it is merely one of those faculties our ancestors developed to a certain point before discarding it in favor of something more reliable, like answering machines. I had never experienced it in anything but the most atrophied form—Chanya and I were occasionally telepathic, usually reading each other's minds with regard to things that didn't matter much; I had never seen anything like this.

For a start the stupa had changed color. It was black. The eyes were an intense, angry red; a great, exaggerated burst of enraged lightning was emerging from the steeple; it was night; a bloated full moon hung in the eastern sky; and, weirdest of all: nothing was happening. I mean, there was no movement. I was looking at a mental painting, an internal snapshot which Tietsin had transferred to me. Later, once the initial amazement had subsided, I would penetrate to a deeper and still more disturbing meaning: this was how Tietsin saw Buddhism, the world, life. Or, you could say this was a picture of his soul he was showing me.

The moment evaporated, the sun came back out, the stupa was a brilliant white again and surrounded by pilgrims in burgundy robes and tourists in shorts and sandals and jolly souvenir shops, and Tietsin was staring at me with that curious look on his face. "Interview over?" he asked with exaggerated courtesy. "Let's take a stroll. We'll be like spies in those Cold War movies who have to conduct their negotiations in open places where there are no microphones and anyone following us would be conspicuous."

I spared him a wild-eyed glance as I followed. "Would you mind telling me how you did that? I mean, excuse me, but for a moment just then you took over my whole mind."

He shrugged. "Blame my meditation master. I was a star student before I disrobed. There was stuff he showed me that shouldn't really be shared with a teenager. To this day I don't know if he passed on those advanced initiations because he thought I would be a lama, or because he knew the Chinese were coming and there was no time left for niceties, or because he was the kind of master who didn't give a shit, which is supposed to be the best kind. Obviously, for whatever reason he felt he had no choice but to risk my sanity." He gave me a quick glance. "Nothing is ever as simple as it seems. Come, let us make merit."

I followed his uneven gait around the stupa, spinning the prayer wheels as we went. He had a specific technique, a professional's handiness with the brass. I was less adept.

After the first nine wheels, Tietsin said, "Whoever is angry, harbors ill will, is evil-minded and envious, whose views are delusive, who is deceitful, he is to be known as an outcast."

I tried to remember where I had heard that before. Surely it was nothing less than the *Vasala Sutra*? I said, "Whoever destroys life, whether bird or animal, insect or fish, has no compassion for life . . ."

"Whoever is destructive or aggressive in town and country and is a known vandal or thug . . ."

"Whoever steals what is considered to belong to others, whether it be situated in villages or the forest . . ."

"Whoever, having contracted debts, defaults and when asked to pay, retorts, 'I am not indebted to you' . . ."

"Whoever is desirous of stealing even a trifle and takes such a thing, having killed a man going along the road . . ."

"Whoever commits perjury either for his own benefit, for that of others, or for the sake of profit . . ."

"Whoever has illicit affairs with the wives of his relatives or friends, either by force or through mutual consent . . ."

"Whoever does not support his father or mother, who are old and infirm, being himself in a prosperous position . . ."

"Whoever strikes or abuses by words either father, mother, brother, sister, or mother-in-law . . ."

"Whoever being asked for good advice teaches

what is misleading or speaks in obscure terms . . ."

"Whoever having committed an offense wishes to conceal it from others and is a hypocrite . . ."

"Whoever having gone to another's house and taken advantage of the hospitality there does not reciprocate in like manner . . ."

"Whoever deceives a priest, monk, or any other spiritual preceptor . . ."

"Whoever abuses by words and does not serve a priest or monk coming for a meal . . ."

"Whoever, being enmeshed in ignorance, makes untrue predictions for paltry gain . . ."

"Whoever exalts himself and despises others, smug in his self-conceit . . ."

"Whoever is a provoker of quarrels or is avaricious, has malicious desires, is envious, shameless, and has no qualms in committing evil . . ."

"Whoever insults the Buddha or his disciples, whether renounced ones or laymen . . ."

"Whoever not being an *arhat* pretends to be one, he is indeed the greatest rogue in the whole world, the lowest outcast of all . . ."

"Thus have I exposed those who are outcasts . . ."

"One does not become an outcast by birth, one does not become a Brahmin by birth. It is by deed that one becomes an outcast, it is by deed that one becomes a Brahmin."

The celebrated sutra had taken us one half turn of the stupa. We had started in the west, I suppose because Tietsin wanted to finish in the east. He was

79

silent for the whole of the second turn of the stupa, then he said, as he spun the wheels with particular vigor, "I guess we have a deal."

"I guess. How much can you ship?"

"Our movement needs forty million dollars. Whatever will get us that sum, we'll ship."

"Your movement? Is it political?"

"Sure. We're going to invade China."

"What with?"

He stopped short, as if the question surprised him. "With the inexorable power of Tantra, of course."

I assumed this was some kind of macabre Tibetan joke; we were talking, after all, about a Communist republic which suppressed religion wherever it could, so I focused on the practical issue. "How can you do what no one else can do and export so much at one time?"

"Contacts and know-how. The stuff is shipped raw from Afghanistan into Waziristan, that is to say tribal Pakistan, where it is processed. From there it is moved to Ladakh, which used to be known as Greater Tibet, all under our supervision. People forget, Buddhists were active in that part of the world for a thousand years before Mohammed. Our contacts predate Islam. From Ladakh we ship it directly into Chinese-occupied Tibet. That's the key. Tibet is mostly pure emptiness, and anyway our people are the only ones who can tolerate the climate—the Chinese all get very frail at that altitude, especially when stationed outside of Lhasa, where there are no hospitals and no oxygen bottles. We have total free rein. No one can stop us."

"Does the Dalai Lama know?"

Here Tietsin stopped. It was the first time he had frowned at me. "Of course not. His Holiness is the greatest living Tibetan. Actually, he is the greatest living human being, he is the incarnation of Avalokiteshvara, but his mission is not to save Tibet. He has invaded the world instead. Anyway, he has said he will not reincarnate, or if he does it will not be in Tibet. Do you understand what that means?"

"You and your movement are left to defend it on your own?"

"No, we've already lost it. I and my movement are going to take it back on our own. From under the noses of two billion Chinese."

"How many lifetimes will it take?"

"That is the only unknown in the whole equation. It is also irrelevant."

My next question, obviously, involved the sensitive issue of morality. However worthy the cause, Tietsin was involved in shipping poison in bulk. I didn't need to ask it. He said, almost apologetically, "I follow my dharma. That's all I can tell you. At the end of the day *I am* is an unfathomable mystery."

We had come to a stop, our three and one half turns of the stupa were complete. We had landed in the east. As we shook hands and he gripped mine with those two fingers, Tietsin said, "We'll ship it to any address in Thailand, Laos, Cambodia, or Burma.

We'll talk about offshore bank accounts nearer the time. We prefer to use Lichtenstein."

I was about to take my leave, but those two fingers of his were pressing into my palm, refusing to let go until I looked into his eyes. Naturally, he had one more spectacular little trick to play that day. I saw it again, in each of his eyes this time, in perfect miniature clarity: the black stupa, the lightning, the rage.

"Nice meeting you," Tietsin said, and turned to make another tour, spinning the wheels as he went.

I should have let him go, but instead, in my ignorance, I stared after him, willing him to come back. So he did. Now he was standing in front of me again, rolling his eyes back, as if he hated having to preach but felt he had no choice. "There's only one real instruction. Forget the Eightfold Path if it doesn't apply to your situation. *Be one of those who travel to the Far Shore.* The Buddha doesn't give a broken alms bowl how you get there, just do it before it's too late. There isn't a lot of time left. That's all I can tell you."

Then he was gone.

9

When the how-to publishers produce a handbook for aspiring consiglieres it will emphasize the wisdom of getting the hell out, once the main deal is done. Any good mafioso would have gotten on the next plane, right? Even a mediocre, 9-to-5 type of consigliere would have done so. Even a tenth-rate thug who operates on animal instinct would have known to go to the Thai Air offices on Durbar Marg and have them change the ticket so he could leave that same day and rush back to Colonel Vikorn with the wonderful news that we could expect to receive however many tons of poison for retail within the next month, probably enough to put our main rival General Zinna out of business—wouldn't he? And did I?

Well, I rushed, but it wasn't to the airport. It was to the Pilgrim's Bookshop on Thamel. (You have to remember how I got into this: I was a monk manqué who found himself ensnared in a nefarious process for which he could only feel partially responsible; if that sounds like a cop-out to you, *farang*, try being an Asian head of family.)

Now, reader dear, would you permit a pause in the breathless narrative while I sing praises? Briefly, if it's God you're after, or some variation thereon, the Pilgrim's Bookshop is the outfit for you. Maybe the Library of Congress is better for general inquiries, but if it's the allegedly nonexistent that interests you — say, the lesser-known habits of Shiva, Vishnu, and Brahma, or which color Tara would be most suitable for the thanka in your living room, or which particular cave in the high Himalayas you should choose for your summer retreat, or how to be a sadhu without giving up your day job, or which plants, mushrooms, and toadstools in the Kathmandu Valley will really get you stoned (there's a whole wall dedicated to them) — trust me, you need the P.B. (Yes, they do ship overseas, and they *are* on the Net, and no, I don't have shares in the company.) In the end I bought eleven volumes of transcendental obscurity and five DVDs, only one of which turned out to be of direct relevance. Entitled *The Shadow Circus*, it went into detail about the CIA-sponsored rebellion after the Chinese invasion of Tibet. I got the management of the Kathmandu Guest House to lend me a DVD player and holed up for the day with my books and my disks. By afternoon I felt I knew a lot more about Tibetan Buddhism, aka Tantra, aka Vajrayana, aka Apocalyptic Buddhism. I guess I ended up with a more nuanced concept of the Far Shore, the biggest nuance being that it was not susceptible to concepts.

And still I didn't go to the airline offices. Or call

them. When my eyes grew tired and I couldn't focus anymore, I decided to do some sightseeing. I took out a map of the city and after a lot of wrong turns wound up at a backstreet shrine near Asan Tole which is dedicated to Vaisya Dev, the god of toothache. There were half a dozen dentally challenged citizens wearing scarves around their jaws looking miserable; the trick is to nail a single rupee coin to the wooden shrine with an ancient hammer which is tied to the shrine with a string, mutter your favorite mantra—and Bob's your uncle, no more pain. You almost wish you had a mild toothache yourself so you could check out the magic. Then I thought maybe old Vaisya was also good for preventive medicine, and fished out a rupee to nail up: *Oh, Vaisya, let me never suffer toothache again*. There is no denying superstition. It's part of what's out there, *thathagata*: like toothache.

After that I walked on Thamel, then down to the Vishnumati River, across the iron bridge next to the Hindu temple, then the long trek to the foot of the Monkey Temple. Even the stairs did not cool my fevered brain. At the top I impatiently paid my tourist rip-off fee and almost ran around the stupa spinning the wheels and then stared out over the valley thinking, nay, screaming silently to myself, *The mountains, the mountains*. Then: *Tietsin, oh Tietsin, I want the Far Shore*. That old Tibetan witch had pressed my big red emergency button. I was in a fever.

Why was I not surprised when a Buddhist monk in his plum robes with the right shoulder bare surreptitiously passed me a flyer for a seminar that was being held that very evening on the top floor of a tea shop at the great stupa of Bodnath? He was gone before I could ask if he knew Tietsin personally. I had a feeling every Tibetan in the city knew Tietsin personally. *Listen,* I whispered to the sublimely beautiful black stone Buddha just behind the miniature mausoleum and next to the Kodak shop (before you get to the alley that leads to the Café de Stupa—I didn't think much of the food, but the rooftop views were transcendental), *I'm supposed to be a mafioso, a despicable international drug trafficker, a poor sucker among six billion poor suckers ensnared irrevocably in karma from which there has never been any escape and for which therefore I experience no responsibility even if it is all my fault. I really don't know if I can stand too much fresh air.*

Cut the crap, was the black Buddha's terse reply. *I don't give a broken alms bowl how you do it, just get to the Far Shore, there isn't a lot of time left.*

That evening I gave myself half an hour to get to Bodnath from Thamel, which should have been ample, but there was a traffic jam on Thamel Chawk at the junction with Tridevi Marg (I'm sure the noise was all from frustrated Hindus; Buddhists don't honk like that), so when my driver finally got me to Bodnath I expected the seminar to be almost finished. I saw no sign on the door, no flyer, and the door was shut; maybe everyone had gone home?

When I knocked softly, a Buddhist nun opened and stared at me suspiciously for a moment until someone behind her murmured something in Tibetan and she changed her attitude. She let me in with a great sudden beam of loving-kindness and nodded at a seat at the back. After I was seated, she locked the door again. Tietsin was on his feet, limping across the floor as he spoke, ruthlessly using his stump as theatrical device. "What was at issue was not Tibetan autonomy, it was the soul of the world. The world decided it didn't need a soul and couldn't use a heart. If there had been a lot of oil there, that would have been different. If we were on some geopolitical trigger point of interest to the West, it would have been different. But there was not, and we were not." He paused. "You could say that in the year 2076 of our calendar there began a process long prophesied by which the bulk of humanity—I'm talking ninety per cent—will get trapped in the continuum of materialism and will therefore be destroyed. The way leading to final destruction is superficially pleasurable, until we're snared, then it gets old real quick. Even on the best view, we're looking at three thousand years of un-enhanced mediocrity, before the Maitreya Buddha comes. Does that ring a bell? I guess it must, or you all wouldn't be here, would you?"

He looked over the audience without appearing to see me. All the seats were full, and it struck me that the one I was sitting in had been reserved, because there were people standing and leaning against the walls. The room was packed, lending a feeling of intensity, even passion, to the atmosphere. As I took it all in, I realized that perhaps half the people present were Buddhist monks and nuns in their robes; most of those, however, were Westerners who I supposed had been ordained here, maybe kids on their gap year between high school and college who got snared—by Tietsin? The others in the audience, lay listeners like myself, seemed to come from a variety of different countries and ethnic groups, but these laypeople seemed older and more serious than those at the afternoon seminar. I had a feeling they had been handpicked, like me. Without exception we were all mesmerized by the crippled giant in the open parka who strolled up and down unevenly in front of us, now with his hands in his pockets, now using them to emphasize a point; and this fixity of focus gave his words a terrible penetrating power.

A couple of people coughed in the silence, and I realized that questions were now permitted. A black man who was leaning against the wall at the back not far from me put up his hand. Tietsin nodded at him. When the black man spoke he had an educated New York accent and seemed to be intensely interested in what the Tibetan had been saying.

"I would like to ask an impermissible question," he said with a smile.

"There is no such thing," Tietsin said, reflecting the man's smile in every particular.

"Right. Well, a politically incorrect question,

anyway. This stuff you were talking about earlier is not exclusively Buddhist. A lot of people are talking this way. Back in the States you hear it a lot, but it tends to be from non-Caucasians. I mean, black, brown, red, yellow, Buddhist, Hindu, Moslem, whatever—the ones who get it at the deep-heart level don't tend to have Caucasian genes. Is there something fundamentally wrong with white people?" Titters from the audience, especially the white monks and nuns.

"No," Tietsin said with surprising force, "there's something wrong with the rest of us for not stopping them. The Caucasian people, especially the Anglo-Saxons, have a specific task. Without their technology life on earth would now be impossible for human beings. But they pay a high price for their genius. The very price you just mentioned. The heart chakra shrivels and starts to die. Not only is all taste for the transcendental lost, the mere mention of it induces rage and hostility—the Managers of the World fear the spirit the way a rabies victim fears water. The rest of us were supposed to help them with that. Instead, we got ensnared in their materialism. Now we're all rabid. Don't blame them, blame your black, brown, yellow, and red brothers and sisters for not standing up for the heart chakra. After all, we outnumber them by at least eight to one."

I watched the black man nod thoughtfully, then look up at Tietsin and smile.

There were a couple of other questions, one from an American nun who seemed to want to show her

Buddhist erudition by asking a question about the Digha Nikaya, which Tietsin dealt with in an equally erudite way. Then the seminar was over. The Tibetan nun unlocked the door, and everyone trooped out, including Tietsin, who used another door at his end of the room. I was left alone for ten minutes, contemplating the great stupa on the other side of the window with its giant eyes, which were spectacularly lit up. Finally the door at the far end of the room opened and Tietsin limped in. He seemed surprised to see me.

"You still here?"

"You knew I would be."

He shook his head. "Actually, I did not. You should not overestimate me. I'm not a Buddha or a bodhisattva. I'm not even an *arhat*. I'm not even a monk. I learned a few party tricks along the way, that's all."

"I don't believe you. I think you know what I want."

Now he was frowning as if contemplating the possibility that I was slightly insane. "Actually, I expected you to be on a plane back to Bangkok by now, asking for your bonus from Colonel Vikorn." He paused. "By the way, what *do* you want?"

"I want you to initiate me. I want the same initiation your meditation master passed on to you."

If his shock was faked, he was a damn good faker. He really looked as if it had never occurred to him in his wildest moments that it would come to this: a little mafioso from Thailand, whom he would surely rather not have anything at all to do with, demanding access to his deepest secret.

"You have no idea what you're asking. Look at me, d'you want to be like this?" He flaunted his stump and even stood up to limp exaggeratedly.

"You're the most complete man I've ever met. You're the only complete man I've ever met."

"No, I'm not. I'm a freak. I'm like someone who took too much LSD when they were young and had to live with the psychotic consequences."

I slipped off my seat onto my knees on the floor. "I am asking."

"Get up, you idiot. You have a life, a wife, a child."

"You already know about family. It's not an answer, it's a trap. Of course I love them, I love them more than life, and that's the problem: they drag me more and more into flesh until I feel so heavy sometimes I can hardly get out of bed. The responsibility is hard to stand, and worst of all is the worry that something might happen to them. And they always want more. And more and more. It's all exactly as the Buddha said: *Took, Anija, Anata.*"

"Say again?"

"*Took, Anija, Anata,*" I repeated with a touch of exasperation: these were pretty basic Buddhist concepts, after all: suffering, impermanence, lack of substance.

"That's the way you pronounce those words in Thailand?"

"How do you pronounce them?"

He replied with the same three words, which I could just about recognize from the Pali root. "Anyway, the answer is no."

Still on my knees I put my palms together in a *wai*. "I am asking."

He stared angrily at me. Then as he stared his features softened. He was looking into my eyes when a great sadness seemed to come upon him. "Get up."

"Is it because I'm not Tibetan? Or because I'm made of inferior stuff, the magic wouldn't take with me?"

"No, none of the above. There is no magic. Only science of the mind. I told you, I spent seven years, from the age of eight to the age of fifteen, in a monastery, subject to disciplines that would stagger grown men. Even then, the initiation I was given was too powerful for me. Look what happened." He waved the stump.

"There's something you've just seen? Your features just altered. Am I really that lost? Will something bad happen to me? I don't care. I want to reach the Far Shore. That's what you said."

"Serves me right for being so damned sancti-monious. It's a virus you pick up in monasteries the way you pick up staphylococcus in hospitals." He paused, then said in a patient voice, "You're supposed to take a slow ferryboat to the Far Shore, not an unstable kayak you've never learned to paddle."

The moment hung for a while in an electric atmosphere. We both knew why. There was a rule here.

When a sincere aspirant asks three times, the master cannot refuse. I made another *wai*. "I am asking for the third time."

He blew out his cheeks, shook his head, but said, "Okay, get up. You win. But I need a drink first." He limped to the door and yelled something in Tibetan. We waited in silence until the woman who ran the tea shop appeared, wearing a long donkey-brown dress with striped apron, her hair in thick braids; she brought *chang*, a barley-based alcohol.

We drank in silence for a long while. The *chang* didn't seem very strong and had a sweet and sour taste with some fizz, as if it were still in the fermenting stage. When Tietsin finally started talking it was in the voice of a very ordinary, humble man.

"They tortured me for seven days. I was fifteen years and ten months old. My comrades in arms were tortured to death before my eyes, and I didn't know why I was surviving. Nor did my Chinese tormentors. They couldn't believe it. Neither could I. We had all fantasized about it, of course: how we would react under torture. My comrades had ordered me, *Don't hold out, you're still a kid, no one expects you to resist. You don't know anything important about the resistance, you can't compromise any of our operations, just tell them everything you know. Promise?*" A couple of beats passed. "So I did promise, eagerly. I didn't think I'd last an hour under that kind of agony. Then, when they caught us and took us back to Chamdo at gunpoint, I felt such fear in the back of that van I couldn't move. I was frozen. My comrades had to carry me to the prison, I was so out of control, pissing and shitting in my pants, vomiting. But the next day, when the torture started in earnest, something happened. It's as much a mystery to me as it was to the Chinese and everyone else. The pain they inflicted seemed to be happening to another body. I hung above it all, watching myself twitch when they touched me with their cattle prods. I literally put all my consciousness in a sixty-watt lightbulb, if you can believe that. I can't. But it's what happened. When we got to day seven and I still wasn't dead, I finally understood why my master had given me such a powerful initiation. He had seen that I was going to need it." Another pause. "And that, my friend, is the only permissible reason for passing it on. I'm not sharing it with you because you followed some arcane formula by asking three times. I'm passing it on because in asking three times you've told me that you are going to need it as much as I did. And may all the Buddhas have compassion on you."

He turned his eyes away from me, as if he could not stand to look at my future suffering. Of course, that is an observation of hindsight; in the heat of the moment I felt only excitement.

"Go back to your guesthouse. Tomorrow morning someone will come to start the preparation. It takes seven days—you know how weird the gods are about the number seven. I don't know if it's really necessary, but we may as well follow the system while we can."

From the cab on the way back to the guesthouse, I called Vikorn to say I was sick with giardia and wouldn't be back until after the weekend.

I can't tell you about the initiation, *farang*, it's against the rules and they made me swear not to. I can give you something of the preparation, though. The nun who came to my suite at the Kathmandu Guest House, thereby shocking the whole establishment, was the same woman who had begged from me at the stupa on the first day. She looked just as decrepit as she had at the stupa; her face was terribly lined and shaggy and a number of teeth were missing from her mouth, but her mind was as sharp as a razor and she spoke perfect English, with a UN accent. The conversation went like this:

Nun: Do you ever wake up scared in the early hours of the morning?
Me: Almost every night.
Nun: And does this fear seem to originate somewhere in the area of the navel?
Me: Above the navel, somewhere between the navel and the solar plexus.
Nun: And what do you do about it?
Me: My mind finds specific things to worry about, and the fear gets absorbed.
Nun: These things you worry about, are they to do with recent acts, statements, events you have set in motion?

Me: Always.

Nun: Good. We want you to develop that. Soon you're going to be worrying about things that happened a long time ago. Then you're going to be worrying about the unbelievable atrocities you committed in previous lifetimes. You're not going to understand immediately, but this vulnerable area around your navel is the only thing about you that is fully human. The rest is animal and devil. We're going to increase the fear to make you more human. It is going to turn into a karma blade wheel which will tear your ego apart. We don't expect you to survive psychically without outside help. You might be on medication for years afterward. Don't blame us. You have insisted and the master cannot refuse you.

Me: It almost sounds like you're going to divide me in half and set the two sides at war against each other. It sounds like schizophrenia.

Nun: Exactly. When we've finished with you, you're going to live in mortal terror of entertaining a single ego-based thought, because one ego-based thought will be enough to land you in a mental institution for the rest of your life. That's why this path is only for the terminally desperate—spirit-starved fanatics, the suicide bombers of the internal world. D'you want to change your mind before the master tells you the mantra?

Me: No.

10

On the plane back to Bangkok, with Tietsin's mantra clattering around my skull like a broken bell, I asked myself the question, *Why am I a crook?* Because my wife whom I loved convinced me that my son whom I loved even more needed an expensive education to keep him from ending up as a bent cop like his dad; but my noble sacrifice of integrity only made me feel like I was drowning in a sewer. I blame the version of capitalism which is destroying the world: you have to be a shit to survive, but your spouse and kids will hate you for turning yourself into a shit and failing to protect them from—yourself. Being born rich may be the only solution, except they always find a way of getting you on taxes. But why Tibetan Buddhism, and most of all, why Tietsin? I didn't really have an answer except for the rather lame one that good old Theravada was fine for rice farmers, but it didn't seem strong enough medicine for stressed-out cops. Now I couldn't complain about the strength of the medicine.

I'd had the check-in clerk give me a window seat on the left. I couldn't resist them: the mountains, the mountains. Each one fully realized, spectacularly different, taking its inevitable place among the others. Sure, they were built by gods; no human has ever managed that kind of harmony in chaos. Somehow they were the ultimate authority in all this, and I thought they were probably in favor of my decision to dare madness; anything was better than the monkey mind I was born with. I was not looking forward to meeting Colonel Vikorn, though. I had a new and different master now.

Vikorn was, of course, the big problem. I suppose, *farang*, you would advise me to turn over a ruthless new leaf, dump the corrupt third-world gangster cop who was my boss, right? Well, I don't know about the West, but in the East things are never that simple. For a start I owed him *gatdanyu*, a kind of blood debt that every Thai owes to someone who has saved their life. Vikorn saved mine and that of my soul brother, Pichai (before he died and reincarnated as my son), by giving us jobs after Pichai killed our *yaa baa* dealer when we were teenagers. In Thailand to fail to honor *gatdanyu* is the vilest of transgressions, the one that above all others will land you in the lowest hell. And then there was the troubling matter of my certain assassination if I ever betrayed the Colonel in any way. What would my loved ones do then?

After tormenting myself for the three-and-a-half-hour flight back to Bangkok, I decided to take a middle path. I would persuade Vikorn to stop dealing in heroin after this next shipment had given him the means to put General Zinna out of business. Once I'd made that decision, everything was sunny again. I knew I could persuade the Old Man; after all, he was at a time in life when the sane prepare themselves for their next incarnation. I got off the plane with joyful anticipation in my heart.

"What's wrong with trafficking in heroin?" Vikorn demanded from behind his huge old desk. "Why should the pharmaceutical industry take everything? They want to ban all the fun drugs at the same time as turning every human experience into a treatable disease. Drugs for sleeping, drugs for waking, drugs for peeing, drugs for erections. For them the human body is an oil well of maladies that can be exploited. It's the biggest fraud in history. You find a perfectly harmless drug like cannabis or opium, which has the disadvantage of being easy to produce, and what do you do? You criminalize it, find a substitute that is impossible to produce outside of a laboratory, take out the patent, and your corporation is good for another hundred years. Meanwhile people die all the time from prescribed drugs—or suffer worse. Ever hear of Vioxx? Ever hear of thalidomide? That wonderful product that produced such spectacular mutations, babies born with fingers growing out of their eyes and faces on the tops of their heads? And what about Seroxat and Prozac, driving people homicidal? More than a hundred thousand people die in the U.S. every year from prescribed drugs. That's more fatalities in a month than smack kills in a decade. And by the way, what about the killer drug of all killer drugs, alcohol? The breweries and distilleries don't like us because we sell a superior product that rivals theirs."

Vikorn stood up so he could walk up and down in front of me. "Sure, there are casualties, but all a sensible citizen who is contemplating shooting smack for the first time needs to know is: Is the ratio of drug to body weight correct, and did I cauterize the needle? That's why I don't approve of selling it to kids, who tend to take risks. But what can you do? Kids are on everything. Have you any idea how well Xanax is selling over the counter? And what the hell do you think it is? A heroin substitute, of course, and Prozac is an expensive substitute for marijuana, except that it doesn't get you high, just vague. All I do is provide the originals for discerning clients. It's like what you told me about French cheese: Camembert *lait cru* is illegal in Europe, because of bureaucratic ignorance. Addicts have to buy the real thing under the counter."

He wasn't incandescent with rage. He wasn't even angry. He wasn't even disdainful. Buddha help me, he was *amused*. The old bastard was so delighted with the deal I'd struck with Tietsin, I could have spat on his desk and he would have forgiven me. We were in his office with the bare wooden floorboards and the anticorruption poster above his head. He had sat with uncharacteristic patience while I pleaded with him to stop dealing in heroin after this next shipment. Now he was standing behind me patting me on the shoulder. "Take a day off. Take a *week* off."

I blushed and coughed at the same time, my big hope for salvation now a busted balloon that suddenly seemed to belong to a state of mind only available in the Himalayas. The power of the ordinary, the familiar, the inevitably crooked, that non-sacred place where the rubber hits the road, had entirely eclipsed Tietsin and his magic. Obviously, I was some kind of airhead, a space cadet overly susceptible to any little mind gimmick that pointed at the transcendent. "Okay," I croaked, defeated and depressed. "I'll take a week. Maybe longer."

He didn't seem to like the *maybe longer*. "Right. Well, take your time, but if it's not too much trouble, once you've squared everything with the Buddha, go see that mule, that Australian tart your Tibetan chum busted for us. Try to find out how he did it. I can't believe his intelligence about our very own General Zinna is better than ours."

I have an image of myself leaving his office with shoulders bent, head hanging, although I expect it wasn't as bad as all that. Out in the heat, everything seemed normal except me. The mom-and-pop cooked-food stalls, the whores hanging out on Soi 7, the designer-fake stalls all along the top of Sukhumvit, the cynical expressions on the faces of the cops, the pollution, the traffic jams: how come I suddenly didn't seem to fit?

11

I'm still here, *farang*, at the Rose Garden. I've commuted from the bathroom to the bar, but I'm way too stoned to order alcohol. I'm nursing a *nam menau*, lime-and-water, sitting at a table in back, watching the business of flesh take place in accordance with rituals I've known all my life. Just now a well-dressed, professional-class Englishman in his late twenties canvassed the girls one by one, sotto voce, to see which of them would tolerate anal intercourse, and for what price. Having carefully constructed a short list, he chose the volunteer whom, I assume, he found most attractive. He struck me as one of those metro-man types who plans his vacations on a laptop. The decision made and the mouse double-clicked, he escorted his lunchtime bride courteously out the door, no doubt to one of the short-time hotels around here. Now that he's gone, things are quieter than ever. The other *farang* are absorbed in their own conversations, or have dropped in for a quick lunch and to read the foreign-language newspapers. They are regulars who treat the place just like any other beer bar, and the girls know to leave them alone. Finally, I manage to rouse myself to go to the Buddha shrine, just like the girls do when they arrive. I *wai* the tree wrapped in a monk's robe and ask for the mental strength to take me through the last chapter of my personal flashback. It's a kind of pain therapy that forces itself on me, this reliving of catastrophe: the more it hurts, the longer I can maintain the trappings of sanity afterward—until the next bout.

After my interview with Vikorn, which took place immediately after I hit Bangkok that day, I was excited about Chanya and Pichai coming back from deep country in Isaan. I had begun to fantasize about getting enough dough together to retire early—say in five years—and go live the simple rural life up there where the air is cleaner and the grass greener. I liked the idea of a near-silent existence punctuated by visits to the temple, meditation, consultations with monks and abbots concerning my spiritual progress. I yearned for the comfort and cleanness of a life dedicated to the Buddha. When Chanya sent a text message to say they were at the bus station and were on their way, I texted back to say I would be there soon after they arrived at the hovel. I figured it would take more than two hours for them to reach home, because the traffic was so bad on Sukhumvit and Petchburi Road.

It was then that I made one of those trivial decisions that can have an enormous impact on the rest of your life: I turned off my cell phone. I wanted to take the moment to allow my mind to relax—I'd hit the ground running when I got off the plane from Kathmandu and had hardly stopped for breath. I went to the temple at Wat Rachanada on the river and in the silence allowed Tietsin's mantra to spin without restriction in my head. I cannot tell you the specific Pali words, *farang*, for I am bound to secrecy, but I am allowed to describe the blade wheel, which is imagined as a star-shaped weapon closely resembling the *shiken* used by ninjas, although unlike the *shiken* it has a disturbing way of morphing into other shapes. The blade wheel is the enemy of self-delusion—"self-delusion" meaning just about everything in the field of normal everyday perception, in particular our most cherished delusions about ourselves. I didn't switch the phone on again until it was all over.

It is usual in these kind of circumstances for the bereaved to say, *I knew something was wrong*; but I didn't. Even when I noticed the small crowd outside our apartment and the way they could not look me in the eye, I failed to make any connection with the stain on the road or the private car parked nearby, or the driver in tears talking to some uniformed cops. When a young constable blurted that I needed to go to the hospital on Soi 49 immediately, I realized the stain on the street was blood, and my mind split into pieces. At the hospital Chanya and I could only stare at each other across the bed where Pichai's six-year-old body lay dying.

"It's my fault," she said. "I let him get out of the taxi on the wrong side. The driver of the other car wasn't going fast, he wasn't doing anything wrong. It's all my fault."

Haggard, I shook my head. "No, it's not your fault. This is my punishment."

She let a beat pass. In a dead tone: "For being Vikorn's consigliere? I was the one who talked you into that. You would never have accepted the job if not for me."

I knew then that I had lost her as well as my son. Her sorrow and guilt was of the kind no human agency can assuage. And so was mine. I remember thinking in a savage mood, *Tietsin, Tietsin, Tietsin. Only you can help me now.*

A week later, after the monks at the local *wat* had instructed Pichai's spirit on how to avoid rebirth and burned his small body, Chanya announced she had made arrangements to be a *mai chi*, a novice nun, at a *wat* in the far east of Thailand, near the border with Laos. They were a radical sect composed entirely of women dedicated to a life of meditation and contemplation of the most extreme kind: four hours sleep per night, near-starvation rations, no electricity, and absolutely nothing to do except develop the inner life. They were not allowed real corpses to meditate on anymore, but the local hospitals provided them with photographs of cadavers, which they used as a method to concentrate on transience. I, on the other hand, tried every means I could think of to get hold of Tietsin by phone, or in any other way, but he had disappeared from view. I was left with only his mantra.

But a mantra, after all, is simply a way of tricking the mind into a higher level of consciousness, and this was something I could achieve only intermittently. There were moments when I was flying high, when death really seemed to be the bad joke the Buddha always said it was. There were nights spent entirely with Pichai in his spiritual form—I'm not going to pretend they were mere dreams—when he comforted me and told me he'd decided to abandon his former body and I should not concern myself about it. He told me there will be no opportunities for people to evolve spiritually in the generations to come, for we will be entirely enslaved by materialism, and his spirit had therefore preferred to return to the Far Shore. He told me there were many millions over there, like him, waiting out the next few millennia until the Maitreya Buddha incarnates on earth and we can all be human again.

At this level the mind knows no fear and experiences the joy of absolute freedom. Cannabis cannot lead to such heights, although you can use it to sustain them; but then the crashes are all the more devastating. After Chanya left, I spent a week in bed clawing at my mattress, unable to believe the anguish. When I finally went back to work, I had learned to treat my grief with a combination of dope and meditation. The case of the murder of Frank Charles, aka the Case of the Fat *Farang*, also nicknamed the Hollywood File, was the last thing I wanted to deal with. Who cares whodunit? The grim, mechanical rituals of the world grind on, monochrome now, and entirely without interest to me; although Lek keeps assuring me I'm going to snap out of it sooner or later.

12

Believe it or not, of those few in my intimate circle, Vikorn is the most concerned about my mental health. He insisted on paying for Pichai's funeral and came to listen to the monks chanting over my son's corpse before they burned him. The Colonel seemed quite moved; he wiped his eyes a couple of times and hugged me once when nobody could see. I watched his face as they pushed Pichai's little casket on the rollers into the oven and the smoke started coming out of the chimney. For all his faults, Vikorn is Thai, after all. The Western superstition that karma stops with death is as improbable to him as it is to me; I'm sure that, like the rest of us, he saw himself for a moment being rolled into the oven.

After about ten days, though, he has started to lose patience. His technique now is scrupulously to avoid any mention of my grief; maybe he thinks I'll get over it if he pretends it's business as usual? This morning he called me into his office to give me my orders for the week. I was in a morose frame of mind, so he tried jollying me up—not a strategy he has spent much of his life developing: "Tell you what, if you like I'll give you that stupid murder old Sukum has got his knickers in a twist about. Put your name on the top of the file: you'll be officer in charge. That way you'll be sure to get promoted when the board next meets, even if you are half *farang*. What were the circumstances again, I seem to remember it sounded kind of exotic?"

"Famous rich *farang* Hollywood director gutted from solar plexus to crotch," I heard myself saying in a bored and somewhat sulky voice, "a stone in his mouth, suggesting, probably falsely, that he was done in by the Sicilian mafia, but there was also an imago in his mouth and it looked as if someone had recently feasted on his brains: the top hemisphere of the skull was cut around and removed—probably done by a rotary saw of the surgical kind. Some of the brains had been eaten: a paper plate and a plastic spoon were found in that squalid flophouse at the end of Soi Four/Four. All of which indicates the invisible hand of Thomas Harris."

"So why doesn't someone arrest Thomas Harris?"

"He didn't do it. He wrote the novels the crime is based on, along with Poe's 'The Pit and the Pendulum' and maybe some other noir influences—I wouldn't be surprised to find Baudelaire in there somewhere." To Vikorn's baffled gaze, I say, "I guess you have to be at least half *farang*."

"Exactly. The case is yours."

"I don't want it. I don't want promotion. Let Sukum get the credit; I've already told him I'll help if he wants."

I watch the old man's expression freeze into contempt. "You've been meditating again, haven't you? I can always tell when your monk manqué side starts to show. Was it those bloody hills up there that got you all sanctimonious? I knew I should have sent someone with you." I do not say, *You know exactly why I feel like this*. He went back to his desk shaking his head, pretending to be baffled. "Other *jao por* have to worry about getting ripped off by their staff, normal stuff like that. *You* I have to worry about losing to the Buddha. What did I do to deserve it? Get out. And, by the way, the Hollywood case is yours."

I stand up to go. At the door I say in a humble, half-dead voice, "Let Sukum keep the case, I'll solve it for him—I just don't want the stress of all the paperwork."

He purses his lips ambiguously, and I'm forced to leave it at that.

Now, back at my desk in the open-plan office I'm logged on to Yahoo! to check my horoscope. Apparently, I should avoid antique collectors for the next two days, along with other claustrophobic situations. When I check my Chinese horoscope on one of the other clairvoyant sites, I find that Wood Rabbits like me can expect a clear run of good luck. The online I-Ching (I always use the Wilhelm translation) is less positive:

Hexagram 36. Darkening of the Light, "Line Six"

He penetrates the left side of the belly.

110

*One gets at the very heart of the darkening of the
    light,*
And leaves gate and courtyard.

That sounds more like it. I'm just through the
commentary when I spy Sukum, purple and
apoplectic with rage, charging toward me, drawing
disapproving glances from our Buddhist colleagues.
The open-plan office makes it possible to prepare for
attack from a distant desk. I find myself wanting to
huddle, somehow, while I watch him negotiate desk
after desk, monitor after monitor, where mostly
uniformed cops try to figure out how best to prioritize
the relentless storm of crime reports. He is too Thai to
really make a scene in public, so when he finally
arrives at my desk he hisses rather than yells.

"You brown-nosing hypocritical asshole, you just
forced the Old Man to give you the Hollywood case
because you cut a big drug deal wherever you went
last month and now he's eating out of your hand. You
make me want to vomit. You're not fit to be a cop.
You should be in jail."

"Would you like to repeat that to Colonel Vikorn,
Khun Sukum?" I ask softly.

Now he's all crestfallen, and I feel pity for him. He
so very, very much wants this next promotion, so very,
very much wants to show his wife and best friends he
can beat me at the art of detection, that he has
violated my mourning without even thinking about it.
I feel sorry that he is so deeply in the grip of the third

111

chakra, the one responsible for greed, aggression, and dominance. (I'm afraid I often think of it as the *farang* chakra, which is horribly unfair to you, I know; after all, look how it is destroying poor Sukum's peace of mind, and they don't come more Thai than him.) I sigh, pick up the phone, watch Sukum's eyes as I speak to Manny, Vikorn's secretary, of whom we are all terrified.

"Khun Manny, forgive the question, but did you just call Detective Sukum to tell him he has been taken off the Hollywood case in favor of me?"

"Yes."

"Please tell Colonel Vikorn I am not accepting the Hollywood case. He can sack me if he likes, but Detective Sukum has already put in more than three weeks' work and is doing a very fine job."

"What did you say?"

"Just tell the Old Man what I just told you."

"Did you just call him *the Old Man* in my hearing?"

"Yes. Now get on with it," I say, and replace the receiver.

Not only Sukum, but the whole office is staring at me, expecting the roof to fall. Now the phone is ringing on Sukum's desk. He looks at me in bewilderment, then races back to his post. We all watch while his face goes through a fascinating collection of emotions, from enraged to obsequious in less than two seconds. To give him his due, when he's put the phone down he walks back over to me, gives a high *wai*, and says, "Thank you. I will be grateful for any assistance you can offer. I know you are very busy and a better detective than I. I humbly apologize for troubling you in your time of grief. I hereby admit I now have *gatdanyu* with you."

I wave a hand. "Please," I tell him, "it's not *gatdanyu*—you can't owe a blood debt to a half-caste. I'm just not in the mood for promotion this year."

He gives me a baffled glance and shakes his head. As he's about to leave, I give him the name of Thomas Harris and recommend *The Silence of the Lambs* and *Hannibal*—in Thai translation, of course. He's never heard of the learned author or his works. He never reads novels. I tell him he can get the idea just as well from the DVDs, which they sell in counterfeit versions at a hundred and fifty baht (you have to bargain them down from two hundred, *farang*) on Sukhumvit at the stalls opposite Starbucks in the Nana area.

My generosity is too much for him; it's too Buddhist, too un-cop. "A minute ago I hated your guts and was fighting the temptation to have you bumped off," he whispers in a disorientated voice. "Now you might be the biggest benefactor of my life. It must be your *farang* blood that makes you so incomprehensible."

"Must be," I agree genially. Instead of going back to his desk immediately, as he would like to, he hangs around, looking even more apologetic. "What is it, Khun Sukum? If you are stuck, I'll try to help."

He fidgets a bit and does a sort of dance. "I did a little preliminary research."

"Yes."

"The victim's name was Frank Charles. He owned a luxury condominium on Soi Eight."

"Yes?"

"But if you remember, he was found in that flophouse on Soi Four/Four."

I push back on my chair until it balances on the rear legs, and I'm using my feet on the desk to maintain balance. "Khun Sukum, did I not already explain, when *farang* get money they often stop thinking about waste. I mean, other factors come into operation."

"Like what?"

"Like perhaps he was embarrassed that the security at his condo would know he brought a different woman back every night, or maybe more than one. Or perhaps he thought if he behaved like that someone would tell his circle in Hollywood."

"They don't have prostitutes over there?"

"Of course, but *farang* suffer greatly from a disease called hypocrisy. That may be why he was here in the first place. What does his passport show? How often did he visit Thailand?"

"Four times a year for the past ten years."

I open my arms in a sort of invitation to Detective Sukum to share my dubious expertise on the subject. "It may be a safe working hypothesis that he was one of those famous *farang* who are also sex addicts, who make regular visits to Bangkok while pretending to be working on their laptops at home. There are quite a few literary figures like that, and even more from the California entertainment industry, and lots of judgmental British journalists as well, not to mention Hong Kong lawyers. That being so, he might have bought his condo for its proximity to Soi Seven."

"What happens in Soi Seven?"

"The Rose Garden."

"It's a brothel?"

How to explain the Rose Garden? "Not exactly. It's full of freelancers. It suits young mothers who need spending money whether they're married or not, girls with boyfriends they need to service during the evening, women with part-time jobs who can slip out of the office to turn a trick or two before going home to supper." It occurs to me that a homily is called for: "The unpalatable truth is that promiscuity makes men happy, and quite a few women, too, especially when they get paid."

"It's full of *farang*?"

I notice the telltale signs of Thai shyness overcome him. "Do you want me to go with you?" I ask.

He nods in relief and lets me have another of those smiles. Before leaving my desk I send off an e-mail to Kimberley Jones:

All you can share about Frank Charles, Hollywood director?

13

Like a lot of Thais, Detective Sukum has never spent much time in the Nana area, although he has passed through it often enough and reads about it almost daily in the newspapers. Perhaps we got the idea of invisible screens from the Chinese, before they kicked us out of their country about fifteen hundred years ago. The invisible screens in this case produce a kind of psychological enclave for the benefit of *farang* men—men like Frank Charles, for example—who do not know how to be discreet, and so we have to be discreet for them, letting them get away with poor public behavior in a restricted area in the hope it will not corrupt our kids. Therefore I deliberately stop the cab at the Sukhumvit/Soi 4 junction and walk Sukum past the stalls that line the pavement where you can buy DVDs of the latest movies, some of them clearly marked as being for the eyes of the Oscar committee members only. (Not only DVDs, *farang*: designer clothes, fake Rolexes, and every martial-arts weapon of the kind strictly prohibited in your country, including nunchakus, *bokken*, *tonfa*, focus mitts, kick shields, and full-length swords in scabbards you would kill for, which you won't be allowed to take on the plane, not even in your checked luggage—but then you know all this already; it's all there especially for you.)

When it comes to buying, Sukum and I both examine our consciences—no, not in the way you are thinking, *farang* (I wish I could get hot under the collar about designer fakes the way you do): I mean we have to decide whether to reveal that we are cops and thereby get the DVDs for free, or whether we bring good karma to the case by letting the poor Isaan hustler, in this case a young woman with a disfiguring harelip who is also deaf and dumb, have her hundred and fifty baht. It's a no-brainer because Sukum, when not suffering from the vice of ambition, is a good Buddhist. I direct him to buy *The Silence of the Lambs* and *Hannibal*. When the woman with the harelip shows him the lurid covers of her porn collection, the good detective actually blushes. Well, I guess the covers are pretty raw if you're not used to that kind of thing. Then it happens, as I suppose I knew it would.

They are a perfectly ordinary young couple, she Thai, he *farang*, of the kind you see often in this area. It's their son, about six years old, who throws me. He bears only a passing resemblance to Pichai, but that's enough. I feel my lips quivering and something happening to my lower jaw. Sukum has only just finished buying his movies and is shocked to see the transformation of my mood. May Buddha bless him,

117

he's able to make the connection with the kid who just passed us and touches me gently on the elbow. I say, "I'm sorry, I better sit down for a moment."

In Starbucks I order a cold mint mocha, medium size, and a mineral water for Sukum. He politely avoids looking at me, waiting for me to recover. How to explain that at times like this it is not merely grief that gnaws at my guts, but Tietsin's mantra as well? I see his blade wheel vividly, as if it were a physical object, its tiny spadelike edges whirring and ripping through the illusion of identity.

"D'you want to go home?" Sukum asks doubtfully. The idea of visiting the Rose Garden alone is pretty daunting.

"I'll be okay," I say. I do not add, *I wish I could light up a joint*.

The moment passes, as such moments do, leaving me purged and strangely light-headed. Relief even brings a sort of wan joy. Sukum has been watching me in wonder, and I think he has decided I'm totally psycho. I understand. He is a simple man who got upward mobility in a limited form and doesn't quite know what to do with it. He is the only cop in District 8 who bought a car out of his own salary; he cleans it about five times a week. Nobody has seen it in anything less than mint condition, and it forms a large part of his conversation. He is also famous for his underarm deodorant and for cleaning his teeth three times a day; we know all this because he is obliged to carry out these ablutions in the men's room at the

118

station. According to Lek, who, when not urging me on to Buddhahood, can be a terrific gossip, Sukum also has a problem with flatulence, which he deals with through an elaborate exercise involving his stomach muscles and a great deal of inexplicable swallowing. Lek sits near him and frequently bears witness to tiny, nearly inaudible ziplike farts emanating from under Sukum's desk. To top it all, Sukum has adopted the Chinese habit of extended hoiking first thing in the morning, to chase away the throat demons. I'm not telling you all this, *farang*, to be malicious, but rather to reveal the flaw in my own perception, for now Sukum shocks me with his penetration.

"I don't know how you feel. I can only imagine. If my son was killed, I would resign and go to a monastery." I stare at him. "I know what you think of me, I know you laugh at me, just like all the others, especially your *katoey* assistant. I didn't choose the smallness of this lifetime. Don't you think I also would like to live a bigger life? Why do you think I want promotion so much? But it's my karma, what can I do?" He adds, "I often wish I hadn't married and had a child."

"Your home life is not entirely what you hoped for, Khun Sukum?" I ask, rather disingenuously; the detective's fights with his wife are legendary.

"You know very well it's not. Let's face it, this is the age of the booby-trapped pussy. If I tread on her toe, I'm violent. If I smack the kid, I'm a sadist. If I look at another woman, I'm a sex addict and she starts talking about HIV. If I don't want to go to the filthy beach at Pattaya fifty times a year, I'm stifling her and the kids. At the same time I get it in the neck for not standing up for her when she gets into an argument with the neighbors, and if I don't dominate her ruthlessly in sex she can't reach orgasm. Then there's always the threat of bankruptcy if she files for divorce."

He gives me a glance. "Go ahead, laugh." He shakes his head and glances around the coffee shop. Out of the corner of his mouth: "If I could have held out against the sex instinct for a little longer, I might have gotten mature enough to be a monk. But I couldn't, and what can I do now? My whole mind is cramped; there's nothing I don't worry about, and I have no idea where the worry comes from. I don't like my social identity. I don't like identity. I hate having to be somebody, it's so burdensome."

My jaw has dropped, and for a moment all I can manage is a high *wai* to honor his wisdom. On the way, now, to the Rose Garden, with Sukum holding his illegal DVDs in a green plastic bag, I'm thinking, *Hold out against the sex instinct, hmm.*

I was too rushed to describe the bar properly to you before, *farang*. It's a great barnlike structure of the type used to house small modern industries and supermarkets—basically a tin roof on an iron frame with walls added and a great oblong bar in the middle of the enclosed space. What I have always admired is the way the strict Buddhist owners have preserved a sacred ficus tree, which somehow rises through the roof and is the primary source of luck for the girls, who rarely fail to bring lotus buds and *wai* the tree before they sit at the bar and work on being irresistible. I'm a little embarrassed that at least half of them know me and say hi and *wai* me as we walk in, but the good Sukum again shows his generous side. "I know you have shares in one of Colonel Vikorn's brothels. I know your mother runs it and also has shares in it. You must know lots of working girls."

"Let's be frank, Detective—my mother was on the Game. That's the only reason I got enough education to be a cop. It's the only reason I'm still alive."

At the words *on the Game*, Sukum snaps his face away from me, leaving me the back of his head with its crop of spiky ink-black hair. I'm thinking, *I've really done it now and maybe he won't be able to work with me anymore, I'm just too weird*, when he says, still looking away at the tree shrine, "How can you say that? How can you just come out with it like that, as if it doesn't matter?"

"I'm sorry, I didn't mean to shock you. I was just being frank, that's all."

"No, no, no." He raises both palms to press his cheeks. Then in a whispered hiss: "*My mother was too.* That's what has made me so petty. It was because I let rip with the sex instinct in a previous lifetime that my mother was a whore in this one. I feel I can never express who I really am in this lifetime. Even I think it's weird the way I obsess about my car, when it's just an ordinary Toyota. How can you rise above your karma so easily?"

Buddha knows where this might have led if Marli—stage name: Madonna—did not come over to join us. She is joined in turn by Sarli, Nik, Tonni, and Pong. They all once worked at my mother's bar, where I still occasionally work as *papasan*. Girls grow out of dancing on stage at an early point in their careers; most don't like to do it after the age of about twenty-seven, at which point they graduate to less strenuous forms of self-promotion, often going freelance right here at the Rose Garden. I introduce them all to Sukum, who, I know, is trying hard not to see his mother in their faces.

"Sonchai, so long since we've seen you, what are you doing here? Are you looking for girls to dance at the Old Man's Club?"

"Sonchai, dear *papasan*, will you buy me a drink?"

I order beers all around. "I'm working," I say. "You must have heard about the *farang* murder at the flophouse on Soi Four/Four?"

They all immediately drop their eyes—whether out of respect for the memory of a valued customer or fear of bad luck is hard to say. I nod to Sukum, who fishes out a navy-blue passport with an eagle on the front. It is hardly necessary to show them the photo.

"We were so shocked."

"He was such a good customer."

"He came about four times a year. He was a good payer. A really nice guy."

"What was great was the way he would usually take two or more of us, so it was fun."

"He was funny about being fat. He would say, *You get on top, honey, I'm scared of flattening you*. He wasn't, you know, the other kind of *farang*."

"That's right. He wasn't *neua*." *Neua* means "north"; we use it to describe people who suffer from a superiority complex.

"Did he take you to a luxury apartment or a flophouse?" Sukum wants to know. He still can't get it out of his head that someone would waste money on a flophouse; it wasn't as if the *farang* had a wife or live-in lover back at the penthouse.

"It would depend. He would get the hots for a girl sometimes for a month, then he would take her back to his penthouse on Soi Eight. But most of the time, when he was just playing the field, he would use the flophouse. I guess he didn't want people at the penthouse to know about his appetite."

"It was incredible. Of course, he used the blue pill a lot. He was one of those *farang* who always have to stick their dicks in someone or other. He was an addict for sure."

"If you did a good job he would tip double, sometimes triple."

"What's a good job?" Sukum asks with sudden urgency.

"Oh, nothing particular. Some customers can be

sensitive. He was one of those. Maybe he was a bit pathetic, you know? He always wanted you to like him, maybe even love him, when you knew it was only for a couple of hours and then he'd want the next one to love him. If you did it in that way, though, like you were a real lover and not just a twenty-minute fuck, he would pay double. After a while every girl here knew that about him, so we all turned into passionate lovers when he hired us. It was kind of fun in a way."

"Even in a group he was like that?"

"Oh, yes. Once on his birthday he broke his own rule and took a whole bunch of us back to his penthouse. It had a giant Jacuzzi, and we all got in with him and he was like the emperor of China with his adoring harem around him. There were ten of us altogether, the bar was almost deserted." Titters at this.

"Did he, ah, do it with all ten?" Sukum wants to know.

Marli frowns in concentration. "I'm not sure. I know he screwed me that night."

"And me."

"And me."

"And me."

"That only makes four," Sukum says with a kind of relief.

"But we all gave him blow jobs. That was standard."

"He wasn't into any kind of sadism, or masochism?" I ask.

All the girls shake their heads, one after the other.

"He was a totally normal sex addict. He never talked about his life back in California, but you got the feeling it was pretty miserable. He was the kind you feel sorry for and want to help, you know? Not the aggressive type at all."

"Real sex addicts never are. I mean, the ones who act it out like that."

"That's right. It's the serious ones you have to be careful about, the ones who probably masturbate all the time and get all intense and stuck on one girl. The ones who fall in love are always the dangerous ones. I wouldn't think he ever needed to masturbate in his life. He was so rich, there was always someone to do it for him."

I let a couple of beats pass while we all drink beers, except Sukum, who sticks to mineral water. "Well," I say, "who has been with him this week?"

Sukum and I watch intently while the girls all exchange looks and shrugs. "None of us. We hadn't seen him in here for a couple of months, even though we knew he was in Bangkok because we used to see him in the street."

"With girls?"

"No, but you can bet he was using another bar. No way he could live without sex."

All this time Pong has been playing with the American's passport, because she was the last to look at it, and Sukum has yet to ask for it back. To break the silence, Pong says, "Look at this giant visa, it takes up a whole page. It's really beautiful. And there's another.

And another. I can't read English. What country is it for?"

I grab the passport to examine the visa. "The Kingdom of Nepal," I say.

14

There's no reason to connect the dead American with Tietsin just because he visited Nepal a few times. You need to be qualified in the finer nuances of superstition to understand my frame of mind when we leave the Rose Garden and head for the flophouse on Soi 4/4. What the circumstantial evidence is pointing at, you see, is my personal connection with Nepal. The cosmos is telling me there's no way out; I'm stuck with Tietsin and his mantra whether I like it or not. Anyway, I lead Sukum out of the bar and down a narrow alley filled with cooked-food stalls, which cater to the girls who work the bars. There are a few sitting at the tables who eye us as prospects when we pass. One, a new girl I've never seen before, tells me she loves me. Sincerity is the first casualty of capitalism.

We emerge out of the alley into Soi 5, which is famous for the Foodland supermarket, which also offers a small eatery, open 24/7 except on Buddhist holidays. (If ever you want to meet a girl when the bars are closed, *farang*, you know where to go, thanks

127

to Jitpleecheep Personal Tours.) We now emerge into Sukhumvit, turn right past Starbucks with the girls hanging around outside—it's a favorite *farang* haunt, after all—keep the bookshop on our right and the martial-arts/porn stalls on our left, then find ourselves waiting at the famous intersection with Soi 4. All trades around here—the bars, the bookstalls, the hair-dressers, the food stalls, the clothing stalls, the DVD stalls, the hotels, and the cops—thrive thanks to the cornucopia of business opportunities created by the most ancient profession. The girls on these streets might be despised in the larger society, but you'll find most locals being polite to them. Looking a gift horse in the mouth is a definite no-no for anyone sensitive to the nuances.

We manage to cross the road at considerable risk to our lives, say hello to our brother cops manning the traffic-control box on the other side of the Suk, then pass the bars and cooked-food stalls of Soi 4 before we finally turn into Subsoi 4. At the flophouse we find two bored security guards sitting outside at a tubular steel table playing Thai checkers with bottle tops. They don't challenge us, so we pass on into the re-ception area, which uses a minimum of space on the ground floor. The *katoey* behind the desk is tall, maybe six feet, seriously overweight (long hair tied back in a ponytail; mascara and rouge), and of the kind whose personality did not improve after he had his goolies cut off. He is also smart, sees we are cops before we open our mouths, and decides not to help.

"We're investigating the murder of the *farang* Frank Charles."

The *katoey* rolls his eyes. "Not *again*. I thought that was all *over*?"

"It's not over. We'd like to ask you how often he visited here."

"I've been told by my management that all inquiries must go through legal channels."

"We are your legal channel," Sukum explains.

"*Lawyers*," the *katoey* says with a sneer. "Talk to the lawyers."

Sukum may be shy when it comes to dealing with *farang* bars and the girls who service them, but here he recognizes a type he knows well. "Do you really want to make us angry?" he asks in a voice of polite intimidation. This has raised the *katoey*'s hackles and now we have a standoff waiting to happen. I touch Sukum's arm. "Later," I tell him. To the *katoey* I say, "Give us the keys to the room," in the kind of voice all cops know how to use. He hands them over with a sulky shrug and we make for the lifts.

There is a romantic couple behind us at the reception desk: a *farang* in his late fifties with a Thai girl in her early twenties. The *farang* rents a room for two hours and pays in advance while we're waiting. They join us in the tiny elevator, and the entire journey from ground to fourth is spent in a tense, precoital silence. There is something fascinating about two strangers who have decided to have sex together within perhaps five minutes of the first encounter.

129

When they get out at the same floor as ours, I cannot help watching them at the door of their room, the man fumbling with the keys, the girl staring at the floor.

"Come on," Sukum says.

While we are walking down the corridor, I fish out my cell phone to call Lek and tell him to get over here and talk to the *katoey* on reception. Now Sukum is jealous because he doesn't have a local *katoey* scout of his own.

In the room where the fat *farang* died they have cleaned up the blood lake and taken the corpse away, but they left just about everything else. No rotary saw or other instruments were found by the forensic team. I automatically make for the bookshelves. The books and screenplays are all still there, although they have been dusted for prints. According to the forensic boys, there were no prints on the books other than the victim's. As for the rest of the room: sure, prints everywhere, from a thousand different sets of fingers. What do you expect? It's a flophouse.

It's the books, of course, which intrigue, fascinate, and baffle me. If not for them, the case might be classified as some bizarre Oriental copycat murder based on a rather literal third-world interpretation of the Western noir tradition. The books make no such assumption possible. I'm afraid they make the whole crime incomprehensible the minute you attempt to profile the perpetrator. On the one hand, we have here as extreme a murder as you could possibly imagine; on the other, there's not a sign of ungoverned rage, the decision to mutilate the human form apparently sustained with surgical discipline. The victim was disemboweled with a single careful incision from solar plexus to lower abdomen; his guts flopped out because he was so obese. Similarly, the whole of his upper cranium had been removed, but the surgery was carried out with considerable care and skill—the pathologist has explained that it is not easy to keep the saw steady without practice. Most telling of all, there are no irrational slashings or stabbings, which may have indicated a psychopathic disorder in the killer. All of this might have been explained away on the grounds that we simply do not have enough information about the perp; but we do: we have the books s/he used as a blueprint. But why? Surely not as a manual? Someone, obviously, is trying to tell us something. And then, of course, there is the small matter of cannibalism.

Now that they have been dusted I am able to pick up the books one by one: *The Silence of the Lambs*, *Hannibal*, an Edgar Allan Poe short-story collection, including "The Pit and the Pendulum," and—what a coincidence!—*The Godfather*, by Mario Puzo.

I'm shaking my head at the impenetrable mystery, at the same time wishing there were a window to look out of. "No window," I say to Sukum.

"Didn't you look at the room rates? A room with a window is double the cost of one without."

"But we're dealing with a successful Hollywood

131

director, the most spoiled subspecies of human being that exists on earth. How could he possibly make a decision based on a five-hundred-baht difference?"

Sukum scratches his head and shrugs: a *farang* issue on which he is not qualified to speak. "Maybe he didn't want windows."

"He wanted a bathroom, though. Rooms without bathrooms are even cheaper."

Sukum and I check out the bathroom: tiny, with a flush toilet crammed next to a shower stall with a torn curtain. There are no clues here. Indeed, that is another paradox. In a case involving extreme violence, you don't normally find the perpetrator's mind organized enough for such a thorough cleanup. Apart from the blood on the floor, there was no circumstantial evidence to follow up on at all. It almost has the mark of a professional slaying; but professionals do not indulge in such a baroque style. Nor do they eat their victims' brains: it would ruin their reputation, and they'd never get any more work.

Stumped! I've never come across anything like it. Violence, you see, is a form of lust, a primitive kind of consumerism: early capitalism, you might say. Just as it is impossible for you to buy a dream house without first fantasizing about it, so with the love objects of killers. They are driven by compelling images just as irresistible to them as dog-snoring-in-front-of-fireplace-while-cute-kids-play-safely-on-lawn may be to you, *farang*—lacking your discretion, however, they tend to end up with an ugly piece of meat, whereas you merely get stuck with a subprime mortgage. Rage turns to ashes: panic. But I see none of that here; nor do I feel it. For the perpetrator to saw open the victim's skull, they would have had to concentrate for as much as ten minutes, being careful not to cut into the delicate, spectacular, crimson spider web of the *arachnoid mater*—the inner membrane which protects the brain. But why would you worry about the *arachnoid mater* of someone you were about to kill, especially when you intend to dig into it for supper? After the perp finished they must have carefully put away the rotary saw and the knife they used to cut him open, neither of which have been found, and coolly departed the premises. I'm not entirely displeased that it's Sukum's case, not mine. Dead end: we stare at each other and shrug.

Downstairs, Lek does not seem to be faring well with the desk clerk. When Sukum and I exit the elevator we walk into a *katoey* shouting match. In Thailand people rarely express their feelings in public; but this is Nana and these are transsexuals, and they both hail from the Northeast, so they are yelling in their own dialect of Lao, which neither I nor Sukum understand. Finally Lek, who, much as he loathes physical violence has no problem with a really good mouth fight on the fishwife model, says something to make the other *katoey* start to walk around his desk. He is big and fat, so Sukum and I quickly come between them. When I get Lek outside he is still cursing the other while repeatedly pushing his long black hair back with both hands; but he quickly recovers. "The victim, the American, he used this place all the time—at least five times a week," Lek explains. "He had an arrangement with the management. He kept the key to the room and rented it on a monthly basis. He got them to agree to change the lock so that only senior management had a key, which they kept in a private safe off the premises. He usually brought girls here in twos, sometimes threes. The sessions never lasted more than a couple of hours. On the other hand, sometimes he would have as many as three sessions in one day."

"So what were you arguing with that *katoey* about?"

Lek pushes his hair back again and shakes himself. "*Somtam* salad. What else? We're Isaan."

15

I'm at the station sitting at my desk staring at the computer monitor after having consulted the online I-Ching for the hundredth time today. I want to know if Pichai has been reborn already, or if he is waiting for Chanya and me to make love so he can come back to us (does he know his former mother is now a nun?), or if my visions were correct and he really does intend to hang out on some higher plane until the appearance of the Maitreya Buddha. (I Googled him, by the way—the Maitreya Buddha, I mean—and I have to report a serious schism in the Mahayana cosmology here. The earliest we can expect him is in three thousand years, but there are others who doubt he'll show for a hundred thousand—apparently what is left of humanity will have had enough of beautiful cars and luxury condos by then and be quite rabid for the transcendent.) The Book of Changes is more than usually gnomic today, however, and the best it can offer is Hexagram 52: "Ken/ Keeping Still, Mountain." There are no moving lines to help me pin down the advice, but the commentary is not without resonance:

> *It is very difficult to bring quiet to the heart. While Buddhism strives for rest through an ebbing away of all movement in nirvana, the Book of Changes holds that rest is merely a state of polarity that always posits movement as its complement. Possibly the words of the text embody directions for the practice of yoga.*

It strikes me, *farang*, that with its insistence on constant movement the I-Ching might be a better guide for you than our Buddhism. I can't see you ebbing into nirvana just yet, frankly, not with all those lovely wars going on, and all that restless money sloshing around all over the planet. (Sorry, I'm in one of those moods.) As for yoga, I'll believe it when they're doing headstands at the New York Stock Exchange. Anyway, I see from a pop-up that the FBI has just sent me an e-mail:

This must be one of the easiest assignments of my career. I got most of it from the Net and the rest from a few contacts in LA. Frank Charles was a phenomenally successful TV and movie director, if you measure success in terms of dough. He incorporated as Patna Productions Inc. and got rich from making sloppy romantic B movies, then selling the franchises to TV for serialization. He had the smarts to make sentimentality look respectable for the middlebrow educated without losing the masses. Looks like he started out wanting to make art-house feature films, based on French and Italian movies of his generation: Truffaut, Bertolucci, Fellini—all that crowd. He did make one film—his first full-length feature—in the American noir genre called *Black Wednesday*, which got a lot of critical acclaim but wasn't a great commercial success. Looks like he took the hint and did a deal with the devil. It was mostly schmaltz schmaltz schmaltz all the way to the bank after that, with a feature film every eighteen months. He married neurotic starlets five times, had one child, a girl, by one of them, let them take him to the cleaners on divorce, but it didn't seem to dent his wealth. After the fifth marriage fell apart he started using professionals in a regular way, which is what took him over there about ten years ago. Like a lot of men, one visit was all it took for him to get addicted to your red-light districts. He hasn't done any serious film work for a decade and Patna Productions was formally dissolved about six years ago. After that he seems to have gotten involved in Asian real estate (stories about him buying in Hong Kong, Malaysia, Taiwan), which made him yet another fortune. The more money he made, the more miserable he got: there's an exclusive interview with Vanity Fair in which he comes out with a full confession of disillusionment with the system, money, etc., I mean, he just about breaks every American taboo, and especially every Hollywood taboo, by saying how miserable money and success have made him and maybe he should have done something else with his life that would have left him with more self-respect and less money. Actually, he comes across on the Net as having been a nice guy who hated his work but couldn't give up the wealth. Which I don't quite buy. I mean, the subtext of this interview with *Vanity Fair* is that his soul was somehow damaged by the notorious bad taste of America. That may be true, but he has been a major contributor to our philistinism, and let's face it, no matter how much irony and cynicism he brought to his work, to be that good at the sunset ending he must have had a generous dose of Jell-O in his own heart. Also, he was said to be ferocious in business. No criminal record as such, but quite a few run-ins with Hollywood cops regarding prostitution. He escaped prosecution, but everyone knew what he was up to. Now here's something you might be able to pick up on. After he first started going east, he tried taking Thai girls back with him to LA to be his companions for a week or two at a time (occasionally, more than one girl at a time). He made the mistake of showing up in public, at parties, etc., with these girls, and got the cold shoulder from the matriarchs, so he had to stop. Instead, he spent more and more time in Bangkok without anyone knowing: he simply had his phone calls patched through to his hotel or condo, and then e-mail came along to make it all easier still. Lately, he seems to have tried to mend his karma by taking up various forms of mysticism. There are reports of him making a fool of himself telling people at LA dinner parties about Hinduism, Buddhism, mystic Christianity—he didn't seem able to make up his mind.

Frankly, with that kind of background, I would follow the money. I'll try to find out if anyone over there knows of a will—I mean, who stood to benefit by his death? His daughter and her mother would be the first place I would look. I know that doesn't fit with the cannibalism, but who knows? Maybe the macabre is just a smoke screen here? Money does strange things to all people.

Kimberley

In the meantime, the Chief has summoned me to his office. Do you think he's worried about our slow progress with the Frank Charles murder? No, neither do I.

"He wants the money next week," Vikorn says in a tone of bewilderment.

He is standing at his window looking down at the illegal cooked-food stalls in the street, which specialize in the cuisinary preferences of District 8 cops: *somtam* salad, chicken satay, *tom yum gung*, pad thai, crispy duck for Vikorn and his two deputies, steamed broccoli with peanut sauce for his secretary, Manny, fried rice, spring rolls, mango with sticky rice, lotus-root water for Lek, vegetable dumplings, fried mussels in butter, spicy roast beef—those are the main ones. There are so many stalls eager and ready to assist the Royal Thai Police—each of which must have its own set of chairs and tables that it will not share with other stalls—that the whole open-air kitchen stretches for more than half a mile on either side of the station; any cop foolish enough to complain about street congestion gets traffic duty at the Sukhumvit-Asok interchange.

"Who does?"

"Your Halloween Buddhist up there in those fucking mountains. Who does he think I am, George Soros?"

"Tietsin? But he doesn't get paid until he delivers."

My Colonel glares. "That's the point. He wants to deliver next week. He's the keenest wholesaler I've ever heard of. How can anyone get hold of forty million dollars' worth of smack that quickly? Did you do the math?"

"Five hundred and thirty-three thousand, three hundred and thirty-three point three recurring." (Of course I did the math, I'm the consigliere, aren't I?) "Basically, five hundred and thirty-three kilos, or eleven hundred and seventy-six pounds, which is a little over half an American ton: point five eight eight of a ton, to be precise." I stop to take a breath. "You don't have the money?"

Vikorn holds up his arms. In a tone of confusion he says, "No." I wait for the coda. "Sure, I can get it, of course, but it takes time. Nobody moves money around like that these days. It's unheard of. Forty million in liquid, or as good as?" He smacks his forehead. "I was expecting to receive the stuff in installments, a million's worth here, two million's worth there."

"Can't you sell something? What about your row of chalets on Phuket? Or that strip of prime riverfront property on the Mekong up near Nong Kai?"

These sound like desperate measures, but I am factoring in the great carrot Tietsin has dangled: the money and the power to establish total dominance over General Zinna, to literally wipe him out.

"It's the wrong time to sell real estate. Anyway, you can't sell stuff like that overnight. And I'm not even sure I'd get forty million. Everyone's shifting to Phnom Penh for real estate, and Sihanoukville, on the Cambodian coast. Thailand has screwed itself by being standoffish toward foreign investors. Apparently Cambodia is pristine and wide open, everyone's scrambling to get in on the ground floor. Then there's Vietnam and Malaysia. There's even a rumor the Laos Socialist government is about to collapse, or do a quick double shuffle into unrestrained capitalism— imagine the profit for those who've already invested there."

I stand with arms hanging. "So, why not tell him he has to wait?"

"I did. Politely. After all, he's potentially a huge business partner, and I don't want to offend him. But he's not happy. Can he really deliver all that dope next week?"

"I have no idea."

"Why is he in such a hurry?"

I shrug. "He didn't say. He just said his movement needs the money."

Vikorn's eyes sharpen. "What's he planning, the invasion of China?" I do not say, *I wouldn't put it past him*. "Have you been watching the news recently?"

"No."

"Those demonstrations in India and Lhasa, led by Tibetan monks. A hundred of them blown away by the Chinese. That wouldn't be anything to do with him?"

"I have no idea. I think it's inevitable, they're trying to embarrass Beijing before the Olympic Games."

Vikorn looks at me. "Yes. I guess if you're a Tibetan, this is your big chance. Now or never."

"They don't have *never*," I say with one of those superior smiles he hates so much, "only *now*."

"Get out of here."

When I reach the door, he says, "That Australian mule, have you followed up on her yet?" It is not a question. It is an order.

Back at my desk I call Lek over to tell him to find a taxi that will take us to the women's holding prison over the river at Thonburi.

16

I've told Lek very little about my trip to Kathmandu; he is fascinated, like any *katoey*, by the spiritual dimension.

"It's because you're so spiritual yourself that the Buddha gave you the chance to go up there," Lek says in the back of the cab, pushing his black locks back with both hands. As usual when alone with me, he has taken the liberty of applying just a touch of mascara, using a tiny hand mirror. "You must be so thrilled to be *called* like that. If it were me I would have felt like a pilgrim on hajj."

"Lek, please, you must have guessed I only went up there to do some filthy job for Vikorn."

"But that's how the Buddha works, darling, you must know that by now. Maybe you're a tad too proud. You have to bend your knee."

"Lek, I feel as dirty as a glass roof in Thonburi. I feel like I'm covered in shit, inwardly, like my soul has one tiny source of light left. The rest is so caked in corruption and degradation and guilt and bad karma, if I do one more bad thing I'm going to die, I know it."

Lek turns to me to make a high *wai*.

"Why did you do that?"

"Because everything you just said points to a man on the threshold of nirvana. Normal people don't think like that. Normal people don't worry about their souls. Only *arhats* like you and ladyboys like me."

I sigh and give up. Maybe it's not such a bad thing to have one human being on earth who still believes in my integrity.

We sit in the traffic jam at the Asok-Sukhumvit interchange in silence while a kid with a broken windshield wiper and a face streaked with dirt makes a token gesture of cleaning the window on my side. I wind it down to give him a hundred baht, which is about ninety baht too much. Lek is shocked at first, then gives me a great beam when he connects the gesture to my spiritual progress. The cabdriver says, "You shouldn't have done that. He'll tell his buddies and they'll all come and one of them will get hit by a car. It happened right here last week."

"I didn't do it for *him*," I retort, to Lek's delight. That's one of the great advantages of Buddhism, by the way, *farang*: it's not results-oriented. There's no way you can ever work on someone else's karma, only your own.

Vikorn's influence at the women's holding jail is less than at most men's prisons, and we don't get much of a reception from the governor. In Thailand female prison officers tend to fall into two categories: bull

144

dykes and morally aware housewives who feel they have a Buddhist duty to fulfill. Khun Kulakon belongs to the latter category. She is also shrewd in the ways of gangsters. She lets me know that she has been expecting a visit from Vikorn's camp and takes me aside to whisper, "If anything happens to her after your visit, there'll be trouble. I'll keep at Vikorn even if he takes out a contract on my head. I don't care how you deal with this, just don't waste her while she's with me."

I whisper back, "It's not like that, she doesn't work for us, she's one of General Zinna's mules." She frowns at me. I feel a little strange, explaining mafia politics to her, but, piety aside, she's nosy as hell and keeps jerking her chin at me to get me to talk. "A third party busted her. It wasn't us, but Zinna is going to assume it was Colonel Vikorn. I have to try to get to the bottom of it before Zinna declares war again, and you know what that means."

Khun Kulakon knows. She is of a generation that remembers very well the secret civil war between cops and soldiers that endured for decades and reached a climax up in Chiang Mai in the fifties with a shipment of opium that the Kuomintang brought down from the Shan States with the connivance of the CIA. The two sides hung in an armed standoff at the railhead with a train loaded with the drug, until the director of police made Buddhist peace by promising to take the opium and dump it in the sea. Nobody posed the crucial question until decades later, for fear of more conflict. When a journalist finally asked a retired senior cop, "Well, did you dump it in the sea or not?" the answer came back: "Yes, but there was a ship in the way."

The governor casts a few inquiring glances at Lek, who, now I think of it, has never been to a women's prison before.

I say, "We're only here to talk. Maybe we can save her life. Buddha knows what Zinna will do if she looks like she's going to talk."

She checks my eyes and manages a slight smile. "Thank you, Sonchai. Anything I can do to help?"

"How is she taking it?"

"She spoke to her best friend on the phone yesterday." Khun Kulakon shrugs. "Apparently, in Australian culture best friends have a special significance—deeper than family, I think." She shakes her head. "It's tough to watch these cases, even after all these years. She's just a stupid girl with a great body who was brainwashed by her culture to think she deserved more from life than she was getting. Corporal punishment would be so much more compassionate, but *farang* have made it out of style. As it is, even if the King pardons her eventually, which he will, she'll be a basket case by the time she gets out. But you can't see psychological scars on TV news, so that makes it all okay."

As with men's jails, the women prisoners spend most of their time in an open-air compound surrounded by rows of cells in a rectangular formation. For Thais, *riap roy*, or neat and tidy, is not an exhortation so much as a way of life. Even though at first glance the compound looks like a refugee camp, with towels and other pieces of fabric used as something to lie on, some cooking going on over small earthenware charcoal stoves, disheveled women shifting in their sleep or moving listlessly from place to place, to any Thai it is obvious that a detailed order prevails. Basically, each six-by-four-foot space staked out by towels or newspapers possesses an invisible number in the hierarchy, with longer-term inmates owning the most highly prized places. On the other hand, the old-timers are expected to help the newcomers learn the ropes and the elaborate rules which the women impose on themselves. That is true of the Thai women, at least. About 10 per cent are foreigners. I recognize a couple of very big and very black Nigerian women who were caught with heroin-filled condoms in their stomachs, a German woman who murdered her Thai husband after she caught him in bed with a prostitute, a couple of English girls who got caught forging checks and copped an eight-year sentence in a case hardly worth a hundred dollars. They were left to find out for themselves how the system worked. Sooner or later even the weeping and screaming Nigerian giants would learn to conform.

Rosie, though, is in a different category because she has just arrived. The head screw takes us to where she occupies one of the most highly prized positions in the middle of the compound; positions are rated as to how far away they are from the cells, where mosquitoes breed and plague the flesh of everyone in proximity. Nights in the cells are a torment during which all but the toughest find it impossible to sleep; daytime is for catching up on lost slumber.

Coming at her from behind one cannot help but be aware of a shapely backside; the curves of her body, though, are brought together in a compressed fetal posture. When we arrive at her spot, we notice she is sucking her left thumb and appears to be unconscious.

"She's not sleeping," the screw explains. "She's blocking out. *Farang* women do this a lot—it's kind of weird. A Thai woman who comes to us for the first time usually sets about learning the rules, studying the power structure, and making herself useful so she can earn some privileges and make friends. *Farang* don't see life that way. They feel either destroyed or superior. There's no middle way."

Well, Rosie does not look superior. The screw bends down and whispers gently in her ear. When that fails to have an effect, she shakes her with increasing vigor. Finally she says, "Sorry about this," and twists Rosie's ear until she opens her eyes.

"You have visitors. Stand up—or do you want to be closer to the mosquitoes?"

I think the name of the insect does the trick. She seems to force herself to stretch her body, as if taking a step in an icy sea, trembling all the while and squeezing her eyelids shut again, clenching her face against the world. When she finally manages to stand, she has the white, crumpled face of an old lady. Once she starts to speak she seems unable to stop, although it's unclear if she is talking to us or simply vocalizing a monologue constantly playing in her head: "I'm finished, my life is over, I'm all fucked up, destroyed, finished, they're going to waste my life here, my body, I'm all eaten by mosquitoes, I'm going to be old and wrinkled by the time I get out, I've had it, I'm dead, this is hell, the mosquitoes are hell, hell, hell, there's nothing left for me, nothing, I'm wasted, finished, I'll never experience childbirth now, I'll never marry, my mum will drop dead with shame, my friends will disown me, I'll get hate mail, I'll be so ugly no one will want to look at me, I'll be bitten all over by insects, I'll disgust people, me, look, don't you like my tits? Don't you want me? Have me, you can fuck me here in front of everyone, I want you to, this might be the last chance I have for good sex, I don't care, I don't care, I'm dead, can't you see, I'm dead, gone, it's over for me, I've got a decade to go in the valley of death, I'll turn to stone, I'll be just a shadow, a frightened little old lady scared to leave the house, I can feel it, I'll be a total nutter, can't you help me, please, I have such a good body. Do you eat pussy? Want a blow job? I'll be your sex slave for life if you get me out of here, I can do things with my tongue you wouldn't believe, I love being tied up, or I can do that to you, whatever you want. HELP ME! THE SKEETERS, THE SKEETERS ARE EATING

ME ALIVE, I'VE GOT BITES ON MY NIPPLES!"

The screw slaps her face and she falls silent. I shake my head at Lek. To Rosie I say, "Maybe we can help, but you'll have to get your head together. Ask the screws for some tranquilizers, something to help you think straight. Here." I slip her a bunch of banknotes worth over a thousand baht.

She stares at me and bursts into tears. "I'm not a criminal, I'm just a normal girl. I didn't want to get into this, all I wanted was a harbor-view flat in Sydney, *it was a one-off*, I was going to open a beauty salon, there's a new development on Rose Bay, I wanted south facing, I was going to be 'Rosie of Rose Bay,' that's all, I was going to have sex doggy-style and look at the view. I only intended to do one bad thing so I could have a real life, that's the only way I could afford it, see? What's wrong with that? It's what everyone does." She stops suddenly, as if remembering where she is.

I hold up a hand and whisper sternly, at the same time passing her more banknotes with the other, "Maybe we can get you out in eight years. That's a long time, but you'll still be in your midthirties. If you keep your mouth shut we can get you special privileges, insect repellent, the right food with vitamins and protein—maybe we can even make you a trusty with lots of privileges—maybe even let you have a man now and then. Rosie, we're the only chance you've got. Am I getting through to you? The only chance, Rosie. Rosie, if General Zinna thinks you're going to talk, he'll kill you, do you understand?"

I think I did manage to penetrate to that part of her that was still interested in living. Openmouthed, she nods slowly, like an idiot. She puts a hand on my shoulder and leans heavily on me, blinking all the while at the scene around her. Little by little she musters her strength, forces herself to focus on her surroundings.

"It's shit'ouse here," Rosie says. "Those slimebucket Nigerian bitches are only crying for appearances, soon as the screws turn their backs they get heavy—and there's nothing you can do, look at them, they're giants." I follow the direction of her chin across the towel-strewn prison yard to the two enormous Nigerian women, each of them about six foot six, who are softly sobbing together at this very moment with their arms on each other's shoulders. It's one o'clock in the afternoon, and those who were given the privilege, like Rosie, of a spot away from the insects now pay for it in terms of exposure to direct sunlight. Rosie's delicate northern skin has started to flake a little on her nose and forehead, and she is taking care to keep covered up as much as possible.

"Rosie, I'm working on your case. I really am. We can maybe get you a pardon in eight years, so long as you cooperate."

"What's to cooperate? You already know who the big bloke is, he's that army general everyone in here talks about. Some clumsy fucker by the sounds of it, half the girls are in here 'cos of some fuckup by him or one of his people. I wish I'd gone with the cops, mate, that was my mistake."

"Rosie, look at me, Rosie, just answer me this: do you know a Tibetan called Tietsin?"

I doubt that the fluttering of her eyelids is faked. I think the question is so far out of her range of knowledge she assumes I'm just another local whose mental software differs so far from the Australian that no understanding between us is possible. "No."

"Rosie, you have a Nepali visa in your passport. This interests me. I'd like to know more about your visit to Kathmandu."

She shrugs. "It's on the circuit, i'n'it? Backpackers go up there. Some go trekking, some go for the dope, most go for both. I don't do trekking, myself."

"You smoked dope up there?"

"Sure."

"Where did you stay?"

"Why d'you want to know that?"

"Rosie, if you hold out on me I might not come back. I'm your big hope for an early pardon, Rosie."

She gives me a fed-up kind of a look, as if I've prevailed upon her to sin against her will, but the sacrifice is not excessive. "The Nixon Guesthouse. Everybody knows it. It's on Freak Street."

"I thought nobody used Freak Street anymore."

"It's fairly extreme. A lot of sixties nostalgia. I'm old-fashioned."

"I wouldn't have put you down as nouveau hippie,

Rosie. I think you had a reason to stay in such a place."

She sighs. "Okay, so, it's the place to go if you want business. But don't ask me for names 'cos I haven't got any. You just go there, you hang out for a while, you put a certain look on your face, you use body language—if you don't dress like some clapped-out freak, if you put a bit of makeup on and show you know how to look respectable, but at the same time you hang out with that look on your face, sooner or later someone's gonna come up to you and make a proposition. See, the word is, they have the safest circuits. The safest suppliers. I've met people been financing their travels for years that way, bought houses, flats, fast cars—I've spoke to them, seen the way they live in Sydney. That's what I thought I was getting into, the respectable set. Now look." She jerks her chin at the prison yard.

"They actually give you contacts in Thailand? And the choice between working for the army or the police?"

"Yeah."

"And the people who come up to you, are they Nepali, Asian, Westerners—what?"

"You can't say. See, it's all rotating all the time. Maybe a Westerner will be up there for two months and he or she will do a lot of dealing for the main man and you'll think the Westerner is an important player, then the Westerner disappears, goes home or goes trekking, and it's someone else doing all the business, maybe an Indian man, or a Nepali woman, could be a Tibetan refugee—or a Thai. Course, you never meet the main man. Never. Nobody does. There aren't even rumors about who he is."

"There are Thais involved?"

"Sure, there are quite a few Thais in business up there, mostly in restaurants. And there are a lot of Tibetans looking for money. Not all the refugees are monks and nuns. Not all the monks and nuns are straight."

I say, "Thanks, Rosie," and try to slip her another thousand baht, but she stays my hand.

"Look, mate, there's something you can do that's important. Get me a little Chanel No. 5 makeup set? I know it sounds ridiculous, but just for me self-respect, mate, and I've worked out my own little hideout for it—it's just soze I don't feel like I'm going native, see?" I look around the yard, taking in the big Nigerians, and she catches my thought. "Don't worry, mate, I ain't gonna put it on in public. Only when I'm all alone at night. Look, look at what I got hold of last week, just in case. I've got to dream, mate, or I'll end up like those two mad bitches over there."

I like the healthy triumphalism on her face when she shows me a shard of a lady's hand mirror. I tap her on the shoulder: "On yer," I say, hoping I got the 'strainism right.

17

I ask Khun Kulakon's secretary to call a cab to take us back to Krung Thep. Once we're on the road, the obscenity of the women's jail, and Rosie McCoy's disintegration, weigh on both of us, though I suspect for different reasons. I pay little attention to the unusual number of times the driver looks in the rearview mirror, though I'm vaguely aware of his nervousness.

Lek, like most Thais, assumes that *farang* are a different order of being, like extraterrestrials, whom it is ridiculous to try to understand. Rosie's performance has only reinforced this impression. The idea of committing a grave crime in order to have a better life and be a better person also is incomprehensible to him. In Thailand people become criminals because of bad karma from previous lifetimes; to actually choose, of your own free will, to blacken your karmic future without compelling reason seems quite Martian. I, on the other hand, understand only too well. I wonder how I would react if they told me I was to spend the next twelve years in a Thai jail?

"D'you think Zinna will kill her?"

"I don't know. If he hears she's lost control of her mind and her tongue, he'll have someone slip her something to make it look like an overdose. Exactly what Vikorn would do."

"Excuse me, I have to take a pee," the cabdriver says, and turns off into a rest area near a clump of trees. I watch him walk toward the trees with a hand on his fly, then he starts to run. I react too slowly. The army truck that has been following us, an open-backed five-ton model used to transport troops, comes to a halt immediately in front of the cab, and suddenly we are surrounded by brawny young men in camouflage fatigues. An energetic fellow with lieutenant's stripes walks toward us accompanied by a couple of kids—they are hardly more than that— holding assault rifles at the ready. Now they are pointing them at us on either side of the car. "Get out, please," the lieutenant says.

I cannot help casting a glance at Lek. He and soldiers don't mix too well. "Look," I say, "I can guess what this is about. He doesn't know anything. He's just my assistant, hardly more than a cadet. Why don't you let him take the taxi back to town?" The soldier looks closely at Lek, takes in the mascara, the long black hair, the unmistakable femininity, and leers. "Let him go," I hiss, which only increases the leer; obviously the military mind has concluded Lek and I are lovers. They are going to have fun on the way back to base.

* * *

156

And so they did. By the time I'm standing outside General Zinna's command suite in the military compound, my ears are ringing with Lek's screams, including the unbearable: *What have I done to offend you?* prior to a squeal of pain. I decide to use the line on General Zinna.

He dismisses the two armed guards as soon as I'm shown into his office. He may be about five inches shorter than me and more than twenty years older, but there's no doubt about how easily he would beat me in a fight. He possesses one of those enormous chests and outstanding musculature with which the Buddha sometimes compensates the short. I envisage him deciding what to be when he grew up and narrowing the short list down to two: army general or operatic baritone. Except he wouldn't have considered the second. The irony of it all is his notorious lust for young men; but he belongs to that section of the gay community for whom erections are a kind of night-stick with which to beat the lover-victim, which makes it all okay, whereas Lek is all about love, hardly does sex at all, and is therefore despicable.

"What have I done to offend you?" I ask.

His hair is gray and so close cropped it is almost shaved; at his height he cannot help but strut. He stands up and walks around his desk, making the flagstones ring with his steel-tipped boots. When he is standing about an inch from me, he pokes my chest with one index finger, as if to push me over with it. Only the rage I feel on Lek's behalf gives me the courage to grab it and turn it back. Instead of flinching he stares into my eyes, waiting to see if I will have the guts to break it—then what? *Go on*, his eyes say, *make my day*. I hurt him as much as I dare, stopping just short of breaking it, before letting go. I have to admit his pain threshold is a lot higher than mine. He looks at his hand curiously for a moment, then nods at me to sit down on a crude wood chair while he stands.

"Explain why you were at that women's holding prison with your geek and you can go."

"He's not my *geek*. He's my assistant, and whatever you're up to, he has nothing to do with it. Are all your men queer? They seem to have fallen in love with him."

The question seems to amuse him. Some laughter lines open around his eyes. "Suppose they are, is it against the law? Are you going to arrest them?"

"No," I say, "might is right. Obviously."

"Obviously." He nods in agreement. "A great pity your boss Colonel Vikorn still doesn't understand that after all these years." He takes a couple of steps back to assess me. "I think you went to see that Australian cunt." He pronounces the word with a contempt you can taste. "Are you the one who busted her?" When I don't say anything he yells to his secretary on the other side of the door and a private soldier in his thirties comes in. That he is more than six feet tall and built like something made of iron is not as disturbing as the mind behind the body. This is not a

158

mischievous young recruit; this is a killer who enjoys his work.

I cough. "Look, I think I can cut this sh-, sh-, short," I say. "You think Colonel Vikorn busted your mule to get an edge because your ten-year agreement with him is coming to an end and you're both maneuvering for position. Well, you're wrong. Vikorn would never be that crude, and anyway it's not the kind of strategy that could succeed against a man like you. Everyone knows that. There's a third party involved here."

I have raised a flicker of interest. "Oh, really? Who?"

"A Tibetan." The word produces a strange effect. The General exchanges a glance with his enforcer, then draws up a chair to sit down and watch me. More than five minutes pass without anyone saying anything. Finally, Zinna says, "Name?"

"Dr. Norbu Tietsin."

I have the most curious impression that both Zinna and his enforcer twitch at the same time. Now Zinna stands up and paces up and down for a while, hammering home his authority with every ring. Finally, he tells his enforcer to go. "Talk," he orders, as the door closes.

"No. I'm not talking until I see my assistant in good health standing on the other side of your window."

"Are you giving orders here?"

"You can get the answer by torturing me, but it will take a while and Vikorn will feel obliged to retaliate.

It would be a much more efficient use of your precious time if you just put Lek outside the window. It would also make negotiations for the next ten-year treaty that much smoother, don't you think?"

Zinna shrugs and picks up his phone. "Looks like true love," he says to me with a leer before talking into the receiver. "The *katoey* the boys just brought in, take him into the compound where I can see him/her from my window. If there are any visible signs, someone's going to get their ass kicked."

During the interval, Zinna and I find ourselves incongruously reminiscing, for want of small talk. He asks me if I remember the last summit meeting between him and Vikorn, more than a decade ago, when I was only a few years out of cadet school. I surprise him with my total recall of the event; it wasn't something anyone could easily forget.

Both men were in their fifties at the time, at the height of their power and eager to demonstrate prowess in the most extravagant pissing contest I have ever seen. The negotiations took place over the border in Burma, where Zinna had set up a *yaa baa* factory capable of producing a million pills per day, manned by Karen tribeswomen whom the Burmese military had enslaved and made available to Zinna for his operation—in return for a big slice of the profits, of course.

I replay the fragments I have retained while Zinna and I are talking about it. In my mind's eye I was no more than a kid: impressionable, fascinated, excited, and totally under Vikorn's thumb. He sent me up into the tribal area, traditionally owned not by the Karen but by the Hmong, to reconnoiter prior to his arrival by helicopter. He astonished everyone by arriving not in one black chopper but in a squadron of thirteen which he hired for the day from an arms dealer based in Cambodia. Zinna was infuriated and intimidated, but tried not to show it while the two men negotiated at a military-type table in a valley mostly given over to poppy cultivation by the Hmong. Then something went wrong, and some very angry-looking soldiers with shoulder-fired rocket launchers appeared over the brow, running toward us in what bore a close resemblance to a charge. Now we were legging it like loonies to the last chopper to remain on the ground— and there we were, swinging away while making obscene signs at them indicating their genetic proximity to buffalo, while at the same time keeping our fingers crossed that they wouldn't be able to get their rocket launchers on their shoulders and fire while we were still in range.

"Close one," Vikorn sang out after a beautiful corkscrewing incandescent missile (which put me in mind of a fully realized soul zooming back to nirvana and made me kind of jealous) went shooting past.

But when the chopper tilted the other way, I could see the Hmong women below collecting their little packets of opium sap in piles for other women to hump back to the village by means of a bamboo rod across their shoulders, as they had done for a thousand years.

"Never saw Vikorn move so fast in my life," Zinna chuckles. Obviously, he believes he got the better of Vikorn in the somewhat fraught negotiations that followed, even though Vikorn worked loopholes into the agreement you could ride a buffalo cart through.

Zinna jerks his chin at the window. Two soldiers have brought Lek to stand in front of the glass. He looks thoroughly humiliated.

Now I'm so angry I'm fantasizing about kicking Zinna in the crotch; I can even feel the blow as I would deliver it with the tip of my shoe. I would enjoy him writhing on the floor, it would be worth the beating. Then something odd happens to my mind. Tietsin's mantra starts repeating itself automatically in my brain. I experience the same sensation as in the teahouse, a kind of floating in which consciousness is withdrawn from the tyranny of the here and now. All of a sudden even Lek's suffering is unreal. Now Zinna is staring at me.

"Well?"

I force my attention back into the five senses. "The day the Australian Rosie McCoy was arrested, we got a tip-off. The call came from Kathmandu in Nepal. We checked the origin of the call. Apart from the fact that it came from the Himalayas it was the standard sort of thing. Ninety-nine per cent of the time it's a trafficker stabbing a former partner in the back. When

162

the tip-offs are specific we notify Immigration. This was very specific, so I showed up and assisted with the bust. That's all I can tell you."

"But you went to see her today?"

"Of course. I wanted to see if I could get any more information. I'm a cop."

Zinna sneers. "You're not a cop, you're Vikorn's poodle. You jump at your master's voice." He lets a beat pass for the insult to sink in. "But you knew she was one of ours, didn't you?"

"We didn't know anything." I scratch my ear. "But she was carrying a lot of smack. Since she wasn't one of ours, we did rather think she might belong to you."

I'm waiting for Zinna to ask more about the Tibetan connection, and not at all sure how I'm going to answer.

"The informant, he actually gave you his name. A *Doctor* Tietsin?"

I raise my palms. "Anyone can invent a name."

The General stares at me with unnerving intensity for more than a minute, then seems to withdraw his interest. "That's right, anyone can invent a name. Even a name like that."

"Maybe it's some kind of joke in Tibetan," I offer. To his skeptical frown, I add, "You know, like someone might say Mickey Mouse or Napoléon Bonaparte—a joke in Tibetan culture, I mean."

"What do you know about Tibetan culture?" he asks suddenly.

"Nothing."

To my surprise he seems reluctant to pursue the subject. "Okay, you can go."

When I stand up I say, "She didn't talk, by the way."

"Who?"

"The Australian, Rosie McCoy. She didn't say a thing. I don't think she knows anything. You run a tight operation, don't you? There wouldn't be anything to connect her to you or your people?"

"There wasn't anything to connect her to your Tibetan either, until you busted her."

"D'you want me to talk to Vikorn, see if we can persuade Immigration to drop the case—I mean as a kind of preliminary sweetener to your upcoming negotiations?"

He thinks about this, before saying, "No. This is something I want to deal with myself." He gives a sudden phony smile. "I shan't be troubling you." As I'm leaving he surprises me with a final comment. "That whole thing up in Nepal, the crown prince massacring his family in June 2001, the collapse of the monarchy, the success of the Communists—you know what it was all about, don't you?"

"No."

"Well, now you do. They've been moving stuff from Tibet down into Nepal for twenty years. It's a bigger operation than anything we have in Thailand. Whoever runs the government runs the trafficking. Actually, it's a lot bigger than Colombia, but it's Himalayan, so nobody knows, not even the Americans. The CIA have no real intelligence about

Tibet at all, except what they get from the Dalai Lama's people in Dharamsala and a few spies in Lhasa." He looks at me. "And they know better than to talk about the Business."

At the door I say, "How do you know?"

"A Tibetan told me."

"Tietsin? He was here? He called you from Kathmandu?" Zinna jerks his chin to indicate that he doesn't answer questions. "But why move it through Tibet? Why not through Pakistan and India? Mumbai, New Delhi, and Calcutta are notorious trafficking centers."

"That's why. Those places are notorious. All the big Western security agencies are in India in invasion numbers, not only the CIA and the DEA, but all the French and German and Dutch, too, along with the British MI6. But when the product disappears into Tibet there are no traces. No tip-offs. And apparently there are hundreds of routes from Tibet into Nepal, routes only Tibetans, Sherpas, and Gurkhas know about. It arrives by foot without a history. Nervous buyers prefer it that way." He gives me a quizzical look.

In the cab on the way back to Krung Thep, Lek and I are silent for most of the journey. When we finally reach the outskirts, Lek says, "You want to know if they fucked me or not, don't you?"

"No. I don't want to know anything you don't want to tell me."

"There are so many ways to fuck someone like me, aren't there? What does it matter how they did it?"

Ten minutes later when he's getting out of the cab, he says, "I suppose there's nothing for it but to go home and have a good cry. I expect I'll be all right in the morning."

18

If I know I'm crazy, does that mean I'm not? I ask this question because it's three twenty-two a.m. This is the time I awake with a groan every night: three twenty-two exactly. And I know that the noise I just heard, the one which woke me up, although it sounded like someone moving in the yard outside, was a pure product of psychosis. Yes, my heart is thumping wildly, my head is sweating so much the pillow is wet, and I'm supine with terror. Surely I'm not yet insane enough to be able to hear imaginary noises in full, normal, daylight consciousness? Oh yes I am. There it goes again: not out in the yard, but inside my skull: a weird and terrifying chirping, like that of a trapped bird warning the others: *Danger, don't come here.* It's just like the nun said: I'm breathing deep into my solar plexus in which a loose nerve is causing havoc. I look down with fascination at my heaving chest and close my eyes. *Now,* I tell myself, *now, choose this moment to face it, whatever it is.* I swallow. *Okay, now, I'm going to look this devil in the eye. I'm going to stare it down.*

I'm afraid of having to see Pichai's small body sliding into the oven all over again. I'm afraid of the depth of grief, how far down it might take me, like a subterranean river roaring all the way to hell. How impossible will it be to return? Like a diver slipping at night into a freezing sea, I force my breathing to steady, to slowly dominate my wildly jumping mind. *Okay*, I say to myself, *okay, now: look!*

Isn't it always the way, that when you finally screw your courage to the sticking place, the phone rings? It's a real ring, not an imaginary one; I can still tell the difference. Blinking rapidly, having been jerked so violently back into the mundane, I grope for the cell phone and manage to press the green glyph as I lay it on the pillow next to my ear.

The caller does not declare himself. He has no need. "What's happening?"

I let a beat pass. "Where the hell have you been? I've been trying to get hold of you forever."

"When the seeker is ready, the master will come."

"Have you spent a lot of time in California?"

He chuckles. "See, it's not as bad as all that, or you wouldn't be capable of sarcasm."

"I was expressing disgust. I don't need Spiritual Quest One-oh-one just now, thanks."

Another chuckle. "Good, you're getting stronger. Just tell me what you were doing just now. I'll tell you what it felt like at my end. It felt like you were dressing up in a suit of armor to get ready to skewer a dragon."

"I hate the way you've perfected telepathy. If it weren't for that, I could dismiss you as a charlatan in a heartbeat."

"You can do that if you like. Go ahead, dismiss me as a charlatan. It's a basic early step. We might have to postpone your enlightenment for this lifetime, but that's okay. Just make sure you rebirth in a decent body with the right cultural influences. That's not so easy, of course. The best estimate is a few hundred more screwups in disastrous socioeconomic circumstances before your chance comes around again. And that's only rebirths in the human form. For the rest, I would choose mammals with short life spans. It'll save time."

"Now you're really sounding like a salesman," I grumble.

"I told you, I once did my best to join corporate America."

I sigh. "Just tell me why you called me."

"Actually, *you* called *me*. I tried to contact you on the other side, but you were all closed up with fear. Clairvoyantly, if you must know, you looked like a fetus with its eyes sewn up."

"I was just about to face my deepest fear."

He clears his throat. "That's what I called about. Your courage is noted, but this is not the moment."

"Why?"

"You're still too weak, there are too many holes in your subtle bodies—that demon would smash you if you attacked symmetrically. Just relax, let go."

I exhale slowly. "Look, while you're on the line, there's business we need to discuss. A little matter of import and export."

"This isn't a business call." His voice is suddenly smooth as silk, like that of an experienced mother soothing a disturbed child. "Are you still in bed? If so, turn onto your front and place the pillow across your shoulders. Have you done that?"

"Yes."

"Okay, now I'm going to repeat the mantra to you in a certain tone of voice. You will concentrate on the tone, not the words. Just relax. You may not know it, but you did well tonight. You summoned the courage to face the dragon. That's good. Now all we need is to train you so you have a chance of winning the bout. Feeling sleepy yet?"

The next time I open my eyes it's late morning. When I finally get to the station, I find a new e-mail from the FBI:

I got the nerds at Quantico to run a check on your victim, Frank Charles. I was wrong about him emerging unscathed from his divorces. The first two hit him pretty hard, but he was still young and had this amazing capacity to suck money out of the Hollywood system. The third, though, took most of what he had—feminism was in top gear and it was all his fault (it was the Filipina maid while the wife was visiting her mother), so he started looking around for sources of dough. Somebody persuaded him that

Nepal had been underexposed in America, and maybe some kind of feature film, or documentary, might be an idea. He went up there for a preliminary reconnoiter, liked what he saw, went up a second time, then something happened that nobody can quite explain. Now, get this. He finds funding for his film. The press releases claim the film is to be about Tibetans fleeing over high passes to Nepal, third-world suffering, dying kids, menfolk tortured in jail, women with newborns having to fend for themselves, frostbite, et cetera—but he never shows it! It's never released to the public, so it never makes any money, and strangest of all, this man who is such a show-off by nature never shows it privately, either. At least, not that I've been able to ascertain, and I've spoken to some real knowledgeable film buffs—you know, the kind who remember who was second grip in Gone With the Wind. That's all for now. Next time you're gonna Skype me. I can only go for so long in Virginia without needing to look at a genuine foreigner.

Kimberley

Sukum refuses to meet me in Soi Cowboy, so I tell him to wait for me at the Asok Skytrain station. I take the train myself to save time. It's an education in the healing power of money. Eight years ago if you rode the elevated line, you saw dozens of unfinished buildings doomed to remain skeletal cadavers, uninhabited save by squatters and dogs. That was after the financial disaster of the late nineties. Now the market god has changed his mind and speculation is pushing up steel-and-glass towers again like mushrooms after rain.

Sukum is waiting at the entrance to the station, wearing his usual generic black pants, white shirt, black shoes; he has dared to leave his jacket at the office, however. We take the pedestrian subway under Asok itself and emerge a few paces away from Cowboy. It is one of the oldest red-light districts in the city and was popular with Americans on R&R from the Vietnam War. Perhaps the names of the clubs and bars say it all: Suzy Wong's, Rawhide, Country Road, Fanny's, Toy Bar, Vixens, Fire House. We start at the British-looking pub on the corner with Soi 23, where an outdoor system of air-conditioning emits wonderful clouds of condensation. The mist splits the light and makes rainbows over our heads as we sit at a table on the street.

Now we've done twelve bars in Soi Cowboy, including Fire House, Vixens, Rawhide, and Suzie Wong's. In other words, I've been studiously avoiding the Old Man's Club, my mother's bar. It's about six in the evening, which is not a bad time to be asking questions. Few of the bars are officially open and a lot of the girls have only just gotten up. They are mostly on the street in shorts and T-shirts eating take-aways from the cooked-food stalls which line the soi, all manned by mom-and-pop teams of Isaan clans-people, frequently from the very villages the girls themselves hail from, so there's a kind of country-fair

172

atmosphere right in the heart of Krung Thep.

Regarding the Case of the Fat *Farang*, we've had a few hits; in fact, Frank Charles visited all these bars in his time, some of them fairly recently, but he didn't take any of the girls out, although he paid generously for some intense groping. In the Pussy Cat he allowed himself to be fellated in a quiet corner by a team of three professionals who took turns.

"He was a good customer," the *mamasan* of the Pussy Cat said, "very polite, paid well, bought me a drink—and the girls said he was a gentleman, the best kind of *farang*, a pleasure to work with. He paid as much for the blow job as if he had taken them upstairs."

Out in the street I see Sukum is getting hungry; he's not quite Isaan himself, hailing from the great plain north of Bangkok, but his village is far enough east for him to have a taste for *somtam* and sticky rice. I have to say the noodle fritters with tuna and ginger salad look pretty good, so I give in, and we order *somtam*, *tom yam gung*, green curry with pork, and five little wicker cartons of sticky rice to take back to the Old Man's Club, where Nong is presiding. Until recently my mother seemed resigned to the generous lines of skirts and jackets designed for middle-aged female executives, but after watching a biography of Tina Turner she's gone back to the tight leggings and fashion T-shirts of her working years. She's looking pretty sexy, I have to say, although there's no denying the wrinkles as she pulls heavily on a Marlboro Red

173

and takes out her reading glasses to look at Sukum's photo of Frank Charles.

"Sure, he's been in here," my mother says. "I had him down as a good prospect so I put Salee on to him. She worked hard, I watched her, and she was really pulling out all the stops, but he wouldn't take her upstairs. I asked him why not—after all, they were almost doing it right here in the bar, and it wasn't as if he couldn't afford her bar fine—and he said, 'She's great, but I'm looking for something even wilder.' Then he left, and I happened to look out onto the street a couple of hours later and who should I see him strolling down the soi arm in arm with but Mad Moi."

A stunned silence, after which Sukum and I say in unison, "*Doctor Mimi Moi, the chemist-cum-pharmacist?*"

Nong nods over a sneer of tobacco smoke. "Well, he said he wanted wild, and I guess that's what he got."

Suddenly I remember that my mother knows Moi from a short and stormy acquaintance years ago, a brief and ridiculous moment when Doctor Moi decided she would try prostitution for a while—as a sort of reflex of ennui—and intimidated the hell out of the down-market johns who frequent Nong's bar, without consenting to sleep with any of them. When she wasn't too stoned to do it with the hairy red-faced middle-aged punters in walking shorts from the Northwest, she was terminally disgusted at the notion of even sitting next to them at the bar. In deference to her social position, Nong waited a whole week before she sacked her.

Now it is my turn to look at Sukum with one of those complacent, triumphalist grins—for Sukum, as everyone knows, has made his career on the back of Mad Moi. "Over to you, Detective," I say, and slip behind the bar to grab a beer. (I have to have at least one a day, on Lek's instructions.) When I've drained the bottle, I hear a bleep on my cell phone. The message is from Manny:

Col. V. ballistic. Get over here.

Feeling the blood drain from my face, I pat Sukum on the shoulder. "If you need any more help, give me a ring."

"Where are you going?"

I show him the message from Manny.

"Congratulations, Khun Sukum, promotion is within reach, and the case is all yours."

19

Colonel Vikorn is standing again, but not at the window; he is pressing his back rhythmically and insanely against a wall. He is white as a sheet and suffering from periodic shudders, which in him are a sure sign of homicidal rage.

"That midget general, that toy soldier, that sodomizing fucked-up dinosaur, that spiteful little creep—d'you know what he's done?"

"No."

Shuddering so hard he can barely speak, he says, "*He's busted one of ours.* Get the fuck over to Immigration at the airport, do something about it. It's someone called Mary Smith. What the fuck do I pay you a quarter-million baht a fucking month for? You're supposed to deal with this, not waste your time on some dumb murder you've already declined to investigate. Didn't you explain to Zinna it wasn't us who busted that Australian woman? Where the hell have you been all morning? I tried to get you on your cell phone, but it's turned off. Consiglieres do not turn off cell phones—it's in the movie."

I do not remind him that cell phones were not invented when Brando and Pacino got together with Coppola thirty years ago. Instead I say, "Yes, sir," and stride for the door, silently promising myself that whatever the state of the traffic I'm not taking a motor-bike all the way to the airport. As I descend the stairs I marvel at the way Vikorn's rage has displaced the Frank Charles case in my mind. My master's anger is my business now. When the Old Man gets into one of his psychotic states, the whole station takes on an unhealthy green glow and everyone feels it. Look at it this way:

You are chairman and CEO of an exceptionally profitable commodities business which you have built up from scratch using such talents and opportunities as life offered to improve the hand you were dealt with (apart from an elder brother who is an abbot, every other male member of your family is either an alcoholic or a rice farmer; most are both); you officially left school at fourteen, but in fact you looked after the water buffalo and your younger siblings after the age of eight. Nevertheless, you felt greatness beckon, and your big break came, naturally, via America, in the form of the Indo-Chinese war, particularly in northern Laos, where a certain commodity—named *fin* in the local tongue, but called *opium* by your new colleagues—was trading at roughly double the price of gold, thanks to unceasing support from Air America.

Using your war profits as a base, you parlay your

way into a commission in the Royal Thai Police and conscientiously build up your business while selflessly serving the public. The way has been long and hard; during tough times many have had to be laid off in circumstances that made survival unlikely; you have to constantly keep your eye on the competition. Nevertheless, your efforts are heroic, inspired, and unceasing: truly a great example of capitalist courage and imagination. By dint of iron control of every aspect of your organization you finally achieve, in late middle age, the kind of dominance over your market and your environment which you so totally lacked in the circumstances of your birth. Your rivals fear you, your people respect you for your benevolence, and there is nothing between you and a yearly doubling of profits for the duration . . . except that someone has told your bitterest enemy your most important trade secret, which tiny flaw will sink your whole operation and land you in jail for the rest of your life if you don't do something about it. *Someone knows who the mules are.*

I am so much a part of the Colonel's unique rags-to-riches fairy tale that I experience his rage, urgency, and paranoia as if they were mine. It only remains to dash downstairs to pick up Lek, who happens to be standing at my desk with a frown of his own. Before I can tell him we're off to the airport, he blurts out the source of his anger: "D'you know what Sukum just did? I saw him do it."

I suppress impatience, for Lek can be stubborn in indignation. "What?"

"He just flipped a case over to you, as if he's already been promoted and you're now his slave." He nods at the monitor on my desk. Sure enough, a file bearing Sukum's initials has appeared on my own list. Lek is consumed with resentment on my behalf; I calculate it will save time if we do a quick check of the new file, so I double-click on the attachment, which is hardly enlightening.

The report is very brief. It seems that a member of a Japanese trade delegation to Thailand decided to commit suicide in the time-honored Samurai fashion by slitting his guts with a sword, in a three-star hotel on Silom, opposite the Hindu temple. The case summary reports little else, except that the trade delegation in question was comprised of senior members of the Japanese gem industry. Mr. Suzuki was in his early fifties and had recently been wiped out financially by some fraud or swindle, which was one of the subjects on the agenda when the members of the delegation met with medium-level Thai government officials. After the meeting, the delegation returned to Japan—except for the deceased. It seems Mr. Suzuki chose to take his life in Bangkok because he blamed Thailand as the prime cause of his bankruptcy. No further explanation is given.

I shrug. On the one hand, Sukum is clearly in serious breach of protocol in flicking the file over to me without authority; on the other, it is a very minor case which was going to end up untouched at the bottom of someone's electronic in-box in any event.

Does it really matter if it languishes in mine rather than Sukum's? "He's just making a point, Lek," I explain. "He feels eclipsed, upstaged. Let it ride, okay?"

So we're stuck in a cab, Lek and I, in a traffic jam near the entrance to the highway. There are about a dozen vehicles in front of us and there's nothing to do but watch the human form reduced to automaton as each driver sticks out a hand with a banknote, the tollbooth clerk in her mask hands back the change, the car moves on. I'm thinking about Tietsin's termite nest and about being worker number one million and twelve acting out my sub-Orwellian karma and thinking, *He's right, my mind master, this is exactly the continuum we're stuck with, and for ninety per cent of us there really is no way out.* Hold that thought for long and you develop a revulsion toward insecticide; I'll never squash another mosquito.

In my extreme boredom I note that my *katoey* assistant has brought an iced drink with him into the cab; it is based on modified soybeans which glow with a Chernobyl-green hue and are the fuel rods for the experiment in the transparent plastic bag with its rapidly melting ice cubes. Buddha knows what will happen when the thing reaches room temperature. Lek pulls on an extra-large-caliber straw—designed not to block when you suck in the fuel rods—which is transparent save for an orange spiral, so you can see the glowing green beans shoot up the tube into his

mouth. When an ice cube blocks his miniature re-
actor, he switches to blowing instead of sucking,
keeping his fist around the top of the bag to save himself from nuclear blowback.

Lek fits precisely with the run-down cab and the
kid—not the same one as last week—who arrives with
his broken windshield wiper to make a desultory pass
across the window, which gesture would certainly
morph into a great show of industry and alacrity
should any of us in the vehicle look like we're ready to
spring for twenty baht. But we don't, and it's four-
o'clock hot, which is by no means the same as midday
hot, even though the temperature is roughly the same
as it was four hours ago. The day itself has curled up
with a yawn; it is exhausted, worn-out, dried, clogged
with untold tons of carbon monoxide and human
frustration, so the kid doesn't try for more than thirty
seconds before retreating into the shade of a pillar on
the corner, not even attempting to extract money from
any of the other thousands of stationary metal boxes
pumping out pollution. It's just too hot to be hungry.

"Why the airport?" Lek wants to know. He's
finished his drink and is looking around for somewhere to dump the empty bag. He settles for a flat
space on top of the driveshaft casing.

I tell him, "One of our mules got busted by General
Zinna," but I don't mention the Tibetan connection.

Lek whistles. There's a lot about Colonel Vikorn's
operation he doesn't know, but there is one rule everyone knows: don't mess with the mules. Over the years,

Vikorn has managed to attract the best kind of carriers: middle-ranking business executives in need of a small pile to regulate a tax problem, respectable *farang* housewives with kids who see a way to get funding for a house improvement they've been longing for (that new veranda—or do you call them patios?—could be yours for just twelve hours of heart-stopping excitement beginning at an international airport near you); and, best of all, business travelers in their sixties or older (successful aging hippies, for the most part) who always fly first-class and are never searched and who carry junk just for the thrill and greed of it. And the reason the Colonel has been able to attract such quality is the same reason other successful enterprises are able to attract the finest in human resources: reliability and high pay. Sure, the sales force is augmented by lower-quality foot soldiers, but they are kept at arm's length, and even then they are given protection and security way above anything Vikorn's rivals provide. For that reason the busting of Smith is an image-control emergency as well as a deep wound inflicted by Zinna, and it will have to be avenged sooner or later.

Except that Vikorn and Zinna might have to form a temporary partnership if they want the Tibetan off their backs. Sooner or later it must occur to their lordships, as it has occurred to me, that there are plenty of other potential buyers in Southeast Asia, including someone in Phnom Penh said to be very close to the chief of police, who might jump into the vacuum and buy up the whole of Tietsin's stock. But can these two old barons suspend their feud for long enough to protect Thailand from a hostile takeover by a Khmer upstart? Do sharks share lunch boxes?

"We just have to make sure she doesn't know anything," I explain. "Apparently she keeps shooting her mouth off about cops being behind her, but she doesn't seem to have any names or contact numbers."

"Who was her contact here?"

"Some *farang* in Kaosan Road. He's just a low-level platoon manager—he never has more than five mules working for him at any one time, and he doesn't know anyone above his manager, who is another *farang* who doesn't speak Thai."

"So how did she get busted at all?" Lek wants to know.

"Exactly. Someone's infiltrated our organization at an overseas outpost."

"Kathmandu?"

"Right."

"Vikorn has people in Kathmandu?"

"Not exactly. They are remote subcontractors, but they do supply quite a lot of low-level mules, like Mary Smith."

"So why not just go to the subcontractors in Kathmandu?"

I scratch my ear. "You ever have anything to do with Hindus? They have such huge extended families. You start out thinking you're with the eldest son, then it turns out he's fronting for an uncle, who is fronting for one of his cousins, who's fronting for the patriarch on the mother's side, and so on." I raise my palms to the Buddha: "We don't really know who they are."

"You don't have names?"

"Sure. Narayan or Shah. Same as fifty per cent of the phone book."

"No addresses?"

I cough. "That's what we're trying to get. The address of our subcontractors in Nepal. Our firewalls are so good, only the mules seem to know."

When my phone explodes with *Must be some way out of here*, I see that it is Sukum calling, and share a wink with Lek. I've already told him that the Fat *Farang* Case has taken a bizarre twist which may have Sukum and Mad Moi working together again.

"She's gone," Sukum says in an excited voice. "Fled. I checked with her probation officer. I even called her sister, the one who talks to me, and the pharmacy where she usually gets her prescription drugs for her mental problems. None of them has seen her in more than five weeks."

"Five weeks? That's a long time before he was killed. Doesn't sound like proof of murder to me."

"Five weeks, three weeks, two days, what's the diff? I'm being intuitive here, cutting out unnecessary paperwork, like you. The point is, she hasn't been near her probation officer, so she's risking jail time. So it's drastic. She's on the run. Look, do I know her or not?"

"Nobody knows Doctor Moi like you, Khun

Sukum," I say, sharing a grin with Lek, who has gone into a devastating mime of Sukum, including his compulsive teeth cleaning and his zippy little farts. This colors the tone of my voice, which causes Sukum to suspect flippancy. Sukum loathes flippancy because he doesn't understand it, even though he's been trying all his life.

"You're being flippant?" he wants to know.

"No. Not at all."

"You're putting two and two together, yes? Just before the murder she disappeared?"

"Okay, Detective Sukum, okay, I accept your expert advice. But we do need to know exactly why she disappeared, d'you see? A suspect who disappears five minutes after the criminal act is not at all the same as a suspect who makes themselves scarce a month before the event."

"What's the difference?"

"Assuming guilt in both cases, the second will have a cast-iron alibi."

"I'll check," Sukum says without nuance, and closes his phone.

What with the day going to sleep on us, and the traffic hardly shifting—even though we have made the crucial turn from Asok onto Sukhumvit, we are now stuck behind a builder's truck in the gridlocked outside lane, which we need in order to access the turnoff for the highway, so it looks like we're in for the long haul—Lek and I cannot resist running through some of the old Sukum and Moi stories, and the way she always seems to get the better of him.

After a low-speed chase that lasted for most of Sukum's career as a detective, he was only able to bust her on cannabis cultivation and tax evasion, even though everyone knows she arranged for the deaths of two of her four ex-husbands and ran her own *yaa baa* production unit as a cottage industry for more than ten years. She took revenge on Sukum by paying a tea lady to slip LSD into the detective's morning iced lemon tea; Lek mimes Sukum on a paranoid acid trip to a disturbing level of accuracy: Sukum crawled under his desk, curled up in fetal position, and shivered there for almost an hour, periodically yelling for his Toyota, before we called the medics to give him a tranquilizer and take him away. The LSD had to come from Moi—this was the midnineties, when acid had disappeared more or less completely from world markets and nobody except a trained chemist like the Doctor herself could have synthesized it.

When the cab finally passes the tollbooth and we're speeding toward Suvarnabhum we're entertaining each other with speculations of how Doctor Moi will stitch Sukum up this time. I have to say, it's fun sometimes to watch Lek's darker side. As he points out, *We're all dual, darling.*

"But what's so *amazing* about her is the way she always manages to look so good in those HiSo magazines. How does she even get *invited* to those fantastic parties, that's what I would like to know."

"She's old money," I explain. "Teochew—her

people originally hailed from Swatow about a hundred and fifty years ago, where they were members of one of the triad societies. Apparently her family is quite senior in one of them. While she was growing up her grandfather maintained mob connections and ran the triad's secret banking system in Bangkok, which has tentacles all over the Pacific Rim. Most of the capital came from opium in the thirties, so she and her sisters were brought up like princesses. Her father encouraged her to follow her interest in pharmacy right up to the doctorate level. He thought she was going to start a retail chain, financed by his money. He didn't know she'd fallen in love with drugs for their own sake in her midteens. She was one of those people who see life in terms of chemicals at an early age, and there's nothing you can do about it. She started one corner shop on Soi Twenty-three, which was closed most of the time while she experimented with her stock. After being patient for nearly a decade, the respectable drug companies wouldn't supply her anymore, and she let the business go bankrupt, even though she's fantastically rich. Her family have not disowned her—after all, she's only got convictions for minor offenses, and it's not certain she killed two of her husbands."

"Each of them died tragically in mysterious circumstances."

"Right. While she was out of the country. But HiSo is HiSo. As long as she plays the game and turns up in those amazing ball gowns at those society events, they'll protect her. They may even be proud of her. How can you tell with the Chinese?"

Lek and I fall to pondering in the taxi, which is speeding now on the highway to the airport. "When you think about the Fat *Farang* Case, though, and then you put Moi in it as a suspect, it does all seem to fall into place," Lek opines with a yawn.

"It does. I've been racking my brains trying to think of anyone in Thailand who could possibly have done it, and Mad Moi simply didn't occur to me. Now that Sukum's onto her, though, I'm wondering why I never thought of her."

"He's going to claim all the credit, you do know that? Even though it was Nong who first mentioned Doctor Moi—if it weren't for you, he wouldn't even be thinking along those lines."

I sigh. "It doesn't matter, Lek, it really doesn't. I don't want promotion anyway. I'd feel even more of a fraud than I feel now."

"Don't talk like a fool, darling. The minute he gets his promotion they'll start to put pressure on him to take money. White turns to gray at that level, and soon after that you get to black. They've only let him keep his innocence because he's so junior. You watch, he'll turn up to work one day in a Lexus, and you'll know that's another soul sold to the devil."

While we are leisurely discussing Sukum and his imminent forensic triumph, he calls on my cell phone: his name is flashing on and off to Dylan's heartfelt *There is too much confusion, I can't get no relief.* I wink at Lek.

"I've traced her," Sukum says.

"Well done, Detective."

"She's staying at the Somerset Maugham Suite at the Oriental."

"Ah! Old money! Don't you love it? They always know how to hide in full view. When are you going to take her in?"

"When are you free? They told me you're on your way to the airport doing something dirty for Vikorn."

I frown at the phone. "Why do you need me, Detective? Call the media, do what Vikorn does, make a career-building event of it."

"Suppose she denies all involvement?"

I cough. "Detective, you will have to do some work. She might fight against the prospect of death row— some do, you know."

"I know that," he snaps. "I'm talking about how clever she is. She's educated and thinks like a *farang*. I might not understand what she's talking about. I want you to be there."

"Is it the LSD from last time that's got you all nervous, Khun Sukum?"

"You're not kidding. Have you ever had someone slip you some acid and you think you've lost your mind for the rest of your life? And suppose she's HIV-positive and she's got spikes hidden in her hair like in that movie you made me watch."

"*Hannibal?* There were hair spikes laced with the AIDS virus?"

"I've watched it five times now. She was a black American named Evelda Drumgo. That's put me right off, I can tell you. I'm just not qualified to deal with sophisticated foreign women, I don't have the exposure. I only know Thai housewives and factory workers, the other kinds are more your field."

I'm puzzled by his reluctance, given the decade he spent on the Mad Moi files. I shrug at Lek. "I might be a while. We're not at the airport yet, and the traffic's going to be pretty bad on the way back, I can tell from the way the cars are all slowing on the other side of the highway."

"I'll wait."

"Suppose she makes a run for it?"

"Then I can arrest her, can't I? But she's so cunning, I bet she won't commit a single crime while I'm watching."

Lek can't believe he said that and is repeating the phrase over and over and shaking his head while we arrive at the airport's taxi drop-off.

20

They're not supposed to keep a suspect for more than twenty-four hours without handing them over to the police. They've made an exception in Mary Smith's case because they had to take her to the hospital for a laxative, where she was kept under tight supervision with a special toilet to catch the condoms. Now the condoms have all been sent off to forensics for tests and nobody thinks they contain anything less than high-quality smack.

Immigration took the opportunity to throw Mary Smith in with another offender, a French woman who was caught with a small amount of cannabis. The French woman speaks perfect English, and Immigration secretly filmed and voice-recorded Mary's night with her. I watch the part of the video where Mary slips a hand between the French woman's thighs and they turn to kiss like old lovers.

"Recidivists," the customs officer says, "both of them. You can tell by looking. These girls love jail, they just don't know that they love it."

Smith is in her midtwenties, longish, light brown

hair which needs washing, crumpled backpacker pants and shirt. An unhealthy paleness haunts her otherwise unremarkable features; she looks like a young woman who is frequently sick from junk. She speaks English in two shades of gray: estuary and Cockney. During my interview with her, I understand completely where the customs officer is coming from. It's not something you can explain to anyone who is not in the business, but cops come across it all the time: people in the grip of a psychological need for incarceration. It's a fatal attraction like any other. Some people scare themselves to death with vertigo as a precursor to jumping off buildings; young men with a morbid fear of violence join the Marines and get themselves killed; there are leprophiles and AIDSphiles, most of whom succumb to their chosen diseases in the end; and there are recidivists, people who, from a fantastically early age, know that their destiny lies in prison. Mary Smith, for example, knows all about Thai jails, even though she's never been in one. She knows they will likely hold her in the women's holding prison at Thonburi, where Rosie is incarcerated. She also knows the name of the prison where she will likely serve out her time. She knows about the punishments, the occasional sexual assault by bull dykes, the likely effect eight or more years will have on her mind, and there is a quiet joy behind the shock, a slow-eyed relief that all the important decisions will be made by someone else from now on—and love will be simply a series of stolen opportunities with short shelf lives. The world recently got very simple for Mary Smith.

I say, "Maybe I can help with the sentence. There's a huge difference between eight years and twelve—believe me, I've seen it."

"What difference?"

"Eight years, there's still something left, some tiny memory of how to function in a free society, something you might just be able to build on—and you're still quite young. In eight years you'll be—let me see—"

"Thirty-six."

"Right. Thirty-six. Still of childbearing age. Still with a lot of future in front of you."

"I don't want a future. I hate future. I definitely don't give a fuck about having kids."

I nod sagely. "But twelve years, that's something else, every programming you ever received out of jail, from birth onward, will have been erased from your mind. All of your responses, even the most basic, will have been replaced with jail responses, even down to using a toilet—you're going to be doing it our way for the rest of your life."

"*Our* way?" She uses a sneer to convey the allegation of hypocrisy.

I scratch my left ear. "Let's cut the crap, Mary. Twelve years is too long. As the jail's little *farang* whore you might just about get away with eight and still be viable, after that you'll be some toothless toy for the dykes to play with, you won't even get to choose who uses the dildo or where they shove it, much less what they make you do with your mouth. Better talk."

My plain words seem to have had an effect. "I don't know anything. If I did I would have talked by now, wouldn't I?"

"Who told you where to go when you got to Bangkok?"

"Someone on the road."

"Where did they tell you to go?"

"Kaosan Road. Some little side street behind the Coca-Cola truck."

The Coca-Cola truck is famous; it hasn't moved for more than thirty years. Actually, it's a *Pepsi-Cola* truck, but we always think *Coke*. "Where were you when you heard about business to be had on Kaosan Road?"

She shrugs. "Everybody knows. It's one of those things people talk about on the road."

"Backpackers?"

"Sure."

"But the precise address—where did you get that?"

"Nepal. Kathmandu."

"From?"

"The place where I was staying."

"What was the name?"

"The Newar Guesthouse."

I let a couple of beats pass. "The Newar? Where's that?"

"Up the top of Thamel, just behind where they sell all those kukri knives."

"Not Freak Street?"

"Freak Street? Of course not, nobody goes there anymore. The Newar is the other direction, I told you, at the top of Thamel, nowhere near the market. Freak Street is next to the market."

"Who gave you the name and address to go to in Kaosan Road?"

"A backpacker."

"Man or woman?"

"Woman."

"*Farang?*"

"Yes, *farang*. But she was only fronting for someone else, someone who had shares in the guesthouse. She happened to be doing business when I got there. She left before I did. I never heard from her again."

"And who owns the guesthouse? Who is the real supplier?" A shrug. Of course a girl like her would never be told a thing like that. "Ever heard of the Nixon Guesthouse?" She gives a blank stare.

On the way home the traffic moves like molasses, and it's about eleven in the evening when I drop Lek off at the Asok-Sukhumvit interchange so he can take the subway to Klong Toey, where he recently took on a small illegal house at a knockdown rent. I think he's finally settling his home base in preparation for the operation that will turn him into a woman.

The first thing I want to do at my hovel is check my Kathmandu guidebook. I am unable to find either the Newar Guesthouse or the Nixon, but that doesn't necessarily mean anything, except perhaps that these two establishments are too basic even to qualify for the "budget" category. Or maybe they don't need to advertise?

Now I have a good reason to go back up to Kathmandu to investigate, and when I call Vikorn he's enthusiastic: "Yeah, find out who's doing the snitching up there." I immediately *wai* my little red electric Buddha in the shrine I put up in my bedroom after Pichai died, roll a joint, and try to stop my mind from slipping, slipping, slipping away. Too late, a tiny dying body attached to a respirator pops up in my mind's eye and I feel my heart starting to sink and hear the whirr of blade wheels. Then: *Businessmen, they drink my wine.* My cell phone is ringing. I forgot to turn it off before I lit the joint.

It's Sukum. His voice is glum. "I finally managed to talk to her over the phone."

"Who?"

"Mad Moi. Doctor Death."

"At the Oriental? She talked to you?"

"Yes. Only to let me know she has a cast-iron alibi. At the time the American was killed, she was at one of those HiSo parties, with photographers everywhere. I didn't need to question witnesses, there's a whole web-page dedicated to the party, with pictures of her nearly naked in one of those ball gowns HiSo women wear, cleavage all the way down to her belly button. I guess her drug diet keeps her slim. She said the photographers will all have date and time features on their cameras, so I could probably work out to the minute where she was and who she was talking to for the whole of that night."

"Why is she staying at the Oriental?"

"Because she is having her house on the river renovated. She's booked the Somerset Maugham Suite for two months. That's more than a year's salary for me."

Maybe I'm too sensitive, but I don't like the "for me" coda. I think it's a reference to cops like myself who have alternative sources of income. I feel one of those twinges you get when someone activates the guilt chakra. Sukum adds, "Of course, there is such a thing as remote murder."

"Sure, but it's a hard case to argue when the homicide is aggravated by cannibalism at the scene of the crime."

Sukum giggles. "I really think you should speak to her. She just won't take me seriously. It's quite insulting."

"Okay, I'll see what I can do."

Everything that happens in Thailand happens thanks to go-betweens; it's our Chinese side. When I call my mother to tell her I need to get in touch with Doctor Moi, I can hear drunken *farang* and whores laughing in the background along with "California Dreaming." Over the noise of the bar, Nong says there's no way she knows of getting directly in touch with the notorious aristocrat, but she'll leave messages all over town for Moi to call me if she deigns. To my great surprise, Nong has a response from the doctor before dawn: she would be delighted to meet me to discuss the case.

By the time I've showered and shaved, though, another mood kicks in. I remember I'm consigliere first and cop second; I'm despising myself all over again. Now that Pichai's dead and Chanya's in a nunnery, why the hell am I stuck in this predicament? Because it's a continuum. Karma. I'm thinking, *Blade wheel, I need the blade wheel.* But when my cell phone starts ringing and I see from the screen it is Vikorn himself, I cannot resist pressing the green glyph.

"So?"

"Smith won't talk," I say. "She doesn't know any-thing." I hear a provisional sigh of relief.

"You're sure?"

"Yes."

"Sonchai, I'm asking you as *jao paw*. You know what I'll have to do if you're going soft here."

"I'm not going soft. She's a typical low-grade mule; I would guess she was born into a one-parent family and brought up in city housing with no real prospects, considering her attitude, emotional underdevelop-ment, and general lack of inspiration or ability. If she'd been talented she might have started her own pharmaceutical business by now, but being essentially of peasant orientation, she has turned herself into a dumb animal ideal for your operation. She couldn't talk if she wanted to."

"Thank you, Consigliere," Vikorn says.

21

I'm in a four-button, double-breasted blazer by Zegna, a spread-collar linen shirt by Givenchy, tropical wool flannel slacks, and patent leather slip-ons by Baker-Benjes, and I smell terrific as I stroll nonchalantly past the security guards on the great entrance doors to the Oriental Hotel. The guards speak out of the corner of their mouths into their lapel microphones; security is one of the hotel's selling points. Another is the full-strength British Raj nostalgia of the Authors' wing with its light-flooded solarium where potted bamboo soars while staff in traditional Thai silks do all they can to spoil you, especially at tea time.

Now I am seated on one of the high-backed rattan thrones under the wrought iron staircase at a woven rattan glass-topped table amid a riot of pastel shades and incredibly pretentious HiSo types, mostly of Chinese extraction, with a few English ladies who may be old enough to remember the original Raj. They have the best of it, these memsahibs, who are not only too old to care about their figures but have also given up worrying about their health, since they are days away from losing it altogether and therefore free to tuck into the clotted cream, strawberry jam, and scones with insouciant abandon, washing it all down with lashings of the best Darjeeling. I just wish I'd had the foresight to roll a joint to smoke in the men's room, instead of hanging out here like a mouse in a trap.

Well, she has taken forty minutes, just for me, but now here she is, making her entrance at the top of the stairs in a black-and-white silk trouser suit which hangs perfectly on her emaciated body. As a connoisseur of criminal integrity, I cannot help admiring the way she is still able to pull it off, the HiSo sangfroid yes-I'm-bad-but-try-to-catch-me performance, even while her liver must be showing signs of domestic violence.

Doctor Moi is forty-three years and two months old, and although there must be organs owned by her which possess the characteristics of those double that age, nevertheless she learned enough at the Swiss finishing school to pay special attention to the parts exposed to the view of others: she looks pretty good. Her skin is Han white, as translucent as jade, and her features—a fine Chinese face with delicate, intelligent lines atop a Modigliani neck—strike one as the last word in good breeding. She is tall for a Chinese of Teochew race, almost six feet, and knows how to use her height to project elegance. Similarly, her hair: it is thick, black, and long, falling from the crown of her head in a series of sine curves and slow-motion bounces as she moves across the floor attracting all the attention she can use. A long string of large pearls loops around her neck and provides something for her to play with on her approach. And there is a black velvet choker around her neck with a precious stone of some kind in the middle, occupying the soft cavity under her Adam's apple. The stone is orangey pink and cut with a thousand facets that reflect light. Naturally, I stand, give her the high *wai* that her social position deserves, then take the hand she has extended for me to kiss.

"How wonderful to see you again, Sonchai. I don't think we've met since I had that silly misunderstanding with your mother."

"You're looking terrific," I say.

"Am I? I suppose I am, but I'm afraid I was born about thirty years too late. You have no idea of the kind of drugs that will come online during the next decade. Any girl with the sense to start using them early in life will never age beyond twenty-two. Isn't that amazing?"

"You mean they'll be immortal?"

She smiles. I had forgotten how twisted her lips go when her demon reveals itself. "Better than that. I mean still looking perfect at my age. Older. There will be women who will pass themselves off as twenty-five until they die at eighty. Imagine!" She waves a hand at the orchids, the wrought iron, the balcony from which she just descended. "It's quite splendid, I suppose, but I'm bored with it. I wish they'd hurry up and finish my renovations so I can go home. I miss my maid. I've sent her back to her people for a week, and I have to call her every day for help. Her ancestors come from the same village as mine in Swatow. I've had her all my life, and I'm only half *me* without her."

"You still keep up with latest developments in pharmacology, then?"

We have ordered the full cream tea, but now that it arrives neither of us knows quite what to do with it. Moi smears the thinnest coat of cream and jam over the extreme end of a scone, nibbles at it, then sets it down. For my part, I have never developed a taste for deep dairy, I gave up on jam and other sweet things about a decade ago, and scones make me feel stuffed without contributing anything nutritious. I am not surprised that the people who invented this sedentary decadence were the biggest narcotics traffickers the world has ever known.

"Of course, I keep up," Doctor Moi says. "If they would only give me back my license you would see what I could do."

I knew the subject of her license would come up sooner or later. "They won't give it back to you? After all these years?"

"No. And it's nothing to do with either of my convictions, which are so minor nobody remembers them except the police."

"So why?"

"It's because cops like you keep telling everyone I murdered two of my husbands. This is Thai society:

it's not the law that destroys you, it's the gossip."

"Ah!"

"It's so unfair. You probably don't understand, chemicals are the future which is already here. The great thing for any pharmacist with brains is that only a few have realized we are now in a position to take over the world." She takes a sip of Darjeeling, and the gesture is so well executed that a couple of Thai women sitting near us immediately begin to drink their tea with fingers in the same position, imitating the Doctor's perfect poise.

"You don't think oil, the economic crisis, the environment, wars, fresh water, and radical Islam will hold our attention more than chemicals?"

"Chemicals are the only way we can cope with such things. That's the point. More than fifty per cent of Westerners depend on mind-altering drugs of one kind or another. We now know that everything—love, war, money, the environment, attitude, work—everything is just a question of chemicals reacting with each other. At the end of the day bliss is all about dopamine, and anger is all about an imbalance in the blood. People are already controlled by the pharmaceutical industry, have been for more than five decades, but we're scientists, we just don't know how to use the power which is now in our hands." The subject has excited her. Her long skinny fingers are shaking slightly as she raises her cup. I wonder what customized chemical she is using today. "Don't you see, the future isn't uncertain at all, it is quite obvious, and if I had my license back I could take over. Within less than a decade the average person won't be able to look at the evening news without taking some kind of tranquilizer. Once the general population get hold of some of the superdrugs that are coming onstream you'll get total, one hundred per cent addiction to a family of molecules over which only a tiny percentage of the population have any control. Our power will be absolute, like having a monopoly on air."

I have a feeling she hopes to use me in some way to persuade the authorities to give her license back. I have to stare into her eyes and shrug.

"I need a senior cop to put in a word for me. All they would have to say is that I didn't kill any of my husbands."

"No cop is ever going to say that. All anyone can say is that there is no proof."

"You could get Vikorn to say that in writing?"

I'm thinking, *Not for the sake of clearing up a little murder inquiry that does not interest him in the least.* I say, "I'll ask him if you like." In an attempt to distract, I add, "That's an amazing stone," and look directly at the large, brilliant, orangey-pink gem at her neck.

She touches it for a second with one of her long fingers, not sure if she wants to let me get away with changing the subject. "Hmm, it's a pad." To my blank look, she adds, "A padparadscha. A rare kind of sapphire."

"Is it as expensive as it looks?"

"It would buy the room," she says without

emphasis, waving a languid hand to include the entire wing of the hotel. "But let's not get into that. I wear it to amuse myself. There's no one here worth impressing."

I clock the gem, thinking, *Buy the room!* It's true, she is far too proud to lie about such a thing, and maybe the hotel, with its army of security guards, is the one public place in town where she can safely wear it.

She lets her eyes rest on me for a moment, then looks away. "So, why did you want to see me? Your little colleague Khun Sukum seems to think I had something to do with a dead *farang*. I can't think why."

"Khun Doctor, how good a customer of yours was Frank Charles?"

She smiles faintly at the question, as if giving it seven out of ten for ingenuity. "Customer? What do you mean? I think your mother saw me walking down Soi Cowboy with him shortly before his death. What does that prove?"

"Arm in arm. You were walking with him arm in arm. You don't let any man take your arm unless he is HiSo or important in some other way. So I assume he was a customer. Also, he had been in Soi Cowboy for a few hours, doing a tour of the bars. He seemed in a strange state of mind—perhaps despair, depression, middle-aged paranoia. He was looking for excitement, then a few hours later you were in the soi, where you had not been seen for years. I think he called you. He needed you."

"You mean he wanted to hire my body?"

"No. You know I don't mean that."

"But I don't have a license to operate as a pharmacist. How could he be a customer?"

"You have contacts in the industry. You got away with a lot for more than a decade. That means someone senior was helping you. You frequently boast you have access to state-of-the-art drugs few people know the names of. Of course, it would be possible for you to do a little dealing on the side for a HiSo friend." I lean forward to whisper, "Khun Doctor, we don't know the details, but we do know you use the canals and the river for transportation. Do we really have to post river police all over your patch?"

She takes another sip of tea, gives the cream and scones a cursory glance, replaces the bone-china cup on its saucer. "You'll get Vikorn to put in writing there is no evidence I ever killed anyone? It's the implication of an induced heart attack in the case of my third husband that has the poor little disciplinary committee so excited."

"I'll ask him. I can't promise he'll do it."

To my surprise she seems to accept this offer and says, "Anyway, they weren't the sort of men you'd want to keep alive if you could possibly help it."

I shake my head. That's the sort of comment she's famous for; nobody knows if, at such moments, she is being outrageous, or if she's merely telling the truth as she sees it. Or maybe she's just nuts?

She looks away again, at a bamboo tree soaring out

of a gigantic pot. "I met Frank Charles years ago. It must be almost a decade. He didn't know Thailand so well at that time and was using contacts he made in LA to introduce him to society people over here. I met him at a ball that was part of a film festival." She flashes me a glance. "Of course, I knew he was fantastically rich, so I spent some time with him. He was very good-looking—that was before he got so fat. We were never lovers, if that is your next question. I don't do sex. It's a mug's game, if you ask me."

"But you saw him from time to time, after that ball?"

"Yes. For a while he showed up at a lot of society events, mostly balls and dinner parties. I think that was before he decided the red-light districts were more interesting. He dropped off most radar screens pretty quickly after that."

"But you remained friends? Let me be frank, Khun Doctor. Your conversation is intelligent, witty, educated, and charming. You also talk openly about drugs. For a *farang* new to Thailand who would certainly have been familiar with that kind of recreation, you would have seemed like an oasis."

She makes a face, then her eyes sweep the room with the peculiar intensity of one who finds few of interest among our species, but who nevertheless lives in hope. "You'll have to give me immunity if you want me to talk."

"If you mean immunity from prosecution for

sharing a few of your favorite molecules with him, yes. Nothing beyond that, though."

She thinks about it, takes another sip of tea, shrugs. "He'd been to a lot of parties in Beverly Hills. He knew the names of a lot of chemicals. I told him I could get him anything he could get in LA, usually at about twenty per cent of the price. Pharmacists over there really know how to turn a profit. I never made any money out of it at all. I let him have stuff at cost."

I lean forward a little for emphasis. "Khun Doctor, I will approach Colonel Vikorn just as you have asked. But you know as well as anyone that there are many ways of asking a favor. If you want me to ask my Colonel to help you in a way that will have effect, if you wish me to give my plea on your behalf the urgency and importance it deserves, you will have to be more expansive. You are making this interview hard work for me, Khun Doctor."

She looks at me curiously, as if it has been a long time since anyone pressured her about anything and she is finding the experience novel. One more sip of Darjeeling and she starts to talk.

"He was not so unusual for a *farang*. He was very smart, sensitive, aware, clever with money, but frustrated, disillusioned, and thoroughly self-obsessed. In his youth he had wanted to be a great artist of the big screen—perhaps even a kind of cinematic Shakespeare. He was convinced of his own talent, but he never seemed to produce anything beyond the obvious. Actually, his problem was the eternal adolescence of America—emotionally, he never got past the golden-sunset school of fucking." She pronounces the vulgarism with perfect aplomb. "You know, as if one apocalyptic screw is going to provide the meaning of life. So, of course, he's in a permanent mess, psychologically. The girls in the bars may have been social and economic simpletons, but they were happier than he was. He was fully smart enough to see the significance: dirt-poor Asian whores in better psychological shape than the very flower of American manhood. His incredibly expensive, constitutionally guaranteed pursuit of happiness hadn't even gotten him into the third-world league. He needed chemicals, and I found them for him in the name of friendship."

"There must have been something in it for you, Khun Doctor?"

"Beyond endless invitations to watch private screenings in LA, which I never went to? Yes. We were friends. Different as we were, we were both pariahs of an unusual kind. The rich and successful kind. Our talk would probably have been considered dangerous and revolutionary, if anyone had overheard. We offered each other the opportunity to be intelligent without restraint. He cried on my shoulder about his condition of chronic mental and emotional unease, I moaned about not having a license anymore to practice pharmacy and play with drugs. We sort of understood each other."

"Khun Doctor, this sounds very much like a real friendship."

209

She nods. "I hadn't thought of it that way. He was certainly more fun to talk to than any of my women friends."

"And so it remained until he died?"

She shakes her head and speaks slowly, thoughtfully: "No. Not really. There was never any kind of schedule, any consistency in our friendship. If he heard of some new drug he wanted to try, or if he wanted industrial-quality cocaine or LSD, I would get it for him. He was a child of the sixties: he liked acid and saw value in it. When he needed to talk, we would meet. Sometimes I felt like a kind of nurse." She shrugs. "To be frank, there was the thought in the back of my mind that he might one day be able to put in a word for me with the Thai authorities through the U.S. ambassador, with whom he was friendly. But our meetings were intermittent. He commuted between here and LA. I was often out of the country myself. And when he stopped going to society events, we ceased to have any acquaintances in common."

"Did he speak to you about visits to Nepal?"

A quick glance from her shrewd black eyes. "Sure. I think it was Nepal that screwed him up. I would look there for the reason for his death, if I were you."

"Why?"

"He got involved with a girl up there. It sounded quite ridiculous. She was some Tibetan refugee who knew a little mystical mumbo jumbo, and because it was the Himalayas he fell for it. I lost respect for him then. He felt he couldn't talk to me about this new mysticism of his because I would laugh at it. When I told him it was all about chemicals—with the right dopamine precursor I could introduce God to anyone—he got all passionate and evangelical and I left early. It was more than a year before he called me after that. And he'd started to get so horribly fat. It was like watching a catastrophe happen in slow motion, the way he just grew and grew—he stopped shaving, too, and I hate beards. I urged him to take some orlistat, or sibutramine, but he was weird about his obesity. It was as if it were part of his new path, his very own personal martyrdom."

"How long ago was that?"

"It was an estrangement that happened gradually. We never fell out, we drifted apart. Since we had never been lovers there was no need for formalities— much less for murder," she adds with a smile: one of those in which the extremes of the lips crawl slightly up the incisors.

"So you were surprised when he called you that night from Soi Cowboy?"

"Not really. I didn't think he would be able to stay away from me forever. I supplied the two *farang* necessities he couldn't shake: chemicals and intelligent conversation in English." She takes another sip of tea and scans the room. "He was in a bit of a state, though. His Tibetan dream had gone badly wrong and he needed a pharmacist. I'm afraid I was quite merciless. I gave him some Depo-Provera to kill the sex drive, crystallized THC so he could get to God

211

without a mandala, cocaine because that was what he was used to. And some acid."

"How did you get LSD? I haven't heard of it on the street for ten years. Have you been synthesizing again?" There is no need to mention Sukum in this context; she knows what I'm talking about.

For the first time she shows signs of discomfort. She pulls girlishly on a section of her long black hair and makes an apologetic face. "He begged me. And it wasn't easy to get. I didn't dare make it myself, so I had to go underground. It came all the way from Goa in a baby's dirty diaper, if I recall."

"And that was the last time you saw him?"

"I had to get the stuff, he had to pay me, we had to pretend to be friends again—there were meetings over a period of a few weeks."

"About two months before he died?"

"Yes. About that."

The interview is over, so she asks after my mother and the Old Man's Club. She has not heard my son is dead and Chanya gone to a nunnery. She shows no sympathy when I give her this news, merely suggests a few chemicals to help with my grief.

22

The interview with Moi has sent my restless mind on a new track, and I feel a residual professional pride that urges me to go a little deeper into the Fat *Farang* Case. There is also something about Doctor Moi herself, the most exotic criminal in Thailand, which makes it hard to focus on anyone else. I decide to postpone the second trip to Nepal for a few days.

The obvious duty call is the American's penthouse on Soi 8. Sukum has never been to a well-appointed *farang* apartment building and is taken aback mostly by the vast glittering empty space on the ground floor. He is imagining how many Thai flats he could fit here. I flash my ID at reception, then collect Sukum, who is now mystically fixated on some flourishing tropical plants about twenty feet high which reach up to the diaphanous glass roof. Where he comes from they don't house plants in multimillion-dollar structures. The banks of elevators are at the back.

A woman from reception in her early thirties, accompanied by a security guard, shares the elevator and opens the door for us. It is because we are cops that she does not trust us. Neither of us is surprised that Frank Charles's property is on the top floor. She and the guard have to split up to follow Sukum and me, since we take different routes around the apartment. Sukum gets the rather attractive receptionist; I get the grumpy middle-aged guard.

Sukum is most interested in the vast reception room, while I am attracted to an impressive film library in what was originally the fifth bedroom. There is a communicating door to the fourth bedroom which has been converted into a home cinema, with projector and roll-down screen about ten feet by five. I check the shelves that dominate the other walls.

However sloppy his sex life, Frank Charles was meticulous about his film collection. It is divided into tapes, of which there seem to be thousands, and smaller DVD cases, presumably representing more recent movies, and, stacked up in one corner, I see some unused cans of film. Now I find I'm starting to like Frank Charles. I'm pleased with him for treating his girls well and spreading his despair in small doses so it didn't hurt any one person too much; but I confess my opinion is colored by the classic movie collection which forms part of the greater tape collection. He has all of Bertolucci, Fellini, Truffaut, Altman, but best of all he has what look like much-used copies of my four favorites: *La Strada*, *Satyricon*, *Les Enfants du Paradis*, and *La Règle du Jeu*. (In case you're wondering how a Thai pimp-cum-cop acquired such erudite taste in movies, *farang*, it's all thanks to

214

one of my mother's former clients, a Frenchman who happened also to be named Truffaut and who taught me many things. In his seventies, he went and had a heart attack on us, forcing us to hightail it back to Bangkok just when we were getting used to Maxim's as our local cafeteria. Thanks to his tuition I later wrote film reviews for *Thai Rath* to help bring in a few pennies when I was starting out as a cop.) I just can't bring myself to believe that a man with that kind of taste can be all bad. Then I get to the porn. I call Sukum.

There is no time to watch every erection penetrate every orifice or every tongue explore every erogenous zone, so we fast-forward about a dozen of the DVDs, searching for clues. At least, *I'm* searching for clues. I have the feeling that Sukum might be indulging a hobby. After a dozen lightning-fast fornications in which the naked players snap around each other like actors in a Chaplin comedy, it's pretty clear that Frank Charles was just plain mainstream. To judge from the collection, he wasn't even into sodomy, which to my way of thinking makes him charmingly old-fashioned. But these are all the works of other directors. Did he not play around with a movie camera himself? I see no signs of home movies and decide to leave Sukum alone in the room. I admire the way he negotiates a change of the guard. Now the attractive receptionist is following me while the security is ensconced with Sukum and grinning like a monkey who found a banana.

I find what I am looking for in the master bedroom, next to the bed and opposite the panoramic window which looks over the whole of the northern part of the city and must be spectacular at night. It's a steel safe covered with a piece of Thai silk, and masquerading as a bedside table. The key has been left in its lock, but that is because you can't open the door without the combination; the key is superfluous. I try using Charles's birth date and passport numbers to crack the combination, but that proves futile. I blow out my cheeks for want of a better idea, then my eyes alight on a small stack of DVD cases on the table on the opposite side of the bed. They are all from Nepal, perhaps bought from the same shop where I bought my collection a couple of weeks ago; they include the DVD I watched about the Tibetan resistance to the Chinese invasion in 1950, and the betrayal by the CIA. The other movies are all about Tibet, mostly the cruelty of the Chinese aggressors and the Tibetan struggle for survival under a barbaric invader, although a few are dedicated to Tantric Buddhism. I decide to check the Jacuzzi.

It is just as the girls described: gigantic and designed for orgies of the Roman type. It occupies a windowless room about thirty feet square done up in antique stone tiles with murals out of Pompeii. Some of the wall tiles bear profiles of Caesar-like men and Messalina-like women. There is also a bust on a pedestal. The bust is unmistakably that of Frank Charles. Every detail is of the highest quality. Kitsch as the idea may be, the execution takes it to a higher, and very sophisticated, level; it could almost be a bathhouse from Pompeii.

All this while the receptionist has been growing more and more irritated at the time Sukum is spending in the movie room with the security guard. It doesn't help that every now and then some of the synthetic cries and groans escape into the corridor. I knock and tell Sukum to come examine the bust of the victim in the Jacuzzi. He emerges shame-faced, rubbing his eyes, unable to look into mine. The porn seems to have done something to his head beyond the obvious. I think I can guess where his mind is going.

When Captain James Cook sailed into the harbor the British would impertinently call Sydney, the aboriginals on the shore did not see his ships, because they had no mental concept of such things. They learned the hard way. I think something of the kind has happened to Sukum. He is seeing Frank Charles's condo with new eyes, and his suspicions are confirmed when I point out the likeness the bust in the Jacuzzi bears to the American's passport photograph. What Sukum had taken for the respectable residence of an eminent man of towering talent and ability—a level in life so exalted he did not trouble even to form an opinion of it and assumed the decor was no more than standard for a billionaire tribe he knew nothing about, a top-of-the-range lifestyle, in other words, which is perhaps the only grail the West aspires to— he is now experiencing as the most elaborate and useless expression of self-indulgence he could possibly imagine.

"It's all just appetite," he says, glaring at the bust. Then, like a good Buddhist, he turns his anger on himself. "This is where *farang* are leading us, isn't it? Like me with my Toyota. If I had money I would fall into this trap, just the same. And maybe end up like him, thoroughly lost in an ego dream."

I smile because he has jumped way ahead of me. I did not directly link the American's narcissism to the exotic manner of his dying, I have too much *farang* blood for that; but to Sukum, who has no overview other than Buddhism, the operation of the law of cause and effect is obvious. I think he loses all motivation to find the killer for a moment, because, after all, the perp was the victim of nothing more or less than the inexorable law of karma. And also, just for the moment, the demon of ambition has quite deserted him, leaving only disgust. Now I'm seeing the penthouse with Sukum's eyes. It's the detail, the extraordinary effort by talented tradesmen and interior designers, the obscenely expensive *perfection* of the place which represents a blasphemous waste of energy and time by all concerned.

Then his mind, stretched to the end of its elastic, flips back to his factory settings. He turns almost aggressively to the receptionist. "Did the deceased own a car?"

"Yes, a Lexus."

"What model?"

218

"The LS 460—top of the range." Clearly she, too, has the Bangkok automobile virus.

"What color?"

"Gray with metallic finish."

"Did he ever drive you in it?"

"Once he gave me a lift to the end of the road. It was like floating on air."

Sukum nods solemnly, takes another glance at the bust, and shakes his head. He has inspired me, though, and I start to hunt around the penthouse.

"What are you looking for?"

"Something incongruous."

Sukum has revealed to me an inadvertent flaw in the place: it is flawless. This is not natural; there must be something that does not fit, something that reveals whatever lays behind the American's extravagance, something driving the self-hate that resulted in his obesity. I find it surprisingly easily, in the corniest of places: under a pillow in the master bedroom. *The Dark Night of the Soul*, by St. John of the Cross. I hold it by the spine upside down to see which pages the deceased most favored. It opens naturally at page 46 of the Peers translation. A thick horizontal pencil mark draws attention to the last paragraph of Book I, Chapter III:

> *But neither from these imperfections nor from those others can the soul be perfectly purified until God brings it into the passive purgation of that dark night whereof we shall speak presently.*

When I try to figure out what resonance those words have for me, I find Tietsin's blade wheel lurking in the shadows of my mind. At the back of the book someone has written in pencil, *This burden is very hard to bear.* Curiously, there is a date: September 21, 2007. Why would anyone bother to date a cry from the soul? Because (I check his passport again) it was his birthday. He was a Virgo on the cusp of Libra and exactly sixty years old when he wrote those words, assuming it is his handwriting. In the Chinese system, he was born in the Year of the Fire Boar; Fire Boars are horny and lucky with money.

So far I have not examined the computer in the bedroom that served as an office. When I do so, I find I need an entry code. What I am most interested in is e-mail messages which might not be downloaded onto the PC but could equally well be hanging out there in cyberspace requiring another code to access them. I decide to leave the computer to the forensic boys.

Back on the ground floor, Sukum resists the temptation to go look at the Lexus, and I ask the building manager to check with the company that runs the surveillance cameras to provide video copies of everyone who entered Frank Charles's apartment over the past six months.

Sukum hangs next to me, apostate, and watches the residents come and go. Most are not *farang*, but neither are they Thai. The majority seem to be Taiwanese and Hong Kong Chinese, with plenty of

Japanese, too. For the most part the *farang* residents do not seem to be American, but rather wealthy Swiss and German. They all have about them the careless sangfroid of the impenetrably rich, which was perhaps the only club to which Frank Charles could possibly have belonged. I think about that and ask the building manager to also provide statements from his staff that would enable us to identify regular visitors during the entirety of his residence. The manager checks his records and informs us the *farang* bought the apartment about five years ago and spent about half the year here in intervals of about two months at a time. A casual questioning of his staff suggests the American had very few visitors—perhaps none at all except when he brought girls back, which he did rarely, although there was a night when he arrived drunk at the head of a convoy of three taxis carrying ten young women whom the night staff automatically classified as prostitutes because of their Isaan accents. In accordance with the building's strict security rules, copies of their ID cards were kept and will be made available to us as soon as they have been retrieved from the archives.

"Ten," I say. The number, which did not seem out of the ordinary in the Rose Garden, now strikes me as grotesque.

"To go with the apartment and the Lexus," Sukum says.

221

23

Forget men with long magic fingers who listen to the subtle sounds of locking mechanisms with mystic concentration; forget explosives, too. There's only one sane way to bust open a safe in someone's home: oxyacetylene. And for that you need steel bottles— one for the oxygen and one for the acetylene—some sheet steel to protect the floor, a guy in leathers with a giant cutting torch and a full face mask—and you need to move all the furniture out of the way.

Half of reception have come up to watch, and I couldn't very well exclude Sukum and Lek. Women squeal while men grunt at the great cascade of sparks as the oxygen eats the iron. The cutter is making a circle around the safe's lock, which glows dull red. The safe is of the kind you can buy on the main street, and not particularly strong. Even so, hardened steel plate doesn't yield that easily, and I'm wondering if there is going to be anything left inside not charred to a cinder, when the door finally swings open a couple of inches and we are left standing in the particle-charged air with that peculiar stench of burnt iron.

222

Now everyone is looking at me. The cutter hands me a thick wad of leather to use to open the red-hot door. The heat is pretty intense, but localized. What I'm most interested in is a DVD case in the bottom right corner. I gingerly put my hand into the oven, pull the case out. It's only slightly molten, but when I open it, I see the DVD inside has curled with the heat. No way it's going to even fit into a DVD player, and the microscopic laser etchings on the plastic will have been destroyed. There is no label on the disc, but someone has written on it in felt-tip pen: "Nepal/Tibet 2001/2." There is nothing else in the body of the safe except for a sheet of paper that looks as if it had personal identity codes written in hand, but is now too burnt and brown to decipher.

When I show the disc to the forensic boys, they shake their heads. DVDs are not like computer hard drives; you can't reconstitute them. I say, "Okay, at least check out the computer, see if we can get into that and onto the Net."

So now we're in the *farang*'s office with the generic tower PC and seventeen-inch monitor; one of the forensic boys has brought a laptop with code-busting software, which he's all excited about; he's never used it before on a real case. We all watch while he attaches a cable from the laptop to the PC, switches on the PC, and red and green lights on the laptop start to pop on and off at an amazing rate. Then the Windows XP screen appears.

We all *koo* dutifully as the kid with the laptop grins.

223

Trouble is, we don't know the code for Internet access, and although we know Frank Charles used Gmail, Yahoo!, and a couple of other engines, we don't know which one he favored for personal matters, or what the log-on code might be. The kid says his software won't work on Internet access, the security is too good. I keep quiet, but make a private note to ask Kimberley to help; she has a whole raft of nerds at her command in Virginia, and since the deceased was American, I guess there is a good enough excuse to bust his privacy rights, which he won't be needing anymore. While I'm thinking, the kid checks out the Windows address book. "Look," he says to me, and points. I stare. There I am: name, title, address—

Sonchai Jitpleecheep, Detective in Royal Thai Police, District 8—

with my cell phone number and e-mail address.

Everyone looks at me, and I know that Sukum and Lek are both thinking this has to do with the private position I hold in Vikorn's organization. I myself am merely dumbfounded.

I'm also stung. Embarrassment and fear spur me into action. (If he knew my name and address, what else did he know?) There are things you pick up in ten years of detection that lie in the back of your mind, little techniques you've forgotten twenty times already, but which come back when you've convinced yourself the case is worth the extra effort. It's true, I'd not been treating the Fat *Farang* murder as if it were my own case—until now. I stride back into the bedroom and grab the leather wad to open the safe door again. It has cooled a lot, although it is still too hot to touch. I use the leather to spring open a semisecret tray in the top of the safe, then use one of my own keys to flick out a small metal box, which lands on the protective iron cover the welder has laid on the floor and bursts open. Naturally, we all stare. The contents of the box appear to be small rough stones of a grayish hue. One of the women from reception has gone to the bathroom and returned with a glass of water, which I pour gently over the stones. To the touch they are surprisingly hard, but small and unattractive, the translucent gray of shrimp before they are boiled. I shrug. It is difficult to see what connection they could have with the spectacular murder of Frank Charles. The stones strike me more like something you might pick up on a beach during a seaside vacation, put in your safe, and forget about. They are too small, ugly, and colorless to be precious.

I shake my head and tell Sukum I've seen as much as I wanted.

"Where are you going?"

"First the Rose Garden, then Kathmandu," I say, sparing a brief glance at Lek as I leave the condo.

From Soi 8 it's only a half-mile walk to the Rose Garden on Soi 7; I call my travel agent as I'm walking. I'm also thinking that Frank Charles walked this way himself, probably every day, for there's nowhere to park a Lexus at the Rose Garden—or did his weight force him to take a cab? By the time I reach the bar I have a ticket to Kathmandu for that afternoon.

It's ten-thirty in the morning, which is early in this part of Bangkok. There are a couple of girls sitting at the bar, both of them reading Thai newspapers and taking a quiet moment for themselves before getting in the mood for action. A lot of the women here make a point of putting in a full day's work, arriving at ten and going home at six, whether they have had a successful shift or not. I order a beer and watch the entrance while I'm waiting.

The Chinese-looking girl, who goes straight to the Buddha shrine under the bohdi tree, lights her incense, *wais*, bows, takes a seat at the bar, and orders a coffee. She is not from Isaan but from Phuket, where her family owns a mini-market. She got bored with filling shelves and working the checkout register and finds prostitution more exciting. The girl behind her, very dark, almost Indian in her features, is from Nong Kai, on the Mekong and next to the border with Laos. She used to be married to an Englishman, who dumped her for another whore six years younger. She nods to me in recognition; when she smiles she reveals her diamond-studded braces. Now here is Sarlee: her whole family, including herself and her two kids, lived off her brother, a fanatically hardworking entrepreneur on a motorbike, until he got killed in an accident. Without any kind of life insurance to claim, the family agreed Sarlee would have to sell her body. Good-natured Sarlee didn't object; she had been working in a clothing factory wondering why the Buddha had made her beautiful and itching for an excuse to do something more interesting—but prostitution was forbidden until karma and despair beckoned. If her father doesn't get his heart drugs regularly, he will be unable to work the rice fields, and if that happens not even Sarlee's body will save the family from hunger.

Now here, striding across the threshold, is a tall, skinny Indian man in his late thirties; I happen to know from eyewitnesses that he is exceptionally well endowed, and only a few of the girls (proud, in turn, of their own prowess) are prepared to repeat the martyrdom-by-member after the first tryst. This does nothing to suppress his bright-eyed, oat-driven eagerness as he looks around the bar for his eleven-o'clock lay. He is followed by a youngish, heavyish Englishman, who is so overpaid in the profession of boilermaker in Essex that he spends three months of the year here, which sojourn is easily recompensed in tax rebates. His vacations begin with modest lechery and end in unrestrained alcohol abuse. I deduce from the signs that he is at the beginning of this one; when he reaches the bar he takes out a copy of the *Daily Mirror* and casts shy glances at the entrance from time to time. Now, finally, comes Pong, then behind her, Nik, Tonni, and O.

I take Pong to a side table, buy her a drink. "That

time the *farang* Frank Charles took ten of you back to his condo, do you remember when it was?"

She frowns. "Not sure. It was during Khao Phansa; I remember because my brother is a monk and we always visit him for a day during the rainy season." Her face brightens. "But you can check with his passport. It was his birthday, I've just remembered. That was his excuse for having ten of us in that tub at the same time."

"What kind of mood was he in?"

"Oh, he was really lapping it up, fondling and kissing and telling us how happy he was and that we were his only family and could it get any better than this, that a man could have ten beautiful lovers as close family? Then, later on, the Viagra wore off and he burst into tears and we all left. He didn't seem to react to alcohol very well, and he'd drunk almost a whole bottle of champagne because none of us liked it. He said it was the most expensive champagne in Bangkok and it cost more than three hundred dollars and he had a refrigerator full of it for the party, but to me it tasted awful, like drinking perfume or something, and none of the other girls drink alcohol either."

"Did he suffer from mood shifts generally?"

Pong thinks about that, then shrugs. "How can I know?"

"You slept with him regularly? More than the others?"

She nods. "Yes. At least, I was his favorite at that

time. He went through phases, as if he was looking for a wife but got addicted to the search."

"After sex, was he melancholy?"

Now Pong is concentrating. I think she wants to make sure she's got the right *farang* when she says, "I've worked here five years and I've never met a *farang* who was at peace. I suppose it's because they're not Buddhist like us? Sometimes I wondered . . ."

"What? If he was gay?"

"No, no, nothing like that. I wondered if he was looking for a mother." She flashes me a self-conscious look: amateur psychology is not popular with our working girls. "He talked about a film, once. One he was making. I think he said it was in the Himalayas. He told me it was the most important thing in his life. But he couldn't complete it. He told me he kept a copy of a half-finished version in his safe and watched it every day hoping for inspiration. He said if he ever did finish it, he would feel whole again and would probably find a Thai wife to live with. I think he wanted me to believe there was hope for me. But when I talked to other girls who had been his favorite, they said he spoke to them in the same way. So I suppose it all depended if you were the flavor of the month or not. I guess the film really was the most important thing in his life. But sometimes he would let slip something about a woman in Nepal." She shrugs. "It was all so vague, though. After sex men go vague, if they don't fall asleep."

I ask if Frank Charles ever mentioned me, or asked

229

for the name of a Thai cop—or if, generally, she knew of any connection at all between him and me. She shakes her head with the right element of confusion—why would he have anything to do with me?—so I get her to run through all the girls who attended the American's sixtieth birthday party, and any others who she knows to have gone with Frank Charles. Then, one by one, I call the girls over, slip them a hundred baht, and ask the same questions. The exercise takes up the whole morning with zero results: none of the girls is aware of any connection between the dead man and me, and they certainly would have remembered if the American had ever used my name. I am experiencing guilt by association, as if I have been fingered as a suspect. I need to speak again to Doctor Mimi Moi. I call the travel agent to cancel the Nepal trip.

24

Doctor Moi has vacated the Oriental and returned to her place by the river. (Sukum has reluctantly admitted she was probably not on the run after all, merely playing one of her elaborate games with him—or maybe she really was having her house refurbished?) I could make an appointment to see her, but her capacity to elude is legendary and I have a feeling she was not planning to grant me a second interview. Everyone knows that witches are best approached by water at night without prior warning, right?

Which, in the case of Doctor Mimi Moi, just happens to be possible. I know the address because I once had to spend a few days at a crime scene over in Thonburi, not far from her house. After she collected on the deaths of the two husbands she denies murdering, she broke yet another taboo of her class by buying a piece of land on the unfashionable side of the river right next to a *klong*, a canal, along which a large shantytown had grown up. Mad Moi's land abuts the shantytown: rickety wooden huts on stilts, filthy kids, and subsistence car-repair businesses, which spread inland for at least one square mile. Little by little she has built up a position of godmother to the locals. She is known to provide free medicine for the needy, communal feasts on holidays, and even legal advice for those who have fallen foul of the cops. Everyone owes her, everyone worships her, and no one is going to betray her if they intend to go on living in the shantytown. Nobody knows how many packages containing what chemical exoticum are carried to and from her house by little old ladies paddling sampans across the river and up the *klong*.

I take a cab to Klong Toey, to a point on the river, then walk down a path by the side of a bridge that brings me out on the riverbank where a couple of motorized canoes are waiting. I agree on a price with the ferryboat man—an emaciated alcoholic in his late sixties who has not shaved for three days—and he starts the tinny little motor with a pull on a cord. Now we are turning upstream in order to take account of the current, with the high black bows of cargo ships, mostly Chinese and Korean, looming up at us as we pass the docks.

Although the Doctor's land abuts the Chao Phraya River, it sits on a loop which forms a kind of bay and protects her from the wash of heavy ships. As we navigate the river, slowing to allow a loud and brightly lit restaurant boat to pass on its way to the Grand Palace, we head for a specific patch of dark emptiness on the other side, then slow the motor to a tick as we slip across what could be a black lagoon.

When we turn toward the bank, I see the house. Although constructed of modern materials, it is strictly in the old style, sitting on high stilts with a riverfront terrace about twenty feet deep which runs the length of the building and gables that look like garudas' beaks. As we approach it is obvious that Doctor Moi's fine eye has produced a kind of perfection of form: a soft golden light illuminates a generous window through a gauze curtain; classic Chinese furniture in blackwood can be glimpsed from moment to moment, along with chaise longues with pastel upholstery. There is a vast abundance of hanging plants on the balcony, mostly orchids, which gives a forest atmosphere, and a maid in full livery appears for a second to serve a beverage to the figure in a rocking chair, a bare-shouldered form in white jacquard silk cheongsam (high collar, pearl dragons writhing), smoking a cheroot and reading a magazine. When she hears our motor she looks up languidly. It is not until we have docked at her jetty that she sees it is me, but she shows no sign of surprise. Indeed, she even sends the maid down to the jetty to greet me and bring me to the house. Little Red Riding Hood must have felt the way I do now.

The maid is about ten years older than her mistress, which is to say in her fifties, quite tall and slim like Moi, silent—she does not speak to me—and very Chinese; I doubt there is a single Thai gene in her porcelain flesh. She wears the white cap, white blouse, black skirt, and white apron of domestic service, as if she works for an English duchess.

Doctor Moi gets up to welcome me as I climb the stairs onto the balcony, and I give her a high *wai*. She does not seem put out by my visit; on the contrary, a faint smile hovers around her thin lips. Nevertheless, she says, "What a surprise, Detective." She is way too cool to ask why I didn't telephone first. "Won't you sit down to join me? I've just told the maid to bring a pot of cocoa with cognac."

"Thanks. I thought you didn't drink."

"My British husband got me addicted to cognac in cocoa before he tragically died. Something about brandy makes one feel rich."

I sit down on a wicker chair with a silk cushion in exactly the right place to support the lower back; the sense of instant relaxation is increased by the silence. A gibbous moon hangs over the black river, the rest is emptiness; I can see why Moi likes it here. When the maid comes back, a ginger tomcat emerges with her and jumps heavily into the Doctor's lap. I mumble, "I was expecting a Persian female," because I can't think of anything else to say. While the maid is pouring the cocoa—her hand is long, pale, with skinny fingers; there is a curious ring on the index finger of her right hand, a band of silver in which eight tiny orangey-pink gems have been set—Moi clears her throat. "I haven't even had him neutered. He's the happiest tom in Thailand. He goes slumming and gets laid twenty

234

times a night, but comes back here for silk sheets and gourmet fish."

"What's his name?"

"Hofmann, after the chemist who first synthesized LSD. But Hofmann prefers smack, don't you sweetheart?"

Right on cue, Hofmann growls and buries his head under her arm. I let a few beats pass. When she makes no attempt to speak, I say, "Doctor, I have a document here signed by Colonel Vikorn—"

To my surprise she holds up a hand. "Please, let's not do business yet. So few distinguished visitors come by river, I feel a need to show you around. And it's such a beautiful moment in the evening." A gracious smile without a hint of irony.

So we just hang there for a while, the Doctor and I, suspended in the night as if we were swinging on hammocks slung between stars, drinking our cocoa. Moi seems in a kind of trance, unwilling to face the practical challenge of standing up again. It occurs to me that by this time in the evening she might have taken something stronger than cocoa with cognac. I insert my first forensic question as gently as I can, hoping to reach a mind which has dropped its defenses.

"Did Frank Charles often join you here?"

"Mmm." The murmur is so low it is almost inaudible. "Lots. He loved it here. He even tried to buy me out. I said no. Anyway, he could never have survived next to the shantytown—they would have eaten him alive. He was a bourgeois, he didn't know how to deal with slaves. He would have been too nice." She lets a beat pass. "He used to smoke cannabis here that I got for him from Humboldt County. He would smoke dope, get despondent—his love problem kept cropping up—and then, of course, the whole beautiful evening was forgotten. One would have to watch his mind shrink all the way back into his testicles—which, being a *farang*, he mistook for his heart." A grimace. "You know, I would never consent to be a man. I'd simply have it all cut off and become a *katoey*."

"You've never wanted children, Doctor?"

She shudders by way of answer. "Pets die. Children are a pain in the ass for the duration."

She seems unwilling to leave the balcony or to waste time on talk, and I feel pretty much the same way. I try to intuit my way into the skin of Frank Charles: how exotic it must have seemed to him at first, to hang out under a tropical moon with an authentic Chinese murderess—and a beauty, in her austere way—who spoke better English than he and whose conversation was wittier than his. And a pharmacist, too! Surely he would have wanted to develop the relationship further? Not sexually, of course—Moi was not joking when she said she despised carnal love—but I think he sought one of those kinds of friendships *farang* nowadays dream of: more reliable than family, and a lot more fun. "Did he talk much about his film?" I mumble, hardly audible

236

even to myself, but I've noticed how good Moi's hearing is.

"Mmm."

"You know the one I mean, Doctor?"

"Mmm."

"What did he say about it?"

"I can't remember. Mostly it was the artistic self-pity thing with him. How much he'd put into it in money and effort. How it consumed him but he never got it finished. He liked to make sure I realized it was not a schmaltz production like the others, it was serious, he was giving it his best shot, every detail had to be perfect."

She takes a toke of her cheroot and exhales so slowly I've given up hope of more information, when she adds, "He couldn't seem to get the ending right."

Maybe she feels she's said too much, for she stands slowly and invites me into the house. We cross the great polished teak balcony together and she steps inside to formally welcome me with a *wai*.

A finely carved Taoist temple table in blackwood: incense writhes upward and curls around two portraits of a man and woman in Qing dynasty costume, with their hair pulled back in queues, staring at us out of the past. I cast an eye at Doctor Moi.

"My great-grandfather on my father's side, with his third wife, my grandfather's mother. If not for Mao and the revolution I probably would have been brought up on the family estate in Swatow, with ornamental gardens and pavilions where one spent

237

the summer. I might have had my feet bound, and I would certainly have been an opium addict." She looks at me. "I long for that lost elegance. After all, I love opium and I never walk anywhere."

She has taken the cheroot out of her mouth and straightened her back, as if the portraits are realer to her than the living and more deserving of respect, while I take in the rest of the room. There's an underlying masculinity in the discipline, but the colors are subtle and fine. I say, "I'm looking for a teddy bear."

She nods thoughtfully, as if in agreement. "I know. For the past twenty years I've kept him in a syringe."

She takes me to a small and cozy library and even offers me a peek at the main bedroom. I'm wondering why she is being so hospitable, when I feel a sudden lift in the area of my brow. I turn to her in surprise.

"That wasn't cognac in the cocoa, Doctor."

"Did I say cognac? I must have had a blonde moment. Don't worry, you didn't drink anything I didn't also drink." She snorts. "And anyway, we're not married, so there's no need to kill you."

"Can I at least know what it is?"

"No, it's too rare and exciting, and the name wouldn't mean anything to you."

"What's it going to do?"

"It's going to solve the case for you. Isn't that what you want?"

I don't know if the reason I can't concentrate is because the drug has started to work on me or because

I'm afraid it has started to work on me. "Can we go back out on the balcony?"

As soon as we get there I slip with a sigh into the wicker chair and become mesmerized by the moon. Now I'm beginning to understand the mood she was in when I arrived. "You were already on this stuff when I showed up, weren't you?"

"Mmm. How do you like it?"

"It's too good. You're a witch."

"Mmm. Now, what was it you were saying about a letter from Colonel Vikorn?"

"It's not going to work, Doctor, I'm not giving it to you until you've done a lot of explaining. That's what I came to tell you."

"A pot of cocoa for the letter?"

"No."

She lets a few beats pass. "Do you realize that without my help you will never in your entire life feel as good as this again?"

I groan. "Yes."

"But unlike earlier versions of this family of molecules, with this one you remember every ecstatic minute the next day, in glorious color, but without the ecstasy, which is replaced by an unendurable nostalgia for the lost high that will have you crawling up the wall."

"I see."

"But the worst of it is, you are only at the beginning of the trip. It's going to get better and better and better—so good you won't believe it. And then it will end. Unless I give you some more cocoa."

"I got the picture, Doctor Moi."

"And don't even think of trying to bust me. That stuff is prescribed by my personal physician in Amsterdam, and it's not my fault you came here un-invited and drank my cocoa before I could warn you what was in it."

"I already know what your defense will be."

"You have unusual resistance," she says with a touch of chagrin.

"Whatever this is, it can't compare to the blade wheel."

"Blade wheel?" She repeats the phrase as if she has heard it before and tuts irritably.

"It cuts through everything. Even your chemicals."

After a long, languid pause. "I see. Well, what was it you wanted to know?"

I find I am unable to answer, not because my mind has gone blank but because it has acquired such a crystalline clarity, such a sharpness of definition in both thought and sense, that I don't want to waste the moment on work. Especially when I can read the file in the night sky. Time passes, but I have lost the measure of it.

"Solved everything yet?" Doctor Moi inquires.

"Yes."

"There never was a problem, was there?"

"No."

"More cocoa?"

"Yes."

240

"Letter first."

"No."

"Detective, I believe that letter is addressed to me."

"It's addressed 'To Whom It May Concern,' and whether you get it or not is entirely up to me."

We hang there like that for fully two hours. It really is good stuff. Finally, Moi says, "Just tell me exactly what you want from me."

"A sign, Doctor, a word, anything that will confirm that what I've just read in the sky is all true. That it isn't just chemicals screwing my head up."

When I raise my head as a follow-up to my words, I see she is thinking profoundly. She picks up a little bell to ring for the maid, who brings a new cheroot and helps her light it, then goes back into the house without a word. Moi stands up to look at the river, which is black and shiny as an oil slick under the climbing moon. All I have of her is a three-quarter back shot with her long black hair trapped loosely in a tortoiseshell clip with silver inlay, the white silk of her cheongsam catching the moonlight thread by thread.

"The life of a pariah is not easy, Detective, even if you are lucky enough to be a rich one. He and I understood one another. We even talked about it. He told me that when he made his films—not the one good one, but the two dozen schmaltzy ones—he always kept a typical member of the public in mind. That person, for him, was a middle-aged librarian he met just once in Arkansas when he was running around the country promoting his first movie. She was a woman with a college degree whose taste remained mainstream and somewhat redneck, a product of a tribe and culture so complacent, so certain of her own goodness—because everyone in her vicinity agreed she was good—that he was able to identify her as a perfect ersatz muse. Although she didn't know it, she was the golden one for whom he made the films. And she, in her unlimited mediocrity, is the one who made him rich."

Moi turns to me for a moment to show the mirth on her face.

"When he first told me that I thought it was so funny—and so *clever* of him—I couldn't stop laughing. He didn't see it that way, though. He told me that this middle-aged librarian in Arkansas had come to dominate his whole life. He had thought that after his first ten million he wouldn't give a damn about anyone in the audience anymore, but somehow it didn't work out like that. This librarian had avatars everywhere, especially inside his head and among the matriarchs of Hollywood. He'd done a deal with the devil, you see? That's who she was, that perfect, good, clean-living, no-nonsense, mainstream, somewhat-redneck librarian from Arkansas. For any pariah, especially an artist, she was the opposition. Poor Frank had done a deal, and the devil had kept her part of the bargain. Frank Charles was very rich. And very lost. There was no way he could get back to that other Frank Charles, the young one who was going to shock and delight the world with his originality and genius. That was all gone. Sold."

"No way out?"

Doctor Moi nods slowly and profoundly. "He begged me, you know, over and over again. He kept begging me to help until I finally gave in."

"Yes," I say, "I can see that." And so I can. Moi's mood of sorrow penetrates me as if her aura has quite eclipsed my own. I do not analyze what she might mean by "help"; I feel it with such intensity that no analysis is necessary—or possible. I can actually see Frank Charles here on this balcony in a morose mood, begging Moi, and Moi, elegant and gracious to a fault, doing all she can to help; it's like watching a scene from a play, with the balcony as stage, but instead of dialogue there is a visible exchange of emotion. I experience her "help" more as a kind of mood of infinite abundance than as anything with practical application. It occurs to me that the drug may be compromising my mind, but then instantly discard the idea as too ridiculous for words. I say, "Are you really telling me the truth, Doctor?" while at the same time asking myself if she has actually "said" anything. But as I speak I'm holding Vikorn's letter over her shoulder. "Just nod, Doctor, just nod once. You're far too stoned to lie." She nods, but I take back the letter. "Just tell me one real thing, Doctor. One real thing."

She stares at me. I think she is a little annoyed that I still retain some resistance. "There is a film," she

243

says, as if the statement has cost her dearly. "He finished it in the end. I have a copy."

As I hand over the letter, I say, "What will you do with it?"

She bites her lip. "Watch it a few more times, then destroy it. I have the only copy in the world. It's not the sort of thing that could ever go on general release. Even though it's a masterpiece. He trusted me to destroy it—but he had to have at least one viewer, do you see?"

"For this film, you were the ideal viewer?"

"Exactly. I was the devil he had to deal with for this very special work. I was his authentic muse. You could say he made it just for me. The first time I watched it, I couldn't believe that any man could portray life so accurately." She turns back to speak to the moon. "He escaped, you see? In his way, he finally escaped. You may not believe me, but that was the real reason I helped him. If I'd wanted his money, I could have married him, couldn't I?" She lets a long beat pass. "It was a kind of love we had. Not sexual, much better than that. Artistic, you might say."

"Doctor, please, may I see the film?"

"No. Never. I promised him. I don't break promises to the dead."

I make as if I'm about to leave when I ask, "Khun Doctor, why did you give Frank Charles my name?" The question has startled her, and now she is blinking rapidly. "Of course, I am not certain it was you, but there really is no one else I can think of who might have supplied him with my name and address. No one at all." Now she is looking at me as if I am slightly crazy. "My name, private telephone number, and home address were found in the Microsoft address book on his computer."

She turns her head to one side with a frown, then smiles. "Ah! Detective, you are a little too smart for your own good. I remember now. No, it was not me who brought your name to his attention, it was you. You used to be a film buff, no? I think a long time ago you wrote a review of the only film he was proud of— his first one. What was the name? *Black Wednesday*, no? I think you accused him of plagiarism."

"I did?"

"Ages ago. You must have hardly been out of the academy."

It's coming back to me. It is years since I made a point of remembering the names of directors, or the plots of old movies. I sort of remember an American noir entry at a film festival. It's very vague, though. If I remember correctly, it was well put together but disappointing in that it seemed to imitate other films. Not very original. Did I really say "plagiarism"? I was one of those passionate young men who mistook the movies for a form of religion.

Moi nods. "When we were on cocaine together one evening he told me about it. He was sort of laughing at his own chagrin, that a third-world Eurasian cop would have the effrontery, et cetera—all quite ironic. Don't ask me where he got your details from, I'm sure it was nothing sinister. More likely he intended to ask you out for a drink one day and never got around to it. He was very civilized, you know, an urbane bon viveur when his chemicals were properly balanced. If only puppy love hadn't screwed him up."

I take my leave, but instead of asking her to call a cab, I decide to go back by river the way I came. She calls a ferryman to take me across. When I'm home and preparing for bed, I remember her threat, that the drug would haunt me the next day with its memory of a lost nirvana. When I wake up in the morning, I experience no symptoms at all. As a matter of fact, I feel terrific. It occurs to me she was lying. Not only about the drug, but also about everything else she said last night. Did Frank Charles really make that film? Does she really have a copy?

25

So I'm finally on a plane to Kathmandu and settled in a window seat (on the right), with my camera this time, and I have a moment to allow my stressed-out brain to relax. I let go of everything using Tietsin's blade wheel technique, and only then I notice a question that the subconscious seems to have been working on without telling me. Something suspicious, it seems, that someone told me during the past twenty-four hours? Ah! Yes, here it is: the thought emerges like a worm dragged out from a hole. Picture it this way: you are a financially successful filmmaker who got caught in flagrante delicto by your third wife at a time when a good percentage of emotional and forensic energy in *farang*land was dedicated to punishing men like you and Bill Clinton, and as a consequence you find yourself suddenly in need of dough. So, do you rush off to Nepal to make what could never be more than an art-house-type documentary or feature film, more or less destined to flop commercially even if you do put it on general release, which you don't? Does this make sense? If you are the king of schmaltz and it's schmaltz that got you where you are today, wouldn't you just turn on the taps in the schmaltz factory until you'd paid your debts? If you had a twinge of conscience and wanted to help the poor enslaved people of Tibet, or the poor free people of Nepal, come to that, wouldn't you put that on the shelf until after you'd reestablished yourself financially? *Hmm* to that. And no way the film would explain all those Nepali visas: to make a movie does not usually take up more than three months on location, so Frank Charles should have used up only one visa, maybe two; his passport contains about ten, which cover a six-year period. He seems to have stopped visiting regularly about nine months ago. About the time he reached sixty.

As I relax further another strange fact rises to the top of my mind and escapes like a trapped wasp into the free air: none of the movies that Frank Charles directed was in his collection at the penthouse on Soi 8, not even his very first feature film, *Black Wednesday*, which, according to critics other than myself, was a very decent attempt to transpose French and Italian noir into an American genre. None of his schmaltz features on his shelves either. If he had been a man sensitive to opinion, one might have deduced he was ashamed of his life's work and didn't want to flaunt it before discerning friends. But as far as we know, Charles brought few guests to his enormous condominium, and they were usually Thai working girls who could not read English and knew nothing of

Western intellectual snobbery. Maybe the one person whom he didn't want to see his own movies was himself?

My mind flips back to how fat he was. To hate one-self in a complete way is impossible; to hate one half of oneself with the other half is not only possible but frighteningly common among *farang*. But I cannot take the thought any further because I'm slowly falling asleep. When I wake, it is because people are rushing around the plane trying to take pictures. *The mountains are back.* I fumble with my camera for a moment, then decide to concentrate on seeing them. They'll be here on the return journey.

At the Kathmandu Guest House I take a suite on one of the upstairs floors near the antiques showroom. The first thing I do, as a kind of homage before I begin unpacking, is to climb to the flat roof of the guest-house to look out over the city. Nepal is two hours behind Thailand, so it is just at the point of twilight, when translucent indigos and purples repaint what little is left of the mountains, and other people on other rooftops bring in the washing and prepare the evening meal. From the rooftop I call Lek.

"I want you to call the Thai Chamber of Commerce here in Kathmandu, if there is one, or whoever at the embassy deals with this kind of stuff. If the Thai govern-ment can't help, ask Kimberley to contact the American Chamber of Commerce. I want to know the names of all the agencies here that might be involved in film-making, you know the kind of thing?"

"Of course I don't, I haven't got a clue what you're talking about. I suppose I'll work it out, though. And by the way, what did your last slave die of?"

Naturally, I try all the numbers Tietsin gave me to contact him. Naturally, none of them are in operation, either because he's turned his phones off or because the network is not operating just now. I go to my room to unpack, then stroll down the driveway, through the iron gates manned by impressive men with black moustaches and military uniforms, out onto Thamel.

26

Once on Thamel, though, I realize I simply cannot resist a visit to Bodnath, even though I've not been able to contact *him*.

It's almost dark by the time I arrive, with just the faintest glow in the west, when I begin my ritual journey around the giant stupa. Its brilliant white breast disappears with the last of the sun, but the two great eyes benefit from spotlights. There are not so many pilgrims and tourists spinning the brass prayer wheels at this time of day, and the eyes have an intimidating aspect to them. Without the certainty of clear daylight, it's easy to imagine the mind behind them as master of the night.

The journey all the way around the stupa takes much longer than during the day. Strange thoughts assail me; my mind changes. It occurs to me that a stupa was originally a means of contacting the dead, that it is a Neolithic burial mound that I've come to pay my respects to. It occurs to me that the *Far Shore* is never all that far away, had we not been programmed to pretend it doesn't exist. It occurs to me that our ancestors, long before the Gautama Buddha arrived with his clarifications, knew more about death than we know about the motions of the stars. With their short, hard lives they must have faced the mysterious disappearance of loved ones every year; it must have seemed as if the whole stream of human life led straight back to the stupa—the sepulcher, you might say—and the more enduring world of the dead. And it occurs to me that nothing has changed, except that the extra twenty or thirty years we can expect to spend on the planet these days seem to have blinded us to a truth that for our ancestors was brutally obvious.

This meditation takes me one complete circumnavigation. I deliberately began in the west so after three and a half turns I will end in the east. When I start the next round, I am thinking, *I know he is watching. He knows I am here.* Nevertheless, the second round with the brass I spend in a kind of trance state in which thought, though it still exists, is relegated to a secondary function while some kind of emptiness, a beautiful, indescribable *absence*, takes its place. So it's not until the last leg, the half turn from west to east that will finish my tour, that I remember what the stupa looks like when I see it through Tietsin's eyes. And suddenly there it is: black under a bloated full moon, quite still, no people anywhere, only me dwarfed by this great dark mountain of death from which a lurid lightning bolt seems to split the sky.

But this time the vision doesn't fade. It stays with

me in the cab on the way back to the guesthouse, and when I lie down to close my eyes it becomes obvious that this is where Tietsin's blade wheel has been leading. That all the great fuss I've made about my state of mind is as nothing compared to what comes next. And it's not Tietsin whose name I call just before nodding off. I hear myself whispering, *Pichai, my brother, my self. Pichai, tell me, what happens after you die, really?*

Well, what happened to me at that crucial moment in my spiritual development was that I fell asleep. Now it's some awful predawn nightmare that has awakened me; no, wait, that really was "All Along the Watchtower" I was hearing in my sleep. I find I've not corrected the clock on my cell phone, so I can tell at a glance it is six a.m. in Bangkok.

"This is your *katoey* secretarial service. I hope you took plenty of clothes, I hear it's *freezing* up there. I got a short list. Actually, there are only *three* agencies worth considering, only *two* of those do high-altitude locations—I'm assuming that's what we're talking about here—and only one really looks like the kind of outfit Charles would have used, I mean with fluent English speakers, contacts in LA, et cetera."

"What are you talking about?"

"The agencies—the people who assist foreign film crews, especially Americans, to make a movie in a foreign location. Sorry, I *am* speaking to Detective Sonchai 'Never Left a Case Unsolved' Jitpleecheep of Bangkok and Kathmandu?"

I blink. Sarcasm and work are two different modes of consciousness, and I can only cope with one at a time right now.

"There's only one agency?" I say with considerable relief. I was not looking forward to spending the day talking to wannabe Asian Hollywood producers in dark glasses and black T-shirts. "So, what are the details?"

"I've sent them by e-mail. I don't trust you to get the details right this early in the morning. Have you been smoking?"

"No. I forgot to score. Too busy. I'll try today, thank you for reminding me."

"Sonchai?"

"Yes?"

"Master?"

"Yes?"

"Is there really no such thing as love?"

For a moment I'm tempted to spill bitterness all over the cell phone. Then I see the inherent irony in the question. You could say Lek has been chasing love all his life in his own way, lifting the rock every morning, watching it roll back down the hill every night, just so he can endure the full day. His martyrdom is immeasurably vaster than mine.

"Not for me, Lek, I don't have your strength. I've retired permanently. They amputated my heart—nothing I can do."

There's a click as he closes his phone. When the guesthouse finally opens its business center at eight o'clock Kathmandu time, I have them print out the e-mail from Lek. It contains the address of the agency, which occupies a first-floor office over the commercial area leading to the Yak & Yeti Hotel. It seems I must find someone called Atman.

I eat breakfast in the garden of the guesthouse. It's basic backpacker stuff: bacon and eggs, toast, fried tomatoes, as much yogurt and granola as you can put down, cheese by Firestone. The clientele here is frequently serious about mountains and trekking, but this is not the time of year to lay siege to Everest, for it is spring in the Himalayas: all over the country snows are melting and rhododendron blooming. I know from the guidebook what to do and where to go, so when I feel strong enough for the Thamel onslaught I walk to the taxi rank and take the first in line. As usual it has no handles for the windows in back so they are permanently open, enabling one to feel like a genuine participant in the honking, the jams, and the pollution. But it takes less than thirty minutes to reach a large tree shrine to Ganesh, the elephant god, in a forest next to a river. The rhododendron here are the forest. It's like being in an oil painting that is all about abundance: a million mauve, crimson, and white blossoms, like bursts of awareness in a dark age.

That's all I needed, ten minutes of sanity; or maybe it's the most I can cope with? After I pay my respects to Ganesh with a bunch of marigolds, for which the shrine keeper charges like a wounded elephant, we drive back to town and the Yak & Yeti. When I get there they tell me that Atman is on location. The good news is that the location is Bhaktapur, which is no more than half an hour away. I sigh, find my second cab of the morning, and negotiate a day price.

Bhaktapur: I have been directed to Durbar Square, which is bigger than Kathmandu's, with a charming Grecian atmosphere of deserted plinths on which black goats hang out to be fed and photographed by tourists. Not today, though; the whole square has been cordoned off with yellow plastic tape for the benefit of a film crew, and the goats have been moved on.

"It's a murder mystery set in the fifteenth century," Atman explains. He nods at a group of actors who are standing in the firing line of cameras, up on top of the main dais in the square, which has been brilliantly renovated by a few tricks of the silver screen. The actors are all done up in costumes not dissimilar to Shakespearean players, with the women in traditional long dresses, aprons, and bonnets, the men in tapered pants with swords and knives at the ready: the father, the mother, the lover, the evil cousin, the girl, and the witch.

"We've even got a decent budget—some seed money from a venture-capital fund in the United States. Not much, but enough to give it a good college try," Atman explains. It seems he has been told to expect my visit, and has made assumptions as to who I am.

His English is perfect, but not Western. I think he

learned it in India. I'm afraid he *is* wearing a black leather jacket over a black T-shirt, but there are no dark glasses. Atman explains that as far as plot is concerned, he has little control over its basic themes: fatal sexual jealousy followed by clan wars, followed by sudden enlightenment, followed by a dance routine which expresses inconsolable grief, followed by miraculous forgiveness. These are all cultural givens with which he must work, and Atman needs the locals on his side because of an additional grant he got from some NGO with connections to the UN which tries to cultivate indigenous talent. Therefore Atman is trying to finesse his themes into a style that might attract the Best Foreign Film subcommittee of the Oscar nominations. He has cunningly decided to so construct his oeuvre that he can easily take out the dance routines for the American market without damaging the plot.

"I'm walking a tightrope," he explains, then looks at me. "You are from the producers, right?"

"No. I'm a cop from Bangkok. I'm investigating a death."

He nods, as if this somewhat radical reprogramming were merely a question of the right number of head movements. "Oh! Frank Charles? It was on CNN for about ten seconds. They only said he was dead in Bangkok. They didn't specify how."

"His death is all we have given out until now. I'm telling you because we'll have to go back to the media in a day or two. It was murder."

More nods. "Right. That's a shame. He was a good guy."

"He was?"

"Sure. Very sensitive. Very generous. So they say, anyway. I mean, that's what everyone says who worked with him. I only met him once. I didn't work for this outfit then."

"Is there someone here who did?"

I fancy the nods are somewhat more considered this time. "Yes. Tara. She worked with him on his film. She's Tibetan." He jerks his chin toward the witch on the dais. She is about a hundred years old, and even though she has removed her black pointed hat, her awful jowls, long nose, bent back, and shriveled flesh are enough to make you fear the hex.

I notice that Atman does not call her, but instead mounts the dais to say a few words, which causes her to look my way. She nods and comes down to greet me. When we are face-to-face she giggles and pulls off the mask.

The French call it *coup de foudre*, meaning "lightning bolt." I am thinking, quite objectively, *This is the last thing I need right now*. It is as if I can see my own heart etherized upon a table and I am reluctant as hell to undergo an operation that will mean more life.

27

Beauty creates its own mental environment. You have a choice: adapt or look away. I haven't looked away for more than an hour. The only person not embarrassed at our end of the restaurant is Tara. Needless to say, out of the face mask and the costume Tara is younger—much, much younger. I can't believe what's happening to me, but I'm not looking away.

The waiters have all noticed and made various signals to one another ranging from the *how sweet* to the downright vulgar, and one young Frenchman sitting at the next table (whose companion is not beautiful) has said something despicably sarcastic, which he doesn't know I understood. But who gives a damn? I'm not taking my eyes off my oxygen source. She reminds me somewhat of Chanya, with the same high cheekbones and wide generous face, but Chanya is from peasant stock, whereas this woman has something almost haughty about her. She speaks perfect UN English and hardly uses her left hand, which she likes to leave in her lap except when pressing it to her face in an odd, slightly nervous gesture. She does not drink alcohol, and I'm feeling self-conscious about ordering another beer, but I do so anyway. More as a way of soothing my nerves than out of professional interest, I decide to work on the case a bit.

"So, how was it, working with the great Frank Charles?"

"Great? Is he great in your country? We thought so, because he was very kind and thoughtful and always encouraged us. We said he was a natural Buddhist. Obviously, he had been exposed to Buddhism in some earlier incarnation."

She has a soft voice which includes in its tone forgiveness and compassion for all living things. I'm thinking she reached the Far Shore some time ago and feel intimidated. I say, "He was famous, anyway. And very rich. A successful man and filmmaker."

"Yes. He was always very professional."

"Would you mind telling me what his film was about?"

She expresses suspicion with the simplicity of a child: "Why don't you know?"

"Because it was never released, and I haven't been able to get hold of a copy. Do you have one?"

She smiles. "No. Nobody has one."

"Why not? What's so secret about it?"

"Nothing. There is nothing secret. It wasn't released because he never finished it. After we were through with filming on location, he told us he would finish the work in a studio in Los Angeles. That was five or six years ago. At first some of us would write to him, asking when the film would be done. He was always very apologetic. He would say that he'd run out of funding, but there were always ways of getting money sooner or later and we should be patient. He'd made sure we were all paid, you see? He was very careful about treating us honorably. He knew how vulnerable we are, how impossible it would be for us to enforce any contracts." She looks up and smiles. It is not a seductive smile, nor a mischievous one. It's a smile from the other side, full of lightness and freedom—a smile that really doesn't give a damn.

"So, what was the plot?"

A frown crumples her brow for a moment, then she laughs. "I'm not telling you. We said we wouldn't. We said we would wait for the final version before we talked in public about the plot."

"But he's dead. Murdered. Doesn't that change anything?" She smiles again. "I'm a cop."

"Are you going to arrest me for not answering questions?"

I blush deeply. "I'm sorry. I guess I'm pushing too hard. No, I don't have any investigative powers over here. It just strikes me as strange that you don't want to talk about the plot of a film you spent months working on. Were you the female lead?"

She shakes her head. "There were no leads. It wasn't that kind of film. It was experimental, artistic. We didn't use the star system."

"Can you tell me who else worked on it? Maybe I should speak to someone else?"

"Yes. Perhaps someone else would feel able to talk."

"Can you put me in touch? Do you have e-mail addresses, phone numbers—is there anyone in Kathmandu at the moment you could introduce me to?"

She takes a long moment to think about it. From her body language I believe she is carefully going through everyone who worked on the film with her, before she shakes her head. "You see, almost everyone was Tibetan apart from some of the technical staff. All the players in the Himalayan scenes were Tibetans like me. But most of them were illegals—that was something Frank Charles insisted on. They were illegal immigrants who knew something about film. Or maybe not." She giggles. "A few didn't know anything at all, and of course they couldn't speak English or any of the Nepali dialects, so I had to translate. I don't think they really knew what the film was about either, they didn't understand how movies are made. They just did as they were told; mostly it was inspired improvisation."

"That must have been difficult, even for an experienced director, to work with people who didn't speak his language and to try to improvise?"

"Yes. I think for someone else it would have been impossible. But Frank Charles was very gifted. Very passionate. His inspiration was easy to go with."

I shake my head. "It doesn't sound like a Hollywood director to me."

"How would I know? He's the only one I ever worked with."

"But doesn't it seem strange to you, that a gifted director who was so passionate about the film should not get around to finishing it?"

My question seems to puzzle her. "But he surely would have finished it sooner or later. It's only seven years ago we stopped filming."

I say, "Do you know someone called Tietsin?" I don't believe I gave the name any undue emphasis, but to me it was like dropping a piece of iron on a tiled floor: it clanged in my head.

She immediately whips a hand up to her mouth — it's the left hand that she doesn't like to use very much, but I can see from her eyes she is laughing.

"I know five hundred people called Tietsin, it's even more common than Rinpoche."

"Sorry, it's a *Doctor* Tietsin."

Now she doesn't try to hide her laughter. "Every third Tibetan man is a doctor of something, it's a title many still acquire in monasteries."

"He gives seminars on Tibetan history and Buddhism in a second-floor room overlooking Bodnath."

"I don't go to Bodnath so much anymore. I've decided to try to assimilate more with the Nepalis who have been so hospitable to us."

I take a deep breath. There is no point in pressing the investigation and alienating her; and there's not a lot of point in pretending the case is the only thing on my mind.

Well, here goes. I say, "You are very beautiful."

Corny? I suppose, but I think also honest and to the point. I've given her a choice. She can end the interview in a charming way, which a woman like her knows how to do—or she can pick up on my offer of courtship on any terms she likes.

I watch while her face changes somewhat. For a long moment I am convinced that she alone in the restaurant had not realized I have a romantic agenda. Now she stares directly into my eyes, offering a clear view of her limpid soul. Then she makes a little twitch with her mouth which is not without humor, before raising her left hand in front of my face, then bringing the right hand up to use its fingers to remove the top joints of the three middle digits of the other. She drops the tiny metal prostheses on the table with a clatter, leaving me staring at the black stubs of her left hand, which she then drums loudly on the tabletop. When the Frenchman with the *farang* wife turns to stare, she waves them at him, and he looks furious because she has spoiled his meal.

"Do you still want to sleep with me?" she asks in a tone entirely free of guile, then adds with a laugh, "I promise I don't have anything else missing."

28

I can't tell you about it just yet, *farang*. It's sort of sacred, embarrassing, and comic at the same time. And it doesn't show me in a particularly good light. Anyway, it's all still alive down there in my guts, sending conflicting signals all over my nervous system, killing my appetite for food or work—and all you want to know is did we do it or not, Tara and I, right? I'll get back to you. Meantime, I'm going on a tour of Freak Street in search of the Nixon Guesthouse. If you've forgotten Freak Street, *farang*, here's an aide-mémoire: Janis Joplin and Jimi Hendrix were both still alive; their work formed the sound track to a social experiment which began in San Francisco but was much better tolerated here, where the dope market was a significant segment of the economy. For the full initiation you needed to have traveled overland through those wonderful, exotic countries the late twentieth century turned into impenetrable battlefields in the name of civilization. Pilgrims who survived were distinguished by lice, long hair, dysentery, entry-level mysticism, a massive dope habit, and an addiction to rock and roll.

I could hardly find the place and kept winding up back at the market, where women in shawls squat over gigantic melons, carrots, radishes, and other vegetables of such outlandish size you wonder if the whole Kathmandu Valley hasn't been magically modified. Carbon monoxide, plentiful in the air, does nothing to stunt the spectacular growth of the local produce, nor are conscientious housewives put off by the presence of free-range hens, cows, monkeys, and dogs at the morning market, where the main attraction today is a bucket of fish someone has caught in one of the rivers—perhaps the Baghmati, where all those cadavers crackle and pop on the ghats? After a good deal of searching I find a wan, handwritten sign attached to a lamppost: FREAK STREET THIS WAY.

The Nixon Guesthouse is a large four-story half-timbered converted Elizabethan-style terrace house with a small courtyard where laundry hangs; presumably you could have breakfast sitting between the billowing sheets if you remembered to stock up on your yogurt and granola the night before. I arrive at ablution time: no guests are visible and I retreat into the street while two brawny cleaning women in saris throw buckets of water over the tiled floor, which quickly floods into the courtyard. I decide to hang out for ten minutes until they've finished and go back to the market. I am in the process of examining a carrot more than fifteen inches long—with phallic implications not lost on the toothless, betel-crunching

266

female vendor—when Lek sends me a text message.

Now I have to go back to my guesthouse to pick up a document he has faxed. There are suddenly no taxis, but a trishaw driver miraculously appears and presents himself as an obvious and only alternative. Like a fool I forget to negotiate a price in advance, and by the time he has heroically pedaled me all the way back up to Thamel and the Kathmandu Guesthouse, guilt has crippled my negotiating power, and I give him the small fortune he is demanding while ostentatiously groaning and rubbing his calves and thighs. I realize how badly I've been screwed from the way his eyes pop when I hand over the full sum he named as fairly representing the extent of his suffering. Now he is thanking me with extravagant gestures for bringing early retirement; I think he sees me as an unlikely avatar of Krishna.

In the guesthouse they have put Lek's single faxed document into a brown envelope, a sophisticated touch I had not expected. When I pull it out, all I see is a group picture prominently featuring a man in his late forties whom I do not recognize. From the context—he is with six Asians—I would say he is quite tall, over six feet. He is very handsome, looks American, slightly overweight but not much. He is also clean shaven. I call Lek.

"You're not going to tell me it's him?"

"Darling, that is a *verified* photo of Frank Charles."

"It must have been taken about a hundred years ago?"

"Nope. It's a media pic sent out when he was filming up in northwest Nepal seven or eight years ago."

"That would make him early fifties. But he looks younger than that. It's shocking. Even for an American, it's shocking how fat he got so quickly."

"Mmm, quite a hunk. I suppose they all run to seed in the end."

I close the phone on Lek and meditate for a moment on the photograph of Frank Charles. He is smiling generously, his arms around two women, one of whom is Tara. Others of the group I assume are actors or part of the film crew. Many are in traditional Tibetan costume, and at least a couple of the men look quite wild with their heads tied up in rags, just like highland yak rustlers. I fold the photo in a way that does not distort his face, slide it into a pocket, and go back out onto Thamel.

There are plenty of cabs now; that must be because I've decided to walk. When I finally get back to the Nixon, I'm pleased to see the Augean stables have been flooded back to cleanliness by the Herculean cleaning ladies, and a man can light a joint among the billowing sheets once more.

And what am I thinking while the THC goes to work? You already know the answer to that, *farang*, because you wondered the same thing yourself when I told you about the photograph of Frank Charles with his arm around Tara: did he sleep with her or not? Am I alone in lamenting the way karma from our reptilian incarnations continues to trap us in the sewer of sexual jealousy? Is this the time to confess all I know about Tara? Well, here goes.

As you recall, Tara said, *Do you still want to sleep with me?* shortly after showing the obnoxious Frenchman not one finger, but three, all blackened, the tips lost to frostbite. Naturally, that was the moment when she morphed from a butter-wouldn't-melt-in-the-mouth product of UN social engineering, mostly of the northern European kind, to a beautiful bitch with attitude. Of course I said yes. Three times, like this: *Yes, yes, yes,* not with the shy lust of a young man, but with the full-bodied desperation of one hurtling toward forty whose wife has retreated to a nunnery, whose only child is dead, and who really did, at that moment, see her as salvation in the form of a last chance.

She explained it would have to be her place rather than mine. After all, despite appearances, this was a very conservative, third-world town and a girl really could not afford to be seen visiting a foreigner in his hotel room. Bottom line, as a Tibetan refugee she risked expulsion for prostitution. It seemed indiscreet to ask how the situation could be improved by a man visiting her in her own room, but I figured it out when we arrived at what must be a kind of unfinished housing project on the way to the airport. From the costumes of the men and women, their highland roughness, the raggedness of the dress, and an indefinable atmosphere of *anything goes*, I concluded that this was an exclusively Tibetan compound for young people between the ages of about twenty and thirty, who seemed to be squatting in the raw, half-finished buildings made of reinforced concrete. The Tibetan version of the Hindu mandala, thanka, was everywhere, for this seemed to be an artists' enclave; someone was blowing a huge Tibetan horn about ten feet long, sending a low wave of yearning sound to bounce off the walls and out into the city. There were kids who had the air of belonging to everyone and no one, playing in an unfinished house at twilight. There were also Tibetan prayer flags everywhere, making great parabolas on cables which stretched from the earth to the roofs. When we had entered her small room—the communal toilet was outside—and she had locked the door with a sliding bolt, she came close to me, smiled, and quickly found my member with her good hand. It was a strangely familiar kind of reconnoitering caress which puzzled me. I was further puzzled by the tone in which she told me to go wash under the hose outside. I obeyed, returned to the room, and waited while she showered in turn. We had not yet kissed.

Then came the moment of revelation, when she returned wearing only a towel. She grinned at my discomfort, then parted the ends of the towel in a theatrical manner. I smiled and paid homage to her breasts. When she took me to the mattress on the floor and had me lie down, she examined my penis carefully, using both sight and touch, as if she were looking for something. Now I was laughing at myself.

I said, "It's okay, I'm clean." She seemed not to understand why I would say that, but the signs were too many for me to be fooled any longer. I said, "Look, I understand. You've found the one guy in the world who is not going to judge you. My mother was on the Game, I help out in a go-go bar she runs, I could fairly be called a part-time pimp. I have no moral objection to any woman from a poor background making an extra buck or two—especially a refugee."

I thought I was saying the right thing, but I only succeeded in making her frown. She shook her head, then told me to relax and close my eyes. "I hope you don't mind," she said. "I want to do it a little differently. Ask me about it afterward. All you have to do is lie there the first time. Try not to come too soon."

When I was about to speak, she covered my mouth with her left hand—I felt the rough edges of the stubs resting on my forehead—then with the long finger of her right hand found a pressure point between my anus and scrotum, which she pushed on forcefully. It had the effect of diminishing the immediate need for orgasm without ruining the erection. How could this not be a professional? And one of a skill level I had never before encountered. When she leaned over so that her breasts were dangling around my chin, she whispered, "Don't get emotional, you'll ruin the ecstasy."

This was not a line I'd heard before; I could not even imagine it coming from my mother, Nong, who

271

could be pretty adventurous with the right customer, and I was thinking, Wow, *these Tibetans really are different*, while allowing her to play me like a penny-whistle.

Except that the music was somewhat more sophisticated. Fine-tuning was achieved by means of the long-finger technique heretofore described; once when I was *really* about to come, she leaned forward to whisper gently, "Imagine a wheel, a spinning wheel, a spinning wheel with tiny spadelike cutters . . ."

But the rest of the time she was astride me, arched back, head high, eyes closed, a clear light (almost visible) emanating from her forehead, which was free of all furrows; hanging from her neck—she must have put it on in the shower, for she had not worn it at supper—there was a silver medallion in the form of a *vajra*, the Himalayan symbol for the thunderbolt.

Her room was without electricity; her naked eternal motion I found best viewed in black silhouette against the left wall, thanks to moonlight entering through a window on the right, which also captured a piece of iron sticking out of one of the incomplete buildings, which now appeared to me like a piece of iron bamboo, thick as a fist, black as a stump, painted on a relative paleness.

Well, I'm prepared to swear on the whole of the Pali Canon that, with the help of Tara's finger, I held out for a full forty minutes. After that I figured she'd had her fun and if she wanted any more she could pay me.

A full condom later, we were lying in each other's

arms. I allowed a couple of beats before the grumpy words fled my mouth: "You didn't come."

She stretched out a hand to cover one of mine; I was tempted to withdraw it, but I opted for good manners and let it lie there. "I haven't come for a very long time, Detective. My partner went back to Tibet and the Chinese threw him in jail."

I gulped. "I'm sorry. Really. Stupid of me."

"He was not my lover. He was my partner."

I took a deep breath. "What does that mean?"

"Don't tell me you haven't guessed? Do you still think I'm a prostitute?"

I shook my head. "Oh, no. I'm starting to get the idea about Tibetans. Prostitution would be way too simple an explanation—and far too worldly."

"But you really are a part-time pimp?"

I coughed. "You're a yogin? You do Tantra?"

"Of course. Didn't you like it?"

"It felt terrific, but it would have been nice if you'd remembered me from time to time."

She smiled. "I think it is difficult for people with a Western background to understand how impersonal bliss really is."

So to her I looked thoroughly Western? I mulled her revolutionary worldview for a moment, before descending to the mundane. "You *do* know Tietsin."

She frowned. "Why do you say that?"

"Blade wheels. They're a dead giveaway."

She rolled to one side; when she rolled back I could see she was laughing her head off. "What's so funny?

Don't tell me, blade wheels are ten a penny in Lhasa?"

"Of course. Blade wheels are central to our culture, like traffic jams in Bangkok." She thought this very witty and cackled for a while, making her breasts shiver.

"You win," I said. "Your blade wheels hurt, but they don't do as much damage to the environment." She nodded, as if to a backward child who was starting to get the idea.

Like an old-fashioned hostess of good breeding, she would not let me search for a cab on my own. When we found one, she insisted on sharing it with me, to make sure I got back safely to my guesthouse. Actually, she wanted to talk. I sensed a burden of responsibility toward me she needed to get off her chest.

"It's all to do with Tibetan history. Buddhism came quite late to us, around about the eighth century, but didn't really get going until eleven hundred. Tibetans then were wild people who lived in the most in-hospitable region of the earth. Only the strongest, most virile men and the most resilient, fecund women survived. They were very physical people and very warlike. And eating meat was the only way to survive—it still is. So there was a lot of sexual energy to deal with. We weren't going to go the Brahmin route and suppress it all by standing on our heads and living on weeds. Something had to be done to divert

274

that energy into the higher chakras. So we developed Tantra, also known as Vajrayana Buddhism, also known as Apocalyptic Buddhism."

I thought this was a way of explaining herself to me. But then she said, "I don't know this Doctor Tietsin personally, but I've heard of him. He's famous among some Tibetans, even revered. He helps a lot of people, especially newly arrived refugees. He gives them money. Some say he's a kind of godfather with connections to the Nepal government. Some say he's a throwback to our atavistic past. Some say he is the reincarnation of Milarepa."

"Milarepa?" I remembered from the guidebook: the patron saint of Tibet.

"Yes. You see, like in every religion, there is the orthodox and the spiritual. Milarepa was a wild man, crazy, radical beyond belief. He started off as a black magician and slaughtered lots of people before he found the dharma. Maybe that's why we love him so much."

"Tietsin isn't even a monk."

"That's his strength. He isn't bound by anything. Some say he is beyond the path—that he is already free from suffering. He is just using that damaged body as a vehicle to help Tibet in its time of crisis."

"And what do the others say?"

"That he's quite mad and about seven hundred years behind the times." She giggled. "He gave you a mantra, didn't he?" I nod. "That's what's secret, not the blade wheel."

She fell silent for a moment, just as we were turning in to the guesthouse. I said, "He gave me a mantra—what about it?"

"Oh, only that with him, you could be fully awakened in seven years—you won't be interested in women at all." She let a beat pass. "Or you could be the permanent inmate of a mental hospital. He doesn't mess around. What you call psychosis, for him is a path to health. Or you could say that to him we're all psychotic anyway, so there isn't too much of a risk."

When I was standing in the driveway, handing her money for the cab, she leaned out to say, "I don't think it's wise for us to meet again. I've opened your heart chakra too much, there's a serious risk you'll fall in love with me. Sexual slavery is the last thing I need. It creates such heavy karma. I'm sorry if I misled you. Goodbye."

Well, how about that! I was doing a little jaw scratching when one of those niggardly, academic questions struck, as they do at times like these. I returned to the cab, which was in the process of turning around, and, feeling more like a traffic cop than a lover, knocked on her window and had her roll it down. "Just out of interest—why did you go with me tonight?"

She looked away and took a deep breath. "Male energy. The power that comes from all that boiling sperm. A girl has to have it from time to time, and there aren't so many opportunities now that my partner's in jail. You've restored balance and power, and I no longer feel I'm about to come down with the flu—and you were cute, too."

That was it, *farang*. My one and only affair since I married Chanya, and the lady turned out to be a perfect yogin. I finished the joint about two hours ago, and I've been sitting among the billowing sheets of the deserted guesthouse all that time in a pleasantly ironic reverie. When I come out of it I realize what should have been obvious. There is no management, and the guesthouse is not open for business. The cleaning ladies are gone, and when I find a cop at the corner of the street he tells me the Nixon was busted last week for drug trafficking and won't be open again until the owners have paid off the cops. He gives the impression that this is a routine event. There is also the suggestion that large-scale drug-running operations need government approval if they are to survive up here for any length of time.

29

I'm supposed to check out the other hotel at the top of Thamel, where the English girl Mary Smith claims she first made contact with the Thai network run by none other than our very own Colonel Vikorn.

But I can't summon any enthusiasm for another trek around Thamel and decide not to follow up on the other guesthouse that Mary Smith mentioned. I have come to the realization that most of my psychic energy today will be spent resisting the temptation to call Tara on her cell phone, or—worse—go visit her on set at Bhaktapur. Now, wouldn't that be the last word in *adolescent needy*? What's really annoying is the tone of genuine compassion when she said, *Sexual slavery is the last thing I need*—in a motherly tone. It was as if she'd dressed me badly for school and now I was going to be uncomfortable all day. I'm caught between indignant rage and erotic fascination. I have never known a woman like her. Of course, I want to see her again. Best would be for *her* to be in the needy mode, but that is too much to hope for in this Himalayan town where the attention is directed skyward. The easiest thing of all would be to go see Tietsin for some kind of confrontation: we really can't have him going around busting our mules to General Zinna. But when I make another visit to Bodnath, and look around the teahouse where he holds his seminars, there is no sign of him. It's starting to look as if I have a day to myself and, strange to relate, my superstitious Asian genes will not let me leave without another three and a half turns of the brass.

So I'm halfway through the first round, spinning the wheels like there is no tomorrow—there never is—following behind a couple of nattering Tibetan nuns who are creeping steadily up on some inexpert Scandinavian backpackers who keep stopping to make sure they didn't miss a wheel, when my legs start to feel heavy. It is an extraordinary moment; the strength suddenly leaves my body, and I feel about a hundred years old. Most scary is the way my mental environment starts to change. The white stupa is getting blacker, people disappear. In a moment of extreme physical weakness I lean against the stupa, and my cell phone rings. I had forgotten to turn it off.

"Get the hell out of there, right now."

"What?"

"You're way too weak for this. The stupa is draining you. If you don't believe me, take one good look at it."

I do so and have the impression, suddenly, of being able to look into its interior—the small dingy river, the ghouls taking charge of souls, the pyramid of enlightenment with those of blackest karma at the bottom and the translucent at the top—and I realize how profoundly I am being sucked in.

"There's no point going to the Far Shore if you're never going to come back—what's the use of that? Come away from the stupa."

I have to physically push myself away from the wall of the stupa, and I stagger somewhat until I'm a good ten feet away, when my strength starts to return. I'm still holding the phone to my ear. "Where are you?"

"Look up; I'm standing on top of the stupa."

I look up. There is no one on top of the stupa; its slope toward the top is too steep, and there is no place to stand. It would be quite outlandish to see anyone up there. "No you're not, you're just doing my head in."

He adds a note of extreme exasperation when he says, "You're about to be sucked into death without a protest, but you can't see beyond the conventional. Look again."

I make a face at the phone, look up again. Now I see there are white stairs which lead up the breast-shaped mound. And there he is, right on the top, waving his stump just for me. Then, also just for me, he turns, lowers his pants, and moons me. To my own astonishment I find this hilarious and burst out laughing. My laughter is quickly followed by tears.

"You're hysterical," Tietsin says, "which is the worst state of mind. Better to be depressed, or even grimly suicidal. I can work with those states. Hysterical is no good. Calm down. Go and have a beer."

"Will you tell me where you are?" I'm suddenly irritated. He is not really on top of the stupa; I just sneaked another look, and there was nobody there. It's some kind of telepathy he's using.

"Never mind where I am—you'd be too shocked to know. Suppose I tell you I'm in bed with Tara—how about that?"

I gasp as if I've been kicked in the gut. "So she does work for you?"

A tut-tut. "She does no such thing. I've never heard of her before. She called me because she is a responsible yogin who got worried about you after you told her you were one of mine. She's afraid you're way too open at the moment and that little bout with her last night could kill you. You're already badly weakened. You need to know, female yogins have something extra we don't have, and they're not responsible for the effects they have on us. You just don't understand the forces you're working with. You don't have the protection of ordinary people—you lost that when we initiated you—and you're not strong enough to live the dharma all on your own."

"I don't understand a word you're saying."

"Now you're lying. You don't want to understand because the implications are too great for your fragile worldview. You thought you would take a little sex vacation yesterday, crawl into the first womb that came your way, get all gooey and lovey, just like a wandering ghost in search of a body, *any* body, to escape the spiritual anguish—and start the whole psychotic process of birth and death all over again. Stop kidding yourself. You've left a big piece of yourself between her legs. If she wanted, she could crush you like a bug. Instead she comes to me, worried about you. If I were you, I would make amends to her."

"But I didn't do anything. She used me."

"Up to you. Etiquette can be important, though. The guardians like good manners. And what the hell are you doing in Kathmandu anyway? Do you realize how unprofessional this is, for you and me to be in the same town when the deal is being processed? *We're delivering next week.*"

"Well, maybe your behavior is less than professional, too," I mutter. "The main reason I'm here is I want to know who your informants are, the ones who tell you who is carrying for who in Thailand. Zinna and Vikorn are quite upset."

"My informants? Why didn't you ask before? One's called Narayan, the other's Shah."

To my astonishment and rage, he has suddenly closed his phone. I stare at my own for a moment, then go to the phone's log to try to find the number he was using, but the log shows it as an anonymous call. Stumped, I close my phone and slide it into my pocket. This has the effect of triggering another bout of paranoia, because I feel diminished without the gadget in my hand.

Now I'm recovering from the moment and my energy is returning. I know Tietsin is right: I have to get away from the stupa. Its great, looming, sepulchral whiteness is too much, and when I look at it I start to feel ill all over again. With no doubt in my heart this time, I have a cab drive me to the Thai Airways offices on Durbar Marg, where I book myself on the next plane to Bangkok.

When I land at Suvarnabhum Airport, it is about six in the evening. I have no luggage to collect, so I grab a taxi and I sit in the back with my eyes closed, exhausted. When I reach home, I remember to switch my phone back on just before crashing.

30

A tiny voice makes insect noises in the depths of my cell phone's miniature speaker, after shattering my fragile sleep with "All Along the Watchtower": "So, how's it going? Feeling better?"

I hold the phone closer to my ear. He's not using his UN accent tonight: it's straight New York with a touch of Brooklyn that penetrates the blackness.

"D'you know what time it is?"

"Sure. For you it's four o'clock in the morning, for me it's two hours earlier than that, but I don't sleep much. Four o'clock is when all good monks get up to start their daily practice."

"I'm not a monk."

"Who are you kidding?"

I let a beat pass. "My son died. I didn't tell you. I thought you'd see it, you being enlightened and all. I was testing you. He was killed in an accident. You didn't know, did you?"

We hang in silence for a moment. "No, I'm sorry. Very sorry. I didn't know."

"But you knew I was going to be hit by something devastating. You said so."

"The spirit is always devastating on its first visit. When you insisted on the initiation, I knew you were going to take a hit. Same as me. I didn't invent dharma. You have Western blood, you wanted the karma of ten thousand lifetimes all rolled up into one hit so you can take the fast track to enlightenment and get the gold medal before anyone else. Well . . ." He sighs. "But I'm still sorry. There is no worse feeling than the first time you get whacked, no matter what any of the old hands tell you. I'm just glad it's you and not me—and you'll feel the same, one day."

"Thanks." I decide to change the subject. "We're having a little problem here, a girl, an Englishwoman in her late twenties, a mule named Mary Smith— somebody busted her. She has a Nepali visa in her passport. D'you know who busted her?"

"Sure, General Zinna. You know that."

"I mean, who busted her to Zinna?"

"I did."

The unadorned confession leaves me speechless for a moment. "Are you crazy? D'you know what Vikorn is going to do when he finds out? It's my duty to tell him."

"So tell him. I don't mind. In fact, I insist. I don't want you trying to make me responsible for your failure of duty."

"But I thought you had a deal with him—with us. D'you think he's still going to deal with you after this?"

"I'm sure of it. In fact, he'll want to deal even more."

I'm lost. All I can think of to say for the moment is, "Why?"

"Vikorn doesn't have the money. He told me. I need forty, and the most he can raise on short notice is twenty."

The full implications of this take a while to dawn on me. "You're trying to muscle him? Look, one: he doesn't muscle easy, in fact he doesn't muscle at all, and two: he really can't raise that much in a week. He just can't do it."

"I know that."

"So?"

"His chum, General Zinna, he's in the same boat."

I'm so aghast I can hardly speak. I'm also disillusioned: Tietsin is coming across as a dangerous amateur. "You went to Zinna when you already had a deal with us?" I pause to allow myself a cooling inhalation. "Look, you may be a great guru or yogin or whatever, but that's one big no-no. Over here, I'm sorry to have to say, that's dumber than dumb. You have just screwed the whole thing up. Maybe you should look somewhere else for a deal, how about Amsterdam, or somewhere not less than five thousand miles away?"

"No. I like you. I'm sticking with you. I told you, Tibetans are a naturally loyal people. We don't give up on someone we take to—not in one lifetime anyway. I might have gone off you before the

286

Maitreya Buddha arrives, but there's plenty of time."

"How can you be so cocky?"

"It's not cocky. Think about it. Think out loud for me."

"Okay, I'm thinking out loud. I'm thinking that you have double-crossed the most powerful drug lord in Thailand, after having first busted that Australian mule who was working for the second-most powerful drug lord in Thailand. That's two very big enemies and no friends except me, and from a business perspective I'm also starting to have my doubts. Maybe you should stick to teaching enlightenment through voluntary psychosis."

He has the audacity to sigh, as if I'm a slow learner. "You're too Western in your outlook. It's too black-and-white. People are driven by psychology. What does Buddhism tell us about that? What are the three motivations of ordinary men?"

"Fear, lust, and aggression."

"Right. Why was your Colonel so keen to deal with me?"

"Because what you're offering is so big he'll be able to annihilate Zinna. Aggression."

"And what would be the reason why General Zinna might see me as a gift from heaven?"

"Okay, so he can get big enough to annihilate Vikorn, but—"

"Stop, you're too stuck in the here and now. Make the blade wheel work for you. It doesn't have to be a full-blown internal workout every time, you can

287

calibrate it a bit. Take a full minute to let it enter your mind, let it rise up from the subconscious, where you have carefully buried it."

I close my eyes and relax. Damn him, it starts to work. But I still don't understand how he's going to get away with alienating his main business partner.

"So," he says, "how far have we got?"

"Well, like I just said, it's all about fear, lust, and aggression. You don't have to be Buddhist to know that."

"And what happens when aggression collapses, as it inevitably does?"

"You start again with fear. It's the vicious circle in the middle of the mandala: snake, pig, and eagle, usually."

"And what would Vikorn fear most in these circumstances?"

"Easy. That he might get annihilated by Zinna."

"Right. And what does Zinna fear most?"

My eyes start to open. I'm stammering at his audacity when I say, "You're, you're, you're playing them off against each other? But how—?"

"When I spoke to Zinna he said the same thing as Vikorn. He can only get twenty at short notice. That's when I knew the dharma was on my side. Two and two make four, right?"

I gasp. "You really think you can get them to work together? Form a partnership to raise forty million?"

Another of those intimidating sighs. "You just told me they will. Fear: what choice do they have?"

Still gasping: "Each one has to be in because the other is in? You're amazing. But I don't think you'll get away with it. They'll kill each other first. Assuming they can't get to Kathmandu to kill you."

He pauses to let the darkness speak, then: "Hmm, you may be right. I don't like to be complacent. That's why I've got you."

"I only work for Vikorn; I don't work for Zinna."

"You are a peacetime consigliere—after you left I watched the DVDs. I thought Brando was terrific, as was Pacino, and you are a perfect Hagen. So, do peace. After all, you're only trying to make your boss richer."

I'm exploring my left ear with my left pinkie. "I still don't get why you had to bust the English girl."

"It wasn't my idea. Zinna insisted. He had to start on an even footing, he said, and I'd already busted one of his. The trouble is, he's psychotic, and with psychotics you have to accept there's a wall in them they can't get around. He can't get around his jealousy of your boss. Vikorn has a better mind, and he's not psychotic."

"So what is he?"

"Go figure—I have never come across anything like him before! When I was in the monastery we spent a whole year on *citipati*, which is a highly specialized kind of fire demon, and Vikorn could belong to a sub-species, but I'm not sure. You really need an expert. It's as tricky as sexing a kitten. Anyway, I think you get the idea, and the General is expecting a visit. I wouldn't take Lek if I were you, he gets the soldiers all excited."

"How do you know about—"

He's closed his phone. Now I realize I forgot to ask if he had ever met Frank Charles; after all, the American didn't have just one Nepali visa in his passport, he had about a dozen. It's four-thirty in the morning. I also forgot to ask him how he knew the names of those two mules in the first place. Joint time.

That's better. I'm not encouraging you to break the law, *farang*, but if on your next trip to Amsterdam and those wonderful smoking cafés (funny how many software companies hold their office parties there), or when you're hanging out in good ol' Humboldt County, home to the medicinal herb (they say at least 1 per cent really *are* on chemo), or maybe you make regular trips to the Riff Mountains over in Morocco, or you contribute in some other clandestine way to the global community of secret smokers (do you realize that the number of people who voted in the last American presidential election were only a tiny fraction of the number of people who smoke marijuana, worldwide? Globalism cuts both ways)— if, as I say, you find yourself partaking perhaps out of mere social duty, as is de rigueur for all presidential candidates these days and I'm glad to hear it (if the last president had taken a toke before bedtime, how many lives might have been saved?), then allow me to recommend the humble herb not only as a meditation aid, but also for the purposes of forensic investigation: it's not good on detail, but it provides a terrific overview. For example, what do we have here exactly, at the present time of smoking? One hell of a tangle, is what we have. Mellowing it all out under the influence of the life-giving weed, I find as follows:

I am investigating the most colorful and photogenic murder of my career under the name of my most serious professional rival, who will get all the credit when I solve it—which I will do because I'm drearily good at that sort of thing—while trying to arrange a huge smack shipment with a rogue Tibetan yogin, who happens also to be my meditation guru at my own insistence, despite a life-threatening conflict of interest with regard to my boss, Colonel Vikorn, who is most interested not in selling smack but in ruining General Zinna, who is equally keen to ruin Vikorn and couldn't really give a damn about commerce as long as Vikorn goes to jail for longer than he does at the end of the day, and the task of your investigative reporter-cum-consigliere-cum-detective at this stage is to persuade these two old bull elephants to join hands in joyful harmony for the purpose of buying said karma-laden poison from the most selfless and enlightened being I have met in a lifetime of search-ing, who has turned my head upside down with some ultra-powerful magic from the ultra-powerful but not very well-known Vajrayana school of Buddhism, also known as Tantra, also known as Apocalyptic Buddhism. Can you blame me for rolling another?

31

Just because it's dawn doesn't mean I'm sober. My assisted meditation got a little off track toward five o'clock this morning and I started to develop this question for you, *farang*, which I'm having trouble getting out of my head. This hand-started universe of yours, this *Big Bang*—for Buddha's sake, what kind of cosmology is that? Was the guy who invented it also responsible for the Virgin birth? And now there are strings attached. Did you know that according to Wikipedia (which is never wrong), the relationship of one *string*, in terms of mass, to one atom is roughly the same as the ratio of an apple to the sun? Frankly, I prefer the original Sanskrit.

Okay, I'm in my bathroom staring at the unshaven guy in the mirror and watching my image of him, which is really his image of me, getting fleshed out as memory floods back. I am becoming more recognizable to myself by the second. Did you ever observe that there are two quite different forms of waking up available to the human species? One when you're happy, the other when you're not; there's no comparison, right? These days Guilt and Horror stand guard at my bedside every morning. Their karmic sources seem interchangeable: Pichai's death can fill me with guilt or horror, depending on which demon happens to prevail. Similarly, the heroin: I can be crippled with guilt or crippled with horror, according to the way my mood is running. Right now, I can hardly move. I am transfixed by what has happened to the guy staring out at me from the glass, the very one who from time to time in his life has seemed really quite close to the full spiritual awakening promised by the Buddha. Not this morning.

And the whole agony of the thing seems bound up with Tietsin's blade wheel; I have never had to get to know myself so well before. The consequence is like waking in a shallow grave and having to shake off the clay before you can start work. I groan when I remember my duties today.

It seems I have to moderate a meeting between Vikorn and Zinna, who have been impatiently awaiting my return from Kathmandu so they can move forward with structuring a temporary partnership which will allow them to pool resources to buy forty million dollars' worth of smack from Tietsin. There are a lot of points to cover. Vikorn has written some down for me, but I have issues of my own, the most basic being how to get the dough to Tietsin safely.

This is deep consigliere stuff, and not without a certain dignity of office. I imagine the chairman of the World Bank often has to tackle this kind of thing, though with less visible threat to his health. Vikorn conceded the venue, which will be Zinna's army HQ, in return for naming me secretary to the board. Zinna is putting up with me because I seem to have a way with the supplier; that, at least, is the story Vikorn has sold to him. Anyway, I am the only one on the Thai national team who has actually met Tietsin, and now that Lek has spread the word about what a terrifying witch the Tibetan is, having more or less turned me into his zombie and slave, no one else is keen to step up for the position of lead negotiator to Free Tibet. On the downside, colleagues have started giving me strange looks; I have the feeling people are reluctant to find themselves alone with me. Sometimes I'm tempted to turn them all into frogs. (That was a joke, *farang*.)

No doubt bearing in mind Vikorn's extravagance at the last summit meeting ten years ago—when, you will recall, my Colonel showed up with thirteen black helicopters, which he hired for the day from someone close to the government of Cambodia—Zinna, we are told, has pulled out all the stops today. So has Vikorn. His taste in spectacular military uniforms (even though he's a cop) has often caused me to speculate that he might be a reincarnation of Field Marshal Göring. (But the dates are wrong: Göring took his cyanide on October 15, 1946, which is four months after Vikorn was born; however, occultism posits alternative ways to invest a body, using vile, black means to kick out the present occupant so you can take over the bivouac for the duration—sounds like Vikorn, doesn't it?) Today he is sporting full colonel shoulder boards in gold on starched white, with gold braid, brass buttons, beautifully tooled leather belt, black boots brought to a shine a girl could use as a hand mirror, a terrific lowbrow white cap with shiny black visor, an ebony swagger stick, his summit-meeting solid-gold non-fake Rolex wristwatch with diamond insets, and Wayfarer wraparound sunglasses: he is the very model of a modern mafioso. When we get into the back of his Bentley, he hitches up his white pants so as not to lose the bayonet-sharp crease: yep, the boss is taking no prisoners today. As soon as we're off he orders his driver to play "Flight of the Valkyries" on the sound system.

General Zinna's HQ is about twenty miles out of town, but he starts to make himself felt at about half that distance. Army trucks full of soldiers in camouflage fatigues start appearing parked on the hard shoulders; then motorbike squads come close to *our* motorbike escort, like medieval louts looking for an off-course jousting match; then, about three miles from the army compound, tanks start to line the road, parked perpendicular to the turnpike with their guns raised ambiguously. Is this a gauntlet or a welcoming committee? Maybe Vikorn wasn't expecting quite so many tanks; he frowns for a moment and tells the driver to turn up the Wagner. By the time we get to the threshold of army land proper, the tanks are lined up tread to caterpillar tread, producing a funnel-like effect which drives us like game into a net with shriek-ing Valkyries infesting the air.

And there he is! I have to say I feel a twinge of admiration, the way he has tried to imitate Vikorn's theatrics, and done a not-bad job of it. He is standing in full army-general parade dress, with *his* shoulder boards, et cetera, all shined up, the thick rawhide band across his great chest, his men—hundreds of them—all at attention with eyes forward. He's the little guy with power to spare waiting with the deter-mined dignity of the short to welcome our own *capo di tutti capi*.

Vikorn, though, is a natural at this kind of thing. The effortless, slightly foppish way he gets out of his Bentley—just slightly limp-wristed here, to point up and impishly mock Zinna's military correctness—then, just as the General is provoked into beaming and moving forward a couple of steps to greet his guest, Vikorn decides to have a girlish moment—*Whoops, I forgot the champagne*, his expression says—and instead of ordering his driver to get it he dips back into his limo himself to bring out what is surely a sym-bolic single bottle of Veuve Clicquot '86 (there is more on ice in the trunk) while Zinna hangs there wondering what to do with the hands he just raised to his eyes in a *wai*.

"So our negotiations go all the more smoothly," Vikorn says with a debonair smile as he hands over the bottle at the same time finally returning Zinna's *wai*.

Sensing that he might have been upstaged, Zinna

blushes as he takes the bottle; but it is clear he has built up an arms cache of extravagance to hit us with. Sure enough, once Vikorn has strolled nonchalantly through his inspection of the troops, with Zinna bouncing up and down beside him, the General declares it is time for lunch and takes us into his mess, where a banquet has been prepared. The banquet, though, is all for the supporting cast; under heavy police and military escort Zinna leads Vikorn and me to a smaller mess room for senior officers; only the three of us and Zinna's valet, a trusted member of the inner circle who hails from Zinna's own village, enter here.

Now Zinna demonstrates how he has grown in stature and grace over the years, because the feast consists of soul food from Vikorn's home village in Isaan. A mere glimpse at the table tells me we are in for quite a treat: noodles, Mekong River catfish, grilled chicken, salads loaded with minced meat or fish, steamed fish with mint leaves, chilies, garlic, lemongrass, lime juice, and galangal. Boneless duck tossed with deep-green long beans. Salt-cured crab, and crunchy pork skins. *Num tok* with rubbery beef balls, slices of pork, cuts of liver, and tripe, squid in *gal kua*. Green curry, eggplant, and basil leaves with pork (chicken, beef, or seafood is also available, but less appealing), in a sauce thickened with coconut milk. Red curry with cinnamon and chili. I have been told by Lek—who, since his ordeal at the hands of the army, has become the recipient of the most salacious military gossip (he claims one of his guilty tormentors e-mailed him with an apology and an offer of marriage once he's had the op, and they've been pen friends ever since)—that Zinna himself interviewed a short list of chefs to produce Vikorn's extra-special favorite homebody version of *somtam*, which takes a full day to prepare and is not complete without a few blessings and spells from the local shaman.

My Colonel's mien is grave but respectful as he bows his head for the first taste of the *somtam*, with Zinna himself holding his breath. Vikorn's expression is all the more solemn when he replaces the fork and spoon, dabs his lips with a napkin, and declares, with an air of defeat, that the dish is perfect, very nearly as good as his grandmother made it. No, he will not bend the truth simply to score a point, he confesses, before the two of us, Zinna and me, that it is even better than his grandmother made it, no doubt thanks to the chef's more delicate hand with the holy basil and the Kaffir lime leaf. Gratified, Zinna exhales slowly, and with considerable relief; how could they not reach an agreement now? Of the two of them, it is Zinna who most needs the money, and no one doubts it is Vikorn, the gilded civilian, who is the supreme patriarch of dough.

The rest of Vikorn's champagne is brought from the back of the Bentley, along with its silver ice bucket. Zinna offers all known cocktails, spirits, beers, wines. We plunge into the Widow Clicquot in silence. Now soldier-waiters arrive with vegetable filo parcels, steamed crabs, chicken satay, Thai dim sum, pan-fried fishcakes, barbecued pork spare ribs, spring rolls, grilled seafood with pineapple, bean sprouts and tofu soup, quail-egg salad with prawns, red snapper with three-flavor sauce, *turia* with pork—I'm giving only the unusual dishes, *farang*; all the old favorites are represented as well.

I am floundering under the weight of the banquet, but those two old bull elephants seem able to pack it away without a stomach rumble. Finally, it's over. Zinna has someone bring the cigars and the Armagnac for Vikorn, a single-malt whisky for himself, while I surreptitiously undo my belt a couple of notches. Suddenly, both men are looking to me for the next move. It dawns on me that some kind of unwritten protocol has forbidden either of them to speak first; indeed, the entire meal has passed without anyone saying a word since the *somtam*—not even "Please pass the *nam pla*." Zinna coughs. Vikorn coughs too, staring—almost glaring—at me. I reflect to myself that one of the great bugbears of conferences of this nature is that nothing is written down—there are no minutes and no agenda—and on the last occasion we got into hostilities before the meeting opened, so there is no historical format to follow. To make matters worse, I don't think either of them has any idea of the proper order of business. Somewhat dizzy, I stand up.

"Gentlemen," I say, then decide to display full consigliere authority by pacing the flagstones a little.

"This is a great historic occasion." They nod encouragingly. "For too long has our great Buddhist country been divided between the military and civilian disciplined services. How can this be? Didn't the Buddha himself favor commerce over war?" More encouraging nods from the old men, as if I were rehearsing for a school play. "And has not the whole of Asia benefited from a trade-friendly religion which has made our half of the world's population into such gifted businessmen and -women?" I pause to glare with righteous indignation. "And is it not a fact that after three hundred years of global militarism, starting with Clive of India, which our people never wanted — is it not a fact that only now is the West beginning to awaken to the need for peace, a need which Buddhism has been explaining to anyone who would listen for two and a half millennia?"

I pause again, frowning like Beethoven. "You see, the essentially sociopathic nature of modern corporations worldwide is easy to explain when one remembers it originated in the needs of professional opium traffickers, viz, the British East India Company under Clive. To see it as anything other than the expression of a criminal mind-set is catastrophically naïve. The long-term effect? The destiny of the world has been handed over to Gamblers Anonymous."

Some cautious enthusiasm now, from the old guys.

"And if we ask ourselves how it came about that red-faced primitives from the far Northwest managed to dominate and militarize the whole world for more than three hundred years, there really is only one answer: opium. Millions upon millions of tons of it. They grew it in India and shipped it to China under armed escort until twenty million Chinese were addicted."

I pause again because I've finally got the full attention of the two oldies, who have leaned forward in fascination. "By the nineteenth century the entire British Empire would have gone bankrupt without the narcotic. The French were similarly active in Indochina, the Dutch sold anything to anyone, the Germans tried to catch up, while the Americans stuck mostly to slavery. What do these countries all have in common? Only this: that through narcotics trafficking and trading in slaves they were able to invest in heavy industry that put them two hundred years ahead of the field, which has only now begun to catch up. But it's a macroeconomic strategy that can only be achieved by a united nation. Gentlemen, for the sake of the global economy, peace, and the evolution of our species, you must join together today in this great venture of sale and purchase—if you do not, the Cambodians or the Vietnamese surely will."

Well, I think that's done the trick in terms of putting it all in historical perspective; at least it's made me feel better about what I'm doing. Both men are now looking suitably self-righteous about the deal, with *Well-I'm-not-going-to-be-the-first-to-break-the-contract* looks on their hard old mugs.

I sit down again and adopt a less statesmanlike tone.

"The structure is a little complicated, but it's the best we can do on short notice. You both will agree to own equal shares in a trading company based in Lichtenstein. The trading company's bankers over there—based in Zurich, of course—will send the paperwork, which your lawyers will check. If all is in order, you will sign before notaries on a date and time to be approved by your astrologers, but in not more than five days from receipt of the documents. For the sake of simplicity, the value of each share will be one million dollars. You each will buy twenty shares, and you will bear the administrative and other costs and disbursements equally. As soon as forty million dollars has been deposited in the trading company's bank account, the bankers will issue an irrevocable letter of credit in that sum in favor of whatever person or vehicle the Tibetan specifies. The letter of credit will be held by a nominee whom you both trust. I will accept the responsibility if you wish to so honor me. In any case, the letter of credit will be brought to the site where the goods are to be tested. When chemists approved by yourselves have examined the product and found it to be ninety-nine per cent grade four in the agreed quantity, the letter of credit will be handed over to the Tibetan or one of his nominees. Are we all agreed?"

32

How did the meeting end? Answer: I don't know. Those two old pythons started knocking back the booze and reliving old battles as soon as I'd established substantial agreement on all terms of the proposed partnership and deal. Zinna had never owned a corporation before, so this was a brand-new ego adventure to get all puffed up about, and Vikorn had to gently dissuade him from designing the stationery; this wasn't going to be the kind of operation where you do a lot of letter writing. Vikorn, of course, owned hundreds of corporations in various corruption-friendly locations around the world, but his sophistication did not extend to letters of credit— his were still mostly cash-only sales—and this new business tool also excited *his* ego: he was keen to try it out on his partners in Miami, who bought most of his *yaa baa* and liked to tease him about being a third-world ignoramus. So they got drunker and friendlier and after a while out came the *jao paw*'s favorite fantasy tool: the pocket calculator. If the Tibetan was on the level, their markup of the product on delivery to Europe or America would be 200 per cent. Zinna saw an endless line of beautiful and cooperative young men visiting him in a six-star villa overlooking the Andaman Sea somewhere. Vikorn saw a massive global empire: he was not too old to go into something legal after the first five-year plan had leveraged his dough; maybe video games? In short, *farang*, both of them slipped amicably into that form of masturbation capitalism with which I am sure you are familiar, while I felt worse and worse. I couldn't stop thinking about all the people we were going to poison, and how black my karma was going to be. When the two of them were too drunk to notice, I persuaded one of Zinna's officers to find me a car to take me back to Krung Thep. He found a white Toyota limousine and a sergeant in fatigues to drive it. Then, just to honor his boss's high spirits, he threw in a motorcycle escort as well. His intentions were good, but the effect was to increase my self-disgust. In fact, I was searching my mind to find something about myself that I still liked when my cell phone rang.

"Call me back, I don't have any money," a woman's angry voice said in a UN accent.

The number on the log began with 977: Nepal. Not that there was any doubt about that. I called the number, and she let the phone ring for quite a while before she answered it.

In a hoarse, hard voice: "So, where the hell have you been?"

"Huh?"

"Thought you'd take advantage of a poor third-world girl while you had the chance, then just dump her like a Kleenex, didn't you?" She managed to insert a great, self-pitying clot of bloody, low-grade emotion into her tone, which had me frowning at the telephone, not believing what I was hearing.

"Tara?"

"The Chinese killed all my family. I'm an orphan, and I'm a cripple, too. Is that the kind of man you are, to use and abuse a girl who was only looking for love and shelter? If I still had a brother he would go over there and punch you on the nose." This was followed by what sounded like floods of tears.

"Tara, I can't believe this is you."

She let a couple of beats pass, then said in her normal voice, "It's okay, don't worry, I was exorcising a demon. It's good practice, you should do it too. Since the demon came from you, I thought you'd like it back. You felt slightly raped after our Tantric evening, didn't you? Since then I've had to deal with a whole stream of minor goblins from the Southwest. That's you. You must have been feeling like an abused teen to churn up those guys—you wouldn't believe how ugly some of them are."

"Tara, this is just crap. It's sheer low-grade, bargain-basement, boulevard occultism you're doing here."

"Oh, yes? Then how do I know you had a wet dream about me last night? You did, didn't you? And I can tell you exactly what you did to me in that dream. Listen."

I'm not telling you what she said next, *farang*, it's too embarrassing. I broke out into a cold sweat. "Tara, do one thing: at least admit you're in league with Tietsin, that way I can try to explain you rationally to myself."

"You know very well I never met him until you came into my life like a little orphan left on my doorstep. And what are you doing indulging in a need for rational explanations at this stage? You're not supposed to still be a novice."

I hesitated, then said, "Tara, that was the most fantastic sex I ever had. I mean it. I didn't understand what you were doing at the time, I admit that, but I've been thinking about it and I'm starting to understand. To sublimate like that really is the essence of Buddhism—it's just a little unnatural at first."

"What is?"

"Resigning yourself to only having one orgasm a year."

She giggled. "Try being a refugee—a lot of deprivations come naturally to us after a while."

I couldn't help myself; the question almost asked itself: "Tara, are you enlightened?"

"Who is ever going to say yes to that question, except a charlatan? Let's say I'm conscious of being free from suffering."

"An anesthetic for life? Congratulations. Must play havoc with lovers who aren't at your level."

"It was your idea, you made a pass at me, don't forget."

"I agree. I, of all men, should know the risks of an emergency lay. But let's say you owe me one."

"One what?"

"One question."

A pause. "Okay."

"Did you sleep with Frank Charles?"

A long pause.

"Is that a yes?"

"Yes."

"And you did it with him the same way you did it with me?"

"We said one question."

"Only you didn't distance yourself quickly enough, didn't snuff out the incipient affair."

"Stop it."

"You were younger, after all, and maybe not so disciplined, not so above female vanity that having a famous American director fall at your feet didn't still hold a teeny-weeny bit of temptation. I don't think he first visited Nepal because he wanted to make a movie. I think he decided to make a movie in Nepal after he met you."

"I'm hanging up."

"He fell, didn't he? Oh, he fell. You're not like any woman any non-Tibetan man has ever met. You're a fusion of the primeval wild and the enlightened future with no electricity in between. For this American brought up to believe that the answer to all anguish is to be found between the thighs of the perfect woman—the Madonna thing they all have—

the zipperless fuck that takes you to nirvana without having to meditate first: you were it, all of it, for him, that poor starved angry man from the spiritual third world."

"Detective, I'm not answering, haven't you noticed?"

"He couldn't get you out of his head. But there had to be something else to cause him to deteriorate like that. Something you did to him far beyond what you did with me, causing him to go up there to Kathmandu again and again—to meet you, was it? Or to pathetically pine for you? Or for you to do something to fix his head? He made you initiate him, didn't he? He knew to keep asking until you couldn't say no. And even though he couldn't have been less suitable, being emotionally stuck at the age of about thirteen, even so, you went ahead and irresponsibly shared your mantra with him. That's the real reason you got cold feet about me and called Tietsin. You didn't want déjà vu."

Silence. She had closed the phone.

She didn't kill him, though, I reflected into the silence. Even if it made psychological sense, which it doesn't, she could never get out of Nepal. I saw her travel document; with paper like that she had difficulty leaving Kathmandu, never mind international destinations. A *dakini* of the Far Shore, she is a stateless exile over here on the left bank, frostbitten and occasionally suspected of prostitution. Naturally, all that makes me crazier about her than ever.

33

This morning both Vikorn and Zinna e-mailed to ask me to download a portrait of Clive of India; so there he was for a moment, gracing my monitor in his powder, wig, and ruff, the Shropshire lad himself, that whoring, bloody, racist, suicidal, alcoholic, upwardly mobile, treacherous, opium-addicted narcotics trafficker who started globalism. I think the two of them will put him in a frame high up on a wall and *wai* him daily like any Oriental guru.

Now someone is calling using the 977 prefix. I stare at the screen, not sure who in Kathmandu I'm most afraid of at this moment, Tietsin or Tara.

"So, how did the meeting go?" It's Tietsin.

"Perfect. Everything is arranged. They've decided to entrust me with the irrevocable letter of credit, so you better be nice to me."

"Not a chance. If you run off with the dough we'll turn you into a louse in the anus of a rabid dog. And the date? We have a date?"

"The one you wanted." For the first time with

Tietsin I sense a normal human emotion on his part, like relief.

"Thank you, Detective. That's good. That date is good."

"You're sure you can bring in that much at one time without getting caught?"

"Of course. I'm a magus, aren't I?"

"Where is the drop-off point?"

He snorts. "You still think I'm some airhead from the mountains who doesn't know scat about shifting smack, don't you?"

"Okay, don't tell me. But how are we going to know where to meet you?"

"I'll tell you exactly ten minutes before delivery. Just make sure you have fast transport, because we're not going to wait more than five minutes for you to show up. One thing about poison, you can always find a buyer."

"Doctor Tietsin, I have just one question, a personal one. As a devout Buddhist, isn't there anywhere in your mind just the slightest doubt—"

"No."

"What are you going to do with the money?"

"How many times do I have to explain? I and my movement are going to invade China."

I sigh. "That's just nuts, and I know you don't believe it. You may be crazy, but you're not stupid. How can anyone invade the most dynamic economy in the world, which happens to own a million-man army, with forty million dollars?"

"Ever hear of Gandhi? And there was a guy named Jesus who was supposed to have transformed the world, although the reportage is suspect. They didn't have armies, they used words instead—*and they weren't even Buddhist*. What kind of Theravada wimp are you, anyway?" he says, and hangs up. When I angrily call the number again, I get the engaged tone. When I try Mimi Moi's number, I get exactly the same tone. Must be my cologne. I'm so depressed, I'm taking a cab to the morgue.

I hate autopsies and avoid them whenever I can. If not for the urgency I now feel about the Frank Charles case, I would not dream of being here, in the morgue, while Doctor Supatra is at work on a cadaver. Actually, most cops feel the same way; the only person who really enjoys autopsies is the pathologist. For them it's a wonderful hunt, which 99 per cent of the time ends with a successful conclusion: they find the cause of death. It's an adventure that combines science, art, instinct, and extreme drama, and usually only lasts a day or so. Don't let them fool you with their graveyard demeanors, those pathologists are very happy campers: lords of death to whom cops like me pay reluctant homage.

The good doctor in her medical greens is at this moment showing two students, also in masks and coveralls, how to turn a corpse over. Sounds easy? Just try it at home. In death even the most upright citizen turns into a slippery character. If you do need the information one day, here's how: you wrap an arm around the inner thigh opposite to you, place the other hand under the neck and up and around, then use your weight to push the body over in a roll. The deceased in this case is a slim Thai girl, but I've seen the doctor heave over dead men three times her size.

"Now you try," she tells one of her students, then turns to me for the first time. Her mask covers the whole of her face.

"I've come about the Frank Charles case," I tell her.

"Him! He was gigantic. I couldn't roll him over at all, I had to call for help."

There's a scream from her students, who together have managed to get their cadaver into quite a cliff-hanger: her head and upper body have slipped over the side of the autopsy table; it looks like she is trying to commit suicide. The doctor shakes her head and returns to the job at hand. "You'll have to put on a mask and talk to me while I'm working, if you're really in such a hurry. Better put on some coveralls as well, I don't want to be responsible if you catch something from the corpse."

So now I'm all in green with a mask and no more than six inches from the corpse, and I'm still having trouble believing the kid is dead. Her face is not bloated; she's really quite beautiful, probably in her early twenties. When Supatra takes her boning knife and makes the great Y incision from above the breasts to the solar plexus, then down to the lower abdomen in a single stroke, cutting deeply through the flesh right down to the bone, I turn my face away. When I turn back, Supatra has lifted up the top flap and flopped it over the dead girl's face at an irregular angle; it looks like a wind has blown the corner of a scarlet drape over her head. Now the doctor has peeled away the flesh from the chest area and is using a pair of garden secateurs to snap open the rib cage.

"It's about the list of drugs the toxicologist found in the American's body," I say.

"Hm, quite a list. Traces of cocaine, cannabis, opium, and a few uppers of the prescribed kind." Supatra is a little breathless from the exertion with the secateurs. "It wasn't drugs that killed him though, nor was it the removal of the top half of his head. It was loss of blood from the way the perpetrator gutted him. Of course, to survive long term he would have needed a skull even if they'd left his guts intact."

I watch in revolted fascination while she digs her hands into the corpse and brings out a heart. "Check it for abnormalities," she tells her students as she passes it to them, "use your hands, change to thinner gloves if you have to at this stage, you need to develop your sense of touch, especially with hearts, livers, and kidneys: any hardening, lumps, gritty spots, undue fattiness—the eye can't tell you half as much as a good grope."

"What about the chunk the killer took out of the victim's brains for lunch?"

She cocks her head. "How do you know it wasn't breakfast or supper? I couldn't give a precise time of death. And to answer your question, no, the chunk taken out of the left lobe may have impaired quite a few functions, but it wasn't lethal."

"Okay, if it wasn't drugs that killed him, or the hole in his brain, surely something must have been used to knock him out while he was being scalped? You said in your report there was no sign of struggle."

"That's correct. I had the toxicologist check for all the usual anesthetics, sedatives, et cetera, and he didn't find any. There is no general check for drugs — you use a specific test for each chemical, and you need to have a good idea what you're looking for, because many drugs will be untraceable after a few days, either because they have decomposed or because they have combined with body chemicals to form some other substance." To her students: "Here's the liver. There's nothing wrong with it. Just handle it for a few minutes, start to get a sense of what a healthy one feels like, squeeze, that's right." She watches the student for a moment, then says, "Certainly, I was aware that something must have kept him quiet while the brain surgery was in progress. My guess was that given his size and probable life habits, a little opium and cocaine were not enough to sedate him. So I asked for special tests for various unusual drugs that have come onstream recently, and guess what? The toxi found tubocurarine chloride in his blood."

"That's what I wanted to ask about."

"It's quite exotic, used mostly in the U.S. and Japan as a neuromuscular blocker." She looks at me. "It's made from curare, obtained from a South American plant which jungle tribes use for arrow poison."

"What does it do?"

"Causes paralysis without loss of consciousness."

"But how would someone obtain it?"

"A well-connected pharmacist would be a minimum requirement. Even then, the pharmacist would normally have to explain to someone why they wanted it." We exchange glances.

She stops in her labors for a moment as if she has just remembered an interesting but minor detail. "One thing did strike me as unusual: the neatness of the work. As a pathologist I don't have to be particularly careful with the rotary saw, but whoever removed the skull of Frank Charles was in a class of their own. Even brain surgeons don't work to such fine tolerances."

Now she turns back to what is left of the young woman. The whole of the chest cavity is open, and most of the organs have been removed. A tube is draining the fluids that have washed down the stainless-steel table into the trough below. "So, everything is healthy. Just as I suspected. Now, this is how to hold the buzz saw. Always use both hands or it will run away from you."

It is similar in size and shape to any small circular DIY saw, though a little more gentrified. It makes a screaming noise that deadens just a tad when it bites into skull bone.

"Ha!" the doctor says when she has removed the

scalp. "Just as I thought. A massive subarachnoid hemorrhage caused by a burst brain aneurysm, caused, in all probability, by a serious overdose of methamphetamine. There would have been a pre-disposing weakness in the cerebral artery, probably congenital. The *yaa baa* would have sent the heart racing like crazy, putting pressure on the aneurysm, causing it to rupture. What a waste! Still, she most probably would have died young anyway—any serious exertion, especially from sport, would likely have caused the aneurysm to burst." She smiles. "Did you know *autopsy* means 'see for yourself'?"

"Thanks, Doctor," I say, and catch the look of happiness on her face: another successful hunt. It's a beautiful profession if you don't mind blood. When she has washed she takes me into her office, where we examine her report on Frank Charles on her computer. We've just about finished, when I say, "What's that, on page twenty-one, at the bottom?"

"Diamond fragment," she reads, and rubs her eyes. "That's right, I forgot. Apparently a fragment of industrial diamond was found, but we couldn't be sure where it came from, and anyway it had nothing at all to do with the cause of death."

"And this, on page three of the toxicologist's report. Beryllium. What's that?"

"Don't know, except that it's a kind of oil we found under his fingernails. Once again, it had nothing to do with the cause of death, so we didn't waste time on it."

It wasn't heroin, I'm telling myself in the cab on the way back to the station. I've quite forgotten about Frank Charles; I'm thinking about the anonymous dead girl on Supatra's autopsy table, her internal organs ripped out, her personality defined, so to speak, by her death, whence she derives a certain power over me, even though I had nothing to do with her demise. No doubt she was just a dumb kid who got handed some *yaa baa* and had no reason for not using it. But she was going to die young anyway, so was it really anyone's fault? Metaphysics aside, I feel awful. And I know exactly what kind of nightmare I'm going to suffer through tonight.

34

Ever tried calling your Zurich-based Lichtenstein bankers outside office hours? I mean, even half a minute after five p.m. on a Thursday? You can see why they're strong on clocks. I'm calling the main banking man dealing with the Lichtenstein trust in a small matter of forty million dollars, to tell him to go ahead and courier the documents we talked about when I first spoke to him about my special shipment of Lapsang souchong tea for wholesale to Europe and the need to set up a Lichtenstein trust for that very purpose—a transparent excuse he didn't blink at—and he's gone home. Nor will he answer his cell phone, and his assistant's cosmology is equally clockwork: she's gone home too. Finally, by going through the switchboard I get a secretary on overtime who knows what documents I'm talking about; she agrees to send them, emphasizing that she is using her own initiative and risking a reprimand and that she is an Ethiopian refugee whose English is not great. That done, there is nothing to do but wait for a couple of days. Without having to rush around town, my mind starts to dig one of those big dangerous black holes.

Why am I doing this? *Why?* My son is dead, I don't need to worry about college fees ever again, and my partner has left me to go to a monastery. *I don't need the dough!* But I'm stuck in this filthy continuum. I'm not even particularly afraid of dying. *But I'm stuck in this filthy continuum.* Last night I dreamed of future victims, all of whom looked like the girl on the autopsy table: vivid images of kids with giant hypodermic needles sticking out of their skulls. I'm not made for this line of work, and yet everyone thinks I am, including Vikorn, Zinna, and Tietsin.

Why not concentrate on the Fat *Farang* file, you want to know? Well, apart from wallowing in a dark mood of self-disgust, I've decided to let Doctor Moi sweat for a few days. I also need to rethink the whole strategy. So I decide to go to temple.

This time I go to the hyper-sacred Wat Bowonniwet. On my way in the back of a cab I think I'm too tense, too uptight, too scared for a successful meditation. But when I'm on my knees giving the Buddha the high *wai*, I feel Tietsin's blade wheel start to spin. It is different on each occasion; this time I conceive it as a great Ferris wheel with giant spadelike cutters lumbering toward me. I know not to give in to terror; I know I have to stand my ground. And it turns out that the extreme state of mind induced by the hallucination reveals my true nature: bitter. At bottom with me it is not old-fashioned greed like Vikorn's, or lust, like Zinna's—those two vices show at least a *desire* to be happy, however misguided. No, with me it has always been a clinging to bitterness as the last word on reality—like a modern thriller that leaves out all positive emotion and ends up as just a production line of death. But bitterness about what?

The blade wheel cuts a micron deeper with every turn. If I'm honest, the bitterness seems to have been there all along, a kind of reluctance, even at my age, to be fully born into this catastrophe called life. It has been lying there forever, this perverse reluctance, driving everything. Do you know what I mean, *mon semblable, mon frère?*

Two days later the documents have arrived from Zurich. Wow! Those banking lawyers really know how to pad! The old boys have to sign four copies with initials on every page, so the whole package—which I send out in neat A4-sized envelopes, plus red stickers with yellow arrows which tell them where to put their monikers—is about the size of a large hardback novel and just as heavy. When I get Lek to take Vikorn's copies upstairs and then send the other set to his army chum for onward trans-shipment to General Zinna, he lets his long skinny *katoey* arms sag under the weight. Then I have to nag and cajole both Vikorn and Zinna to actually sign the things; they're intimidated by the sheer size of the package and all that small print. Worst of all, they don't like using their ID cards when they go to the notary to sign. Also, Vikorn is nervous. The truth is that he has never dealt in such a large single shipment. Somehow, Tietsin got both old men into a mood of high bravado, and now that it's pay-up time, our godfathers are getting twitchy; they've never dealt with a Tibetan before. If, by some unforeseeable stroke of misfortune, they lost their forty million, they would both be in serious trouble. Zinna would be wiped out.

Finally, it's all done, and I send the stuff off to Zurich so they can register the corporation in Lichtenstein. I'm not sure there are any people in Lichtenstein; maybe there's just a large population of registered offices with a single robot to post letters and send them. Has anyone you know ever been there? You soon get into the did-they-really-land-on-the-moon mind-set, dealing with the virtual world of high finance. Then, out of the blue, a package addressed to me arrives at my home. It seems to have been sent by ordinary airmail from somewhere in Hawaii. I think: Hawaii? But the package makes the hairs on the back of my neck stand on end. Why is that? Oh, only because the bubblepak envelope is one of those designed exclusively for the shipment of DVDs. I am strangely reluctant to open it. I even leave it lying on the teak coffee table that Chanya and I bought at Chatuchak market on one of our lighthearted shopping sprees about a thousand years ago when the world was still innocent.

When I get to work, I tell myself I'm being quite girlishly silly, and after ten minutes staring at my computer monitor and consulting the online I-Ching and the Yahoo! astrology page, both of which are wildly enthusiastic about my love prospects today, I sigh and take a cab back home. When I pick the package up from the coffee table, I experience the same sensation as before: hairs standing to paranoid attention, something crawling up my back, a distinct premonition of death. Whose? Okay, okay, I'm opening it. Now I have it, an unmarked disk, shining brilliantly on one side; it is a Sony DVD, charcoal black on the reverse side with no title. I blow out my cheeks and scratch my ear before sliding it into my DVD player. At first I think it must be some kind of joke, for nothing appears on the screen. When I check the numbers flicking by on the counter, however, I see it must be a full-length movie of some kind. Finally, the monitor flickers into life—and there he is.

35

The Frank Charles standing before the camera is not quite as overweight as his cadaver. I think he must have filmed the introduction to his movie at least a year before he died. He appears to be looking directly at me when he says, "Hi, Detective Sonchai Jitpleecheep—unless something has gone badly wrong, you are the one watching this movie, and, from what I know of you, you are probably alone.

"I guess you never expected to hear from me, huh? I am assuming you are the one running the investigation into my murder, because you always get the *farang* murders in District Eight. But even if I'm wrong, you have certainly heard of me and my spectacular manner of death. You are aware of the existence of a film. If you found the DVD in my safe, you also discovered it was just a set of preliminary shots of Nepal: not what you were looking for at all. You and your colleagues have also failed to discover whodunit. That will all be explained in the next two hours. What you need to know right now, though, is: why you?"

What is interesting to me right now is that the camera follows Frank Charles as he paces a little with his jaw in his hand; he is not alone, therefore, although you would never know it from his posture of total self-absorption. He carries his weight well, as a big man can, and does not thrust his gut forward in arrogance; one gets some sense of what it must have been like to have lived in the skin of that big, male, energetic, once-superb American animal. From his body language one understands that, before something went badly wrong, the world had belonged to him. Now he thrusts his hands into the pockets of his oversized denim overalls; there is a microphone attached to one of the straps.

"It's ironic, because there is someone else who thinks she's the muse behind this work. Let's say she's mistaken. She's not the muse. She's what you might call a point producer—the one who makes sure certain vital props are at hand. No, I needed someone with your eye, Detective, the one I could not fool, even when I tried my damnedest."

He pauses and makes an almost comic gesture of humility and defeat. "I swear to God, Detective, that as far as I know there are only two people in the world who didn't think much of my first full-length movie. You and me. You saw the plagiarism—so did I. And in your review you had no mercy. The little scene I stole from Truffaut, those long interior shots that Bertolucci perfected, playing with color à la Robert Altman, outdoor shots from John Ford, suspense from

Hitchcock—and a lot of other thefts, too: you saw it all. You must have had one hell of a teacher at film school. Except you never went to film school, did you? That's another thing about you that told me you are the one: your permanent pariah status in your society. Not only are you a *leuk kreung*, a half-caste, but your mother's illustrious lovers taught you way above your station. One of them must have been an old-style French-movie buff, a real *Cahiers du Cinéma* type. Whatever. I'll never know what you will say about what you are about to see. That's not important. What's important is that you understand."

He lets a few beats pass. "You know what's tough about being a voice from the dead? Jealousy. If you are investigating the case, Detective, have you gone up to Nepal yet? Have you met Tara? Have you slept with her? Or is this all just gibberish to you? I'll never know. But what I do know is that you're a Buddhist, and quite a serious one. That also weighed on my decision to show you my beloved masterpiece. You see, my other muse is too much of a cynic; she will see the point but not the pain. You, though, with that uncanny intelligence and sensitivity everyone says you have—you are ideal. I bet you experience my movie just as if it were all happening to you."

He takes his hands out of his pockets and holds them behind his back.

"But the kind of Buddhism I almost got into doesn't bear much resemblance to yours. *Vajra*, the Tibetans call it. Thunderbolt Buddhism, usually translated as Apocalyptic or Tantric Buddhism. It's pretty heavy stuff, and that mantra Tara gave me really did my head in." He pauses. "But at the end of the day, you know, a man like me isn't going to be satisfied with mantras and mandalas; I'm just not that cerebral. And anyway, I belong to the great Western tradition of dramatic expression—and there's no drama in Buddhism, as far as I can see. No, this is how it happened to me."

He seems to falter, like a man shifting gears in his mind and fumbling a little—those might be tears in his eyes, it's hard to tell.

"I was up in Nepal one time, looking for Tara, who had turned invisible on me yet again, and I was that far gone in the disease we call love that I thought maybe if I meditated and spent time at Bodnath and generally turned myself into a Tibetan—maybe she would come back to me. And that, my friend, is no state of mind in which to meditate or make a movie. So I gave up, like a good spoiled Yank, and just wandered around Kathmandu for a while. It happened to be a holy day, that one in October when they make a lot of animal sacrifices. I stood in a crowd of Hindus and watched while the Brahmin priest slaughtered a goat by clamping its head in a stock and cutting it off with a big knife. Then he threw some of the meat on the fire in the center of the shrine. And it was all Technicolor, of course, the great orange flames, the huge vertical crimson *tikka* in the middle of the priest's forehead, his fantastic robes, the chants, the incense. Then when I looked around, I saw the whole square had been converted into a giant slaughterhouse, wherever I looked I saw shrines, priests, smoke, and goats—and for one dizzying moment I realized that most bourgeois of words, *surreal*, was not going to cut it; the squeals of the goats did not permit such an escape route."

He takes a moment to think.

"And it so happened there was one of those Hindus standing next to me who you meet all the time over there: the kind who wear old-fashioned spectacles, speak perfect English with a Welsh accent, and never tire of explaining their culture to you whether you're interested or not. And he told me that, properly understood, the priest officiating at the sacrifice was Brahma. Also, the fire was Brahma. Also, the god to whom the sacrifice was directed was Brahma. And also, the sacrifice—the goat—was Brahma. And Brahma was life itself, the whole cycle."

He stops to close his eyes in concentration, then swallows and begins where he left off.

"And in that tiny moment I understood. I understood how easy it is for a Westerner to play the priest, the god, the fire—anything but the goat. As Brahma, in other words, we are inauthentic; the big joke is that everyone else knows it except us. Let's face it, we much prefer to sacrifice others. Our extreme—you might say homicidal—aversion to pain and suffering makes us the ultimate apostates in the business of life, and this was what was making me so unhappy as an artist and as a man. I never really got to the *ecce homo* moment, when I might have stepped forth from the stone they made me out of. I guess an awful lot of men feel that way in their hearts at the going down of the sun, but I'm one who couldn't give up the struggle, though I tried to suppress it for thirty years and produced a whole bunch of schmaltzy junk in the process. So, for better or worse, this is me. Enjoy."

It is one of those movies which begin at the end of the story, then show you how everything has led up to the present moment. After the beginning, which is also the ending, we find ourselves in Kathmandu seven or eight years ago. It is possible to tell the age of the footage by reference to the body weight of the director, who is also the male lead. Here he is in his fifties, but looking quite a bit younger. Beardless, smooth-faced, handsome; he has about him the bounce, the enthusiasm of a much younger man. He is also smiling a lot as we follow him around Kathmandu. There is a light in his face which might be a form of insanity; the mountains seem to have gotten to him the way they got to me: that sense of landing in the cradle of consciousness itself. There's no doubt about it, that is a very attractive man, glowing with a kind of *metas*, or "loving-kindness," which has nothing to do with Buddhism, but is part of his natural state. Perhaps he doesn't know it, but it is that inner glow of his which has brought him success in life—and right now has brought him all the way to the Himalayas.

I am surprised at how early in the film Tara appears. It seems she is the liaison at the agency he is using for local support for his film. We see her by way of interpreter, using her UN English to listen to the famous Hollywood director, then translating back into Nepali and Tibetan. There is a silver *vajra* hanging on a simple nylon string around her neck. The director explains that he wants to do some filming up near the northern border, maybe even cross over into Tibet if he can get a visa from the Chinese. She explains that conditions are very harsh on the border, which is fifteen thousand feet high. People get altitude sickness at that level. And there is the problem of China itself. They do not much like Americans with movie cameras on the loose in Tibet.

The scene shifts to the mountains. We are very near that high border with Tibet; the landscape is unremittingly barren, with vast flat areas of purple shale fading into gray glacier and then snow. The shale fields aside, nothing is horizontal; mountains rule wherever you look. And up here our director-hero isn't looking so good. If he is not holding his head he is holding his stomach. He has almost no energy and even talks in slow motion. The only cure is to go back down a few thousand feet and wait for his body to adjust. But he is an impatient American, he won't wait. Anyway, he has only so much funding and he cannot afford a break in shooting.

These scenes take place in the presence of the supporting cast and others on the team. From time to time the camera focuses on the other actors, all of whom seem to be ragged Tibetans from the highlands. Unlike the director, they are unaffected by altitude or delay and seem unlimited in their capacity to hang out. Tara here is not merely an interpreter of words, but also an interpreter of men. She is suddenly the central figure, helping the Tibetans to understand the director, and insisting at the same time that the director try to understand the Tibetans. "But they're all so damn spiritual in the way they think, it's hard to get a practical idea across," he complains, only to receive a lecture from Tara to the effect that he isn't going to get anywhere if he doesn't show more respect and sensitivity. *Sure we don't think like you*, she seems to be saying, *and there's a damned good reason for that: we know better.* Eventually things reach a point where the director is too ill with altitude sickness to work. If he doesn't get out of the mountains within the next twelve hours he risks brain damage and death. Now we accompany him on the back of a yak led by the Tibetans, with Tara walking by his side.

The shots here are deliberately reminiscent of Jesus riding a donkey on the way to Jerusalem. We see from his face and posture that he really is very ill, and it is in this paranormal state that most of the rest of the film takes place. We enter flashbacks within the main flashback, but the collage is cleverly executed so the device does not intrude; on the contrary, the way he cuts scenes of his childhood with flashes of him in the Himalayas is brilliant.

But it's a strange kind of brilliance; you might call the whole movie the product of plagiarism taken to the point of genius. At some point in the editing he must have decided that the film would not go on general release, and therefore he was released from any need to obey the law of copyright. As a consequence he does not merely imitate, but blatantly cuts in whole scenes from other movies; for example, the mountains are often invoked by retro shots of James Stewart hanging in space in *Vertigo*. He even manages—and here we cannot deny his eccentric gift—to lift scenes from Truffaut in the original French, without jarring the viewer. You could say one of the subplots is his own obsession with cinema, which is almost pathological.

As the journey down the mountain progresses, however, with Tara walking effortlessly beside him as he's slumped over the yak's neck, we realize in the subtlest possible way that the incomparable Tara (we have already seen her remove her prostheses from her fingers: one of the many things about her, along with her *vajra*, over which the camera obsesses) is slowly but surely replacing film itself as his control center.

I think that to convincingly show a man dumping the obsession of a lifetime for a woman he has only recently met must be very difficult. Frank Charles succeeds only because he is telling the truth: this is exactly how it happened, one has no doubt about that. But his problem is that carnal desire competes with spiritual thirst: he yearns for her with every chakra, but especially the second. (The crotch chakra, *farang*.) And so it is in this near-death fragmented state on a narrow track in the high Himalayas that we are shown the various strands of personal history that have made the man. We see the barrenness of his early life in the Midwest, where his family owned a hardware store. His father is largely ignored; we focus on his Italian mother, from whom he inherited his Latin good looks and his passion; she is portrayed as an exotic Mediterranean songbird trapped in a utilitarian cage. We see him as a kid masturbating in protest against the uncompromising vacuum of a world filled with nuts, bolts, and screws, DIY and plumbing accessories, welding torches and huge stainless-steel hoppers for seed. We see him retreat into film, which can only be viewed in theaters in those distant days. He almost takes up residence in the town's only cinema.

I won't spoil the movie for you, *farang*. You never know, it might find its way on to the black market one of these days; I might even upload it onto one of the illegal file-sharing Internet sites. Suffice to say we are led by an ingenious sequence of cuts and shots to intimately understand the director's psychology, about which he is uncompromisingly honest. One surprise is the violence of his mind. His adolescence is not only filled with erotic imaginations, but moments of extreme rage as well. He knows not where this tendency originates, much less his bizarre gift for marrying exactly the wrong women. By the time we get to the end we are convinced that for him there is no other option; there is no way for him to retain his fragmented self, nor has he acquired the strength to change at root. Can art help?

Well, now I've taken you this far, I guess you'd be vexed if I didn't at least let you have the first scene, which is also the last:

It is that squalid room on Soi 4/4 where we first encountered him. At first his bearded face—he is at his most obese now, the beautiful young director buried under a flesh mountain—fills the whole screen. As he retreats from the camera, he mutters, "Anyway, it's less expensive doing it this way, a dummy would have cost too much."

The camera follows him in a brief tour of the room before he climbs with difficulty onto the bed, and now, finally, I understand the books. They were the one item whose purpose eluded me. I had thought they were a perverse tease by a deranged mind; now I see their amazing innocence. They are a confession not to murder, but to a crime which scarred his soul far more deeply: an inauthentic life.

Once he has propped himself up, he says, "Okay, focus the camera on the top of my head, make sure you've got me from the eyes up, I don't want any nose in this shot, but you have to angle it to take in the ear when the saw cuts above it: drama, I don't want this to be a boring shot, ha, ha. Now get the saw and come over here and wait. Remember everything we practiced during rehearsals. Don't duck down as you work, because the camera will catch your face and you'll be incriminated and this scene cannot be reshot, ha, ha."

A few moments pass during which he keeps his eyes closed, then: "Okay, I can feel the drugs working, my whole mind is slowing. That's when she said to start. Leave the camera now and come over here. If my head starts to slump you'll have to pull it back into the frame. Now, it should be possible for me to use my own strength to dig out the first few spoonfuls from the left lobe, the one that's been causing all the trouble for sixty years, but if I can't, you'll have to help me. Use one of your hands to guide mine, but make sure I keep hold of the spoon."

The hands holding the buzz saw are sheathed in surgical gloves of the ultra-thin, almost transparent kind; it is not possible to be sure, but I would say the hands are female — long, slim, and porcelain white. The glove successfully obscures the details of an unusual ring on the index finger of the right hand, which appears to be quite broad with tiny protuberances suggestive of gems. She proceeds slowly, taking great care not to damage the spectacularly filmatic arachnoid mater, with its great crimson webs of veins and arteries which feed the brain. When she is finished, she raises the skull, much like a waiter at Maxim's might reveal a great dish by whipping off its cover.

"Did I just experience liftoff?" Frank Charles asks in a groggy voice.

* * *

334

What am I thinking? I'm thinking, *Poor Sukum*. I've solved the case for him after all, and with the best Buddhist will in the world it's going to be hard to let him take the credit. Anyway, it's a suicide, so what credit is there to claim? This isn't the stuff that leads to fast-track promotion. It's kind of funny in a sense, but I'm not laughing. The film might be a masterpiece in its own weird way, but for my money, the genius lies in the introduction. The straight, honest, naked confession of a life of luxurious failure has hit a nerve with me; I'm haunted. I send a copy to the FBI by e-mail attachment, then I call Sukum.

36

For the sake of good housekeeping, I need to follow up a little on the Fat *Farang* suicide. After all, records already show that I've interviewed Doctor Moi in connection with the file, so I really need to have her comments on the movie. Then there's the little detail of the familiar hand holding the buzz saw, which I cannot simply ignore. Also, let's face it, every cop loves to bust a triple-A liar.

It was Moi herself who suggested we meet at the Starbucks in the Emporium, a shopping mall on Sukhumvit, which used to be state of the art until they opened the Paragon at Silom. You can only understand the Asian passion for shopping malls when you realize you didn't invent them, *farang*, we did. You added the air-conditioning and the coffee, for which we are most grateful. For the rest, it's the local street market all over again.

Starbucks here is an Atlantic island in the middle of a Pacific Ocean of cooked-food stalls, ice-cream stands, pharmacies, cutlers, bathroom specialists, and, most important of all, vendors of electric rice cookers.

Behind me is a Japanese supermarket, somewhat on the pricey side and therefore frequented mostly by HiSo Thais, Japanese, Koreans, and *farang*. Shopping there is a treat. All over Asia no shopper is ever required to empty their own trolley at checkout; here, though, Japanese rules apply, and you not only have your trolley lovingly discharged before your eyes, but also cop a high *wai* and extra-special *sawatdee-krup*-with-smile from the beautiful clerk, who really does convince you she's pleased to see you.

Just for the record, *farang*, I am not making an invidious comparison with your supermarkets (where they make you feel like a shoplifter with previous convictions who has to be watched all the time).

The café is no more than a large stand with lounge chairs open to the rest of the mall, so while I'm waiting for Moi, who is late as usual, I sit at a table and watch the world for a moment. I see a TV personality who does a lot of commercials, and a senior banker with his young mistress: he rents a suite in the apartments attached to the mall; the girl is so much the exquisite light tan Barbie doll of his dreams that one cannot doubt she has enjoyed previous lifetimes as a banker's moll.

Now here is an Isaan family: the woman battling a feeling of inferiority with brute defiance and a permanent frown, the man looking skinny and humble and nostalgic for his rice field, the kids like miniature tanks which go shooting off in every direction, fall over, come shooting back; they inherit rubber bodies in Isaan. There are plenty of Sikhs, Hindus, Moslems from the South, middle-aged *farang* with their local squeezes, some white women politely waiting to reclaim their men and move to another country; a couple of Thai dykes with spiky cropped green and crimson hair hold hands with exaggerated affection. There are plenty of middle-aged gay *farang* with obedient local slaves, too. Now here's a Nigerian family, the mother in national costume with bright mauves and oranges with a purple turban. There is on average one humble, smiling, lazy Thai sales assistant for each shopper; when there are no customers the boys stage mock kung fu fights in the refrigerator section while the girls apply cosmetics and gossip.

I sit back in the armchair and wait. When she is more than twenty minutes late, I stand up to stroll around for five minutes and check the escalators. When I peer down onto one of the lower floors, I see Moi, her tall, slim figure with long hair tied loosely back with a silver clip; she is wearing a silk blouse the color of old gold over black leggings and seems to be involved in some kind of dispute with her maid, who is carrying some packages. I guess the Doctor has been shopping. Both women seem angry; I'm surprised at the intensity of the maid's expression—Moi seems slightly scared, but gesticulates upward, in my direction. Finally, she shrugs, turns her back on the maid, and gets on the escalator. I rush back to my armchair, but stand to greet her when she arrives. My

338

problem, at this moment, is that I have not yet decided whether or not to start by telling her about the DVD someone sent me from Hawaii. I had decided to play it by ear, but now I'm not at all sure how to guide the conversation. I watch while the Doctor orders a peppermint mocha at the stand, then comes to sit opposite me in one of the armchairs. She is in an unusually alert mood; her smart black eyes take in everyone in a couple of glances, then check me. I have the unnerving feeling that she knows something about the package from Hawaii, and that that was what she was arguing about with her maid. We exchange pleasantries, but when I say nothing about the case, she becomes uneasy. Finally, she says, "You wanted to see me, Detective? I am hoping you have good news for me? An intervention with the disciplinary committee would be nice."

I nod slowly, then take from my jacket pocket my secret weapon of the morning. It is an A4-sized piece of paper with a color printout of a still from the movie. I lay it in front of her on the coffee table and stare at her staring at Frank Charles propped up in bed with a buzz saw cutting into the side of his head. The saw is held by a gloved hand. The hand is long and slim, and one can speculate that the wide band on the index finger of the right hand is silver and set with eight tiny gems.

Moi's porcelain skin has turned still paler. I am fascinated by the elegance with which she raises both hands to her face and presses them against her cheeks.

For a moment I am looking at a woman looking at a personal catastrophe; but she's tough. She recovers immediately, looks up at me, and cocks an eyebrow: *What about it?* I'm not standing for any gimmicks, though, and keep my expression firm. When she tries to pick up the picture to give it back to me, I place both my hands flat on top of it, keeping it there on the coffee table like a piece of evidence so crucial it is radioactive. She takes the cue from my grim determination, then suddenly reaches for her black Gucci handbag to take out a gold pillbox. It is one of those reactions of hers, like the crooked smile, which makes you wonder if everything she's done and said so far is somehow fake. She pops something bright crimson into her mouth and washes it down with a gulp of peppermint mocha. While she is doing so, I point to the hand holding the saw, outline its length with my finger, and come to rest on the ring. She takes a deep breath.

"There's nothing you can prove with this," she says, avoiding my eyes. "Nothing at all."

I nod. "No, I agree. This proves nothing. No judge or jury would draw conclusions from this. But a cop can. A cop can use it to give direction to his investigation. A cop could ride this piece of paper all the way to a full-blown house search—and worse. I could use this as a very good reason to investigate every tiny detail of your life. Assisting suicide is a crime." I raise my eyebrows.

She frowns hard at the photograph, looks away toward the electric rice cookers, seems to come to a conclusion, and nods. "I'll help you, off the record. But I want immunity for myself and my maid. After all, we're talking about a suicide."

I acknowledge the last point with a nod. "First, I'd like to know—is this the reason you refused to show me the movie? Could this be the reason you won't let it be shown even in private viewings? That surprised me above everything else, when I thought about it. After all, if you really wanted to honor the dead, you would want the genius of his last work to be available to the world."

She ignores the question. "I'd like to know where you got this—do you have the whole movie, or only this still?"

I shake my head. "Don't make me say, *I'm the one who asks the questions.*"

A flash of anger crosses her long face, but she smoothes it over with a casual exercise of will. She gives a theatrical sigh. "I suppose I'm in your hands, Detective." She looks around the shopping mall. "This is hardly the best place to talk. If I'd known you were going to pull this trick, I would never have suggested meeting here."

I follow her gaze. It all rather depends on how your sense of security works. To be sure, there are plenty of people around, and it is even possible someone could be eavesdropping; on the other hand, nobody knew we intended to meet here, so it is unlikely we are being spied on. When I catch Moi's expression, though, I see that it is more the need for privacy that

341

is motivating her. I do not say, *How about the police station?*

She fishes out a super-slim silver cell phone and presses a single button. When she speaks, it is not in Thai or English. I am not an expert, but I would bet Wall Street against a Thai mango that it is the Teochew dialect she's using. Now she has closed the phone. "I told my maid to take a taxi home — we've been shopping. But then you knew that. We saw you spying on us." She gives a grim smile. "My car and driver are in the garage downstairs."

It is, of course, a dark blue Benz with a driver in fawn livery designed to intimidate traffic cops and anyone else prone to get in the way. The driver is gaunt, and I doubt there is a single Thai gene in him. I note how casually she exercises her authority, using the Teochew dialect; as with the maid, these two, also, go way back. But there is a sliding glass divider which enables her to shut out the driver altogether as we emerge from the garage into the gridlock on Sukhumvit. After a couple of minutes I have to admire her discretion; surely in all Bangkok there could not be a better or more secure place to hold an intensely private conversation; no one can get to us here, barricaded as we are by a filthy bus on our left, a builder's truck on our right, private cars straight ahead, and traffic backed up behind us all the way to the river. The gridlock is so dense even motorbike taxis are at a standstill, their riders fretting, noses and mouths covered. Pollution radiates steadily and vertically.

Moi looks straight ahead into the infinite traffic. When she finally clears her throat, she begins with the immortal words, "You are half Thai, perhaps there is enough Asian blood in you to understand there is such a thing as the world of the dead?"

I think I was prepared for anything except that sentence. I give her a double take and say, "World of the dead?" But she seems not to hear me. On the contrary, she is sitting bolt upright with a grimace of concentration on some internal object. Then she starts to talk. She is leaning forward slightly, utterly absorbed in some inner vision, and her words seem to be an earnest attempt to describe what she is seeing. Unfortunately, she is speaking in Teochew, so I cannot understand a word of it. Carefully, so as not to interrupt her trance, I reopen the glass partition a couple of inches, so the driver is exposed to her words. His reaction, after a couple of minutes, is to maneuver the Benz to the inside lane, then, when the traffic finally starts to move, he turns into a side *soi*. Now he has picked up his cell phone and is making a call. When he closes the phone, he turns to me. "You better go. The maid will come to take care of her. She took a bright red pill when she was with you, didn't she?"

"Yes."

The driver shakes his head. "It's opium based and the worst in her collection. Every time she takes it she goes into a trance and talks to her ancestors. She's not really here at all. You better leave, she can be quite unpleasant when the effects wear off."

343

I see that for some reason he doesn't want me to be here when the maid arrives. I say okay, get out, and start to walk back to the gridlock on Sukhumvit. After a few yards, I turn to look back. The driver is in the car again behind the wheel. He has opened the partition all the way and is listening with rapt attention to her bulletin from the Far Shore.

37

Sukum vomited at the end of the movie. He watched it all through with unnerving intensity, then threw up where he sat on my floor with the laptop. I had to fetch a towel, then wait while he took a shower and changed into some of my clothes, which are too big for him. All this seemed to take place in a time-free zone, with him in a kind of trance after the film, moving slowly and saying almost nothing. I can understand why he might have been revolted or shocked, but Frank Charles's masterpiece seems to be having a different kind of effect on him. I sense that Sukum understands it on a deeper level than I am able to penetrate. But he's not a movie buff at all; I don't think he's ever watched anything more challenging than *Spider-Man*.

When we emerge from my house, it's raining and I remember we are in for the fallout from some gigantic tropical storm that has been pummeling Vietnam. The sky is slate gray, and the winds from the east are shaking the tops of trees like rag dolls. In a cab on the way to the station, I find his silence unnerving

345

and try to talk about the case. "What about Moi's other two husbands, the ones who survived—did you investigate them when you were trying to nail her?"

"Sure," he grunts.

"And?"

"The first marriage lasted four years, the other six months. Her first husband was a Hong Kong Chinese. The second an American."

I note that he's answering more like a suspect than a cop, giving the minimum of information for each question, but I let it ride. "Four years? It's hard to imagine Moi sticking out a marriage for that length of time."

"She didn't. She was still young and trying to fit into the rules of her class, so she pretended the marriage was working. In fact, it failed after the first few months. Her husband found excuses to travel to Hong Kong and Taiwan a lot and after a while only visited Thailand rarely, until they formally announced they were divorcing."

"And the other, the American?"

Sukum allows himself a thin smile. "That guy was no fool. He got the vibes early on and totally freaked after a year. He jumped on a plane to the States, but kept up some kind of business connection."

I say, "Business connection?" as any cop would, but Sukum won't look me in the eye. "A business connection with the ex-wife, isn't that something we need to explore?"

"Why?" Sukum says, looking out of the window.

"We're not investigating her, are we? We have a suicide, right?"

I decide not to press the point. "And the other two, the ones who died?"

"One was English; he died of a heart attack when he was only in his late thirties. The other was also *farang*, a Frenchman, he was hit by a small truck on Soi Eleven. Moi was out of the country on both occasions, which made everyone suspicious, but the autopsies didn't throw up anything sinister so there were no serious police investigations."

Detective Sukum falls into a heavy silence once again, as if he has returned to a place in which Frank Charles's last movie plays over and over. Finally, I say, "What is it, Detective? I know it's a pretty bloody ending to that film, but you're a cop, for Buddha's sake."

I think he will not drag himself out of his trance, he takes so long to answer. After about five minutes he seems to hear my question for the first time, and turns his face to stare at the streets through the curtain of rain. Already the drains are overflowing with the volume of water, turning the street into a dirty yellow river. Sukum says, "She killed him long before he finished the movie. She sapped his strength, stole his soul. That's why he had to die—that big speech at the beginning, that's just a *farang* caught in a spider's web and trying to be smart and rational about it."

"Moi? How can you know that?"

"It's what she did to me," he says, and holds his

347

head with both hands. "The more I worked on her case, the slower my mind became. She was turning me into a zombie. D'you know how many times I screwed up the paperwork to get her prosecuted on tax evasion? And a thousand little things went wrong with my private life. My marriage collapsed, and now it's just a cold, empty sham. Then she had the tea lady at the station slip me that LSD. Sure, I had a bad trip, but there was a lot more than that behind it. It was a bad trip that's lasted nearly ten years. My life has never been the same since I investigated her. I've had no luck at all. Every day is hard work, battling demons at every turn. I've tried every kind of amulet—cat's eyes, antlers, khot stones, Buddha images. I even had a *salika* inserted under my skin. And Buddha knows how many monk baskets I've donated."

His fear of Moi is so tangible, I reach out to touch his arm. He turns eyes on me that could be described as limpid pools of paranoia. "Look, maybe you were right from the start. This case has your name all over it. I want you to have it. When I get a chance I'll ask the Old Man to formally sign it over to you so everyone will know you solved it, not me." His eyes contract somewhat; he seems to be wrestling with guilt when he adds, "I'm sorry."

When I continue to stare at him, he says, "You still don't get it, do you? You lost control of this investigation the moment you visited her at her house. You just haven't realized it yet. You have no idea how powerful she is." He lets a few beats pass. "Of course, as a cop I could never tell anyone. They would have kicked me out for reasons of mental health. Or snuffed me. I'm telling you now because you're already caught in her trap." He lets a couple of beats pass, then adds, "I think you know what I mean."

Actually, I don't have a clue what he means. The case is over, isn't it? A suicide is a suicide. I'm even more mystified later that day, when Lek sidles up to my desk with a peculiar expression on his face. He makes as if to lean over my monitor, then drops something on my desk, which looks like a piece of paper screwed up in a ball. When I catch Lek's eye, he shrugs. I sense the need for secrecy, so I whisper, "What's that?"

Lek whispers back, "Don't ask me, darling. I'm not even allowed to tell you who sent it."

I frown. "Who sent it?"

"I'm not allowed to tell you." At my stern glance he starts to melt, then giggles. "Who d'you think? He made me swear on my next thousand years of karma not to tell you, but here's a hint: it's a *he* and he owns a Toyota."

"Sukum? Has he gone totally over the edge?" I cast a glance in the good detective's direction. He appears to be fixated on a file he is studying.

Lek shrugs. "I was beginning to wonder if you two had fallen in love and decided to use me as a go-between. I mean, that's what *katoeys* are for, really, isn't it? We're just life's eternal voyeurs, good for carrying messages but not for anything more." He is giving me one of his prize pouts. I cannot help grinning while I dismiss him. When I flatten out the ball of paper I see it is a printout from Wikipedia:

Padparadscha *is a pinkish-orange to orangey-pink colored corundum, with a low to medium saturation and light tone, originally being mined in Sri Lanka, but also found in deposits in Vietnam and Africa. Padparadscha sapphires are very rare, and highly valued for their subtle blend of soft pink and orange hues. The name derives from the Sinhalese word for lotus blossom. Along with rubies they are the only corundums to be given their own name instead of being called a particular colored sapphire.*

I am scratching my head. Now I'm carefully tearing the paper into shreds and throwing the pieces into the bin under my desk, in accordance with Sukum's furtive instructions. When, about half an hour later, I see Sukum get up to go to the men's room, I follow and stand next to him at one of the booths. He instantly moves as far away from me as he can. When I say softly, "Detective," he raises a hand, puts a finger over his lips for a brief moment, then zips up and exits without a word.

38

Sorry, *farang*, if I've gotten you excited about Frank Charles all over again; today it looks as if I'm con-sigliere for the duration.

Zurich/Lichtenstein just called, and would you believe the Swiss banker, who speaks better English than the Queen of England, and with an even snottier accent, actually scolded me for bullying his Ethiopian receptionist into sending the documents, because now he's received them it is obvious they were incomplete?

"Incomplete? The whole package weighed more than two pounds."

"She forgot to include a power of attorney."

"I saw about five different powers of attorney."

"But none of them in your favor. For you to be legally able to do what you are doing—not that I'm making any assumptions as to what you are doing—although everything is subject to attorney-client privilege anyway—as I say, for it to be legal and aboveboard, I need to see original powers of attorney from both share-holders in your favor."

I'm not keen. The thought of asking either Vikorn or

Zinna to go off to the notary with their ID cards all over again is daunting. Zinna, in particular, has been expressing doubts about trusting me with so much responsibility. Vikorn's spies report the General is "quite wired." Read: bag of nerves. The wording of the power of attorney is not without difficulties, either. It gives me absolute power over forty million dollars, for example. I'm not sure even Vikorn will be sympathetic, so to avoid a face-to-face confrontation I send both old men a translation of the power of attorney in Thai, with a notice that this is urgent business. I am feeling exposed, but can't quite put my finger on it. When, after fidgeting for an hour or so, I don't hear from either of them, I try to call Vikorn, but Manny says he's not available. Not available? We're talking about the deal of the year, if not the decade, and suddenly the boss is not available?

Paranoia comes easily to a mind that has been well prepared. My own has started revisiting the Thai translation of the Lichtenstein power of attorney. Even in English the language is intimidatingly absolute, using phrases like "each and every manner or thing of any kind whatsoever including but not limited to . . ." and then there's the bit which says, "the said Sonchai Jitpleecheep shall be assumed to be acting with the full approval and authority of the grantor who will support, confirm, and endorse every such action of whatsoever nature and shall not under any circumstances seek to deny, block, alter, or amend any disposition of the said funds . . ." Well, in Thai, which tends to repeat important phrases so everyone is clear about them, and which has a certain way of emphasizing absolute power, probably due to Sanskrit influence, the whole thing sounds even more stern, like I'm being appointed the viceroy of India or something. Let me be frank: a poorly educated army type who has spent his career in the mind-set of a gorilla hunched over a sack of bananas might find this legal jargon quite threatening. Indeed, said gorilla might decide it is being ripped off. It does not help when I call Manny and she reports that Vikorn has been on the phone to Zinna for an hour. It was an hour ago that I e-mailed the Thai translation of the power of attorney. I feel a stroll coming on.

Out in the street I feel better for a moment. Everything seems normal, the cooked-food stalls are all set up and ready to do police business: it is shortly before noon. The worst thing I could do would be to start running for no reason other than self-generated terror. Is this what they call a nervous breakdown? It's weird, the way I seem to have lost control over my legs. *The worst thing you can do is start to run, it will look bad.* The stalls are passing at an accelerated speed as I walk faster and faster. Something is saying, *No, not like this, don't go out like this, like a crass coward, a fool running from shadows, trying to flee his own mind.* So I apply that thing called will. It is like finding an iron bar in the middle of a brawl, and using it to cosh the enemy: I use this thing called *will*, whatever it is, to beat down the accelerated heartbeat, the jumping nerves, the overheated imagination, the legs which at the moment want only to run.

Okay, I'm at the end of the street and everything is under control, except I'm inexplicably terrified. I tell myself this is crazy, there is no one there, no one checking, no one in the street is interested in me at all. *Oh yeah? You just sent a document to two of the most senior mafiosi in Thailand requesting them to hand over control of forty million dollars, and you think nobody is watching you?* When I force myself to walk back to the station at a reasonable speed, I look up at Vikorn's window. Sure enough, the Old Man is there, staring down at me. When I get back to my desk, Manny calls: "Get up here."

Now I'm standing in front of the Old Man, who is behind his desk. A cold sweat has broken out over my face and hands. But I haven't even done anything. Vikorn lifts a document from his desk and waves it at me. It is the Thai translation of the power of attorney. "Kind of heavy, isn't it?"

"Yes," I splutter, "that's the way *farang* lawyers do things. I didn't draft it."

He is looking at me curiously. "It gives you exclusive power over forty million dollars. You could do a lot of damage if you abscond. You would wipe out Zinna and cripple me."

"I know," I groan. "I just knew he would take it the wrong way. What can I do?"

Vikorn stands up, comes around his desk with his hands in his pockets, looks me up and down. "I saw the way you were walking, down in the street."

"You saw the way I was walking?" My hands are clammier than ever.

"Yes, I saw the way you were walking."

He is now very close. "How was I walking?"

"Like a man thinking of running." He puts a hand on my shoulder to force me deeper into the chair and gazes at me for a long moment. "It's not really Zinna who is making the green balls run down your trouser legs."

"No? So what is it?"

"The power of forty million dollars. You are a monk manqué, you have survived so far by dodging reality. Your life can only be sustained as long as you believe your hands are clean. But they're not. In truth, nobody's are, but people like you, dreamers, like to kid themselves. Well, now you can't kid yourself anymore, can you?" He leans over his desk to pick up a bundle of documents in English from his in-box. "Here." I see they are the powers of attorney, signed and notarized by both Zinna and Vikorn. I look up at him, baffled. "You said it was hyper-urgent, so Zinna and I both got notaries to come to our offices, and Zinna sent me his copy by motorcycle messenger. We were afraid you would scold us again for being third-world morons who don't understand high finance, so we jumped to it. Now you are a plenipotentiary for forty million bucks. Careful how you spend it."

"Th-, th-, thanks," I say.

He is merciless. He won't stop staring at me, but he won't dismiss me either. Finally, he says, "It's okay, Zinna isn't afraid you'll cheat us."

"He isn't?"

"No. He's afraid you'll snap and do something even stupider, like have a nervous breakdown. That would really be hard to deal with. A fraud we could handle in the usual way; a psychotic meltdown would be a problem."

"It's guilt," I explain. "Guilt is warping my mind."

Vikorn frowns. "Guilt? About what?"

"Oh, nothing in particular," I say, shaking my head. How could anyone possibly feel guilty about trafficking in forty million dollars' worth of smack? What a pale and cloistered fellow I must be. "Like you say, I'm a monk manqué. May I resign?"

"No," Vikorn says.

"But it must be such a liability to you, having an honest man as consigliere."

Vikorn points to the documents. "Honest? Those papers prove you're a crook, like the rest of us. Maybe that's what you were trying to run away from."

Obviously, he is enjoying this most excruciating initiation of mine. He even lets me have a jolly *Take care, now* as I leave his office with the powers of attorney.

Back at my desk, though, a sense of relief sets in. Apparently I'm not going to be kidnapped and tortured today. I order an iced lemon tea from the tea lady, and sit back for a moment. Now another side of my mind is getting creative. Forty million! Imagine. I could get on a plane to Zurich right now, have the dough transferred to a numbered account, dedicate—say—ten million to personal security (there are semisecret corporations which employ people like retired SAS and Navy

SEALs), buy five different properties in five different countries, all in proxy names, and live happily ever after, right? Wrong. Not with an imagination like mine. When my endlessly calculating mind projects itself into such a future, I see only sleepless nights during which I am convinced the maid is a spy for Zinna and the security guards all secretly work for Vikorn. Forget it. Cowardice will keep me an honest consigliere.

The silver lining to this unnerving day comes in the unlikely form of a text message from Sukum:

Keep tonight free. You will be contacted.

Except that I'm not supposed to know it's from Sukum; he has used someone else's SIM card. I let that cook in the right lobe while the left organizes the dispatch of the powers of attorney. Even this minor chore is not without complications. I certainly cannot use the police dispatch department, nor can I have a courier company visit the station. Now I have to lie about where I'm going—suddenly I am harboring a kind of internal schoolmistress who frowns at every tiny transgression—and I feel quite Macbethian as I sneak out to get on the back of a motorbike to go find a FedEx or DHL courier office: *Returning were as tedious as to go o'er,* or something like that. At the same time I am able to tell myself that all I am doing at this moment is sending off a bunch of legal documents to a lawyer in Zurich. I'm a white-collar gangster. So why do I feel so awful?

It happens there is a FedEx office not far from Nana. After I've sent the docs I feel the need for a beer, so I hang out for an hour at a bar at the entrance to the plaza. It's too early for the go-go bars, and the girls who serve in the beer bar are not especially pushy, although any of them would "take a shower" with me at one of the short-time hotels if I asked nicely. Suddenly they all seem so innocent. Even the older, more hardened women who have been on the Game for a decade reveal themselves to me as essentially innocent: women who got stuck in the continuum of prostitution but never really allowed it to contaminate their souls. I'm in a bad way, and the best future I can see for myself would be something totally clean and spiritual with Tara. Indeed, she has suddenly popped into my mind as a perfect representation of a pure human soul: inconvenient proof that such a thing is possible in this filthy lifetime.

For the first time in the Fat *Farang* Case I'm actually pleased to hear from Sukum, even though he is using yet another anonymous SIM card. His text reads,

Under the bridge near the Port Authority buildings at Klong Toey tonight at ten p.m.

The bridge is directly opposite Mimi Moi's house on the Chao Phraya River.

39

We are waiting under the bridge at Klong Toey. Sukum has not shaved today and is wearing baggy army-surplus shorts, an old black T-shirt, and flip-flops. He is doing *river peasant*, in other words, and flatly refuses to say where we are going. On the other hand, he has made it clear that he is risking life and limb by taking me to wherever he is taking me; he will not confirm or deny that Mad Moi's house is our destination.

The ferryman, when he arrives, is stunningly ugly. His canoe is old and a couple of the seats are smashed, as if it has been rescued from a wreck; his bare arms and chest are covered in prison tattoos and there are vicious facial scars which spell *knife fight* to a cop's eyes. He doesn't speak when we climb into his boat, and starts the tinny little outboard with a vicious pull on the starter cord. We cross the broad black river in silence except for the motor, which the boatman cuts when we are about a hundred yards from Moi's jetty. Now there are only the faintest river sounds: the diminutive wash of the boat's bows, a fish or water rat breaking the surface, voices from the opposite shore faintly carrying across the river. Moi's house is in darkness. Instead of aiming for the jetty with the motor cut, however, the ferryman takes out an oar and maneuvers us silently around a headland so that we end up tied to a stump of tree, facing Moi's place across the water. I watch in disbelief as Sukum reaches into a bag he has brought and shows me a pair of night-vision binoculars. He raises them to his eyes, makes a few adjustments, and hands them to me.

As my eyes adjust to the green tincture, I see nine monks sitting in a semicircle on Moi's terrace, with their backs to the house, facing the river. They seem to be chanting, but in such low voices they are inaudible even across the water. But they are not monks. I made that assumption because they are sitting the way monks sit and wearing robes. But those are not monks' robes, I now realize. They are black gowns with hoods which obscure the faces of the chanting men. Sukum urges me to scan the rest of Moi's property. When I do so I see that the path from the jetty to the house has been modified so that there are now three makeshift bamboo arches, which you would have to pass under if you were planning to reach the house from the river. I'm frowning at Sukum to ask for some kind of explanation, when the first of the boats arrives. It is a snakehead boat about sixty feet long, and seems quite full of people, who get out at the jetty and stand around, waiting. Now another boat appears, a rowboat, with only three people in it. One of the people—they seem all to be men—is blindfolded and has to be helped from the boat to the jetty, and then led carefully along the jetty to the land. One of the prisoner's minders pulls off the blindfold, causing me to gasp. It is a member of parliament who recently changed political parties. I turn to Sukum, but he shakes his head vigorously and urges me to keep watching. I stare as one of the officials of the ceremony, who seems to act as a kind of hierophant, shows the new initiate a piece of bamboo; it must have words written on it, for the neophyte is reading from it, after which he makes a humble *wai* three times in the direction of Moi's house, then takes off his shoes, socks, and upper garment. Bare-chested now, he is taken under the three arches, at each of which he stops and recites a few words, apparently repeating each phrase three times. Eventually he reaches the terrace of the house, which has been modified for the occasion. Moi's ancestor portraits are now hanging there over the blackwood shrine, which has been brought out from the interior. Moi and her maid are sitting in large rattan chairs with peacock backs that look like thrones. The ones in black gowns continue to chant. There is a pile of something on the blackwood shrine which glitters greenly in the night-vision glasses. The balcony is full of people sitting on the floor, all of whom seem to be men except for Moi and her maid.

All of a sudden our ferryboat man is restless, and Sukum, too, has decided it is time to leave. When we reach the shore, Sukum hands the nervous boatman a large amount of cash, far more than the value of a river crossing, and the boatman races away into the night. Sukum doesn't look at me. We don't talk until we have reached the road and found a cab.

In the backseat, Sukum looks away at the deserted streets, and murmurs, "D'you get it now?"

"I think so," I say. "The one they were initiating, he was who I think he was?"

"Yes. Of course. Didn't you get a view of any of the others?"

"A couple."

"So? Can we just forget about the case now? This is the moment to stop, when you have a clear and corroborated suicide—you don't need to pester Moi or her maid anymore. You don't need to die; you could say she's let you off."

There is something strange about the way he says *suicide* which is hard to pin down; but Sukum is confident that what I have seen tonight is enough to stop any Thai cop in his tracks, even me. He does not understand that all of a sudden the Fat *Farang* Case is my last hold on integrity. I don't care that it's a suicide. I want to know everything that led up to the American's death. I want to prove I'm still a cop.

"No," I say.

When I look at him I remember the detective he used to be, before Moi ruined him. I imagine him staked out on the river somewhere, night after night, brave, enthusiastic, confident that in his case, at least, the system would allow him to grow into full manhood. I remember his breakdown at the end. After she slipped him the acid he was off work for three months.

He turns to stare at me in disbelief. "Half the Thai-Chinese movers and shakers in Bangkok were at that initiation. I risked everything to show you, including my life. Don't expect any more help from me. I've done enough. I've done a lot more than any other cop in my position would have. I've done a lot more than you would do—after all, you're Vikorn's consigliere, aren't you?"

I'm shocked and saddened that the word has entered his vocabulary. It means the whole station must know what I am. I say, "Why didn't you tell me before?"

"Terror," he explains. "For some stupid reason I don't even understand myself, I seem to want to stay alive. Don't you see, if any of those people tonight find out that two humble cops know more than we should, they'll waste us in a heartbeat? Drop it, Detective, drop the whole thing. Whatever that fat *farang* was really doing in that movie, it wasn't what he claimed—or maybe even he didn't know why he was doing what he was doing. You can see the power of her magic from the kind of people who attended her gathering tonight. What's the matter, is your *farang* blood telling you to play the hero? Not in Thailand, Detective. You know that."

I allow a period of silence to do justice to his vehemence before changing the subject. "I didn't know those kinds of societies use women in their rituals."

"They don't—at least, not anymore. We're talking about a Thai version and you know how conservative we are about rituals. It seems at the beginning, long before the Shaolin Monastery stuff the movies talk about, these were initiation rites into an ancient mystery dating back to the Warring States period. Before Buddha, before even Confucius, women were used as priestesses and had a lot of power. Naturally, that's something Moi's family insists upon, seeing as she doesn't have any brothers. Her family members have been the Dragon Heads, Incense Masters, and White Paper Fans for more than a hundred years. Unlike in Hong Kong, in Thailand these are not elected offices, they are inherited."

I let a few minutes pass. I'm finally seeing the world according to Sukum. "Look, Detective, you don't have to help anymore. I understand. You took a big risk tonight and I appreciate it and I have no right to ask more of you. But I have to work this case. I just have to. But answer one question. That other suicide, the Japanese jeweler named Suzuki—it's connected, isn't it?"

He stares at me resentfully, then opens his window and turns to howl softly at the night, like a wolf.

40

I need the vastness of dharma, so I'm sitting on the back of a motorbike taxi on the way to Wat Rachananda.

At the *wat* I pay twenty baht for a set of the following: one candle, one lotus bud, four squares of gold foil, and a bunch of incense—and I switch off my cell phone. Lighting the incense is always a chore because it takes a while to catch fire, but Wat Rachananda has an oil lamp permanently burning for that purpose. I stand in line behind a couple of middle-aged women and a young man to light up, slip off my shoes, enter the *wat*, hold the incense in a high *wai* at forehead level, bow three times to the enigmatic gold Buddha on the dais, stick the incense into the sand pit at the back of the temple, place the lotus bud on the silver platter, walk toward the Buddha, and prostrate three times. The ritual over, I turn to the more demanding business of meditation and go sit in a semilotus against one of the pillars at the back.

Before I met Tietsin and his blade wheel it would take me a good half hour, sometimes double that, before my mind would still itself to the point where any real meditation could happen. Now, though, it takes less than ten minutes. Even while my mind is still zinging with the events of the day I can sense an appetite just under the surface—nay, a desperate, rabid lust—for some way out of here. Just before the attack from the blade wheel, I'm thinking about the fat man, Frank Charles; and Tara; and Pichai; and a dozen small, petty things—then it's suddenly as if I am faced with the prospect of death. Nothing is important except that elusive thing the Buddha advised us not to even try to define; the terror of death does not compete with the terror of surviving death, once you're convinced. The reality of the transcendent, in its infinite and crushing variety, causes synapses to short, hearts to groan, brains to fry. In other words, the blade wheel is here. It can appear as a gigantic terrifying rotary engine with scythelike blades or it can camouflage itself as a microscopic insect that turns metallic when it enters your bloodstream. And it can multiply itself arithmetically, which is what it does right now. With my eyes closed I experience the whole *wat* as filled with Tietsin's blade wheels, all inexorably flying toward me. Like a madman I am muttering, *Yes, yes, rip away, whatever the price get me out of this quicksand only an idiot would describe as life.* And: *Pichai, where are you?* The experience is almost epileptic, the way my nerve-tormented body writhes where I sit in a kind of orgasm, until the grasping which has dominated this continuum for a thousand years melts under the power of the Buddha and I experience a few seconds of peace.

Purged, emotionally drained, but high as a kite, I'm on the back of a bike again. At a traffic light I remember to switch on my cell phone. Instantly there is a succession of bleeps, which chide me for my radio silence. The text message reads,

Skype me.

Using skills honed over the years, I manage to text back, using one hand:

Ten minutes.

"It's a fake," the FBI says. I have her on my monitor at home, although the picture is kind of blurred and jerky and the colors don't really do her justice. Most of the time she's a feisty redhead these days, although all that exercise they put people through over there has drawn her cheeks; she looks like a super-fit sergeant at boot camp, except that her left arm is in a cast. She is hunched over her monitor and moving from side to side as if avoiding punches. I say, "What is?"

"The end of the movie."

I stare at her for a moment, wondering if I've got the wrong conversation. "Huh?"

"I'm talking about the film you sent me. The movie allegedly recording the suicide of one Frank Charles, famous Hollywood director. The ending is faked."

I have to let quite a few beats pass while my brain unscrambles. "Faked? You have ways of telling that from a digital copy? Your nerds have confirmed?"

"Actually, yes, they confirmed, but it didn't need nerds. All it needed was a machine that would play each frame extra slow. You could even try it on your own DVD player. When you play it real slow, you see the saw is touching off concealed strips of skin-colored plastic tubing under the hair—the saw just has to touch it for the ketchup to burst out, so it looks like a real medical operation, but if the saw were really cutting into bone the action would take a lot longer. I spoke to someone who does special effects for the film industry. She watched the movie and said it was a dangerous and unorthodox procedure—the saw could easily have broken the skin and then there would have been a massive civil claim, and maybe even a criminal one. They would never do it that way over here. But it's very clever—it makes for great cinema."

"And the other stuff—we see the whole of the inside of his skull?"

"Apparently, that was the easy part. Just a question of trick photography and a lot of work with plastic models."

"But"—I'm spluttering—"we have the body—that's how he died—the skull was completely detached, parts of the brain had been eaten—there was real blood everywhere—someone ripped his guts out—the murder wasn't faked."

"I didn't say the murder was faked, honey, only the movie."

We both hang there in silence for a long moment. I say, "Wow."

"I agree. *Wow!* I'm jealous—what a great case! Is it the only one you're working on?"

"No," I say, swallowing guilt like something sour in my mouth. "I'm doing something special for Vikorn at the same time."

She's smart enough to take the hint. There is sorrow in her tone when she says, "Ah!"

I am realizing how compromised I am, how my freedom of action has been destroyed by the chains on my spirit. For all her faults and her restless need for love and change, the FBI still has integrity; I doubt she's ever broken the law in her life, or even slightly bent the ethics of her profession. For all her experience, she's less worldly than I am these days. I envy her the unobstructed speed of her brain when she says, "I don't want to tell you how to run the case, Sonchai, but if I were you—"

"I know," I interrupt, anxious, I suppose, to show I still know how to investigate a murder. "The surviving husbands."

As soon as I've closed Skype I find Frank Charles's movie and slide it into the DVD drive. I fast-forward to the ending, then play around with the controls until I've got extra slow-mo. I stare in disbelief. The FBI is right. At this speed it is possible to see the edge of the saw's circular blade touch on the hair, which is covering some kind of skin-colored strip that bulges slightly in the center, and as soon as it does so the strip bursts, shedding "blood." I manage to catch a still and magnify it: tiny shreds from the plastic strip are clearly mixed with the spray of gore. You wouldn't normally notice them, because they look like bone fragments. I'm shaking my head. I need Einstein. I have Sukum.

41

It's around midnight when I finally decide to call Sukum to get the names of Moi's surviving ex-husbands. Then I take a cab to the station to dig out the report from the nerds who hacked into Frank Charles's computer. Then I take a cab to his penthouse on Soi 8.

It's about two in the morning, and most of the action is finished for the night at Nana Plaza when I pass. There is a drunken *farang* who has to hold on to the wooden guardrail of one of the bars in order to stand up, and a *katoey* who is trying to get him to his hotel. A bunch of whores are crossing the street to the Nana Café, where it is possible to hang out until dawn, hoping a customer will show up. There is a line of taxis, too, ready to take stray jet-lagged *farang* to those unlicensed bars where you're scrutinized from behind a spyhole before they let you in (you don't have to be white, just foreign), and where you can drink and play with girls for as long as you have the dough. Soi 8, also, is very quiet but still carries the signs of a party neighborhood: girls with *farang* sitting on iron seats outside a closed bar; a Westerner in his late twenties singing to himself on his way home (an ancient European Cup song to the tune of "Blue Danube": *Vienna are shit, shit-shit shit-shit*); a couple of cops standing by a lamppost, chatting.

At the apartment building they are surprised to see me and not too keen to let me into Charles's suite—can't it wait till morning? I'm in no mood for diplomacy, though, and opt for arrogance as a means of getting their attention. Now I'm sharing the elevator with a sulky receptionist who opens the door to the penthouse and shrugs. She doesn't have the time or the patience to hang around, so she closes the door behind me and returns to reception. All alone in the silence of his death—which, I now realize, has quietly penetrated every aspect of his home—I decide to pause, trying to commune with his spirit. *Were you murdered after all?* I ask the bust in the Jacuzzi. *If so, why?* The response is ambiguous; I sense a kind of relief, even amusement, on the part of the deceased's ghost, while I check out the Windows address book on the PC.

It takes less than a second to find the name, address, and telephone number of Robert Witherspoon, Moi's American ex-husband. Interesting that Frank Charles had found the need to keep the coordinates on his computer. Still more interesting that Witherspoon is located in Hawaii. When I dig a little further into the computer's secret chambers, I find a Skype account with Witherspoon's name and photograph: a square-jawed, balding blond in his midforties, wearing a black T-shirt, is attached to the address book by means of a mug shot. I click on the glyph, and the monitor comes alive with the Skype home page. I double-click on Witherspoon's mug shot. The program tells me my request to speak to him has been sent. My heartbeat seems to have doubled, and I'm clutching the edge of the desk when Witherspoon himself appears on the screen. Now I realize I don't have a microphone or computer camera—but Charles must have owned such items to go with the Skype account. I rummage frantically in the drawers under the desk; a plug-in mike/headphone set and camera are in the bottom drawer. I plug them into the front of the PC, don the headset, and say in a rush, "Good morning—is it still morning in Hawaii? My name is Detective Jitpleecheep of the Royal Thai Police. A few days ago I think you sent a DVD to my home?"

A long pause, during which I imagine my words and image finding their way across the globe to Hawaii. Then: "Yes, it's still morning in Hawaii. What took you so long?" Witherspoon says.

"I'm half Thai," I explain.

Witherspoon blinks into the computer cam as if he is trying to see me more clearly. "Are you?"

"Didn't you know that?"

"I don't know scat. This guy, this Hollywood director, calls me out of the blue one day and asks me to tell him all I know about my ex-wife, the world-class witch named Doctor Mimi Moi. So I told him, which wasn't much. We got chatting. We must have Skyped each other about ten times, so we're bonding in a way. He asked me to do him a favor. I said, *What?* He said, *I'm gonna send you a little package with an address on it. Just keep the package until you hear that I'm dead — then send it to the address that's written on it.*"

"That's it?"

"Pretty much. Look, I'd love to talk more, but I'm due to go on vacation in about twenty minutes with my new girlfriend and I don't want to screw this one up. How about you call me in about a week?"

I say, "Huh?" Somehow, what with the excitement of the chase, the last thing I expected was a key witness on vacation. "Where are you going?"

Witherspoon lets me have a wry grin. "New girl, buddy, I'm being spontaneous. Speak to you." He Skypes off.

42

On Bangkok murder squads, inspiration and paranoia are Siamese twins joined at the hip for life; some of us theorize they are the same thing. I've got it now, the insight into the devious workings of an exceptionally twisted and gifted criminal mind—but whose? I'll find out. I'm 100 per cent certain I've finally got a handle on the Fat *Farang* Case, and for the first time I'm slightly irritated with myself that I've promised Sukum he can have all the glory. This may be a good sign: maybe I'm returning to egocentric normality, thereby rehabilitating myself as a card-carrying citizen of the twenty-first century? Whatever, I am unashamedly pleased with myself this fair morning when I am on the phone to Virginia. The FBI listens to me in attentive silence, then says, "You're a genius, Sonchai, there's no other word for it—I've been racking my brains about your case, but I never would have thought of the solution. You're just amazing."

"There's nothing I can do until you get me some fingerprints, or, even better, DNA samples," I say, not for the first time.

"Don't worry, honey, we'll get them. In the meantime you might try his apartment."

"I'm onto it—but the place was very clean. Any fingerprints or hair samples are likely to be from cleaners or the forensic people—it was never the crime scene, so we weren't too careful."

"What about his car?"

"Yes, I'll try it."

I get the keys to Frank Charles's Lexus from Sukum and take a cab over to the building on Soi 8. Charles's penthouse owns three parking spaces underneath the building, and it takes about a minute to find the metallic-gray sedan parked in one of them. Best bet for prints, always, is to dust the gear stick and steering wheel. I dust both and lift the prints. Even in the rough I think I can see one set of prints repeated over and over again. I also pick up a selection of fiber rubbings from the front seat, pop them into a bag, rush them over to forensics—and even though it's only three in the afternoon, I'm so exhausted from having been up all night I decide a massage is called for. I go to the massage shop at the corner of Soi 39 and Sukhumvit, mostly because of the sense of religious silence that prevails there after lunch when most of the customers have gone back to work and most of the girls are fast asleep.

So here I am, prone and submissive under a muscular girl who is all of five feet tall and in the process of delivering the most delicious torture to my

mind-ravaged body, when—of course—my cell
phone rings. I fish it out of my pants, which are hanging by my side, to check the identity of the caller. I
only deal with emergencies during massage, but when
I see it is the FBI I signal to the girl to hold off with
the torment for a moment while I take the call.

"Got it," the FBI says, "it was an amazing piece of
luck. I just happened to be making some casual
checks on the Net, using Frank Charles as a keyword,
and guess what? He was in some kind of paternity dispute with a Thai woman here in the U.S. a few years
ago. It seems she was trying to tap him for dough on
the assumption he wouldn't fight the claim for child
support, but he did, and the DNA test came out in his
favor—it wasn't his kid. So I got hold of the file and
now we not only have prints, a mouth swab, and some
hair follicles, we have the DNA chart. We already
have his DNA profile, in other words. I'm sending it
via e-mail, you'll have it in roughly ten seconds." She
hangs up.

If I was a cooler kind of cop I'd let the girl finish
with the massage, but I'm not. I apologize and give
her an extra big tip, and now I'm on a bike on my way
back to the station. Sure enough, when I arrive I see
the FBI has already sent me the file. Now I don't need
the prints and fiber from the Lexus. I print out the
DNA chart and hold it to my heart for a moment,
while expressing profound thanks to the Buddha that
I have not totally lost my touch or my luck or my
mind. In fact, I'm wondering why I was so slow to

catch on. Even Frank Charles's obesity makes a sinister kind of sense: who was ever going to doubt the victim was him, the morbidly obese giant with the long hair, fat face, and gray beard? But all those things—the beard, the obesity, the long hair—have the capacity to diminish individual traits. Somehow, Charles found a willing substitute—such things have been known—who was prepared to die a few years earlier than expected (with that kind of weight no one lives long; maybe the proxy was terminally ill?), in return, perhaps, for a generous payment to his dependants? With the corpse mutilated in exactly the way portrayed in the movie, no one was going to doubt the identity of the victim—it was a brilliant device, depending more on illusion than anything else: the one thing no sane person was going to doubt was that the victim was *the* Frank Charles. Amazing! It was only the unexpected revelation that the death scene in the movie was faked that put me on the right track. Now everything is clear and obvious and I'm kicking myself for not working it out before. For some reason, Frank Charles wanted to disappear—why? I don't know. When I call Doctor Supatra, she tells me she'll have a DNA test done using the victim's blood and get back to me. It will take a couple of days.

43

Isn't it awful when the glorious rediscovery of your innate genius and street smarts turns out to be a delusion? That's the trouble with relentless optimism: it leads to suicide. Right now I'm thinking maybe I really have lost it totally; okay, it was a reasonable hypothesis that if the movie was faked, it was to provide Frank Charles with a way of finally liberating himself from an identity which had become a burden. In Thailand it is not unusual for someone with the means to buy a new persona in some other province, or, as often as not, across the border in Cambodia, where the bribes are lower and enforcement rarer— but in the case of a rich *farang*, his refuge could have been just about anywhere in Southeast Asia. I had visions of turning up uninvited and unexpected on some five-star beach, maybe in the Philippines, or Malaysia, or Vietnam, or—my first bet— Sihanoukville, Cambodia, with the bad news that I had come to arrest the fat bearded guy who had only recently bought a beach property in an obscure spot where he had planned on living out the rest of his days in peace and anonymity. Wrong.

Supatra just called with the astonishing news that the deceased really is—was—Frank Charles: his DNA matches perfectly the DNA chart the FBI provided from the paternity action in California. Now I'm scratching my head. Have you ever heard of such a thing yourself, *farang*? A guy takes the trouble to record his suicide message about a year before the event, goes through with it all on film to the last gory detail—except he fakes it. Then, next thing you know, he turns up dead in the same sordid flophouse where he filmed his fake suicide, and not only that, he dies in exactly the way he pretended to die in the movie? Amazing. Maybe you've worked it out already, *farang*, after all, you have the full genetic complement necessary for this conundrum. Myself, I'm only half Western, and I just don't get it.

For the moment, I'm working on the psychologically sound hypothesis that he chickened out the first time, then brooded and dared and cursed himself to the sticking point where he was actually able to go through with it; that's why we have a fake suicide followed by a real one. This is by no means unusual in the self-annihilation community: so often someone is talked down off a high ledge where they were coyly waiting for attention, only to jump under a train a month later. You can't stop human will. I'm uneasy, though; this case has levels all the way down to caverns measureless to man, and my doubting mind is already finding holes in my new hypothesis. If he finally decided to do himself in, why imitate the movie? Why go to that ridiculous amount of trouble when a simple overdose would have done it? There was a case in Soi 11 of a Belgian john who paid the owner of the Twenty-Four Bar for nonstop servicing by not less than two girls at a time for a twenty-four-hour period while he worked his way through a box of Viagra and a bottle of vodka. In his sixties, he died of a heart attack a few days later—it's the kind of ending I would have expected of Frank Charles. Yep, *uneasy* fairly describes my state of mind. I seek relief in doodling on a Post-it sticker, then, feeling somewhat primitive, I decide instead to avail myself of the Internet for its infinite distractions. How about keying in a few names and playing chase-the-clues-across-the-planet? One name holds a particular sonority.

In less than five minutes I have the webpage of one Robert Witherspoon, a Hawaii-based gemologist. It's a professional sort of page, uncluttered, elegant, with no extraneous advertising and a *contact me* panel small enough to ignore. There is no way to order his products online. You get the feeling this is not a beginner who recently graduated from gem school after giving up day trading in pork bellies. Either Witherspoon does not need an army of Internet customers, or he figures discretion is the best marketing device for the global 2 per cent he wants to attract. There are no pictures of his stones set in flattering filigree silver or gold. In fact, there is only one picture on the whole page: a beautiful gem cut perfectly with facets to catch and break light from all directions. It dominates the monitor like a beacon and is only half explained by the caption, which reads, A *perfect Padparadscha Sapphire will be orangey pink in color.*

Properly understood, it's a tap-your-desk-and-wait-for-the-brain-to-catch-up moment, but I seem to be doing a lot of that these days. I'm actually sort of freaked out by the sight of the big orangey-pink sapphire in the middle of my screen. I mean, my intuition is screaming that this is a case solver of a break, but I just don't know why or how. Anyway, it's lunchtime and Lek feels rejected if I don't take him across the road at least three times a week.

Now I'm at the braised-pig-knuckle food stall opposite the station with Lek, who still watches me anxiously for signs of psychosis. Normally he doesn't eat pork except to keep me company, but we both know that if you reach the stall early enough you can have the pick of the choicest pieces of meat braised to an exquisite tenderness so that it melts in your mouth, and even a 90-per-cent veggie like Lek cannot resist. We order a couple of iced lemon teas to finish, then lean back in our plastic seats.

"*Padparadscha,*" I say with an insane smile.

"That's the fourth time you've said that," Lek complains. "At least tell me what it means."

"I don't know," I reply. "That's why I have to keep saying it."

Lek sighs and sucks neurotically on his straw in an

expression of distress which empties the glass. When we're finished I realize the need for some more Internet surfing; I return to my desk, and key in the name *Johnny Ng*.

Well, you can't expect your luck to hold all day long. In Hong Kong, it seems, there are about a million people with the surname *Ng*, and about half of those own webpages. That's what happens in societies with too much money and too few brothels: citizens are forced to play with themselves in cyberspace. *Ng*: I still don't know how to pronounce it. Where's the vowel?

I pause to open my mind to the cosmos. For some reason this cannot be done in the police station, so I take a stroll. It's around three in the afternoon, which is to say between meals and therefore snack time. Most of the cooked-food stalls have closed for an afternoon break, but a nifty new gang of entrepreneurs on wheels have shown up with snacks on a stick. Sausages, fishballs, eggs, shrimp, chicken, whole fish, ice cream, frozen coconut, dim sum, satay, dough balls, watermelon, and dried squid can all be eaten off a bamboo spike: watch. Now I'm tucking into a well-stuffed Isaan sausage and feeling a little better, not so much because I was hungry but because I'm claiming back my city soul. Nobody who wasn't reared in Krung Thep can saunter down the street with a gun stuck down the small of his back, gnawing at sausage, nodding to acquaintances, grabbing an iced lemon tea from the iced lemon tea lady on the corner, and generally walking the walk with the kind of panache

I'm exhibiting at this moment; it might not be much, but it's making me feel like *the man*. It's good for inspiration, too.

Now I'm back at my desk frantically surfing the Net again, with an idea so whacky I'm embarrassed to be following it up, and I'm not going to tell you about it, *farang*, unless it yields results.

Well, it has. How about this: I used a search engine to find people named Ng in the Hong Kong gem trade, and guess what? One Johnny Ng is quite well known and successful in that field. I even have his office telephone number and his Internet address. My instinct, though, is not to give him any room to maneuver: I'm thinking of getting on a plane. But before I do that, I need help. Detective Sukum is out of the station on some minor case at the moment, so I decide to hit him with a question designed to jangle his nerves. I call him on his cell phone, and as soon as he has said hello I say, "What is it about gemologists that Doctor Moi is attracted to?"

"Huh?"

"Witherspoon and Johnny Ng—both jewelers and gem traders. I haven't checked on the two dead husbands—named Thompson and Legrand, I believe—maybe you can save me the trouble? After all, you were the one who sent me that article about padparadscha. You also sent me the Suzuki case." The pause is so long I think we've been cut off—then he lets me have a long sigh. "Get off the phone."

44

Sukum will not speak to me at the station. He will not even communicate via Lek. I think I've lost his support completely, and maybe I'll even have to report him to Vikorn for holding out on me with information vital to my investigation, when I get a text message from an unidentifiable source:

Look under the near left leg of your desk. Be discreet.

Pretending I've dropped something, I do as instructed. Printed on a small piece of paper:

12:20 p.m., Taksin pier.

The important thing about Taksin pier is that it connects the Skytrain to the riverboats: you can take the train to the terminus, walk down the steps to the river, and buy your ticket for any direction: upstream, downstream, or across. I noticed that Sukum was in the same compartment of the same train as me, but he would not acknowledge me, so I make no attempt to approach him at the line for the boat tickets; on the other hand, I need to be close enough to him to find out where he's going. In the event, he helpfully points downstream before scurrying off to wait for the boat on a bench as far away from me as he can find. Now the boat's here, about seventy feet long and ten feet wide, a pilot at the back whistling his lungs out with Morse-like directions to the captain as he pauses for a moment at the jetty. The intense whistling brings excitement and a dash of fear as everyone hurries to get off and on. Finally Sukum and I are forced together by the crowd as we board.

We are hanging on to stainless-steel uprights at the stern of the ferry, designed to help people keep their balance during turbulence. Sukum is wearing an incredibly loud banana-and-mango tourist shirt, shorts which show his unexpectedly powerful legs (he's built like a football player), dark glasses, and a straw hat, which he has to press down on his head when the boat speeds up. I intuit he would have preferred a more temperate climate for this meeting so he could have worn a raincoat with the collar turned up to his eye sockets.

"You're half Thai, so you are the victim of superstition," Sukum explains. He is embarrassed that his security precaution has forced him to shout into the oncoming wind, right into the ear of a *farang* woman tourist, who glares at him. "But you are also half *farang*, so you don't have it in the marrow of your bones the way full Asians do."

"Meaning?"

"You might have guessed. I myself didn't see the connection until your mother mentioned she had spotted Moi with the victim, Frank Charles—then I got scared."

"You've been watching me buzzing around like a fool all this while?" I yell.

"Correct," he yells back. "I admit to a certain ego-based pleasure in knowing more about the case than the great Detective Sonchai Jitpleecheep. On the other hand, I have tried to discourage you. You can't complain that I've been cynically watching you race toward death."

"Like Moi's two dead husbands?"

"Yes. Like them." He screws up his face for a moment and shakes his head. "*Farang* say Asians are corrupt. Maybe we are, but it's a disease we've developed some immunity to—most of the time we keep it under control, because we know in our hearts that too much corruption leads to destruction. *Farang* have no such instinct. Once they get into grabbing dough, they show no restraint."

"You better give it to me in chronological order, Detective."

"Not a chance."

I frown. "What? You wear fancy dress and drag me here in the middle of the river just to give a half-minute lecture on differentials in global corruption?"

"Right."

"Are you going to tell me any more?"

"No."

"Why not?"

"If it is obvious your information comes from me, we both die. If I just give you a few clues to follow up, maybe only you die."

Try as I might, I cannot fault his logic. "Okay. Give me one more clue to take me forward."

"Look in the gem trade journals."

"That's it?"

He scans the crowd around us like a security camera before saying in a superior voice, "Yes, that's it. Let's change the subject. That file I sent you—the Japanese suicide your *katoey* got all worked up about, how's it going?"

I'm so irritated I think if not for the crowd, I would punch him.

45

Not everyone on the street in downtown Hong Kong is talking about money on a cell phone—only 99 per cent. You don't need to be an investigative journalist to realize this place is all about dough. I've been ashamed of my generic Thai black pants, white shirt, and black jacket since the moment I arrived. I don't know why I didn't think to bring my consigliere wardrobe; of course, it was because I'm not here on Vikorn business, am I? Never mind, I am armed with my Armani cologne. I'm staying at a three-star hotel on the Kowloon side, but Johnny Ng, I have discovered, is a jeweler-socialite based on the island itself. I know from the local society press that he is a leading member of the gay community here, and the only leverage I have is that he may not want it known that he was once married to a woman. He is in his midforties and, judging from the pics, still pretty. I have also discovered that everything happens around food over here. The local gem traders' guild is throwing an over-the-top buffet supper at the Grand Hyatt tonight, which I intend to crash. In the meantime, I'm sightseeing in the world's biggest shopping mall: central Hong Kong.

Most people here are Chinese, of course, but there are plenty of *farang*, too, whom the locals call *gweilo* (meaning "foreign devil": I don't know why we didn't think of that—just teasing). I think it's a mistake, though, to talk about race in this city of the future; clearly the citizens here are genuinely color blind, as long as you're a millionaire. Everyone else is second-class, or worse. Here the smiles don't fade on shopkeepers' faces when they see I'm Eurasian; it's the generic jacket and black pants that turn them hostile. Just now I went to buy a necktie for tonight and the sales assistant put all my personal details into a computer before he would hand it over, so they can flood my e-mail account with special offers of three-hundred-dollar ties for the rest of my life. The clerk was so much better dressed than me he could not withhold a sneer as he handed over the long gold-embossed packet containing the tie that cost me more than a thousand Hong Kong dollars. It's a one-off Japanese design which might someday fetch a fortune at Sotheby's; am I being naïve to think it will compensate for the rest of my inadequate wardrobe? No, not naïve, just bloody-minded: I knew I had to have a tie, so I bought the most expensive one I could find, to confuse the hell out of them; for the rest, I'm having an allergic reaction to capitalism and cannot bring myself to buy better clothes. In fact, I don't want to buy anything. The prices are so inflated and the sales clerks so precious, I'm feeling nostalgic for lazy Thais who don't give a rotten durian if you spend your money or just hang around window-shopping for a week.

But guess what—the tie works. I used a fantastically high-tech public toilet that looked like a bathroom out of *Home & Country* to put it on, then tried it out on another sales assistant in another men's clothing store. The clerk offered me a complete new wardrobe—except for the designer tie. Thank Buddha I've brought my Nokia N95 (eight-gig) cell phone, or I really would feel like a third-world refugee. The tie apparently being my sole claim to membership in the human race, I decide to sightsee before attempting to ambush Johnny Ng at the buffet banquet tonight.

Ghosts of the departed British colonial power are everywhere, especially in street- and place-names. Victoria and Stanley are the biggest haunters, with George and Albert as runners-up. Now I'm on a funicular railway climbing a mountain called Victoria at about thirty degrees to the vertical. I get off to do the famous walk on a path called Stanley, which, at a certain point, overlooks a town of the same name. The path is circular, so you end up staring down at a harbor also called Victoria—but it's a magnificent view. High-prowed green fishing trawlers compete for sea space with giant oil tankers, luxury yachts, sailboats, and high-speed ferries plying between here and Macau, where you can gamble legally. You can gamble illegally in Hong Kong to your heart's content, but those homemade roulette wheels are notoriously easy to fix and inevitably lead to fights— better to take the forty-five-minute trip to the former Portuguese enclave where Siberian whores will wipe your brow after every loss, assuming you are not attracted to the local girls.

It's a near-God experience, up here above the mighty throbbing silicone heart of the tiny city-state which took over China ten years ago. (Haven't you noticed how Beijing looks more like Hong Kong with every passing minute?) Your sense of divinity decreases as you descend, though. In the backstreets of Wan Chai, a red-light district that has the effect of making me feel more at home, the clacking of mahjong tiles is deafening, like a heavy sea shifting gravel right next to your ear. And I can't say the local personal habits quite live up to the sartorial elegance. Just now I watched a well-dressed Chinese man in his sixties expertly blow the snot from his left nostril while pressing with an index finger on his right at exactly the point in his stride when he was leaning somewhat to the left, thus ensuring the turbocharged mucus would hit the pavement (or someone else—these streets are jam-packed 24/7) rather than his person, then perform exactly the same maneuver with right nostril, left index, right-inclining stride. I guess in the Asian city that never sleeps people don't have time to blow their noses on tissue.

I'm told there's a good Thai restaurant on a street called George, just off a street called Stanley, so I decide to leg it over there so I can speak Thai. Kathmandu never made me this homesick, and I've only been here three hours. It takes me a while to find the Sawatdee restaurant. When I get there the food is perfect, but no one speaks Thai; the owners and staff are all Filipinos. I say, "I thought you people were experts at imitating music?"

"Filipinos can imitate anything" is the proud reply. "In America, Europe, and Saudi Arabia we imitate nurses all the time and nobody notices. Next challenge will be brain surgery. What are you doing in Hong Kong?"

"Imitating jewelers," I say.

46

The Grand Hyatt is Renaissance Rome with more money and less God: vaulted ceilings, lamps held up by brass cupids at every elbow, more polished marble than you could point a spray can at, prices to bankrupt nonmembers of the millionaires' club. The Gem Traders' Society of Hong Kong is holding its annual bash in the main reception room on the ground floor.

Just my luck that neckties are fresh out of style among the gem-trading elite. Black Nehru jackets with high collars set off with sparkling diamonds in gold or silver are de rigueur, though you can sport rubies, sapphires, lapis lazuli, jade, pearls, opals, and even amber as long as the settings are the highest examples of the jeweler's art; aquamarines and other species of beryl are not big in the Far East, but at the end of the day it's all about the four Cs: *color, cut, clarity, and carat*. After a few minutes I'm sure I hear those words in English and Cantonese repeated all over the room.

As far as male fashion is concerned, *farang*, at this kind of function if you are gauche enough to wear a thousand-dollar sports blazer, whatever you do don't wear a tie with it; no, sir, you just leave the top two buttons of your five-hundred-dollar shirt undone to reveal the independence of your spirit and the success of your business—and perhaps the bijou body-art tattoo just below your throat. Neckties are for the salaried masses and carry the stigma of middle management. So why don't I simply pull mine off? Because if I did they would start focusing on my jacket and pants; better they think I'm just a decade out of date. How did I get into the party? Well, in a town where everyone knows everyone else, security is not that tight. I noticed how the guests casually flipped their gold-embossed invitation cards into an enormous silver bowl in front of a waiter in a starched white jacket, whom I distracted by playing with my gigantic garish tie with my left hand, flopping the end of it in front of him like a silk fish, while I clipped one of the cards from the silver bowl with the other. "Oh, you want the invitation card?" I exclaimed. "Here it is." No billionaire ever chucked a gold-embossed invitation card into a silver bowl with more panache. I deeply impressed the waiter, who allowed me in with a respectful bow.

One thing for sure about Johnny Ng: he's as gay as a fairy light. I spot him from a distance behind a gigantic ice diamond about a yard wide which dominates the central buffet table. Except it's not a diamond, is it? The ice has been dyed orangey pink, and the facets send slivers of light all over the enormous room. One catches Ng as he makes queenly gestures that cause his filigree gold bracelets to shake while he plays with the long thin gold chain around the neck of his Nehru jacket. We're separated by an army of narcissists, though. A lot of the men, all of whom are Chinese, have decked themselves out in jewelry just like Ng, although most are more conservatively dressed businessmen in tuxedos. This night is really for the women, however. I already know from my research that to the cognoscenti diamonds are common rocks compared to the incomparable padparadscha. I see plenty of them, along with other corundums hanging from long elegant Chinese necks of flawless alabaster. As everyone knows, the purpose of gems is to make girls' eyes glitter, and so it is tonight: the whole place is ablaze with photons bouncing from polished stone into black Chinese eyeballs and out again. There's not a female in the room who does not find herself irresistible. Some wear the traditional silk cheongsam, where dragons compete for nipples and there is a tantalizing slit all the way up one thigh, but the vast majority are sporting the very latest products from the best haute culture ateliers of Milan and Tokyo.

The crowd is excited by its own wealth and beauty and it takes me a while to work my way through to the main table: Chinese-style crispy pork and duck; wonton soup; snow fungus soup; dim sum; roast beef, English style; wok-fried vegetables of all kinds;

blanched kaylan in oyster sauce; steamed fish in lemon sauce; spareribs with watercress and apricot kernels; scallops with ginger and garlic—I'm describing just that corner of the table nearest to me. When I catch sight of the shellfish stand on the other side of the room, I decide to load up on oysters before approaching Ng, but I get distracted by the sushi table—then I see that the dessert booth includes crêpes suzette made to order by the short-order chef in the tall white hat, and I gulp. I've not eaten crêpes suzette since Monsieur Truffaut entertained Nong and me at the Lucas Carton, off the place de la Madeleine in Paris. Exquisitely torn between the Sydney rock oysters on the one hand and the crêpes on the other, I pause in the middle of the room—and notice I am being watched. Well, with so much wealth adorning people's bodies you'd expect the society would have taken care of its own security: there are quite a few Chinese men in tuxedos between the ages of thirty and forty with faces like rocks who are not participating in the high-pitched gossip and are certainly not interested in seducing anyone. At least two of them are staring at me. Under such pressure, one is forced into quick decisions. I go for the crêpes suzette and wait patiently while the chef pours the mixture into the pan and adds the orange sauce, prodding the pancakes in the approved way until they are soaked in Cointreau. Conscious, now, that my remaining time as a privileged member of the global billionaires' club is short, I stride as quickly as I can across the room in the direction of Johnny Ng, holding my plate piled high with cutely folded sauce-soaked pancakes that reek with the divinely fragrant sauce. The two bodyguards also adopt fast strides as they converge toward me, and it so happens that we all meet on the other side of the ice padparadscha, where Ng is playing with his gold chain and flirting with a younger man. I just have time to say, "Good evening, Mr. Ng," hoping I pronounced the Ng right, when the two heavies, taken aback because I seem to know one of the stars of the evening, say something softly but firmly to Ng in Cantonese. Now, *farang*, if you think Thai is a singsong kind of language, try getting your ear around Cantonese. It's impossible to tell anything at all by Ng's tone when he gazes at me quickly and shrugs at the security guards. Then he turns to me and says in perfect English, "Would you mind telling me who the hell you are?"

I feel like Clark Kent when he removes his shirt as I pull at my tie to yank it off—it's an identity issue—then take out my wallet to flash my cop ID. What I'm interested in, of course, is his reaction to the Thai script and the royal emblem on the card. Sure enough, his expression flattens and his eyes harden when he looks up at me from examining the card. He says something firm and not at all fey to the two men, who nod and stand on either side of me. "Go with them," Ng says. "I'll join you shortly." Then, with the kind of contemptuous benevolence only the best crooks can muster, he glances at my crêpes suzette and adds, "You can take that with you." Anyone of good breeding would have been crushed, but his disdain has no effect on me at all. I'm still holding the plate and munching on the last of the crêpes when we reach the underground garage, the heavies and I.

47

Have you noticed, *farang*, how even in the very finest of modern buildings the parking garages have all been designed by Stalin? I predict an architectural revolution one day, which will give us underground parking garages to die for, rather than in. (Our descendants will watch ancient footage and exclaim, *How could they ever have put up with such drab parking garages?*) Dismal is the word, and now I've finished the crêpes suzette and don't know what to do with the plate. I feel diminished. I'm going through my usual self-recrimination at having turned myself into a fool while flying by the seat of my pants: *Why couldn't you just play it straight for once, you just had to imitate a frigging Hong Kong jeweler, for Buddha's sake, what the hell were you thinking of, still trying to prove you're a cop and not a consigliere, who are you kidding?* You will understand that in this state of mind, it is quite a relief when Ng roars up in a red Ferrari, opens the passenger door, and snaps, "Get in." He is still in his Nehru jacket, but the gold jewelry has been safely deposited somewhere and his top buttons are undone,

400

giving a quite different impression of the personality of the owner, whose voice has deepened a shade and lost its queenly intonation. I cannot resist handing the empty plate to one of the heavies, along with the silver fork, before getting into the car.

Now we're all about torque as we roar up a turnpike, which leads up the mountain called Victoria fast enough to create our own bow wave. Lesser vehicles get out of the way: wealth here is a sign of power, and every Asian knows from bitter experience that might is right. We've turned off the turnpike before Ng speaks again.

"You have no investigative powers here."

I nod humbly. "That's right."

"And by crashing our party you compromised yourself totally."

"That's true."

"If a Hong Kong cop behaved like that I'd have his balls for batter."

"That's a good expression. Where did you get it?"

He allows himself the ghost of a smile. "One of my mothers was English. So was one of my wives."

"Was your English wife male or female?"

For some reason Ng finds this question very funny. He's still laughing when security lets us into his high-end condominium building.

Now we're standing in a great split-level salon with floor-to-ceiling windows through which dark energy travels from the city below. At the back soft footlights illuminate two ten-foot commemorative portraits: a

Chinese couple in frontal pose sitting on elaborately carved chairs draped in brocade, a lavish carpet at their feet, wearing winter gowns and fur-trimmed robes. The woman's feet and hands are hidden, and they both wear long jade necklaces and elaborate headdresses with gold and silver ornaments. The resemblance to Doctor Moi's ancestral portraits is so strong I want to know if they are the same; but when I step closer I can see that they are not. Ng watches me with curiosity. He is entirely at home, entirely relaxed. I'm the third-world nerd who provides a kind of foil. If I weren't here, who would he feel superior to?

"My paternal great-grandparents," he explains. "Before the revolution."

"You are from Swatow?"

"I'm not from anywhere. Chairman Mao threw Mummy and Daddy into an oven when I was four. They say I cried out loud at the very moment their brains popped—that was my childhood over and the end of identity." He waves a hand to forestall questions. "Distant relatives, foster parents, some of them foreigners—I wound up in Hong Kong. By age fifteen I was already an old man. I met a mind master and a benefactor. For a high price he shared his wisdom: *Don't try to be somebody. Don't try to be nobody. You are already dead. Enjoy.* Of course, the words mean nothing unless part of an initiation—in my case a kind of mental chemotherapy that annihilated all remnants of the notion of belonging." He smiles at me

402

without warmth or hostility—just a smile performing a function. "Shall I offer you a drink? Is it that kind of moment? Or shall I just spill my guts? Obviously, it's too late to tell you to fuck off, now you're my guest. I had to get you out of that party, didn't I? That was smart of you; I doubt I would have bothered with you at all otherwise." He pauses to reflect. "Actually, you were the perfect excuse. I'm so bored with those overblown Hong Kong functions."

He stares out into the city night: quite beautiful, I have to say, with the fattest skyscrapers competing for attention with laser light shows, and the water of the harbor black behind them. When he speaks it is to the window.

"You probably don't realize how mad Mimi Moi really is, nobody does who hasn't lived with her." He spares me a glance. "That must be why you're here, right? Mad Moi, Doctor of Chemistry, the first and only Thai-Chinese woman to do chemistry/ pharmacology at Oxford and get a First?" I nod. "Without her maid she can't even dress herself—she really can't. When we lived together I watched some-times while the maid spread her knickers for her to get into in the morning. She refuses ever to bathe herself, the maid has to do it. And she's hopeless with money. The maid has to control the purse strings." He smiles, perhaps at my reflection in the window. "Now that's a good cop point, isn't it? But you'd be wrong to draw conclusions. It's much, much deeper than that." He shakes his head. "No, that maid doesn't care about money, she's already incredibly rich." He smiles again, thinly. "Now I've really shocked you, yes? Probably the richest slave in the world. And d'you know that's exactly what she is half the time? There's nothing she doesn't do for Moi, nothing she won't do. She even puts medicinal cream on her hemorrhoids. The two of them have been an item since Mimi was born. But Mimi is a baby, Detective. A brilliant, witty, cynical, beautiful, charming, highly sophisticated, perfectly educated baby. Not unusual, perhaps, among the rich in any society. Anyway, the executive summary is that Mimi cannot live without her, and I dare say the maid would probably not consent to live without Mimi. Together they make up the two hemispheres of a perfect private world, and they know it."

"No room for husbands?"

"Oh, as long as I didn't seek attention I got on okay. I was relatively young, but not that young. I needed a trade. She wanted to prove to the world that she could catch a man as well as any other woman—I mean, at that stage in her life she was still pretending to be normal."

"Trade? I thought you were a jeweler? We've already established that Doctor Moi is a pharmacist." By the way he smirks I realize I've given him the information he wanted: how much do I already know? Not much, apparently, for he says, "I'll have to educate you from the beginning, it seems. I'll tell you what, why not stay the night? Don't worry, I don't fancy you in the least. Your wardrobe turns me right off."

48

Johnny Ng has a maid, a Filipina who brings us breakfast on his vast balcony overlooking downtown Hong Kong. Ng points at some buzzards hanging in the sky above the tall apartment buildings. "Their numbers diminish every year," he says. "I think it's a miracle they've hung on this long." After the coffee and fresh croissants, he drives me to the rail terminal in the city center, and I take a train to the airport. It is not an ordinary train: there is a "train ambassador," who walks through the carriages making sure everyone is okay on the twenty-minute journey. She gives me the standard Hong Kong money smile, but takes in my clothes as she passes. From the airport I call Sukum to tell him about my evening with Johnny Ng. Sukum refuses to comment over the phone; all he communicates is fear, so it seems I have to carry the burden of enlightenment all on my own. As soon as I touch down in Bangkok, I call him again. "That was the deal, wasn't it? I do the investigative stuff, then you corroborate or not?"

"Not on the phone. I'll come around to your house.

No, wait, I don't want to be seen visiting you, I don't want them to think we have a personal relationship."

"D'you want me to wear a disguise?"

"Would you?"

"I was joking, Detective."

He coughs. "How about Hua Lamphong?"

"Thirty minutes."

So now I'm sitting at a café in the train station with an iced lemon tea, watching some backpackers hump their packs to the platform from which the train for Chiang Mai and all points north will depart. The station is crowded, as usual, mostly with rural Thais who have come to find fortune in the big city, or to depart in sorrow that they have failed. There are plenty of food vendors and taxi hustlers, as well. There is a big clock under the old-style rotating noticeboard that carries the departure times and makes it possible to imagine it is a hundred years ago when the station and its clock were new. Sukum is late. Sukum is terrified.

Finally he shows up in a pair of jeans, a black T-shirt, and dark glasses. He is carrying a Thai newspaper, which he has opened and raised to eye level, so that he has to take precautionary peeks before every step. He still walks like a cop. When he sees me he makes a sign to say, *Don't say hello*. Instead of taking the seat next to me at my table, he sits at an adjacent table and takes out a pack of L&Ms. Sukum never smokes. I try not to stare as he opens the pack,

406

thumps it to extract one, and lights it clumsily with a butane lighter. Ad-libbing as best I can, I wait for a few moments, then ask if I can have a cigarette. He shoves the packet at me. When I take one I use the opportunity to go nearer to him to beg a light. All the time his eyes are darting, and I see a fine patina of sweat has covered his face and soaked his T-shirt into a still darker shade. "Get a newspaper," he hisses. So I find a vendor, buy today's copy of *Thai Rath*, sit down at my table again but nearer to him, and carry on the conversation as if I am making remarks about the day's news.

"You really met Johnny Ng?" he whispers. Despite his fear, he is fascinated that I may have penetrated further into the heart of darkness than he did ten years ago when he first started investigating Doctor Moi.

"Yes."

"And he talked?"

"Yes, he talked. But that guy is a born survivor. What he said is all unattributable. I need you to fill in the gaps."

He shakes his head at the incalculable depth of the void that has opened under his feet. "Okay," he croaks, "talk."

I tell the tale of a Chinese soldier of fortune whose tragedy was not entirely without a silver lining. True, Ng was shuttled around between family members after Mao's Cultural Revolution had claimed his parents, and finally found a long-term foster home with a British family living in Hong Kong when it was still a British colony. All along, his surrogate families tended to be quite well-off and very well educated. He himself was also very, very smart. The youngish bi-sexual man—he was in his mid- to late twenties—who went to Bangkok to check out the possibilities of a distant family connection with a well-to-do pharmacist only a few years older than himself was cocky, adaptable, fluent in English and three Chinese dialects including Teochew, excessively good-looking, and entirely without moral sense. He married Moi within three months of meeting her, without expect-ing much in the way of love or normal family life. He had no illusions. Mimi Moi was weird within a tradition of upper-class Chinese women and not in the least interested in sex. That made a deal easy to reach. He would provide her with a respectable and attractive front for social events; in return she would have him trained in the most esoteric, and profitable, aspects of the gem trade. Theirs would be a symbiotic arrangement between what one might call "married singles."

When I introduce the word *gem* into the narrative I watch Sukum's face very carefully. He sinks into depression. I say, "Except that Moi doesn't know much about precious stones at all, does she, Detective Sukum?" Sukum groans. "Oh, I expect she can tell a real sapphire from a fake—she would have learned that at her mother's knee, no doubt."

Sukum lights another cigarette. I don't think this one is a prop. "Go on," he gulps.

"The story at this stage, as with everything to do with China, plunges into a historical sidetrack. I'm talking about the 14K Triad Society." Sukum drops the cigarette as he's tapping ash into a tin ashtray, and has to retrieve it; now it's covered in black ash, so he has to light another. "I didn't know how widespread their operations are. I didn't know they'd colonized half of the Pacific Rim."

"You don't call it the 14K outside of Hong Kong," Sukum hisses. "Didn't he tell you the unoriginal Thai name they've adopted?" I raise my eyebrows. "Kongrao. I want you to use that name when you talk to me about it."

Kongrao means "our thing," and, like *cosa nostra*, can be used in conversation without invoking anything sinister. It's a phrase you hear a thousand times a day. I say, "Okay, so, Kongrao goes back to the eighteenth century—"

"Seventeenth."

"Whatever. Chinese secret societies are genuinely religious at their core. All that Westerners see in the ceremonies is a lot of mumbo jumbo designed to brainwash and terrorize members into total obedience. Like with the Sicilians. What *farang* don't understand is that no Asian society, especially not a criminal one, lasts for hundreds of years without a spiritual foundation. The rites work because they have something behind them."

"Right," Sukum says, lighting another foul-smelling L&M with shaking hands.

"And as so often in Asia," I continue, "the priestly line was dominated by one family. One family whose duty it was to provide a priestess to preside at the rituals."

Now that I've really let the cat out of the bag, Sukum seems almost relieved. I explain, "We're talking about an exceptionally successful operation built up patiently over a period of centuries by dedicated men and women who never think of themselves as criminals at all, merely as people making a living in a difficult environment which requires absolute loyalty and absolute secrecy and includes an apprenticeship that lasts more than fifteen years. That's why the rituals are so important and why the priestess has to be perfect for the part. Using this age-old system based on Confucian values, Kongrao has long dominated loan sharking throughout the Rim. All the big illegal logging operations in Cambodia, Thailand, and Malaysia, for example, are financed by Kongrao. But even logging is secondary to the most consistently lucrative trade, which has never failed for three hundred years and is the most closely guarded of all Kongrao's operations. Comparatively, heroin and methamphetamine are like cash crops that, though good for turnover, do not bring in anything like the steady income generated by this business: the buying, cutting, polishing, faking, smuggling, and selling of precious gems."

Sukum has stopped smoking. The cigarette is held suspended between his fingers, and he is staring at it.

He is unable to speak, so I continue: "In many ways Moi is an ideal priestess. As the eldest girl in a family which has dominated the Bangkok chapter of Kongrao for centuries, central casting could not have provided a better one. In other ways, though, she is a dangerous liability—because she really is half mad. So Kongrao needed someone to keep an eye on her: who better than her maid, on whom she has been emotionally and physically dependent all her life? Thus the maid is promoted to a kind of surrogate priestess herself, or perhaps a handmaiden to Moi, who also acts as master of ceremonies. And the maid is very shrewd, very controlled, and very Chinese. Nobody is surprised when she finds a way to make herself rich, this is natural, and she is respected for the way she makes a profit without harming the interests of the society. For the maid took the precaution of learning an awful lot about precious gems, especially sapphires. And especially a particular form of sapphire called padparadscha."

I pause here to take in Sukum. He is still in a kind of terror trance, unwilling to allow his frozen body any freedom of movement. "Tell me, Khun Sukum, for I'm sure you know. Of all those guests at Moi's house that night participating in the rites, how many were connected to the gem trade?"

"All of them," he splutters. "The maid has been recruiting jewelers and gem traders for decades. In reality, she runs all of Thailand's precious stone rackets. No one gets to survive, especially not with sapphires, except by joining Kongrao, which means they're under her thumb. Even the guests who weren't gem traders, the politicians, senior lawyers, top cops — they've all been bought by the gem industry, through the maid's maneuverings."

"Yes. That's what Johnny Ng said."

I stop talking because I want to see what Sukum will say next. This is the most interesting point of the story, after all, but I'm not sure how much even he knows after a decade of investigations, all of which got blocked sooner or later. "And the maid, perhaps better than anyone in Kongrao, saw the risks of too much success — am I right?" I take out a collection of magazines from a plastic bag I have brought with me. Some of them are Western publications, but most are local; all of them could be described as trade publications for the gem industry. "And this is her brilliant strategy," I say, pointing to a picture of a tuxedoed white man in the center spread of one of them. The caption explains at some length that the local guild of jewelers and gem dealers had decided to copy other high-end retail industries by appointing a kind of mascot or exotic representative, called an "ambassador," who will be their public face to the West, where most of the customers live. The guild is proud to appoint Mr. Robert Thomson as honorary roving ambassador of the Thai gems industry.

"Put it away," Sukum hisses.

"It's her third husband, isn't it? The first one to die young and tragically — a heart attack, I believe, while

412

Moi and her maid were out of the country? Interesting that the maid persuaded the guild to appoint her mistress's husband as its ambassador, don't you think?"

Sukum is disinclined to speak, so I take out another, later copy of the same trade magazine. "Once again, the Thai guild of gem traders is appointing a *farang* to be its official ambassador. Once again the ambassador, a Frenchman named Marcel Legrand, also in a tuxedo, is honored to accept the appointment." Legrand is the one who was hit by a truck. I raise my eyes at Sukum.

"She didn't need to persuade them," Sukum mutters. Finally, he decides to cut to the chase. "She had to share her scams with the others—the other gem traders, I mean. You have to look at the big picture. Kongrao wasn't just cheating a few regional traders and retail outlets. It was bankrupting the gems industry in entire neighboring countries. Cambodia, Malaysia, Sri Lanka, Vietnam, even Burma, all got stung."

"I see. Therefore it would have been obvious from the start that sooner or later victims would retaliate. But who would they assassinate to avenge themselves for the massive frauds that had been perpetrated by the Thais? Thailand is a mysterious place not only for *farang*, but also for everyone who lives near us. Our language is largely impenetrable, and our businesses are, shall we say, dominated by families who know how to remain anonymous. And ninety per cent of the

413

trades in wholesale jewelry are never declared, for tax reasons." Sukum nods. "So the smart thing was a form of sacrificial corrosion: let the *farang* mascot take the hit. After all, in such cases murders are largely symbolic. There's never any way to get the lost investment back, but a well-executed vendetta always makes the aggrieved party feel better and allows you, after a respectful pause, to go on doing business in Asia."

"Right," Sukum says.

"I think Witherspoon and Johnny Ng were both too smart to take the bait. But Thomson and Legrand were not so fly. They both died, and in both cases the hit was perfectly executed: the cops did not find evidence of foul play." Despite Sukum's reluctance, I take out the more recent of the trade magazines—it is less than a year old—to flash a picture of Frank Charles, also in a tuxedo, also with a caption which declares him to be the new honorary representative of the Most Honorable Society of Thai Gem Traders. But Sukum is not disturbed by the photograph. He waves a hand at it. "That's after my time," he explains. "I don't know anything about developments after I nailed her on tax evasion. You're on your own now, there's nothing more I can say. You've got the big picture. Whatever you find out from now on has nothing to do with me. You'll have to get the rest from Moi."

I nod respectfully, then notice he is tapping rather heavily on his ashtray. After he has gone I lift it up and find yet another of his newspaper cuttings. There is no date, but the clipping is yellowing:

Kontea, Tanzania: Not long ago Godot passed quickly through this tiny village in the deep South of this sleepy African country. Last year, during a routine pass by a gem-hunting corporation, "gravel" was found here: a technical term referring to certain unprepossessing small pebbles the color of raw prawns. They are near-worthless members of the sapphire family, but can be, and often are, indicators of the presence of their most valuable cousins. For a full six months the village was home to earth-moving and sieving equipment, mobile homes and offices, a cell phone pylon, and a small army of dependent industries including cooked food, laundry, and prostitution. Then, when it was confirmed that such sapphires as existed here were all of inferior quality with poor coloring and other flaws which made it impossible to market them profitably, the twenty-first century withdrew like a high tide, leaving plenty of detritus with the original villagers, who are scratching their heads and wondering if it has all been a dream. Said Mr. Jomo Matembele, shopkeeper: "We really thought we'd all been saved from poverty by God, but God went back North and now we have just a few white devils poking around the riverbed and buying up cheap stones for pennies."

49

It's late morning before I get around to thinking about Moi and the Frank Charles case again. Out of curiosity, and kicking myself for not thinking of it sooner, I check out padparadscha for myself on Wikipedia:

Because of its rarity, it is frequently fabricated via synthetics in laboratory settings, or on regular pink or orange sapphires by a process of beryllium surface diffusion. This diffusion process involves heating the stone along with crushed chrysoberyl, the source of the beryllium in the treatment.

The vast majority of padparadscha sapphires (and most other colors of sapphire) are heated in varying temperatures to enrich color and improve clarity. While this may have a negative effect on the price of the stone, it is an accepted practice so long as it is disclosed to the buyer in the process of the sale.

416

Treating stones with surface diffusion, however, is generally frowned upon; as stones chip or are repolished/refaceted the "padparadscha" colored layer can be removed. (There are some diffusion-treated stones in which the color goes much deeper than the surface, however.) The problem lies in the fact that treated padparadschas are at times very difficult to detect, and they are the reason that getting a certificate from a reputable gemological lab (e.g., Gubelin, SSEF, AGTA, etc.) is recommended before investing in a padparadscha.

The rarest of all padparadschas is the totally natural variety, with no beryllium, or other treatment, and no heating. To find a stone that is certified by a reputable lab as being completely natural is extremely rare and the stone will be very expensive. High-quality unheated and untreated natural padparadscha sapphires will start off in the range of $5,000 per carat and rise by size, color, tone, cut, and clarity, to $20,000–30,000 per carat.

I decide to take a flyer and show up in a cop car at the front entrance to Moi's house on the river.

It's quite a different prospect from this side. You could say the estate is almost conventional, with its long curved drive lined with tropical plants. Orchids of every shade grow like parasites in coconut husks hanging from ficus and palm trees. Scarlet poinsettias, amaryllis, and ivy poke and drape for most of the drive, with a stand of bamboo next to a large pool surrounded by tropical succulents that look as though they could bite your hand off. A large anthurium bush owns slim golden phalli that emerge from bracts exactly the same color as the backside of a red-assed baboon, and just as obscene. Finally, at drive's end, a porch like a Thai temple, and, of course, the shrine in the northwest corner of the grounds garlanded with lotus. Someone has already made an offering of rice, oranges, and bananas to the household gods. I press the electric bell three aggressive times, because I intend to crash, whatever mood she is in. The maid answers, sees the marked police car behind me, and beckons me inside. She is immaculate as ever in her black-and-white servant's livery, tall and elegant with her long sad moon face soaring over the frilly collar. I think it a little odd, the way she directs me across the polished teak floor of the central part of the house, and onto the terrace at back, without first alerting Moi. I can hear the Doctor yelling long before I see her. Why would the maid want me to see her mistress in the midst of one of her early-morning tantrums? Perhaps it is a statement about who is in control. To my surprise, her preferred language of scolding is not her native Teochew, nor even Thai, but finishing-school English.

"And you bloody spilled cocoa on my favorite cheongsam," Moi is howling in a slightly hysterical

418

voice, before she sees me. "How much more of my life are you going to destroy before you kill *me*, too?"

I turn instantly to catch the expression on the maid's face: blank. Moi is sitting up on one of her chaise longues, braless in a large black cotton T-shirt which would be easily big enough to cover her loins if she cared. Even when she sees me she makes no effort, but sits there in a sulk for a moment, her vagina on general view, before she hitches the T-shirt over it with a grimace. "What the hell is *he* doing here?"

For answer the maid returns with a silver tray containing what I suppose is the Doctor's breakfast: a collection of pills of various dimensions and colors, and a tiny medicine bottle with a pipette. The pipette, it seems, is the star of the show, for Moi carefully squeezes the rubber bulb, inserts it into the bottle, lets the rubber bulb expand, then examines the contents of the glass tube. Satisfied, she throws her head back, empties the clear liquid into her mouth, then tucks into the rest of the pills. Whatever was in the pipette, it works pretty quickly. Moi's personality alters in minutes, and now she is standing and brushing the black T-shirt down over her body until it reaches the middle of her thighs, the miracle of elegance somehow retrieved. She holds out a hand for me to kiss; "What a wonderful surprise," she says in a glacial tone. "Won't you please sit down?"

I sit near the guardrail at the edge of the balcony, next to the river. It is quite gay at this moment, with tugs pulling a big Korean container ship into midstream, a couple of snakehead boats with their great bus engines on davits at the stern roaring past, a posse of women wearing straw hats each in her own individual sampan, hauling vegetables, fish, fruit, and whatever else they can sell. I feel a little strange to see a bunch of kids from the shantytown naked, screaming, and diving off Moi's jetty into the river with the fanatical repetition only the young can maintain. Moi is blinking in the merciless light. Suddenly urbane all over again, she refuses to ask me what I want. I say, "I went to see your ex-husband Johnny Ng in Hong Kong."

I kept my eyes on the maid as I spoke the name, hoping that I would succeed in making her pause while she tidied up; not a chance. Moi, on the other hand, has clamped a hand over her mouth. When she removes it I cannot read her expression, not because there isn't one, but because it is too complex to interpret. Amusement? Excitement? Puerile curiosity? Anger? All of those, together with a certain delicious anticipation. I see no sign of fear. "Would you like some cocoa?"

"No, thanks, not this time."

She moves toward me, I assume to take up her favorite chaise next to the guardrail. Before doing so, she brushes by me and—to my astonishment—caresses my face with one hand. "You're so cute. So dangerously innocent, like Lord Jim. You visited Johnny and managed to stay in one piece? I'm surprised he didn't have you for dim sum. What did he tell you? If he talked it must have been because he was bored. Boredom is his only real weakness. I do hope he prefaced everything with the confession that he's Kongrao? That we own him all the way down to his DNA?" I'm shocked at her use of the word *kongrao*; but, of course, technically you could argue that the phrase might have an innocent meaning here; after all, Moi did marry him.

"He didn't need to. The way he left out everything that could implicate 'your thing' made it all too obvious. But he did tell me in a few hours what I would have discovered anyway in a week or so."

She sits down on the chaise, stretches her legs and crosses them, turns languid. "And what might that have been?"

I take out a gem trader's magazine for the month of March 2007, open it to the page which bears the news that the famous Hollywood director Frank Charles confessed himself deeply moved to accept the position of honorary ambassador to the Thai guild of gem traders, then stand up to lay it on her black lap. She takes it in with one glance, sighs, chucks it on the floor, and stares expectantly at me.

I go back to sit on my rattan chair, lean forward toward her, and ask in a slightly plaintive voice, "Why, Mimi? He was your good friend, for Buddha's sake."

She looks at me in blank incomprehension, gasps, turns to the maid, and seems to say in her mother tongue, *Did you hear what this jerk just said?* Or words to that effect. Now even the maid is looking at me as if I have a serious learning disability. Indeed, Moi lets out a long, slow whoop. "Are you sure you don't want some enhanced cocoa? I think you're going to need something, Detective."

In a voice which is suddenly regal, she dismisses the maid, who quickly leaves the terrace. "As a chemist, allow me to ask one little question. The pathologist, whoever it was, they made a list of all the chemicals found on and in his body?" I nod. "And was one of those substances beryllium?" I nod again. "Under his fingernails, perhaps?" I let her have another nod. "Then quite frankly, Detective, I could rest my case right there. Out of respect for your terrifying mother, however, I will tell you more."

The maid reappears with a cheroot, which she pops into Moi's mouth and lights. Moi takes a long pull and exhales dense gray smoke. "Padparadscha came late to the land of Nippon-koku," she begins with a half smile. "You might want to bear that in mind. But let's get poor Frank out of the way first. It's his damned film, isn't it, that's knocked you quite off track?" She looks at me with that form of condescending benevolence that inspires feelings of violent resentment in all sane people. But she won't let up. "That's so funny. And you a cop, too. But that was Frank, you see—the biggest charlatan of all. A real, professional, all-points-covered, state-of-the-art all-American graduate from that most celebrated academy of charlatans called Hollywood." She waves a hand. "Oh, I don't mean he didn't actually do and feel all those romantic, sensitive, self-doubting, spiritual things. But they belonged to the pretend side of what he was, more like aspects of what he wanted to be. But I'll give him one thing. For a full three weeks he really did intend to die just exactly the way he dies in that movie. That's why he forced poor Ah Ting to be in it, you see? He was really going to pay her to kill him in that way, and—umm—Ah Ting didn't mind. She hates all men, but especially the ones that get close to me, so she loved the rehearsals. And, as I'm sure you realize, there is no way any Thai cop who wants to stay alive would dream of arresting Ah Ting for any-thing. Kongrao wouldn't let them—me you can arrest anytime, it won't make any difference in the scheme of things. You see, she's the real priestess now. She copes with the mumbo jumbo so much better than me. In fact, I think she really believes in it. After all, it's made her quite magically rich, and at the end of the day she is a full-blooded, card-carrying, hyper-superstitious Chinese peasant."

"So what happened?" I ask. "Frank Charles got him-self into such a romantically suicidal state, such a lovelorn, obese, self-loathing late-life crisis that he was going to shock the world in the only way left to him—that is, by dying on-screen—thus ensuring the acclaim that had so eluded him in life. What happened?"

"He chickened out, of course. He was a child of cinema, of fantasy. I think he used drugs to keep his mind off what he intended to do, then when the crunch got closer, he stopped intending to do it. He was in quite a state. You see, he had no reliable addiction; even his fondness for chemicals was promiscuous." She pauses to give me a long, appraising stare, perhaps to check if I'm ready for what comes next. "There's only one thing harder to handle than a would-be suicide, and that's a failed suicide." She gives a brief smile. "I'm afraid Ah Ting caught him in a vulnerable moment when I was out, and strictly against my instructions told him about—ah—one of the little things Kongrao gets up to overseas."

"She recruited him because she needed another scapegoat? Kongrao was moving into Japan?"

At the word *Japan* she gives a couple of blinks of acknowledgment. "But, you see, it wasn't a case of 'moving into' Japan." Here her face turns quite merry and she blows a long stream of smoke over the balcony. "We'd been supplying Japan for over a century. But a terrible thing happened to Japan after they lost the war. Half their psyche turned *farang*. That's why they're so confused. They rely on science instead of Asian intuition. It's made them terribly vulnerable." Now she is spluttering, trying not to collapse in laughter. "They have laboratories, d'you see? And in *farang*land, a fully accredited, properly staffed scientific laboratory is like the word of God. And just like God, it can be amazingly unreliable." Now she cannot stop laughing. When the maid comes onto the terrace, perhaps to check on her, she, too, permits herself the ghost of a smile. Once she has seen that her mistress is okay, she retreats again into the dark teak interior. Moi shakes her head.

"Recruit him? Ah Ting recruit Frank Charles? A lawyer might frame it that way. A more accurate way of putting it would be to say she waved a carrot in front of him and he turned into a voracious donkey overnight. After she'd explained the scam to him, pretending to keep it secret so I wouldn't be implicated—she protects me from all forms of reality, especially male—you couldn't have stopped him." She has become quite vigorous, even to the point of raising her body from the chaise. "And this is the point, d'you see? If he'd just heated up a couple of cheap Burmese sapphires now and then and taken a modest profit, the Japs would have accepted the scam as part of the game. But he had to do his American think-big thing and go to that godforsaken village in Tanzania and buy up all their sapphire junk by the kilo. Literally."

I wait and wait, but she doesn't continue. She has fallen into some kind of reverie. I say, "I don't understand."

The words take about two minutes to penetrate, then she says, languidly, "Why not? To understand all you need are two things: sixteen hundred degrees Centigrade, and beryllium."

"You paid off the Japanese labs that check gems for the local industry?"

She waves a hand. "Nothing so sophisticated. Thais don't know how to bribe Japanese laboratories, assuming such a thing is possible. No, you see, the labs

425

themselves weren't up to speed. They simply didn't know, or didn't believe, Thais could be so smart, so devious, and so humble looking at the same time. And apparently their tests for beryllium were very crude and unreliable. And what's more, we never used the word *padparadscha* on any of the invoices—they were simply described as sapphires. The Japs thought they were being clever because they knew these gems were really the hyper-valuable padparadscha and we did not. *They* thought they were fooling us—just as we intended. They're terrible racists, you see; they haven't changed since Nanking. No way they were going to think our decadent brown people would out-smart them. We never sold the product at the market price—thirty thousand dollars a carat—but about twenty-five per cent cheaper. We let them think they were getting a bargain from a genuine Thai padparadscha mine, and Thai pads, when you can get them, are among the best in the world. It was only when the Japanese tried selling their Thai padparadschas—which were actually enhanced low-quality African sapphires—to America, where the labs were more up to speed, that they realized what Kongrao had done. And since there was no evidence of misrepresentation, there was nothing they could do. But it destroyed more than fifty per cent of their gem merchants. You had bankruptcies from Nagasaki to Sapporo." She rubs her jaw. "I suppose one shouldn't laugh."

"But you killed Frank Charles. I mean, you set him

426

up as a mascot knowing the Japanese would kill him sooner or later?"

"Detective, you are a terrible naïf, and this leads you to misjudge human character. You are still thinking of Frank as a victim, just because he got bumped off. Actually, it was the opposite. When *farang* get greedy, they have no restraint. Once he knew how the whole scam worked, he became a fanatic. Ah Ting begged him to calm down, he was selling too much, upsetting the balance. He not only ignored her, he mastered the technique himself. He started heating the gems up to sixteen hundred degrees Centigrade and adding the beryllium—he became very good at it, approached the whole process much more methodically than any of our people. He even invested in proper electric kilns and a cooking recipe that enabled him to control the timing down to the microsecond. You see, Detective, the bottom line about Frank Charles, the source of his being, you might say, was greed. A nice enough guy, and he really did want to make a halfway decent film at least once in his life, but he was thwarted by his own greed all the way. Frank Charles was just greedy, greedy, greedy. That's why he got so fat, and why he had to have ten naked girls in his Jacuzzi on his sixtieth birthday—no fancy psychological component, just old-fashioned greed and the American predatory spirit."

I'm tired of being mocked for my naïveté, so I take a long while to think the whole case through. After

427

five minutes I'm still shaking my head. "But the way he was killed, Mimi—the way he died?"

She takes a cool toke from the cheroot and stubs it out. "Have you any idea how anal-retentive Japanese jewelers are? They are like brilliant insects working at the microscopic level all their lives, shaving off a micron here, a micron there, dominating their world at a level of detail designed to induce madness. No wonder they are all men. The passion to control is off the human scale. Imagine such a man consumed by hatred and the lust for revenge?"

I blink rapidly. "But whoever the perp was, he would have needed a copy of the film, and would have needed to know that the film had not been released, that no one of importance knew about it—"

I stop, because Moi has given a single, short glance toward the interior of the house where the maid has retreated. Obviously, she will not say another word of relevance to the case. I guess she doesn't need to. Nevertheless, I try one last question. "It was in the interests of Kongrao to provide the sacrificial goat? To facilitate both the assassination and the perfect alibi—namely, that the victim killed himself on film? That's why Witherspoon, who is Kongrao, was ordered to send me the movie? You are still trading with the Japanese? I suppose they had to be placated somehow?"

Moi doesn't say anything. The interview is over. I have only one ace left: "Doctor, the toxicologist found tubocurarine chloride in his blood. How would a jeweler get hold of it? How would a jeweler even know he needed it? Frank Charles was *paralyzed but fully conscious* when Suzuki cut into his skull, removed it, and *ate his brains.*"

For an answer, the Doctor gives me that smile, the one where the corners of the lips crawl up the incisors.

I leave and walk through the house to the other side. There is no sign of the maid, but two of Moi's outside guards are chatting to the cop who is waiting in the marked car I came in. They straighten up when they see me, but I can tell they've been smirking over some yarn with my driver. I get in the back of the car instead of sitting in front the way I normally do. "Where to?" he asks. I stare out the side window at Moi's magnificent house, and at the river behind it, and at the kids from the shantytown yelling as they dive naked from the jetty. "It's the strangest story you ever heard," I tell the driver, still staring at the skinny kids. "Once upon a time a rich man arrived here from the West. It turned out he was lost in a dream in which he foretold the manner of his own death down to the last detail."

"What? Where do you want to go?"

I think about that. "Silom," I say. "That dingy three-star hotel opposite the Hindu temple."

The temple is called Sri Mariamman, and there is the usual crowd of flower, incense, and amulet sellers hanging around outside it. I have no idea why there should be a Hindu temple in the middle of Bangkok, but it's incredibly famous and holy, to judge by the amount of ochre and crimson powder people chuck all over its shrines, and the number of half-naked Indian holy men who arrive from places like Varanasi to worship here; generally they like to stay in the same three-star flophouse where Mr. Suzuki, the Japanese jeweler, committed suicide. Strictly speaking there is no forensic need to visit Suzuki's former room; the evidence relating to his suicide will be in storage at a police station somewhere. But I feel a kind of animal need to be in the place where the little Japanese man—according to one of the newspaper reports he was just five foot two—worked himself up into a controlled orgasm of rage. I'm not entirely surprised that the superstitious Thai manager has kept the room vacant for the moment, and even placed some lotus buds to float in a brass bowl of water outside the door. He lets me in without question once I've flashed my ID. It is, indeed, a very small room, renting for only five hundred baht per night. The tiny window, no doubt perfectly clean on the inside, is dark with city pollution. Suzuki moved here from the five-star hotel he was staying in with the trade delegation, after his colleagues all went home. Did they appoint him as assassin? Did they know what he intended? Surely he must have needed help?

Against all logic, I prefer to think of the little guy working on his own. I don't want to believe he used a pack of *yakuza* thugs to carry out his plan, although police reports suggest there were a few accompanying the delegation as bodyguards. I think he somehow maneuvered Frank Charles into his room in the flophouse on Soi 4/4 all on his own through sheer force of personality; how he stuck the lumbering giant with a syringe full of tubocurarine chloride is more of a challenge than my imagination can handle, however. Once he had paralyzed the American with his venom, did he use the room's DVD player so that he could check he was following Frank Charles's own instructions for his gaudy "suicide," or had he watched the movie so many times he retained perfect recall? He would have needed a rotary saw, of course, but for a master jeweler that would not have been a problem.

Suzuki, more than anyone, had been destroyed by Frank Charles and Kongrao's scam—utterly wiped out, according to reports, and left with an impossible pile of debts. It seems he had seen the padparadscha trade as his chance for jewelers' stardom and wagered all his savings, even mortgaged his business, in order to buy the brilliantly colored sapphires that turned out to be worth only a tiny fraction of what he paid for them. A man of honor and a passionate practitioner of the Japanese sport of kendo, I think he was also a dark introvert who told nobody what he intended to do; rather, he expected that the nobility of his last act would redeem him posthumously in the eyes of his society. I think of him working on Frank Charles's drugged body plopped all over that narrow bed on Soi 4/4, carefully marking out on the American's cranium where he had to cut in accordance with the movie. I imagine the demon of vengeance taking full possession of the little man's disciplined soul. *He ate the brains right out of the skull, raw like sushi.* Apparently, a few hours after he killed Frank Charles he returned here to disembowel himself while sitting on the floor cross-legged facing the dirty window.

When I find out from the station where Suzuki's personal effects are being held, I go over to the storage depot and sign a form. I wait in a dusty office while a clerk brings me an unusually long metal box, which she opens in front of me. According to the rules I am supposed to put on a pair of plastic gloves; I do so in order to pick up the heavy object in one corner of the box. It is much smaller than I imagined, far smaller than the kind of rotary saws that surgeons use, but I guess it is just as powerful, if not more so. In any event, the disk is easily big enough to cut through a quarter inch of human bone, and, of course, being a tool of the jewelry trade, the disk's edge is enhanced with industrial diamonds. It is also encrusted with blood. And then there is the other kind of disk, a DVD, black and wordless on the title side; I pick it up to examine it, turning it in the light so I can see where the band of data has been burned into the plastic, then replace it. The other object of interest—and the reason why the box needed to be so long—is a samurai sword; its blade, still bloodstained, is wrapped in a clear plastic sheath. I'm not an expert, but I would judge from the damascene pattern and the perfect heft that it must be of the highest quality.

I am afraid there is not much to do but sigh. I could, of course, have the bloodstains on the saw tested to see if the blood belonged to Frank Charles, but I don't really have the time. Tietsin is dropping the smack tomorrow. And anyway, who cares? As far as the world is concerned, two unrelated suicides, one a diminutive Japanese jeweler, the other a fantastically outsized American movie director, happened to occur within hours of each other on the same night in Bangkok. What else is new? And that's just the way Kongrao and the Japanese gem traders want it left. But I had to solve the case, didn't I?

50

Tietsin is dropping the smack tomorrow: you did notice me coyly slip this dangerous intelligence between the plump thighs of the previous chapter, *farang*? Are your knees trembling the way mine are right now? Don't you wish you were stoned? I do. Under the contract he only has to give us twenty-four hours' notice within a certain time window. I faxed him a copy of the letter of credit so his bankers could check it, and he sent me a text message yesterday consisting of a single word— *tomorrow*—and I've been up all night. I've vomited in the sink twice already and it's only six in the morning. *I'm not going through with it*, I tell my face in the mirror. *Oh yes, you are*, the face replies. My own mind has conspired against me: I have no options anymore. *Supposing some of them are kids who use the stuff?* I ask myself. *You accepted Vikorn's money, didn't you, you took the job. Are you a man at all?* So it goes on, the war of the self against the self. I do believe I might be turning 100 per cent *farang*. But I have one of those wily Oriental solutions up my sleeve, which you'll probably

434

despise for not being confrontational enough, but it might just do the trick, even if Vikorn snuffs me for it, which he certainly will. I don't care. I'd rather die early and (relatively) innocent. Look at my record: more than ten years in the Royal Thai Police and I've committed no major crime, nor even a minor one as far as I can recall. (I'm not including smoking dope; sometimes the law is wrong.) Is there another serving officer who can swear on the Pali Canon that he is equally clean? No, the hell with it, Tara is never coming to live with me in Bangkok, so there's no use kidding myself I have a life at all; what's to lose?

Do you also have the martyr cutoff psychology, *farang*? The kind that says, *Only so much and so far, I prefer death to further degradation?* It's quite a powerful mantra, but you risk having to put your life where your mouth is sooner or later.

Now you're saying, *So why didn't you think of this before, why leave it to the last minute?* Answer: cowardice. I just didn't want to face it. I'm coming out of an extended Hamlet moment: I just couldn't make up my mind. Now I have. And the Buddha, for once, is quite explicit. He visited me last night in a dream, in the form of a child's plastic Buddha. He actually told me how to get out of this fix. The only trouble with advice straight from Gautama himself, though: he doesn't place any value on flesh at all. I mean, to him, there's no difference between the two shores; he is master of both. Now I'm not sure if the dread in the bottom

435

of my gut is from the crime or the Buddha's plan to prevent it.

It is a common observation among Buddhists of all persuasions that after death one is not initially aware of one's altered state; the clue comes from the people around who can no longer see or hear you, and in this sense the condition cannot be said to differ greatly from your basic urban paranoia: *Am I dead already? Have I always been that way?* These are the kinds of thoughts which illuminate a mind focused wonderfully by the knowledge that it may well be slotted before morning. Nevertheless, I'm off to the local hardware store at the bottom of the street, which sells gas bottles for cooking. I choose two of medium size— the kind that can supply the cooking needs of a normal Thai family for a month—then buy two little camping gas burners—are you beginning to get the picture, *farang?*—and take everything home in a taxi. Then I buy my first car. Well, why not? I'm consigliere, I deserve a car. In view of its short life expectancy, however, I go for a secondhand Toyota. The more I develop my secret plan, the prouder and scareder I become. It's now midday. The next few hours are going to be tough; I see quite a few joints coming on.

Now I'm at the station not half as stoned as I would like to be, fiddling with paperwork, making constant checks on my cell phone to see if Tietsin has texted me again, even though I would have heard the bleep if he had. I'm waiting for the final signal that will tell me which of twenty named locations in Bangkok the Tibetan will actually use for the drop.

He has calculated that even Vikorn and Zinna together cannot ambush twenty separate drop-off points to steal his product without paying for it—not without drawing undue attention to themselves, anyway—so he faxed a map with twenty different crosses on it. General Zinna immediately pointed out that half the locations were on the river, so the Tibetan was surely planning to come by water. Vikorn sees it differently: *He's probably trying to make us think he's coming by river because he's not.*

The question—*How is he going to bring the stuff into the country?*—has brought the two old dogs together in a competitive kind of way. I have had to attend bull sessions in the General's map room, as if the Tibetan were preparing to invade Bangkok. Basically, Zinna is convinced the stuff will come by sea and be taken up the Chao Phraya River by sampan. Vikorn doubts there is time for the sea route, which is exactly what intrigues him as a fellow professional: how do you shift that much smack across a modern border and get away with it? As far as he can see there are only two solutions: overland from Cambodia or overland from Burma. But in both cases, the Tibetan has to get the stuff out of the Himalayas first, not easy in the present climate. Even if he has bent people in the Nepali government, there is still India to deal with. Vikorn only pretends to have a view on how Tietsin will bring it off; in reality he is waiting to find out. You can see why the cop is richer than the general.

Five p.m. comes and goes. So does six. The letter of credit is in the safe in Vikorn's room; I can get it in five minutes. The gas bottles are in the trunk of my car. Six-thirty: it occurs to both Vikorn and me at the same time: Tietsin will wait until the last minute. According to the contract, he has until midnight to reveal the precise location; after that we have the right to kill the deal. Vikorn calls me: "What d'you think, he'll stretch it out till then?"

"I don't know. What does Zinna say?"

"Zinna? He isn't even guessing anymore. The Tibetan has done his head in."

Ever felt, *farang*, that you just don't have the constitution for modern times? That theoretically you could see how living a better life might be achieved, but the logistics of the nervous system are against you? I keep thinking about those gas bottles and how I'm going to use my consigliere status to follow the smack once Vikorn has paid for it, to whatever warehouse they're using, and use the small gas bottles to heat up and explode the big ones—and my whole body starts to go into contortions at my desk and *I'm not sure I'm going to be able to carry it off*; I'm not sure my body will obey me.

At ten p.m. Tietsin texts me; within the same moment I'm calling Vikorn and Zinna on my cell phone, grabbing the letter of credit as Vikorn meets me at the door of his room, snatching my car keys— and I'm out of the station. "It's location thirteen," I'm telling Zinna as I'm walking down the steps to the garage. "Location thirteen, that's right, on the river near Klong Toey commercial port."

I get there first, so I position my car near where I think Vikorn will park his van, the one he's going to use for the pickup. I've no sooner killed my engine when a tall camper van turns up with the two chemists, one representing Vikorn, the other Zinna: highly respected professionals, both of whom are aware that honest reporting is the likeliest way to stay alive. I'm pretty sure they are incorruptible, even by a Tibetan psychonaut. Now I hear the fairy crunches of army tires on the tarmac. Yep, Zinna's here, with a twenty-man backup — Vikorn and I had to talk him down from a hundred-man squad. Speak of the devil, here's the Colonel himself, rolling up in an ordinary police van with only a few bodyguards on motorbikes. He took the view a long time ago that there will be no trouble from Tietsin, as long as we come up with the cash.

Our high-tech Tibetan gave us GPS coordinates for the precise location of the drop, and both Zinna and Vikorn are following their lieutenants, who are playing with different GPS handhelds and bumping into each other trying to get the coordinates exactly right. It seems we have to walk a little more toward the river, then turn right onto the dock where some huge, black, and rusted cargo ships from China, Korea, and Vietnam are berthed. We are between a couple of container ships, standing under the bows of the *Flower of*

Shanghai and looking the *Rose of Danang* up and down, when I say, "It's that one."

I'm pointing to a ship on the opposite side of the docks which was previously invisible but has come into view as we try to position ourselves in accordance with the Tibetan's coordinates. I say, "The coordinates he gave are not where he is located. He's taken us to the point where we can see him, that's all."

"See what? I don't see a damn thing."

"The prayer flags," I say, unable to repress a grin. "On that ship over there, all the way up to the top of the mast."

"Why the hell would he do that?" Zinna moans.

"Because we're being watched by his people, have been since the minute we arrived," Vikorn explains in a tone of respect and wonder. "By now he knows everything he needs to know about us. How many men, what kind of weapons, even our morale."

When we finally arrive at the ship that's festooned with Tibetan prayer flags gently swaying in the night air, the Tibetan wild man himself is sitting all alone in his open parka on a black iron bollard, his long gray hair tied back. With his eyes rolling, he looks insane.

"*Sawatdee krup*," he says in a not-bad accent, showing us the equality *wai*, with hands raised to eye level and no higher.

"Told you," Zinna says. "I told you he would come by water."

Everyone watches while I walk toward Tietsin with the letter of credit in my hand. I hold it in front of his

440

eyes, but he makes no gesture to check it. Instead, he jerks his chin in the direction behind us. We turn to look, but all we can see are the high black bows and shadows in between.

Then they start to appear one by one, all dressed in black. One by one, Zinna, Vikorn, and I drop our jaws in amazement.

"Backpacks?" Vikorn says, gobsmacked, his voice squeaking in disbelief. "He brought in the whole fucking five hundred and thirty-three kilos in backpacks?"

I stare slack-jawed in wonder at Tietsin while his men continue to appear in commando-black T-shirts and pants, with black backpacks. When they have finished arriving there are thirty in all, which I calculate produces an average of about seventeen kilos—thirty-eight pounds—of heroin per backpack. Thirty-eight pounds is the maximum load for paid Sherpas in the Himalayas.

"We thought about other means," Tietsin says, rolling his eyes back, "but none of them were viable. In the end I had to develop a customs officer mantra with all the ritual that goes with it. So far so good, it seems to have worked fine." He beams.

"Please tell me you didn't all take the same plane," Vikorn says; the blood has drained from his face.

"Of course not. Half of us came on the morning flight, the other half in the afternoon."

"You, you, you—" I say, then stop. Words fail one at times like this.

"What d'you expect? We're Himalayans. We don't know any better. Now, why don't you tell your little friends to get their chemists working so we can all go home?"

Vikorn and Zinna use their men to seal off the area while the chemists' van trundles up the docks and the two scientists examine the contents of the backpacks one by one. While they are working, a Tibetan, who was not one of those carrying the dope, comes up to Tietsin and whispers a few words into his ear. The yogin suddenly stares at me in a way that is physically uncomfortable, as if some painful ray has emerged from between his eyes to give me a sudden headache. My bowels turn over and the intolerable nerves of the day return to shake up my whole being. Tietsin doesn't take his eyes off me while the chemists are taking their samples, so by the time they have finished and are confirming with smiles that they are satisfied it is indeed 99 per cent smack in each one of the thirty backpacks, my knees have turned to Jell-O.

And all the time, more and more of his men are emerging from the shadows of the dock. Now it is hard to say how many people Tietsin has brought with him. At first I assumed that some of them, at least, were Thais he'd hired from some underworld connection, but after a few minutes I have changed my mind. You can take the Tibetan out of Tibet, it seems, but you can't take the *vajra* out of the Tibetan—there's something about their eyes that says you don't exist in the way you think you do—even if they have all shaved

442

and cut their hair. No doubt about it, these are high-lander yak rustlers armed with cute little machine pistols who overcame hesitation about five thousand meditations ago. For a mystic, Tietsin has quite a practical side. He jerks his chin at me with demoralizing contempt. Now I am standing in front of him like a naughty schoolboy.

He speaks softly. "Detective, did you ever hear of an asshole named Clive of India?"

"Yes."

"And do you know what this asshole named Clive of India did to the world?"

"British Empire."

"Financed by?"

"Opium sales."

"If you put it like that you risk trivializing his achievement. He was the first to make the connection between arms and narcotics. This little thug from Shropshire, who would certainly have been hanged if he'd stayed in England, saw the way to finance a whole private army, and the model proved so effective they repeated it all over the world: narcotics, slaves, and weapons. It's the great tripod upon which our global civilization continues to be based, even if they have changed the labels and the slaves get health insurance. The plain fact is, the sociopathic nature of the modern corporation started then and there with Clive. By the time the British narco empire collapsed, twenty million Chinese were addicted to opium and pink-faced syphilitic alcoholics in scarlet jackets were intimidating the whole world with their Maxim guns. The United Kingdom in its modern form is an opium derivative. And what was the point of the exercise? Answer: so middle-class girls in Kent and Sussex could go to school all dressed in white and play the violin instead of going on the Game. If that is good enough justification for enslaving the world and invading Tibet, don't you think that forty million dollars' worth of smack is a fair price for freedom and democracy?"

He sighs. "You thought you would play the martyr, get yourself a permanent seat in nirvana in return for your sacrifice, your undeniable stinking *goodness*? What are you, some kind of Sunday Christian? Didn't I already make it clear that *good* isn't good enough? You accepted the mantra, kid, and you can't say nobody warned you. Good is even harder to kick than evil. They are a duality, *you know that*, you don't get one without the other. I dread to think what kind of sanctimonious asshole you would have turned into, probably about five minutes before Vikorn snuffed you, if we didn't get to you first." He lets a couple of beats pass while he examines my shocked and terrified mug. "It just ain't that easy, you of all people should know that. And anyway, you have no right to deprive me of my karma. It's all *me* driving this. This is *my* moment, not yours, so who the fuck are you to screw it all up just because you can't live with yourself? If you can't live with yourself, dump your self."

"The Buddha came to me in a dream," I mumble. "He showed me the gas bottles."

"Oh, yeah? Listen, around us you don't talk about the Buddha. Which Buddha? Be specific."

"He was in the form of a child's toy."

"See! Can't you even interpret your own dreams properly by now? The Buddha's showing you it's time to grow up already, dump your infant faith, and get into something adult. Didn't they tell you the great Theravada admonition: 'If you see the Buddha on the road, kill him'?"

"That's Zen," I explain.

"Really? Whatever."

"And what about the gas bottles?"

"You weren't supposed to take that literally, dummy. The gas bottles are you: pressurized gas, that's all any of us is who has not reached the Far Shore." He scratches his head, apparently genuinely perplexed. "I can't understand how anyone could get that wrong."

He stands up, comes intimidatingly close, and whispers in my ear, "Whatever little mind pictures you've got of me by now, kid, you better dump them. I don't have an ego. Those Chinese burned every tiny little bit of it out of me, every root, every fiber with their cute little cattle prods—in the end I was secretly urging them on. I knew even then there was no way I was going to spend the next sixty years dragging a bleeding, damaged, heartbroken, resentful, miserable stump of ego around. If I had, I would have gotten sick and died thirty years ago. But I didn't." He lets a few beats pass while he assesses me. "You need to grow up. That great pile of black karma you're so worried about,

445

that huge Chomolungma of guilt that's looming up in your mind and crippling your judgment—forget it. *The people who will use this stuff are already dead, can't you understand? They are stuck in their diabolic continuum because they trafficked in previous lifetimes.* Whether they buy from us or someone else has no significance, because *buy they must* and *buy they will*—don't you know that Clive himself is out there somewhere, shooting up in some squalid back-room above a supermarket in Shropshire, just another deadbeat with tattoos, paralyzed by the weight of his karma, helpless without his little brown servants and whores, the classic Caucasian male basket case of modern times? This isn't my personal payback, this is world dharma we're talking about. *The earth itself is making this happen, otherwise we would never have gotten the stuff past customs.*" He pauses for breath. "For my part, you know what I'm going to do? I'm going to suck it all up and transform every last lost life into positive energy using the power of Tantra. And do you know how I acquired the means to do that? I'm not a Buddha, Detective; I'm not a bodhisattva; I'm not even a doctor of Buddhism, only of Tibetan history, and I'm not a monk. Detective, I have to tell you, I am one hell of a lot better than all of those things. *I am a man, and I want my country back.*"

He stops for a moment, as if deciding whether or not to speak his full mind. Finally, he leans closer so I can feel his breath on my ear.

"I am a mystery to you because I am psychically invisible. I show up on no one's inner radar. I no longer

446

exist in the way you do. I am your dharma. Get the fuck out of here right now and take your stinking pressurized gas with you."

When he sees I am on the verge of obeying, he adds, "There's someone at home waiting for you."

I'm about ten paces away already when he calls out, "And don't forget to watch CNN exactly one week from today."

But leaving, it turns out, is easier said than done. I'm on the way to my car when I see that it is guarded by some of Zinna's soldiers. I figure the game's up with me, despite Tietsin's help, and I just stand there for a moment, waiting to be shot or, more likely, taken away and tortured to death. Then I see there are quite a lot of soldiers, far more than Zinna's quota, pouring in from the street. At the far end of the dock, Tietsin's men seem to be rushing out of the area, as if they have an understanding with the soldiers. In spite of everything, I feel the need to warn Vikorn. Too late. Zinna is walking toward the Colonel. About five paces away, he suddenly raises one of his arms and clicks his fingers. Great spotlights originating in a military truck on the street suddenly illuminate most of the dock, especially Zinna and Vikorn, who are facing off in stark white light. The spotlights also reveal the extent of Zinna's treachery: there must be over two hundred well-armed soldiers on the dock now, and a lot more outside the perimeter. Zinna smiles triumphantly, and almost apologetically, at Vikorn: "Looks like I won," the little General says.

Vikorn has turned gray and is shaking slightly. When I examine him more closely, I see it is one of those near-epileptic rages that has taken possession of him. I am deeply saddened that he has been double-crossed and defeated; there is nothing to stop the General from simply taking all the smack from under Vikorn's nose. Zinna is about to wipe him out. You could say he has done so already. Why do I feel such animal loyalty to the Old Man? I'm so depressed I feel ill.

"Looks like it," Vikorn says with a groan.

Zinna gives the victor's satisfied nod. "No point in a bloodbath," he says in his brittle baritone. "Especially when all the blood spilled will be yours."

"That's true," Vikorn says, nodding. "That's very true." He pauses, utters the single word "except," and gives the tiniest little nuance of a nod toward the nearest ship to his right. Zinna is too wired not to notice; when he looks up at the ship, so does everyone else. At the same time, someone switches all the deck's lights on. Now they are clearly visible: about a hundred cops who had been waiting in the shadows walk forward holding M16s all cocked to fire.

While Zinna is taking this in, Vikorn jerks his chin at the next ship. We are not surprised, this time, to see it light up to reveal another hundred or so cops. With the improved lighting we can see a great crowd of sampan ladies in their boats tied up against the two big ships, their silent oars hanging. The old bastard must have sent a secret signal as soon as he knew where the drop-off was going to be. At about the same time Zinna sent his secret signal.

Zinna has turned ashen, but is not defeated. "Don't be a fool. I've got men on the streets, are you crazy, you can't defeat me, *I am the army*."

Vikorn nods gravely. "You have men on the street, but my men have cordoned off the whole area. I also have a communications van down the road. If you open fire, the whole country will be alerted that you are staging a coup. I do hope you warned your superiors that they are going to be running the country in the morning?"

Everyone is watching Zinna. Which way will he jump? An awful lot of guns are pointing at an awful lot of men. Well, at this point we need to bear in mind that he is Asian. He rubs his jaw. "Vikorn, you old fool, you've completely misunderstood, as usual. As the most senior army officer present I was just taking care of security." He waves a hand to take in the whole of the docks. "Just in case. I wasn't double-crossing you at all. Can't you understand that I feel responsible for the safety of the operation and everyone involved in it? I can't tell you how hurt I feel at your mistrust."

"I most humbly beg your pardon," Vikorn says with a glorious smile. "My mistake. Shall we get on with moving the smack, half to your warehouse, half to mine?"

Zinna nods and with another flick of his fingers turns off the spotlights. When Vikorn gives the signal for the two ships to shut their lights, we're in near darkness again and I can finally go home.

* * *

Confused is probably the best word to describe my state of mind; very confused. It occurs to me that Tietsin has finally shown me something that should have been obvious all along: he's not human. Not like you and me, *farang*; his brain systems are of a totally different order, and my most basic mental images of him seem to be dissolving even as I drive home. Who understands Tibetans? Maybe he is a reincarnation of Milarepa.

But I won't deny it, I'm human all the way through, blade wheels or not. Sure, the idea of *someone waiting for me at home* sweetens the bitter pill quite a lot, and once I'm settled into a good, hot, late-night traffic jam I cool my fevered brain with imaginations of Tara and me romping in the high Himal, chucking handfuls of freezing spring water at each other, arguing and fighting all the way to Shambhala. To say I'm all eagerness when I reach the door is downplaying it: I'm sort of shuddering with gratitude when I burst in.

Her head is shaved and she's lost a good bit of weight, but those agate eyes still know how to gleam. She turns on a quizzical expression just for me.

"Chanya?"

She lowers her lashes. "I decided to surprise you."

She is waiting for a welcoming smile. I give it. Now she adopts the humble posture of a woman who no longer has proprietorial rights here, while exercising those same rights in a surreptitious search for signs of another woman. Of course, she has already completed her investigation and concluded there are no indications of a live-in other, so the performance is all for me. She uses a slightly pathetic expression to say, "I'm not interrupting anything?"

"No," I say, "nothing."

"I'm so sorry, Sonchai. So sorry I had to leave you alone like that with your grief. You're stronger than me. You took it all without anesthetic. Not me. I needed the *wat*, the nuns, the hardship, the four-in-the-morning wake-up calls, and the endless photographs of the dead to see me through. But I thought about you all the time. I thought about your body. It amazed me to discover I love you more than Buddha. It's almost irritating."

Although her head is shaved, she is no longer in her nun's robes. On the contrary, she is wearing a T-shirt and jeans. When she pulls off the T-shirt and bra, I see how thin she has become, how much her breasts have shrunk. How hard Pichai's death hit her. "Not without anesthetic," I clarify, suppressing a gulp. "I've been stoned since the day you left."

"Sonchai, we're too young to give up on life. Let's try again."

If ever you're in this sort of fix yourself, *farang*, I am able to advise there is a good deal of Buddhist teaching in favor of taking the path of least resistance.

"Okay," I say. Then, as I'm undressing: "By the way, I bought a Toyota."

51

The next day Tara calls me. Do you think this indicates mind reading, synchronicity, magic? Me neither. I think Tietsin told her to phone me. Chanya and I are in bed, and I have to use that most provocative phrase in the English language: "I'm sorry, I can't talk right now." Then, to add a still more sinister note: "I'll call you back later."

So now Chanya is up on one elbow stroking my face with ambiguous tenderness, licking my ear, and murmuring, "Who was that, *tilak*? You can tell me, you know how guilty I feel, I can forgive you anything in this tranquil state the nuns taught me. Who was it?"

Well, what can you do except play out the role dharma has provided? Yes, I do tell her about Tara, yes, I do go into detail about how lonely and needy I was at the time; but I do not give the slightest hint of how fascinated I continue to be by the Tibetan *dakini*. I don't mention Tantra, much less how intriguing the lady is in bed. Though I say so myself, my confession is a masterpiece of common or garden-variety hypocrisy. Afterward, Chanya of the shaved dome—women's skulls are so much more delicate than men's—lies on her back for five minutes, not saying a word, while I watch her diaphragm move up and down, her diminished breasts rising and falling in that half-starved frame.

"You're still fascinated by her, aren't you?"

"Of course not."

"For a cop you're a lousy liar." She stares down at her body. "I'm controlling it, look," she says, almost excited at proof she has made spiritual progress after all. "All that choking jealousy, that awful dark emotion like soy that's been fermenting too long—I'm free of it. Fantastic. Thank you, Sonchai."

"You're sure? You used to have a serious—" Then it comes, from out of nowhere, a lightning twist of her superfine body and—*wham*—open hand to the right side of the face. "What did you do that for?"

"To make it even easier to forgive you. I'm so sorry, did I hurt you?"

That was quite a clout. I'm still rubbing my jaw when Tara calls again. "I'm sorry, Detective, I don't have any money. I want to talk to you. Please call me back."

Chanya's face has tightened. "Call her."

"No, I won't."

"Oh yes you will."

"What am I going to say?"

"You're going to say your wife's just come back and it's all over, dummy."

I find the number in the phone's log and call Tara. "Look, Tara, I have something to tell you. My wife

453

came back last night. We've decided to try again. We're in bed right now. I'm sorry."

A pause, then: "What are you sorry about? Congratulations. I want to speak to her."

I hold the phone away from my mouth and mime to Chanya that Tara wants to speak to her. She mimes back something like *What the hell do I want to speak to your little Himalayan tart for?* I shrug.

Now Tara is saying, "Does she speak English?" At the same time Chanya has suddenly become curious about this Tibetan *mia noi*, or minor wife, who has the balls to try to speak directly to First Wife in a classic three-hander like this. I shrug and pass her the phone. Chanya says yes a few times, then goes quiet. After about five minutes she gives me a quizzical look, says, "Yes, that's right, I've just spent a month in a Buddhist nunnery," then she gets up, throws me a glance both startled and intrigued, and leaves the room. I can hear her voice out in the yard, but I cannot distinguish her words. The conversation goes on for about twenty more minutes, mostly with Chanya listening to whatever Tara is saying. Then Chanya takes a long cold shower and finally returns to the bedroom, where I am sitting up expectantly and nervously with one of those ridiculous facial expressions we learn in school which says, *I didn't do anything wrong, did I?*

"Lie down, lover," she says gently. "Now, all you have to do for total atonement is tell me when I get it right. Where is that nerve exactly? *Somewhere between the anus and the testicles*, she said. Does it really work?"

"Yes, but you're not supposed to come."

"I don't want to, Sonchai. I don't want to come ever again. That friend of yours makes so much sense. I have to admit, I stayed away so long because I wasn't sure I wanted to sink back into flesh. What I really wanted was to be with you on a genuine spiritual path. I think the Buddha sent this friend of yours as an answer. If I press right here, is that the point?"

"Forward a millimeter," I mutter. "She told you her mantra, didn't she?"

"Yes."

"What is it?"

"I'm not telling you."

"Try to remember me from time to time. Bliss can be pretty impersonal, you know."

"Mmm, thank Buddha for that." Then, when she's settling down prior to the primeval rhythm: "You have to send her money for the phone call. The poor thing's incredibly poor. Imagine having a mind like that and no money. She understood everything about me. She's changed my life with one phone call."

"You moved your finger."

"Sorry."

(Try this at home by all means, ladies, but it might not work without the mantra.)

Well, *farang*, you saw it all yourself on CNN, just like me. Those were Tietsin's prayer flags you were looking at on your TV at the opening of the Olympic Games—not only all over Beijing, but in a motley Tantric network all over the country, from Tibet to Shanghai, from Canton to Manchuria, from Yunan to Beijing, from Kashgar to Fuzhou, from Hailar to Lhasa, from Hohhot to Haikou, unmistakably Tibetan in their shaggy insistence, the majestic curved sweep of their cables from earth up to the highest available point, most frequently a telegraph pole, and in the universal magic of their colors: blue for sky, white for air, red for fire, green for water, yellow for earth, generally (but not always) in that order—which are having such an effect on the world. Did you get a chance to see viewers' e-mails and text messages? I guessed immediately that the forty million dollars to invade China was spent not on the prayer flags themselves, but mostly on bribing a whole raft of Chinese officials to look the other way when the flags were hoisted for the benefit of the world's cameras. Not that Tietsin will be too worried about the publicity. What interests him is the exercise of subtle power, the silent invasion of China by Tibetan thought, the promise to its misguided people of a better heaven than that offered by Marx, Mao, or Friedman: the slow but certain remodeling of the World Mind, starting with China, into something more civilized. To Tietsin's way of thinking, he can't fail. It's only a question of time— and he's Tibetan. You did send a message of support, even though there's no oil in Tibet, didn't you? I know how committed you are to freedom and democracy.

Farang, it's time to wind this up. I know you are itching to find out more about my spiritual development. I'm still with the blade wheel—I fear it will be my companion for many incarnations—but, as I'm sure you guessed, Chanya made a family decision that I would give up the position of consigliere. We have discovered the hard way that names matter. As a free spirit, buzzing around Vikorn's ear urging restraint, I feel more myself; call me his consigliere, give me a quarter-million baht a month—and I feel enslaved. In my personal form of Buddhism, morality is organic and impossible to codify. You cannot grasp *the way* with your hand, nor even your mind; you have to let it lead you.

Oh, by the way, Rosie McCoy is still inside, but has adapted with genius: she has bribed the head screw to give her a private cell with computer and Internet connection. Her webpage charges three dollars a pop to download pix of her naked body in various erotic poses. Mary Smith is now in the same holding prison and has somehow managed to find favor with the big Nigerians, who protect her. Although the Frank Charles case remains officially a suicide, Sukum did get his promotion and became impossible to live with for a week, but he has not yet exchanged his Toyota for a Lexus; there is hope for his next incarnation.

Do not judge me too harshly, *farang*. (You know how you are.) In the wasteland where narrative rots, Good Thief may be the highest aspiration. Let he who is without karma cast the first stone.

I am yours in dharma, Sonchai Jitpleecheep.

Epilogue

Farang, I have a question for you: do we have a happy ending? I myself cannot decide, but it might help your deliberation if I share with you yet another anonymous package which arrived a couple of days ago. It is a single yellow Tibetan prayer flag, which has been unstitched to reveal the tiny paper prayer within. The prayer is in Tibetan and Chinese script; fortunately, the anonymous sender has provided a translation in English and Thai. I am not an expert, but I would guess the incantation to be unusual:

> Hey, China, stop being stupid!
> Don't go down this road anymore!
> Look at the West. It may be confused, but it has been down this road of yours and has much to teach: Hitler, Mussolini, Stalin, Franco, Nixon, Botha. And there's a guy called Mao you really need to study more deeply. Know who they all were, these guys? They were the direct cultural products of Clive, Palmerston, Kitchener, Curzon, Younghusband: the kind of

guys Marx hated most in all the world. Remember Marx?

Monocultures with iron fists don't last very long these days. Better get yourself some variety if you want to survive.

Things are looking good for you at the moment, aren't they? Did anyone explain the Third Reich was supposed to last a thousand years?

Listen, China, this is a new age we have here. Freedom isn't a theory anymore, it is an instinct people are born with. So is the longing for the transcendent. Nothing you can do about it: *it's even stronger than money!*

Here's something from your own culture:

> A *cup of wine under the flowering trees;*
> *I drink alone, for no friend is near.*
> *Raising my cup I beckon the bright moon . . .*

Li Po is the greatest poet in world literature. He was also a Buddhist, by the way. So were the Emperor Wu of Han, Yao Xing, Cao Xueqin, Liu Ying, Li Shizhen, Commissioner Lin, and the Emperor Ming.

You better link up again with those guys if you want your good karma to continue. The way you treat my people is filling the Illustrious Ancestors with shame.

Let my people go, China. The alternative is too ugly to contemplate.

Om mani padme hum

Sources

Bayonets to Lhasa, Peter Fleming

Circling the Sacred Mountain: A Spiritual Adventure Through the Himalayas, Robert Thurman and Tad Wise

Esoteric Teachings of the Tibetan Tantra, translated by Chang Chen Chi

Lords of the Rim, Sterling Seagrave

The Madman's Middle Way, Donald Lopez

Opium, Empire, and the Global Political Economy: A Study of the Asian Opium Trade, Carl A. Trocki

Pax Britannica: Climax of an Empire, Jan Morris

The Ritual and Mythology of the Chinese Triads: Creating an Identity, Berend J. Ter Harr

The Shadow Circus: The CIA in Tibet, White Crane Films

Shamanism and Tantra in the Himalayas, Claudia Mulles-Ebeling, Christian Ratsch, and Surendra Bahadur Shahi

Very Thai, Philip Cornwel-Smith

Bangkok Eight

John Burdett

In surreal Bangkok, city of temples and brothels, where Buddhist monks in saffron robes walk the same streets as world-class gangsters, a US marine sergeant is killed inside a locked Mercedes by a maddened python and a swarm of cobras. Two policemen – the only two in the city not on the take – arrive too late. Minutes later, only one is alive.

The cop left standing, Sonchai Jitpleecheep, is a devout Buddhist and swears to avenge the death of his partner and soul brother. To do so he must use the forensic techniques of the modern policing and his own profound understanding of the mystical workings of the spirit world. Both will be vital as he immerses himself in the moneyed underbelly of Bangkok where desire rules and where he will eventually find the killer, a predator of an even more sinister variety . . .

'Cracking East meets West thriller introducing a half-Thai, half-American cop whose Buddhist beliefs are as important as his forensic skills. Terrific'
OBSERVER

'A fantastic new thriller with an avenging Buddhist cop as its central character'
MAIL ON SUNDAY

'Like a modern-day Indiana Jones adventure written by Evelyn Waugh . . . One of this season's cleverest and most stylish entertainments'
WALL STREET JOURNAL

'Quirky and highly entertaining . . . something to enjoy for its sheer bravado'
NEW YORK TIMES

'A thriller as exotic as it is enthralling, and as provocative as it is obscene'
HARPERS

'Impeccably researched, this is sometimes poetic, often exotic, and totally hardcore'
DAILY MIRROR

9780552153560

Bangkok Tattoo

John Burdett

'Killing customers just isn't good for business'

In District 8, the underbelly of Bangkok's crime world, a dramatically mutilated body is found in a hotel bedroom. It looks bad.

It gets worse for Detective Sonchai Jitpleecheep when the self-confessed murderer is Chanya, the most successful 'working girl' at The Old Man's Club, a brothel owned jointly by Sonchai's mother and his boss, Police Colonel Vikorn.

And it gets deadly when Sonchai, in an effort to get at the bizarre truth, is forced to run the gamut of Bangkok's drug-dealers, prostitutes, bad cops, even worse military generals, and the pitfalls of his own melting heart.

'Like no other novel that's come my way lately. Ironic, sexy and trailing an odour that reminds me of a Bangkok street after hours . . . Expect to be enlightened'
LITERARY REVIEW

'Open *Bangkok Tattoo* and you will read on and on, with wide-eyed fascination, some horror or disgust and considerable delight'
WASHINGTON POST

9780552771412